i'm a believer

Also by Jessica Adams

Single White E-mail
Tom, Dick and Debbie Harry

i'm a believer

by

jessica adams

Thomas Dunne Books
St. Martin's Press ⋈ New York

THOMAS DUNNE BOOKS.
An imprint of St. Martin's Press.

www.stmartins.com

ISBN 0-312-32107-4

First published in Australia by Pan Macmillan Australia Pty Limited

First U.S. Edition: February 2004

10 9 8 7 6 5 4 3 2 1

To Cate Paterson, for talking me into it,
and Diana Beaumont, who has always believed.

i'm a believer

one

For the first few days after Catherine's death, I find myself doing all the wrong things – though I'm not exactly sure what the right things are. I'm fairly certain you're not supposed to lie in the bath, listening to ABBA, when your girlfriend's just been killed in a car crash. But this morning, that's exactly what I find myself doing. Singing along with Fernando on the radio. Using Catherine's bubble bath. Mindlessly trying to churn up more bubbles with my hands.

Because what's just happened is so major, anything I do which is minor – and in my life, that's quite a lot – automatically seems wrong. Putting my feet up on the table this morning, reading the sports pages, I caught myself thinking: Is this allowed? And making a triple-decker honey sandwich: Is this too frivolous?

Both my grandfathers are dead, so you'd think I'd know how to behave. You'd think I'd know how it's done. But one died in a Spanish retirement home, and the other had a heart attack years ago, and on both occasions I was either too far away, or

1

too young. I know I wore black to one of the funerals, but that's been the extent of my mourning practice.

I have to buy a black suit for Catherine's funeral on Wednesday. But if you always wear black, which I do – which, in fact, most men of a certain age in London do – then what should you wear to a funeral? Blacker black, just to show that it's more serious? And all the time, part of me is thinking: Catherine doesn't know, Catherine doesn't care. Catherine's dead and almost buried, and anything I do with her in mind now is just a total waste of time.

Some other inappropriate things I do this week: Opening her post, and for the first time in the history of our relationship, looking at her bank account. Frying the honey sandwiches in butter, just to see if Elvis Presley was right. Finally, worst of all, getting into bed at two o'clock in the afternoon, with an old photo of Catherine, lying topless on some Australian beach, and trying to take some comfort in it. I think it's fair to say that this is the low point.

People from school have rung up – other teachers, mostly. Some I know quite well, so I'd expect a call, and some I only know well enough to nod at in the corridor. I didn't know some of them cared. There's a woman in administration I only know because she used to pinch my parking space. She's rung up, and she cried as well – in fact she cried so much she couldn't speak. I've even had sympathy emails, which seems wrong somehow, but maybe everybody's doing it these days.

The people at Catherine's work, at the travel agency, have rung up as well. And so far, everyone seems to have heard how she died, which saves me an explanation, but I've still had the inevitable comments:

'If only she'd taken a different road.'

'If only you'd come to us for dinner that night, Mark.'

'If only Catherine had thought twice about taking the car out in that weather.'

The dinner thing got to me the most. Do some people really think that her death hinges on us not going up to Balham to eat their chicken curry at seven o'clock on a Thursday night?

'If only you'd come to us for dinner that night, Mark.' Sod off.

Catherine's ex-boyfriend Matt, has just rung up. He wants to come to the funeral. And he can sod off as well. He's the one who took the topless photo of her in Australia. The photo I've been lying in bed with. I've just remembered that.

The next day, I see that the morning post contains a book from Amazon for Catherine, and some more sympathy cards for me, and her parents – they've all come to this address. The book Catherine ordered is called *Eat Right, Live Well, Live Longer*. It's up there in the rich irony stakes this morning, along with her low-cholesterol margarine, still sitting in the fridge door, approved by the National Heart Association – and all her cashew nuts from the health food shop. All this stuff dates from Catherine's last big supermarket shop, the day before she died. I chuck the book straight in the bin. Then I chuck the cashews out of the front door, for the pigeons.

It looks as though some of the the sympathy cards addressed to me are along the 'if only' lines too, like the phone calls. Because her accident was written up in the local paper, everyone now knows that Catherine was driving in the rain, at night, swerving to avoid a dog, on a dodgy road, in a very old car. Consequently there's a lot of 'if only' stuff revolving around these details.

The people sending sympathy cards, some of whom I've never even met, divide into two camps. About half of them find her death poignant, senseless and tragic, and something which could easily have been avoided – and the other half seem to find her death meaningful, fated and even proof that God might work in mysterious ways. There's no middle ground. Perhaps the people who have no opinion at all about car accidents – other than the fact that they're just accidents – don't bother to write. I have to say, this is the camp I fall into.

The God and Heaven cards have crosses and flowers on the front – one shows three bluebirds flying around in front of a cloud, smiling. And the cards go on about God having prepared some sort of paradise for Catherine, and in one case there's a message from one of her old school friends which talks about God having set up a nice eternal resting place for her. I think these people are missing the point. If you follow that line of logic, it's God who set the whole bloody car crash up in the first place.

The people who run Catherine's weekly yoga class have written a long letter, on recycled paper (of course) talking about karma. I didn't know they were that far gone. I just thought they did yoga for the exercise.

In any case, the recycled paper letter goes in the bin. But not before I've ripped it into shreds. The yoga people say we might not understand why she's gone, but Catherine's higher self already knows. What higher self? I lived with her for two years, and I never saw it. The yoga people say it's part of a plan – I love this bit – it's part of a plan, somehow, but annoyingly enough, the laws of karma mean we'll just never know.

There's an okay card from Catherine's Aunty Pam in Yorkshire. She was always nagging us to get married, but in such a funny accent that we never really took offence. In Aunty Pam's card, she says that ever since her husband died in 1988, she's learned that you get used to it, but you never get over it. This sounds about right to me.

Just before midnight, though, in the middle of another bath with the radio on – it's the 'if only' cards that end up affecting me the most. My defences are probably down because I'm so tired. And obviously, as everyone has been telling me, there's the after-effects of shock to consider. Either way, though, I seem to be weakening. Other people's obsession with the trivial combination of factors that led to Catherine's death is now – finally – beginning to get to me.

When I get out of the bath, I find myself thinking – if only she had stayed home with me that night, I could have walked around the corner and got a video, and then she never would have driven out in the rain. And if only she hadn't bothered with a shower before the yoga class, then she would have driven off fifteen minutes earlier, and whatever freakish set of circumstances the police are now telling me about, with the dog, and poor visibility, and wet roads, and old brakes, and heavy traffic – well, those circumstances would never have lined up. We'd been wanting to get *Billy Elliot* out on video for ages. I should have got it. That's the bottom line, really. I didn't get the *Billy Elliot* video out on Thursday night, and she didn't stay in with me, and she went out and got killed in a car crash.

If you wait long enough, when your heart has stopped

4

palpitating and your head has stopped thumping, common sense eventually kicks in. I've discovered this over the years, during the odd work or money-related panic attack. And common sense now says, why stop there? I mean, if I'm going to torture myself with these scenarios about what might have been avoided – well. Why not go all the way?

I mean, if only Volkswagen had never exported the particular make of car that Catherine happened to be driving that night, if only the course of the Second World War had been different, and Volkswagen's corporate destiny in Germany had taken another turn. If only the dog who shot out in front of her had never been born . . . and it goes on. If only the rain hadn't been pelting down that night, if only Catherine wasn't shortsighted, and vain with it as well – she never wore glasses. If only she'd set off earlier, if only she'd set off later. If only the council had built better roads.

And to really get at the heart of all those links in the causal chain, I may as well start with myself, because if only I'd never met Catherine Roden in the first place, on a family holiday to a seaside town called Dymchurch in 1977, we'd never have got together anyway. And then Thursday night would never have happened, and she'd still be alive. So take that, those of you who want to ramble on about the endless twists in the chain of fate, and shove it.

Ultimately, if you're going to take this 'If only' thing about her accident to its logical conclusion, then full responsibility for Catherine's funeral next Wednesday rests with me, and me alone. And if anyone else rings up wanting to know about the terrible pre-destined event that's got us to this point where she's dead, it's actually a holiday in Dymchurch, and a copy of a girls' magazine called *Jackie*, from 20 years ago.

Amazingly, I manage to find the same copy of *Jackie* the next day, in a cardboard box on the top of our wardrobe. All Catherine's childhood stuff is there. One of those little plastic machines you make name labels with, and then numerous school folders bearing the same labels, along with a list of all the bands she liked at the time, from The Bay City Rollers to Mud. I wonder if her parents will want this stuff? It's been too soon, yet, to have that kind of conversation. But I can't see myself hanging onto it.

The copy of *Jackie* I find is so flimsy it's not really a magazine at all – more like a 35-page pamphlet for teenage girls, all of whom seem to have spots, and problems with their tampons, and crushes on David Cassidy. It's amazing that Catherine kept it, but then she's also kept other things I don't understand, like a small troll with turquoise hair, and an empty perfume bottle, and an abcessed tooth in a little jewellery box.

Catherine's drawn pictures of herself all over the ads in the back of *Jackie*. She's drawn them using a blue, red and black biro – red for her lips and cheeks, black for the hair, and blue for her eyes. I think I can even guess the pen Catherine was using – one of those magical jumbo biros from the 70s, which you used to flick with the top of your thumb, instantly changing the colour of the nib. I notice Catherine's given herself a boobtube in the drawing, as well. And boobs.

In actual fact, when she was this age – when she would have been reading this copy of *Jackie* at the Dymchurch Caravan Park, Catherine had no breasts at all.

I remember this, not because I was interested, but because a snotty kid called Noel Oliver pointed it out to me.

'That girl Catherine's as flat as a pancake, Mark.'

I remember it well, mainly because I had never heard the expression before, and I immediately had a strange vision of what might be under Catherine's T-shirt. Something fried, and flat, with brown spots, lemon and icing sugar, perhaps.

In any case, Catherine's pancake-chest was more fascinating to Noel Oliver than it was to me. At nine years old, I was only interested in cricket. Girls were Noel's thing, though – unfortunately for them. Because, if you were looking for the ultimate in boring, whining, irritating little tossers, that was Noel Oliver.

In the Dymchurch Caravan Park, where all our parents had booked sites – Mr and Mrs Roden were friends with my Mum and Dad – Noel spent most of his time by himself, banging a racket against a tennis ball, which had been wedged down the end of his mother's pantyhose and knotted to a pole at the top. It was a girl's game, and I told him so. In return, he punched me in the back. After that, our holiday in Dymchurch became a kind of long, drawn-out feud. I can still remember the satisfaction I felt when I smashed him in the arm with the sharp end of a *Whizzer and Chips* annual.

Noel and I seemed to spend a long time hanging around in the local shop that summer, deciding which bubblegum to buy, so we could play endless games of one-upmanship with all the free cards. When we weren't doing that, we were trying to drown each other in the sea, or throw wet, grey sand down each other's swimming trunks, up on Dymchurch beach. It was freezing, of course. And after we had saved up enough money for one donkey ride (the donkeys always seemed to be pissing everywhere, too) all we could do was buy small windmills on sticks, and poke them into the top of our soggy sandcastles.

Noel Oliver was my age, so he should have shown some respect, but instead he seemed determined to wind me up, as often as possible. Someone had given him this phrase, maybe it was his dad, maybe he'd seen it on TV, but anyway, he used it on me all the time.

'Don't give it, if you can't take it, Mark'. And some other classic Noel Oliver phrases from that holiday I remember now – 'Get knotted' (where had he learned that from, watching *Are You Being Served?*) and 'Naff off you prat'.

Because Noel had a crush on Catherine, after a few days I did too – or at least, I tried to fake one. I didn't want to be left out, I suppose, though my knee-jerk reaction to her, whenever she swanned past in a bikini, or rode her bicycle up to the shop, was no less automatic than my knee-jerk reaction to people like Suzi Quatro or even Olivia Newton-John. I knew I was supposed to like girls, because that was the way the world worked, but every silly, soppy face I made at Catherine wasn't driven by a genuine impulse at all. It was the presence of Noel Oliver, standing a foot behind me, which made me do it. It was just like the bubblegum cards. I wanted to keep up.

At school, I noticed when girls had gone through bad haircuts, which was always hilarious, or if they had their arms put in plaster, or if they had their teeth out. But beyond that, I might as well have been blind for the first nine years of my life. I think I was fourteen before I even noticed my own body in a mirror. If you'd asked me about football players at the age of nine, I could have given you all the goals, and all the penalties, and even most of the old chants. Peter Bonetti is made of spaghetti. Georgie Best, superstar, looks like a woman and he wears a bra. But frankly, in 1977, although I was pretty good on football statistics, I didn't even know what a bra was.

And then Noel Oliver came along, with his *Jackie* comic.

Noel had bought it for Catherine, as a seduction gift, leaving it on the front step of the Rodens' family caravan. And at the moment that I saw that particular romantic gesture ('Get knotted, Mark, what are you looking at?') something changed, and Catherine Roden, who had been just another kid on the caravan park I was supposed to go and play with ('Go and see if she wants to go swimming with you, Mark') suddenly became an object of real interest. I suppose, in an odd way, I finally got my first crush.

The copy of *Jackie,* which Noel Oliver bought Catherine, had a free love heart badge on the front. If you were heart-broken, you pulled the two halves of the heart (red plastic, of course) apart, and walked around with this split heart badge on your T-shirt, presumably looking devastated – and available. If you actually had a boyfriend or girlfriend, you just wore the heart, intact, looking smug.

I don't think Noel Oliver even got this far in his understanding of the Jackie free love heart badge, though. To him, a red heart just meant romance, and girls, and love, and it was something he could give to Catherine to impress her, and best of all, you got it free with every copy of *Jackie* which let's face it, even in the Dymchurch newsagency in 1977, was still only 8p. I suppose he thought it was a good investment in the future of his love life.

In retrospect, the Noel Oliver and *Jackie* magazine episode should have been one of those 'Oh, how we laughed' stories for Catherine and I to share in later life, when we finally got together after all. But it never was.

I didn't bash up Noel Oliver in the end, even when he punched me in the stomach for stealing the *Jackie* magazine from the caravan steps. I did throw a lump of soil at him though, at close range, and it had a chunk of brick inside it – which I didn't know. I broke his nose, and he went to hospital, in tears, and I'll never quite forget the way he looked at me when they bundled him into the car, holding a tea towel up against his face.

Catherine wasn't allowed to have anything to do with me after that. Her sister, Veronica, who was four years older, said, 'You're a bloody little racist bastard for doing that, Mark.' I'd never heard anyone calling me any of those things before – either bloody, or racist, or bastard. For some reason I'd got to the age of nine without any kind of verbal attack, even at school – but even so, I knew what she meant when she said it, although I wasn't clear on the racist bit.

My mother explained it to me later, in the caravan. But she was as surprised as I was. The fact that whining, annoying Noel Oliver was black hadn't really registered with me, apart from the fact that he supported the West Indies cricket team and I supported England. 'You didn't say anything bad to Noel, did you, Mark?' my father asked. But no, I hadn't. Not as in, *racist* bad.

My parents packed up early after that, and we went home. We never went back to Dymchurch – and Dad eventually sold the caravan. And it was to be five more years before I saw Veronica or Catherine Roden again.

I find myself thinking about all this now – specifically Veronica Roden, and the way she called me a bloody little racist bastard. When she rings, she manages to say my name, and hers, and then she bursts into tears.

'I'm sorry, Veronica,' I say. 'I've been waiting for this call.'

'Don't be sorry!' she snaps.

Veronica's way of operating is anger, and irritation, in that order. In between, you get the occasional bit of amused silence. In fact, on the mood-ometer of life, Catherine's older sister is mostly stuck on the part where the needle swings from seething to pissed off. She was like that on the unmentionable holiday at Dymchurch and she is like that now, in her late thirties.

'What I mean is,' Veronica says, continuing the phone conversation with a blocked-up nose, 'why are you saying you're sorry to me? You shouldn't be saying that.'

People find this hard to believe, but I went out with Veronica years before I eventually started going out with Catherine. It was really a question of timing. When Veronica and I met up again in Canterbury, years after the Noel Oliver incident, she had turned into the kind of raven-haired, red-lipped, leather-jacketed beauty I used to fantasise about. She had become a classic 1980s sex bomb by her early twenties, with a dyed red fringe, and diamond crucifixes in her ears. By this stage of our lives, she was in a band, and I was in a band. And we were still living about thirty miles apart, on the Kent coast. And our parents still knew each other. So – I suppose it had to happen, really. And it did.

Her band was called The Voodoo Blitz, and their poncey lead singer used to get very annoyed if you left out the 'The' bit at the front. My band was based in Folkestone, which is where my parents had moved to by then. And the name of our band was, I'm embarrassed to say, The Bottom Line. A kind of non-name. Even poor old boring Noel Oliver could have come up with something better than that, though by then I expect he was married, in a proper job, with his first mortgage, and had no time for anything as pointless as bands.

'Will you go to the rest home first?'

Veronica is snuffling into the telephone.

'Yes.'

'To see the coffin?'

'Yes.'

'I'm glad you saw the body, anyway, Mark. I couldn't have done it.'

'It's all right.'

'Was she – okay?'

'Oh, for God's sake, Veronica!'

Sometimes, in common with a lot of people, I expect, I could happily shoot Catherine's sister. I have actually been through all this post mortem stuff about Catherine several times with my parents, not to mention her parents, and it's all okay. It's all fine. It's just something in Veronica's nature that makes her long for a problem. It was exactly like this when we were going out together years ago.

The truth is, I saw Catherine in hospital, after the doctor on the phone had told me she was dead. And they had her lying down in a room, at the end of a lot of corridors, and she was black and blue. Bruises on her stomach, bruises on her legs. I touched her hair, which was a bit sticky, and I noticed that her eyes were closed – I remember some doctor at a party once telling me they put coins on the lids to keep them shut – and then after that, I just left. I didn't break down, I didn't pass out, I wasn't sick in the toilet, despite the nurse showing me where it was. I just signed something, and then I left. Oh no, I had a plastic cup of tea from one of those machines in the waiting room – and then I left.

Veronica is crying properly now, into the other end of the phone.

'It's fine, Veronica,' I hear myself saying. 'Everything is fine.'

I go through some practical stuff with her. Catherine's death certificate is going to the Registrar of Births and Deaths. Her parents are splitting up the paperwork with me – her dad is doing the life insurance, I'm doing the bank. Her parents have taken care of the inquest and the police, and the priest and the crematorium. In turn, because I can't even bring myself to think about the bloody God stuff right now, I'm doing all of Catherine's clothes, and her books, and her CDs, and all the other boxes of stuff she always had shoved under our bed. I'm cancelling her subscriptions, and her classes and her courses. So that's it. My duty done.

I try to keep the conversation with Veronica normal, but it's not easy. In the end, I decide to try to talk to her the same way I talk to the kids in my class at school, most of whom, I should point out, are nine years old.

'On Wednesday morning,' I explain, 'we'll go to the funeral parlour, which is just round the corner from the church, and we'll sit with the coffin, or see the coffin, or whatever the proper expression is – frankly, I think I'll just stare at the wall –'

'Oh, don't say that.'

'And then we'll all drive with the funeral directors to the service, and one of their cars will follow with the coffin in the back.'

A long pause. Veronica is now weeping steadily, so I give her a minute. I've just remembered you call it a hearse, too, not a car.

'I'm in shock, Mark. I'm in absolute shock. How do you feel?'

'The same as you. I suppose.'

'I don't even know if I'll be able to get through the funeral.'

'You will.'

'No, really Mark. I don't know if I can.'

When she was in her twenties, playing in a band in Canterbury, Veronica Roden was not only older than me, she was also better looking, more talented, more intelligent, better off, and generally just – better. I still lived with my mum and dad, and she lived in a brand new block of flats just outside Canterbury, with fake carriage lamps outside, and winding gravel pathways. She shared her flat, which she used to refer to as an apartment, with a film student from Denmark. I drank beer, she drank pina coladas. No wonder she always refused to sleep with me, for the short time that we went out together.

Of course, I'm not even sure you'd call it going out, now. Perhaps our strange, casual, semi-snogging friendship qualified as a relationship then – I know I wanted it to qualify. But basically, it was all about us turning up to see the same bands, at the same time, and me buying her cider, which was her compromise drink when she couldn't get a pina colada. And I remember lying on the floor at her flat on Sunday afternoons, listening to Depeche Mode and drinking white wine. I used to make a move on her from time to time, and she even returned the favour a couple of times (when she was drunk) but nothing ever really happened.

Now, I find myself wondering about her. Approaching forty, Veronica is too thin – it's the kind of thinness that makes women look not very well – and she's got lines on her face from too many cigarettes, and she's in a dead-end relationship with someone who's out of work – but it never seems to break up, despite this – it just goes on and on, like bad weather.

When she was alive (how strange now, to find myself thinking this phrase), Catherine believed that therapy might be the answer for her sister, but I don't know. If you ask me, it would give

Veronica even more things to be dramatic about, to agonise over.

'Anyway, I'll see you at the funeral home,' I hear myself telling her.

'You don't want to talk about anything, do you?'

'Sorry, Veronica.'

'Oh, it's all right. I'll see you –' she chokes up again, and I wait for her to gather her words together, but instead, she signs off.

'Bye then, Mark. Look after yourself.'

'Bye, Veronica.'

A lot of the qualities Veronica has now – the general moodiness and lack of energy, the sulking – were actually pretty hip in the 80s. In fact, the bleak, bored look affected by the members of her long-gone band, The Voodoo Blitz, came so naturally to Veronica that she practically started a one-woman fashion for pouting in Canterbury all by herself.

To be fair, I guess you couldn't wear the black lipstick she used to put on, and go around smiling and waving. The gloom Veronica used to carry around with her went with the crucifix, and the black fishnet tights, and the moaning songs, with agonised choruses, that seemed to be permanently fixed on her record player.

And now, what was so fascinating, so hip and so unapproachable about her then has become that least fashionable thing now, negativity. I've met enough of Catherine's yoga friends at parties over the past two years to work this out, all by myself. Veronica's stance on life just isn't very popular any more. Or as Catherine's mother puts it, 'No wonder she can't get herself a decent boyfriend with a proper job, she's so negative all the time.'

I never even bothered trying to sleep with Veronica all those years ago. It was like trying to scale Everest with a plastic budgie ladder. Why bother getting her drunk, or flattering her senseless, or any of the other sad tricks I used to try on less challenging girls in the 80s?

Back then, Catherine was much less hard work, as she'd grown up to be a softer and easier proposition than her sister. Everything about Veronica was hard – straight black hair, blood red mouth, shiny black boots. Catherine was a gentler prospect altogether – brown curly hair, sweet smile, fluffy jumpers. But, predictably, I just wasn't interested in her. Catherine was my age (and that used to matter then) but she might as well have been living on Mars.

Catherine thought Princess Diana's bridesmaids were really sweet. That was actually one of the first things I ever heard her say, when we were finally reunited, at one of Veronica's trendy band parties, after all those years following the Dymchurch holiday.

I can't remember why we would have been talking about the wedding so long after the event.

I think Catherine was wearing a nice white blouse with a pussycat bow when she said it, which didn't help. Very prim and proper. And there was Veronica, with a sultry pout and a cigarette, hanging around in the corner listening to The Cramps with her head jammed in the speakers. There was no contest really.

Now that Catherine's dead, and I want her so much, I could almost look at that time as the wasted years. These were the years when we could have been together, and weren't – sometimes because I was wasting time with her sister, sometimes because I was just too stupid to see what was right in front of me.

But this is taking me into 'if only' territory again. And that's something I can't afford to do. I'm too tired, for a start.

What I'll miss most about Catherine, if I actually give in and think about it now, if I can actually bear to think about her at all, is her *niceness*. It's not the best word I can come up with, but at least it explains what she had. She was always inherently nice, or kind, or good – even when she was a kid. In fact, when the Roden car pulled away from Dymchurch that summer, towing the caravan behind it, Catherine was the only one who bothered waving goodbye to me – I can still see it now. Just one little hand going, frantically, from the back seat.

I suppose people will talk about this niceness of Catherine's at the funeral, although I know I'm using the wrong word. They might find better words, more elaborate ones, because this is going to be a proper service after all. Sensitivity, compassion, empathy, kindness. All those words will do for Catherine.

To her eternal credit, Catherine didn't fancy me at all in my teens. Then again, I don't blame her for avoiding me.

There's a photo of me from that time taken at a free pub gig in Ashford with The Bottom Line, and I've got a quiff which is going flat, and pointy shoes, which I'm wearing with thick woollen hiking socks, and a pained expression on my face.

One of the teachers at our school has a theory about the bands you were in, in your youth. His name is Felix Saddleton and he has a lot of theories about everything, but this is his favourite. Felix maintains that your career path, your health, your finances, and indeed your love life, can be safely predicted by referring to the musical instrument you played in your first band.

Drummers, according to Felix, end up in middle management, never get promoted, fail to marry or produce children, develop boring hobbies like fly-fishing, and run to fat in old age. Keyboard players, in his worldview, get married young, get into hi-fi systems, get bad eyesight and end up secure, but unhappy. Bass players like me just go bald and get into home renovations, apparently. I have a suspicion that Felix's bass player theory is secretly based on me, but we've never discussed it. And yes, I am going bald. I have what Felix refers to as 'an East-enders hard-man haircut', which means I get down on my hands and knees, on the floor, once a month and mow the whole thing from front to back, with an electric razor.

Felix is one of the people from school who rang up about Catherine on Friday. He felt he should, but I wish he hadn't. He's fine for the staffroom, and for swapping CDs, and for making me laugh, but he was clueless on the other end of the phone. Not quite as bad as one of the 'if only' people, or the God people, but not very good either. I was embarrassed, he was embarrassed. He's coming to the funeral, anyway. We spent a long time talking about the black clothes problem.

Of all my ex-girlfriends, Donna Roberts is the one Catherine disliked the most, so it's quite a shock when I get an email from her, the following day – she must have pestered someone for my address – asking if she can come to the funeral. Her internet address is madDonnagirl.

She's in her thirties, for God's sake, and now she's calling herself madDonnagirl. Her email meanders on about how she's just left her job in a second-hand bookshop, because she was being sexually harassed by her boss, and how her eczema has come back, after all this time. And do I remember the way she sometimes had to wear my socks over her hands in bed, to stop herself scratching? And then, at the end of the email, Donna talks about seeing Catherine's accident in the paper, and she writes 'Mark, I know it's strange, but I just instinctively want to help you now.' I feel like writing back, 'Donna, I know it's strange, but I just instinctively want to press delete and get rid of this email.'

Even though I haven't seen Donna Roberts since email was invented, I know enough about her to guess that she'll have a device on her computer that lets her know when someone's opened and read one of her messages. So if I trash it now, or don't reply, it'll be the end. Or, more accurately, it will be the beginning. The beginning of a lot of intense, sighing phone calls, timed for around midnight, and this time there won't be Catherine there to grab the telephone and slam it down on the bedside table. No Catherine. It hits me again, today – no Catherine.

Catherine didn't like Donna, because Donna wouldn't go away. Catherine tried to be nice about her at first, at the beginning of our relationship (which, let's face it, is when everyone tries to be nice about everything), but after a while, she couldn't stand her any longer.

My attitude was, I was Donna's boyfriend, and then her friend, long before Catherine came along – and I couldn't just tell her to piss off overnight. Catherine's angle was that Donna wanted me back, and the friendship thing with me was just a ploy. Catherine thought she was a game-player and that she wanted to sabotage our new relationship. I totally disagreed. Catherine thought I was encouraging Donna. Once again, I couldn't agree with her.

For Donna and I to stay friends after our big break-up – two years before Catherine and I got together – made both of us feel like civilised people, and more than that, it took some of the sting away for me. It made our separation seem less scary, and less final, because, after all, I was in love with Donna once.

By staying friends with Donna (and it was she who left me) I was able to console myself that splitting up had nothing to do with not really loving each other, it was more that we weren't cut out for a relationship. Just the usual stuff you tell yourself. Anyway, it ended up causing a lot of problems with Catherine.

The first morning that Catherine and I ever spent in bed together, Donna rang up. I have a vivid memory of it even now, because it was such an historically crap moment – Catherine propping herself up on the pillows, flushed in the face, with a couple of condoms on the floor, and me trying to talk to Donna, trying to sound normal to both of them, and consequently sounding very abnormal indeed.

I suppose I thought it would take a couple of weeks to sort out the old friendship and the new romance. In the end, it took two years. One year of being with Catherine – and continuing to be friends with Donna, who needed me more that year, because she was with some guy who used to hit her – and then another year, when Catherine and I were apart, but trying to get back together. In the second year, Donna edged over from being friends to being my lover again, on at least two occasions. Needless to say, that held things up with Catherine yet again.

Throughout this second year (the bad year, before the good third year, when Catherine and I finally bought this house together) I became Mr Wobbly. I know this because Catherine was bitching about me to one of her friends once, on the phone, and that's what I was being called. Or, as Catherine so delicately put it, 'Frigging Mr Wobbly'.

I wasn't made of jelly, though. I just had no good reason to choose either her or Donna for a very long time. In fact, for a full year, I just didn't feel passionately enough about either of them to make it any kind of three-way contest. So we all carried on having these kind of . . . low-fi pseudo friendships (with sex thrown in) and almost-relationships (with sex frequently thrown out).

I didn't really want Donna as anything more than a friend, but I was angry that Catherine could demand (and she did demand, often) that I give Donna up. And I wasn't sure enough about Catherine to make a commitment, because – quite honestly – her jealousy made her ugly. I suppose I can admit this, even to myself, now that she's dead.

Reading Donna's long and rambling email to me now, I can only think, more wasted time. I could have had another two years of potential all-Catherine days, when I was going through the Donna thing, and I blew it. Catherine had me all wrong. I wasn't Mr Wobbly, I was just Mr Stupid, and I've been stupid about a lot of things. But then, how the hell was I supposed to know that one day, when I least expected it, there would be no more time left, and Catherine would be dead?

One day later, I'm still thinking about Donna. How do you tell someone they can't come to a funeral, if they've specifically asked if they can come? It seems wrong to let her turn up, given that Catherine couldn't stand her. But then again, Catherine is gone, so it's nothing she either knows or cares about. I keep telling myself this, anyway, in the hope that it will sink in.

We do a subject called Change and Decay in science classes at school. All the kids in 4B bring in jam jars, and we put in bits of bread, and apple cores, and watch the mould grow. Then we go walking in the woods behind the school, looking for rotting leaves under holly bushes, and I get the children to organise the leaves in order, from most decayed to least decayed. It's all I can think about right now. That, and the crematorium.

Catherine is definitely dead, I have to keep reminding myself, because in the course of daily domestic trivia, it's so easy to forget. I find myself playing cruel self-inflicted tricks, like getting two cups out when the kettle boils. And separating out sections of the paper for her and me. And letting the phone ring on, automatically waiting for her to answer it, because it usually is for her. Or was.

I have to head Donna off right now. She's not coming to the funeral. And this is something I can do for myself, rather than for Catherine. I have absolutely no opinion on what the entire Roden family, including Veronica, would say if Donna showed up at the service tomorrow. I doubt that they'd even notice her, to be honest. So, the only person left who could possibly care about Donna being at Catherine's funeral is me. And I've already decided. She's not coming. Perhaps, in a way, it's my small way of compensating for the Mr Wobbly years.

My experiences with Donna have taught me that the best way to sort anything out is to be as direct and as blunt as possible. It would be so much safer and easier to send her an email – luxurious, even – but I also know this is the one thing that will set her off. Being fobbed off at a distance is not something Donna's ever coped with particularly well – in fact, it's always been her main trigger. Something to do with a father who was never there, apparently.

I call her eventually, finally finding her number after tracing her via yet another of her bouncer ex-boyfriends.

'Mark, we'll have to get drunk together,' Donna says, in her familiar, breathy, pseudo-posh voice, when I finally find the number. 'We'll have to go out and take lots and lots of drugs together!'

'No time to get drunk!' Why do I sound so hearty, suddenly, like some English actor in an Ealing comedy?

'I can take time off work. I can come and stay with you,' Donna says.

'No, don't do that.'

'I'm just thinking of you.'

'I'm fine.'

'Oh, God, I want to get drunk with you right now! It's the only, only way, Mark. You know, I've been through death. I don't think you have.'

What Donna means is, she's lost both friends and boyfriends, whereas I've only lost grandfathers, who apparently don't count. Her friend died of a heroin overdose, about five years ago, and she once had a boyfriend who drowned in a swimming pool in Los Angeles. She spent a lot of time talking about it when we were together.

'How is the family?' she asks me. 'Is it hell?'

'It's fine.' I suppose she means the Rodens.

'Is it a church funeral?' Then without waiting for me to answer, 'But Catherine wasn't religious at all, was she?'

One of the things about Donna that both attracts and repels is her ability to cut through the crap. It can either make you feel that she's invaded all your defences at once, in which case you hate her for it, or alternatively, you want to hug her, because she's just spotted what everyone else has missed. So – in the space of a five-minute phone call, Donna has correctly identified that I want nothing more than to sit in a pub and get drunk. And more impressively still, Donna has just identified the biggest problem in my life this week, which is the way death has suddenly forced Catherine into the big church machinery she spent most of her life not believing.

'So is it a religious funeral?' Donna persists.

'The family want it.'

'Oh, screw the family. Put her in a hole in the back garden, she never went to church, did she? And Lord knows, you don't believe in anything.'

'Donna.'

'Come on, talk about it, let's have a real talk.'

The next part of this sentence is, predictably, 'You'll feel better', but annoyingly, I already do. What is it, this feeling with Donna? Perhaps it's the freedom that comes from being honest. After a week of baths and honey sandwiches, she's unzipped my soul. Mind you, I still don't feel it's entirely safe to talk about anything yet.

I put my feet up on the table and tell Donna about the funeral plans instead.

'The families are both converging, at the same hotel in Paddington. Catherine's are all Catholics, so there's loads of them. I've just got me, the dog, Mum, Dad and Uncle Ray. He used to go camping with us sometimes, so he knew her. Ray's not stopping at the hotel, though. He's going to get the train in from Manchester early, and go home the same night.'

Donna sighs. 'And what else, Mark?'

'I get the feeling I'm being protected, not just by her parents, but by mine too – at the same time that I get the feeling I'm being left out of a lot of stuff.'

'More!' Donna insists.

'I am being left to my own devices, I can see that.'

'More! More!' Donna pushes me. She's got that almost-giggle in her voice that is usually a sign that she's stoned. It's eleven o'clock in the morning, and she wasn't expecting this call. So, from long experience, I'd say she probably is.

Everything I've just told Donna is true, of course. The Roden family have given up on me in the middle of Catherine's death, just as they gave up on me when she was alive. In their world, girls go on a few dates with different sorts of men, they sort out what they want, then they fall in love, then they get married and have kids. The Rodens are not the kind of people who understand men who fiddle-faddle around emotionally the way I do. They never quite fathomed what was going on with Veronica in Canterbury, during the white wine and Depeche Mode years, and they certainly didn't get my Mr Wobbly period, with Donna and Catherine feuding over me. I wasn't quite excommunicated in those years, but her mum and dad have never really been very sure of me, either. Both their daughters, and me. I suppose it must have seemed like some terrible test to them, sent by God, of course.

'Catherine's father rang me up and asked me if I was in shock,' I hear myself saying.

'Well, you are,' Donna says. 'I can hear it in your voice. You've gone blank. Haven't your parents offered to come round?'

'They offered, but I said no. Anyway, Mr Roden kept on asking me, did I feel numb? Then I told him Veronica had rung me up too and he couldn't get off the phone fast enough.'

'Funny about that,' Donna smirks.

'Well, it was another reason to leave me out of the funeral plans – the reminder that far from being content to stuff up one of their daughter's lives, I also managed to ruin another one.'

'So you never married either of their daughters, you total cad, you should be punished!' Donna half-laughs. She's using the voice which I sometimes used to joke was her telephone-sex voice.

'I've had a lot of cards about God,' I hear myself saying.

'No wonder you want to get drunk with me.'

'But I haven't said that.'

'But you do. And it would be good for you. Come on, let's get stoned.'

'Donna?'

'Yes, my love.'

'I've just realised something.'

'And what's that?'

'You can't possibly come to this funeral, because you're

basically doing something that's well out of order.'

'I care about you, you idiot. You're going to need me. Especially in the next few days. I know you, Mark. You've got no friends. You always were a miserable anti-social bastard.'

'No. You're not coming.'

'I'm not calling to see you because I think we can finally make it, now that she's dead. I swear to God, that's not why I'm ringing.'

And the ouch factor from this typical Donna statement is like someone ripping out a row of stitches.

'For God's sake, Catherine's only just died,' I tell her, after searching for something to say. There is a pause, and then finally she reacts.

'Oh, go screw yourself.'

And then she slams the phone down. I call back, which feels very familiar – these compulsive slam-and-answer games go back years with us – but Donna has already switched on her answering machine.

There's no point in talking into it. What is there to say? But for all Donna's ancient ability to get to the core of me, I can also get to the core of her, and I can guess three things from this conversation – first, she's still doing a lot of drugs, second she's probably broke and wants to borrow money, and third, she genuinely thinks there might be a place in my life for her, now that Catherine is dead. In typical Donna style, it has taken her exactly four days to reach this disgusting conclusion. It's enough to make you sick. And I am – it happens when I'm in the bath again, listening to the radio. In fact, I only just make it to the toilet.

The next day, I wake up panicking at about five o'clock in the morning. I think I'm even grinding my teeth when I wake. I have to be at the funeral parlour at 9 a.m., and the church service is at 10 a.m. We then go down to the church hall for morning tea at 11 a.m., and then me, Veronica and the rest of the Roden family need to be at the crematorium at noon. As I run through these things in my head, I automatically reach for Catherine's side of the bed. And then I see her.

Catherine is sitting on what used to be her chair on the left-hand side of the bed. She's close enough for me to touch. She's wearing the Snoopy T-shirt she always wears to bed, which is bizarre, because I packed it up along with a whole lot of other stuff for Oxfam.

I look at her feet. She is wearing bedsocks. I packed them up for Oxfam too. Then the lower half of her body starts to fade out from left to right, as a fuzzy electric green light starts to wash over her.

'Concentrate, Mark!'

I think that's what I hear. Although it's like something coming out of a wind tunnel, or the wrong end of the hair dryer. A voice that's not quite in the room, but not entirely inside my head, either.

This is obviously a dream, or a hallucination, but at the same time, maybe I *should* be concentrating. It seems to be what she wants. It might make the green light stop wiping her out. And sure enough, when I do this, it stops.

Finally, I find some words. If I'm going to play this mad game with myself, I might as well talk to her – to it – the bright, transparent apparition thing.

'Is it really you?' I hear myself say.

'Love you,' she says, which she always did, dropping the 'I' off the front. And again, it's like hearing something rush through a tunnel. And then she's gone. When I wake up again, I've slept through the alarm, and it's quarter to nine. I'm going to be late for the funeral parlour.

two

I almost expect to see Catherine again, either next to the coffin, or at the church, so it's a relief when nothing happens. I suppose bad dreams are part of the territory when somebody dies. It's stress. Tiredness. All those things. Your unconscious mind needs to deal with the shock of a loss, the same way that your conscious mind does.

And then Catherine starts talking to me at the crematorium, which ruins that theory.

The pallbearers are at the stage where they have to slide the coffin into the furnace – which is shiny stainless steel, and clean, like some hi-tech new kitchen appliance – and push the big square buttons. Veronica and her parents are standing well back, and to the left, and I'm out on my own, to the right, with my parents standing behind me. It's at this point that I hear Catherine.

'I'm not in there.'

Although, am I hearing at all? It's not a voice, not something with volume and texture, not like last night. There's no sound, no loudness, no tone. It's more like Catherine is inserting a line of words into my head.

And my immediate reaction to her voice is, I *know* she's not in there. I teach science to nine year olds, after all. Whatever Catherine was, in terms of firing neurons and her parasympathetic nervous system, ceased to exist about a week ago.

'Talk to me,' she says, suddenly. And it is definitely, inarguably, her voice again, though once again it feels as if it's being fed noiselessly through my head.

I can't see her, but I can definitely hear her.

'Push your thoughts towards me and I can hear you too,' she says.

What thoughts? My immediate thought is, I need to see a psychiatrist.

'You're not going mad, this is natural,' she replies. But it's all in a rush, almost too fast to take in.

I push a thought towards her.

'Catherine. Where are you?'

'Losing you,' Catherine says, but in the same speeded-up way as before. Then I realise my attention has wandered, for a second, to Veronica.

She is crying, with her father hanging onto her arm, while her mother tries to say something polite to the funeral director.

'I can't keep this connection up, Mark,' Catherine says, more slowly and clearly.

And this time, something else happens. I get waves of shivers through my body. Very mild electrical currents, in a kind of sequence of five or six repeated waves. It's all I can do to stand there in front of her family and not react.

'Sorry.' I push the thought back. It's like last night, when I stopped looking at her. She started disappearing.

'I'm not sure I can do this,' I push again.

'It's okay. Later. Love you.' The voice comes in a wild rush of words again.

And then she's gone. And it occurs to me that the only thing making me even participate in this hallucinatory experience is the fact that I need her so much, I'll cling onto anything. Even madness like this.

Catherine's well and truly gone too, as far as the funeral

director is concerned. She's over, basically. And maybe it's time for the next cremation, but in any case he's practically wiping his hands together in a 'That's that' gesture. You can't blame him, I suppose. They've got a lot of people to get through, and it's been a long day. I suppose after a while it feels exactly the same as working for KFC.

'Mark.'

It's Veronica. She's been avoiding me since this morning, even when we were sitting in the same pew. I suppose it's because I refused to say anything at the service. Or maybe it's the fact that my black suit is partly cobbled together from stuff I used to wear on stage with The Bottom Line. She's probably offended. And God knows, it doesn't take much.

'What will you do now?' Veronica asks me.

'Go home, have a cup of tea.'

'Then what?'

Her face is red and puffy.

'Go back to work.'

'You can't go back to work! Honestly, Mark, I think there's something wrong with you!'

Her parents look at her, then at me. Then they look at my parents, who are now hanging around by the exit, politely waiting for everyone else to leave first. Then Veronica does her almost-pouting look.

'Of course I can go back to work,' I tell her. 'If you must know, it's going to keep me sane.'

Then I walk away, far ahead of them, in the direction of the car park, leaving the coffin, and the gigantic stainless steel cremation machine, and everything else, far behind me.

At home, I find some flowers on the front doorstep, from one of Catherine's old customers at the travel agency. I'm now thoroughly sick of flowers. In the last week or so, they have come to symbolise death, and who wants that around them? The only thing that stops me from throwing them in the bin is the suspicion that Catherine might be watching.

'There, I've said it, Catherine. The only reason I'm not putting these in the bin is because you might be watching.'

I push the thought, and I say it loudly as well, to the empty kitchen. If I was expecting a response, though, I don't get one.

And it's a relief. *Tea*, I suddenly think to myself. She's not here. Good. Normality. Tea. Back to my old self.

Then I pick up the phone and ring the Head. I'm going back to school tomorrow.

I teach 4B at a place called Rivett Street Junior School. The children there are aged between seven and eleven, and they all come from the edge of the same South London suburbs – Brixton, Stockwell, a few from Clapham, and some from Balham. I've been there for five years.

As I get ready for work, I realise just how many gaps there now are in my normal pre-school routine. Catherine would always line up the jam and marmalade, next to the toaster, after she'd finished with it. This morning, there is no line-up. When a good song came on the radio in the morning, I would always turn the volume up, and then as soon as it had finished, she would turn the volume down again, giving me a jokey, pissed-off look. This morning, there is no radio – and no look.

Despite this, after seven days of death, and honey sandwiches, and long baths, it feels good to be back in the centre of life again, even if it does mean having a clueless ten year old run over my foot with a metal scooter.

'You know you're not supposed to have that inside,' I tell him. He's been riding up and down the corridor on it.

The child turns around and I instantly recognise Scott O'Grady, known to several staff members as Grotty Scotty.

'Mr Buckle!'

Scott gets off the scooter and makes an attempt to fold it under his arm – which at least makes me feel like I'm having some effect.

'I'm not having a very good day, Mr Buckle!'

'Yeah, well, that makes two of us.'

'Can I tell you something?'

Scott, predictably, has a breakfast stain on the collar of his school shirt, a pierced ear which is going septic and he's shouting at me.

'Mr Buckle, I can stick my fingers up every single hole on my recorder!'

'Yes, I did hear you, Scott. I'm the wrong teacher, though. You need Mr Saddleton. He's the one with the recorders. I'm the triangle and castanets man.'

Felix Saddleton has an older class, who are apparently capable of doing more than banging bits of metal and wood together, so they get to play recorders – which means, he gets to shake the spit out of them, at the end of the day. Felix also plays them a lot of extremely boring national curriculum songs on his guitar. A small sample from Felix Saddleton's 6B Hit Parade: *Song Sung Blue*, *Puff The Magic Dragon* and *Kum Ba Ya*.

'The thing is,' says Felix later, taking a drag on his cigarette, 'they don't realise *Puff The Magic Dragon* is essentially a song about Class B drugs.'

We are sitting in the smoker's corner of the staffroom. It's where we always sit, with Felix in a tatty orange vinyl armchair, leaning half his torso out of the window, in order to avoid offending the non-smokers. He's wearing one of his brown nylon shirts, which means there are big patches of sweat under his arms. He's also wearing a 70s kipper tie, with wavy lines all over it – and gravy. We haven't discussed yesterday's funeral yet, or even the fact that I've returned to school so quickly after Catherine's death – and I can see we're not going to.

'I saw Mr Blount making love to his alsatian again this morning,' Felix drawls, in his strange, camp Australian accent. 'It was disgusting.' He mimes something which might be a salivating dog, enthusiastically rolling its eyes, inserting its tongue in a human being's mouth.

Mr Blount is the schoolkeeper. He and his dog live in something called The Hut, at the back of the school. They basically control the school, in a powerful two-way dog-man combination. People think the Head is in charge, but actually it's Blount and the alsatian.

'He's turned up the temperature in here again,' I add.

Our schoolkeeper is famous for fiddling around with the central heating. There can be a temperature variation of up to ten degrees Celsius, depending on which room, in which part of the school, you happen to be standing.

Felix sighs. 'It was like the bloody Arctic five minutes ago, with 6B. Now I'm in the Sahara.'

Felix has been doing Crazy Shoe Music this morning. This means that the children in 6B bring in assorted footwear – wellington boots, flip-flops, clogs, ballet shoes, plimsolls, their mothers' platform shoes – and bang them together violently while Felix plays *Ta-Ra-Ra Boom-De-Ay* on the piano.

'I won't describe the smell of the shoes,' Felix says, wrinkling his nose. 'Or the look of them. I mean, it went beyond the bounds of sartorial decency. All those gum boots and thongs. And those stinking sandshoes!'

'Wellingtons, flip-flops and plimsolls we call them in England, Felix. But what did it sound like?'

'Oh, it sounded all right. Anything sounds all right when you've been forced to listen to Close Encounters of the bloody Third Kind all week.'

The children are also doing Outer Space Dancing, along with Crazy Shoe Music, and after some child stole most of Felix's CD collection, he's been left with just one album in the classroom.

'I am so absolutely, irrevocably tired of these children who constantly want to take over my classes!' he sighs, ashing out of the window.

'I know,' I sympathise.

'Scott O'Grady!'

'I know.'

'Of course, Scott O'Grady wasn't content to be the sun,' Felix says in disgust, 'he also had to be the moon, the stars, a meteorite, a dust storm, a gas cloud . . .'

'Well, he's definitely a gas cloud,' I interrupt. 'In fact, some people say he travels with his own private gas cloud.'

'I hate him, I hate him,' Felix says. 'Outer Space Dancing used to be so relaxing!'

'Felix, we're not allowed to hate the children, have you forgotten?'

'Well his mother, then. His father. Whatever human life form spawned him – I hate them.'

Having seen Scott's parents for myself, on the one and only occasion they turned up to parent-teacher night, I have to admit that human life form is probably a good description.

Felix is from Sydney, and gay – and camp with it. It's hard to describe the way he talks. Think Kenneth Williams crossed with Crocodile Dundee, maybe. Or Russell Crowe doing the Jeremy Irons monologues from *Brideshead Revisited*. Sometimes, when

Felix is drunk, he even makes a sound approaching a moo. He also tuts a lot. The kids have picked it up, of course – there are quite a few brilliant Felix soundalikes in 6B. The best Felix soundalike of all, though, is definitely Felix himself. He's the only man I've ever met who can do his own impersonations.

'Tch, Mark, let me tell yoooou, I was at the gym this morning and I saw a man who convinced me that it was time to drink freely from the goblet of Adonis again. On the Princess Diana-type equipment. But Maaaark, he was with his mother! So what's a boy to do?'

Felix is always telling me about his failed man-hunting expeditions to the gym, and this is one of them. The other men, presumably gay, all seem to go with their boyfriends – and occasionally one of their parents. Consequently, Felix has been single for all the time he's been at the school, which must be about two years now. He says he doesn't miss Sydney, but at least he seems to have had a love life there.

He got the job at our school because of me, and that was in turn because of Catherine. She got to know him during one of her Australian holidays, back in the days when the travel agency she worked for, had tickets to spare. Catherine and Felix became friends right away, after she met him at a party at Bondi beach, and eventually he moved to London. Despite the fact that Felix can't, or won't, talk about Catherine now, I also happen to know he left probably the biggest and most expensive wreath. No card.

'Oops, here's trouble,' Felix says, leaping out of the orange vinyl armchair. He has, of course, been sitting in Alison's spot for the past twenty minutes. In our staffroom, this is almost as bad as taking someone else's mug.

Alison is our age, I suppose, although she always seems older. She's the only teacher I know with a share portfolio. She has a horse called Molesworth, at her parents' house in the country, and a lingering boyfriend called Charlie, who also seems to be permanently stationed with her parents. Felix's private theory is, she's frightened of horses and she's frightened of Charlie, and she hates her parents – which is why someone posh like her continues to teach at Rivett Street.

30

Alison arrived here years ago, for reasons involving the Head – which she never talks about. He's married, of course. But the gossip and speculation is so old now, that it's become part of the furniture in the staffroom, like the orange vinyl chairs, or the plastic wood coffee tables.

Alison mock-thumps Felix now, and sits down, making space for herself by moving all his copies of *The Guardian* out of the way. Her arse is at least one *Guardian* wide, and possibly more. Then she gets out her packet of Silk Cut. The three of us are the only members of staff who still smoke. As Felix says though, it's actually an advantage. We practically own almost a quarter of the staffroom, with views thrown in.

Alison was at the funeral too, I remember, though we didn't actually get to speak. She was just another big black hat at the back. I suppose I should apologise to her, but maybe I won't have to. I get the sense that I'm being given a lot of mileage at the moment. People are like the Red Sea, parting in front of me, wherever I walk.

'Mark!' Alison says, 'you're back!' I can tell she's embarrassed, but then a lot of Alison's time is spent being embarrassed – about quite a lot of things. She resorts to mock surprise when she's faced with what she thinks is a tricky moment. I'm used to it, but it just compounds the awkwardness.

I'm tempted to reply 'Yes! Alison! Isn't it surprising! I'm back!' But I don't. Felix gives me a look, and slopes off to make himself another cup of tea.

'Me too,' Alison interrupts him, hopefully waving a hand at the tea urn.

'Only if I can have one of your special bags,' Felix says. 'I mean, call it vulgar excess, but I can't face PG Tips today.'

'Oh, go on then,' Alison says, 'do have a special bag.'

Alison brings in her own box of Earl Grey tea, which she hides below the s-bend underneath the sink. We all hide things in the staffroom. Felix hides his copy of *Time Out*, which is permanently dog-eared at Gay What's On, under the stack of old *Guardian*s on his armchair. I hide a razor, and a toothbrush, and a tube of toothpaste, in a plastic bag behind the digestive biscuits.

While Felix is getting the tea, Alison gives me a look. It's a silly look. Her mouth is turned down at the corners, and she has big, blinking eyes, like Bambi.

'Okay?' she asks, meaningfully.

I nod my head. 'I'm fine. I just want to get back to work for a while.'

This could obviously lead to more awkwardness – a moment when emotions might start to well up, perhaps, so Alison briskly changes the subject to her dog. We hear a lot about her dog in the staffroom. It lives with her parents as well. It's called Cedric – hilarious name, ha ha! – and it's a labrador.

'Cedric's got worms again, he's scooting along the driveway on his funny old furry bottom.'

'Oh dear.'

'Cedric's been trying to lick the television again, whenever *Teletubbies* are on. He gets so excited. We had to tell the cleaner to switch it off.'

Then Alison thinks of something else.

'I just had 6A on traffic census. God, it was odious.'

Then she realises this means the kids were standing around on the street outside the school, watching cars go past, and this has a vague, tenuous connection to car accidents, and thus Catherine being killed, so she shuts up – and goes bright red.

Felix hears the last of this sentence as he brings back the tea.

'You know,' he says, putting the mugs down, 'this school now has eight filing cabinets filled with hard traffic census research. Years and years of this incredibly detailed minutiae, gathered by thousands of eleven year olds, all based around – where is this bloody school again?'

'Near Clapham,' Alison says. It's actually nowhere, in South London terms, somewhere between Brixton and nowhere, but we try to rein it in towards Clapham to make it sound like it exists.

'Anyway,' Felix continues, 'we have reams of notes from these poor, confused children. Microscopic detail about all the complex permutations of South London traffic patterns 1970–2000, all of it illustrated by coloured-in bar graphs and questionnaires, all of it wildly inaccurate.'

'And why are we saving it?' Alison sighs.

'Well, I've got a confession to make,' Felix smirks. 'I chucked all mine in the incinerator.'

Alison teaches 6A, so she often compares notes with Felix. They also compete. If Felix organises Crazy Shoe Music or Outer Space Dancing as part of his music lesson, Alison will then be moved to come up with some bright idea of her own. This is how she came up with Rap Lessons, or specifically, a terrible song for assembly called *Tower of London Rap*, the mention of which, even now, reduces Felix to howls of laughter.

'Your feudal aristocratic English background, Alison, oh my God, it cracks me up. What a cack that was, the *Tower of London Rap*! Exquisite! I can't belieeeeeve it!'

Felix can still recite the lyrics to *Tower of London Rap* by heart, though I don't think Alison can. The children of 6A, for their part, probably try to forget. 'I was sittin' on my steed in the merry month of May/And some dudes with suits of armour came lookin' for some hay.'

It goes on. Other ideas of Alison's over the years – painting Egyptian hieroglyphics on the toilet walls when they were doing history (Mr Blount is still trying to get them off with a sponge) and some weird upper-class game called quoit tennis, which resulted in several children being injured by flying rubber rings.

Alison sips her Earl Grey tea thoughtfully.

'One of the children told me that Scott O'Grady was feeling them up in your Outer Space Dancing,' she says, looking sideways at Felix.

'Not at all, my dear.'

I try to help Felix out. None of us likes to look as though we've lost control of our kids.

'Scott O'Grady just wanted to be everything at once, as usual,' I say.

'Yesss,' Felix hisses. 'Not only the sun, the little bastard, but also the moon, the stars, the asteroids, the rings around Saturn, the entire Milky Way . . .'

'Anyway,' Alison says smugly, crossing her legs and smoothing down her skirt, 'O'Grady was definitely rogering someone while he was pretending to be Jupiter and it was in your lesson.'

'I hate to say it,' Mark smirks, opening his newspaper, 'but you're talking out of Uranus, Alison.'

She groans at his attempt at a joke, and wanders off to the toilet – or, as Alison calls it, the lav – and I wonder if I should get my notes on friction and ball-bearings together for 4B, or go back home instead.

Something in me needs to take another bath, or have a nap, or maybe just collapse – I'm not sure. It's tempting to cycle home now, while it's still sunny, so that I can avoid the empty shock of going home at the end of the day, when it's darker and gloomier, and the house will seem emptier and bleaker. In the end, though, the decision is made for me.

Alison comes back from the toilet and tells me that I have to look after another class, along with my own, this afternoon – some female teacher's just gone home with PMT. I suppose, if there was a competition for time off, I could probably defeat this sickly feminine creature with my new widower status. There isn't any contest, though. And apart from anything else, I'm not even really a widower, because at the end of two years, I still couldn't bring myself to propose to Catherine. It's a thought that stays with me all the way until the start of the next lesson.

three

There are too many objects in this house which belong to both Catherine and I, rather than just one of us. It would be so much easier if the weird spiky plant in the corner was a Catherine object, because then I could put it out with the rest of the rubbish on the street, or at least put it out and hope one of the neighbours might nick it.

Instead, the spiky plant is something that is ours, and even though every time I look at it I think of her, I still can't throw it out. Why? Because I paid fifty quid for it. Catherine chose it, and I paid for it. It was a peace offering from me, because on the day we bought it, we'd had a huge argument over the new rug. Catherine had ordered it without telling me, and when the delivery van men unrolled the rug in front of the fireplace, I just walked straight out of the room. And sulked, as is my habit, until it was time for the news.

The rug had – and still has – one yellow triangle, one red circle and one white circle, on a purple background. We looked after Veronica's cat one holiday, and it pissed all over the white circle, and then someone else (probably me) spilled red wine on the yellow circle. But still, that's another mutual Catherine-and-me object, not in spite of the argument and the sulking, but because of it. I can't throw the rug out now, any more than I can throw out the spiky plant. Plus, the floorboards get freezing in winter.

I can deal with the reminders of Catherine that are months, or years old. It's the most recent bits and pieces of her life that have the power to throw me. I'd forgotten about the pink razor that's still stuck to the bottom of the rubbish bin, in the bathroom. It's lying in a pool of hair gel, or some other goo. It still has her leg hairs in it, or her armpit hairs, or something quite recent. Catherine was also one of those people who are always leaving little reminders to themselves everywhere. I found one of her yellow square notes stuck to the inside of the kitchen cupboards today. It's for an appointment with her naturopath. It would have been tomorrow, at four o'clock.

She cut herself on the pink razor, when she was shaving her legs, the night that she died. We were shouting at each other through the bathroom door, which is how a lot of our arguments seemed to take place. That night, it was one of those shopping-list arguments, where you start shouting about something that you think is at the top of your own directory of grievances, and end up working through six, seven issues in the space of an hour.

It began with my failure to pay the TV licence. It then segued into her failure to cancel our subscription to *National Geographic*, and ended up, inevitably, with the biggest problem of all – the baby that she wanted to have, that I didn't.

She was in the bath, fuming, shaving her legs, when I shouted something like, 'You don't want a baby any more than I do', through the door. And I heard her swear, and then she got a bit tearful, and then she yelled back that I'd made her cut herself, and that she had – finally – had enough. Of me, of our life together, of everything.

I'm walking around the house in a daze, trying to collect all these razors and sticky notes, and other Catherine reminders, when my father rings the front doorbell. To be caught red-handed with all her stuff in my hands, ready to throw it out, looks callous, but at the same time, why cover anything up? He's been through death – his own father died – he should understand.

My father is standing on the front doorstep with a Tupperware container full of spaghetti bolognaise. It smells. And it also has a label, in my mother's handwriting, saying SPAG BOG.

'There's more in the boot,' he says, 'but I thought I'd borrow your brolly to go back for them.' I can hear his engine running, and it's pouring with rain now. And my father has pushed his hair back, which he always does when he gets wet, so he looks like an otter.

It's now raining on all the black plastic rubbish bags of stuff I've left near the bins. Oxfam was supposed to collect them today, but they haven't. So I can see the arm of one of Catherine's cardigans, drooping over the side of the bag, getting wetter and wetter.

Dad puts up the umbrella in the hallway, and is back from the car seconds later, with a stack of even more Tupperware containers crammed up to his chin. As well as spag bog, I can see from the labels that I'm getting beef borg, shep pie and fet nap. A wet cat is now following my father up the pathway, sniffing the mince in the air.

'Go away you bugger.'

Dad doesn't like cats, and he shuts the door in its face. It has one blue eye, and one green eye, like David Bowie. Apparently Bowie got eyes like that after being in a fight in Brixton in his youth. I'd say it's the same with the cat, except it was probably a fight with a squirrel on Clapham Common.

'I'll put these in the freezer,' Dad says, moving all my microwaveable pizzas to the back, and stacking all the Tupperware, labels out, at the front.

'Well, I'm not going to starve,' I say.

Dad puts the kettle on.

'Beer,' I say, finding two cans in the fridge, and waving one of them at him. I don't feel like tea, I've had enough tea. It's funeral fluid.

We sit in the living room, watching the rain, and the cat with odd eyes rubbing itself up against the window.

'Bugger off,' my father says again, waving a hand dismissively.

I switch on the television. It's a game show for kids. Everything is, at this time of night.

We watch for a while, mentally answering every question except the ones about Destiny's Child and *Dawson's Creek*, and we joke about this for a while, then Dad eventually says what he has to say.

'Mum and I were wondering about Catherine –'

'You mean Mum was wondering and she's making you ask.'

'Just about – had you ever made any plans?'

The plus side of this embarrassing conversation is, I suppose, that my mother actually makes very good shepherd's pie. And there is now enough in the freezer to feed me for a week.

'As in plans to get married,' I say, eventually. 'Or have kids.'

'It would make a difference, a slight difference, if we knew,' my father says, but I'm speechless now.

'Chops was up all night worrying about it,' he adds. Chops is my mother's nickname.

Not because she has big jaws, mainly because her maiden name was Lamb. I let him go on.

'She was up all night,' he says again. 'She had a bit of a cry over it.'

'Oh, God.'

'It would make a difference to her to know,' he says again.

'There are other options in life, you know, apart from automatically having to get married or produce kids, just because you've passed the two-year mark.' And I realise, as I say this, that I'm using my teacher's voice. 'What makes you think,' I continue, a few seconds later, 'that Catherine and I weren't just going to live together for the rest of our lives?'

My father gives me a brief sideways glance that exposes this for the rubbish it is. He knows as well as I do, that I'm not like that – my family's not like that. We do all the normal things, really. We have mortgages, we get married, we go and see ordinary doctors instead of naturopaths, we eat cornflakes for breakfast.

'Of course you would have got married, if you were going to,' he says. And he's right. Part of me knows about that awkward two-year mark, just as much as he does.

'You wouldn't be asking if Catherine wasn't dead,' I say,

38

feeling childish about it all of a sudden.

'No, I think we'd still be asking,' he shakes his head, 'but perhaps only each other, rather than you. I think it would make a difference to Chops to know,' he tries again.

I think about my mother not being able to sleep, and crying in the middle of the night. If I think about it too long, though, I'll just get angry, so I focus on the kids' quiz show instead. Why the hell was she crying about us? There are other things she could be crying about. Like East Timor, or Africa, or something.

My father always wears his coat inside, even when the central heating is on. It's a big, olive-green parka with a drawstring hood. In all the years I've seen him in it, though, he's never once drawn the strings. I think his head's too big for the hood.

'Talking about funerals,' he says, although we haven't been, 'I died once.'

'What do you mean?'

'When I had my operation. I was dead for a minute. For some reason' – he looks genuinely baffled now – 'it's come into my mind to tell you. But don't tell Mum.'

'No.'

'I was on the ceiling.'

'Oh, yeah?' It's as if we're talking about his last holiday in Greece.

'I could see everything. The top of the surgeon's bald patch, everyone talking about me, everyone looking worried.'

'So you were really dead?'

'Definitely dead. Because I was told to go back. Not so much a voice telling me, more an impression.'

'Just when you were beginning to enjoy yourself too.'

He ignores this, and the kids' quiz on television roars on.

'It's not what you think, Mark. I didn't hear any harp music.'

'No pearly gates?'

'It was nothing that I expected,' he goes on. 'Although I never expected anything, to be honest. Like most people. I just assumed you died, and everything stopped.'

And really, I'd like to leave it there. But I can see from the look on his face that I'm not allowed to.

'And how long were you dead for?' I ask politely. It's like asking him how long he was in the army for.

'Well, the surgeon told me it was eighty-eight seconds, something like that, it's on my medical record. But those eighty-eight seconds!'

'Oh yeah?'

'I was on the beach, Ryestanon beach in Cornwall, where we used to go when we were kids. During the war. And I was there, as much as I'm here now. But the sun was brighter, the sea was almost white, everything was like they say, the big, white light.'

'You thought you were on Ryestanon?'

'Well, obviously I wasn't there, but I was there,' he says, thoughtfully. 'But the point is, my mind was still working.' He slurps back more beer and adds, 'Fascinating.'

'Well, they chopped off someone's head at the Tower of London, didn't they,' I reply.

'And you know her lips were still moving. It was Queen Mary or someone.'

My father shakes his head. 'To be specific, although my heart had stopped beating, I could see, I could hear what they were saying about me, on the table – and I could hear one of the nurses coughing. And there was more, as well.'

'What more?' I put my beer can down on the ugly rug.

'It was like my soul was flying, and I didn't even know I had a soul, to be quite honest.' Dad suddenly puts his fingers halfway up his spine, and cracks his back. It sounds terrible.

'Don't tell Chops about this,' he says again. 'She'll only worry.' He cracks his back again. 'I'm not totally sure why I'm telling you all this now.'

'You know I teach science, Dad,' I say at last. And just in case there's any doubt about this, I can hear myself using my teacher voice again.

'Yes.'

'Well, it might be a relief to know you were just dreaming. Or hallucinating.'

'I had no feelings for my body at all when I saw them working on it,' my father says. 'It was just like another person. Or an object.'

'Strange things happen under anaesthetic. You probably imagined you saw the surgeon's bald patch.'

'And there was a ringing noise in my head, too,' he says, 'like brrring-brrring.'

'What did the surgeon say?'

'He gave me a book to read about it, it was in the hospital waiting room. I never looked at it.'

'The oxygen supply to your brain got cut off, and your brain was dying. It was like a last gasp for your brain, probably.'

'And it happened to Ronnie.'

'Oh, for God's sake.'

Ronnie is my father's friend from the pub. He's fat – there's no way around it, he's extremely fat – and he had a heart attack last Christmas.

'Ronnie was dead in the ambulance. He was watching television, when he went.'

'Must have been a luxury ambulance, then.'

'No, it was like an imaginary television, and all these pictures of different people were coming towards him, on the screen. A picture would start coming towards him, then go past, then he'd get another one. After a minute, he realised they were all pictures of people who'd died. All the people he knew, family and friends, all dead.'

'Wow.' This is what I say to the kids when I pretend I'm impressed with something they've drawn, or written, or found underneath a hedge in the woods, even though I think it's utter crap.

'There's no wow about it.'

'A neurologist would be the person to speak to, Dad. Not me.'

But that's it. Whatever compelled him to tell me his secret story has now gone. Still with a wet patch of rain on the back of his green coat, my father gets up from the sofa and takes his empty beer can into the kitchen.

'Thanks for the food.' Something stops me from saying thanks for the talk. Perhaps it's too much exposure to slushy American TV programmes as a child. And anyway, it's insincere. I'm not grateful for the talk at all.

'I'll tell your mother I spoke to you.'

He means about the not marrying bit, I suppose.

I see him to the front door. The rain has stopped, and howling wind has taken its place. The cat with the David Bowie eyes is long gone.

'There's something on your back.'

My father motions me to turn around, and picks off a yellow note. It's the note about Catherine's naturopath that I thought I'd thrown in the bin.

'Stuck right on the middle of your back,' my father adds, picking it off.

I say goodbye, and I let him go out into the night, and then I open another beer. And what I don't say, and what makes me feel so uneasy, even though the beer is making me mellow, is this – sticking Post-it notes on my back is a Catherine thing. It used to be her little joke. Without even looking at the note again, I grab it off the table, screw it up, and throw it in the bin.

four

It's amazing how lack of sleep can make the smallest things irritating. When I arrive at the staffroom the following morning, Alison is sipping Earl Grey tea and twanging an elastic band, repeatedly, on a shoe box. The shoe box has a Harrod's price sticker on the side adding up to half my weekly salary, which is bad enough. Worse, though, she insists on twanging the rubber band more violently with each separate ping.

'I'm going to get the children to draw the sound actually *travelling* through the atmosphere,' she says, pinging away with a silly look on her face. It's like watching David Attenborough get excited about something boring under water.

'Well, does the sound have to travel around my head in particular?'

'Oops!! Sorry Mark!'

As always, Alison is speaking in double exclamation marks. She then puts the shoebox and rubber bands away, with a lot of fuss, which is somehow even more annoying.

'I might need to borrow your oscilloscope later,' she tells me.
'I'll think about it.'

'Well it's not exactly yours, is it?' she presses the point. 'It belongs to the school.'

'I lent you my slinky spring for a lesson last year, I still haven't got it back.'

'Oh, do you know, I think Cedric might have buried it in the back garden! Sorry!'

She laughs at this, as she always laughs at anything involving her ageing and worm-infested labrador, Cedric. In any case I know it's a lie. Most stories involving her dog are. It's not his fault, but Cedric is the excuse dog. And also the joke dog. Some other things that Alison has borrowed for her class from me and lost over the years: a box full of empty margarine containers, all of which Catherine had saved and in fact washed up for me, a bunsen burner, and an aquarium, which Catherine was hoping to nick from the school and grow cactus in.

Alison now goes through her class notes, drawing a line through every other sentence with a fluorescent green pen, and making a serious face. She then starts muttering her notes aloud.

'Get the children to strike the tuning fork on a piece of cork,' she mumbles.

'You know, that's not really the best way to go,' I hear myself saying.

'Why not?' She shifts around in her armchair, sending the cushion sideways with a slight farting noise, which predictably enough makes her all twitchy and embarrassed and upper-class again.

'The cork's too soft,' I tell her. 'You want to try something else with a tuning fork, like felt on the edge of a table.'

'No, no, I've had success with cork before.'

I can't believe I'm doing this. I'm actually arguing about the finer points of a tuning fork experiment for ten year olds as if I care about it.

'Are you a bit stressed, Mark? You poor thing.'

Alison says this in mid flight, as she waddles off to put the kettle on again, for more vats of Earl Grey tea.

'Well, I'm stressed,' Felix Saddleton answers for me, striding into the classroom with his cigarette already half lit, collapsing into his chair.

Today he is wearing a purple shirt, which looks like a bottle of French wine went through the wash, and a horrible brown tie. He's also perspiring profusely. Mr Blount must have been mucking around with the central heating again. Felix's armpits are always like this – two patches of darkness, no matter what the weather's like outside. But today the armpit stains are spreading.

'So why are you stressed?' I ask him, because I know that the nicer I am to Felix the more it pisses off Alison. Funny, really, how being surrounded by children all day can also make you more childish.

'The children all went back home with the wrong tooth-brushes,' Felix says.

'What?' Alison picks up *The Guardian* and sits down.

'I was doing Teeth, remember?' Felix prods her.

'Oh, Teeth,' she interrupts. 'You know, when I did Saliva the other week, I actually had someone chewing the bread for twenty minutes before she generated anything.'

'She was probably an alien,' Felix counters, 'most of your children are. No, I tell you, this toothbrush disaster is really the nadir of my career. We could be talking legal action. I could be jailed. Imagine. My children with foot-and-mouth, passed on by toothbrushes!'

Waving his arm out of the window, with a fag attached to it, Felix manages to look genuinely upset for a moment, before his face reverts to the placid, tanned, dimpled Australian look that the school knows so well.

'So what happened?' I encourage him. If nothing else, it's better than listening to Alison twanging rubber bands on the lid of a shoe box.

'Well, I was distracted in class,' Felix says lamely. 'I took my eyes off the ball. Namely because we had School Dentist in. Who of course is the great love of my life.'

'School Dentist is actually married to one of the parents and he's not gay, because he made a pass at me once,' Alison observes, although I already know this.

'Shut up, witch, don't shatter my dreams,' Felix moans.

'But he's not very happily married, if it's any compensation,' I offer. 'So who knows, you could get lucky.'

'Anyway,' Felix continues, 'in came spunky old School Dentist –'

'I hate that word spunky you always use,' Alison interrupts.

'So spunky old School Dentist came in,' Felix continues, ignoring her, 'with his special dental disclosing tablets, so the children could all watch their teeth go bright red, and then I realised –'

'You didn't get the children to label their toothbrushes, you silly arsehole,' Alison interrupts.

'No, I didn't get the children to label their toothbrushes,' Felix finishes, sadly, with another little gasp on his cigarette.

'I've got nowhere to run, nowhere to hide,' he concludes. 'Jane Costello has a Barbie toothbrush. She went home with Trevor Sutton's Bob the Builder. And he went home with Nathan Taylor's manky green toothbrush from Poundstretcher. God, I just know I'm going to get sued.'

At this point, I realise that someone in the staffroom has turned up the volume on the radio, which must mean Felix has been louder than usual.

'Anyway, you were saying you were stressed, Mark,' Felix counters, leaning over to shut the window, and stubbing out his cigarette.

'Alison was accusing me of being stressed, but I'm not,' I say.

'Oh, yes you are!' Alison says, smirking.

Then they both remember that Catherine being dead is why I'm stressed, and it suddenly goes quiet.

'Is that the news?' Felix says quickly, craning to hear the radio.

'Well, I'm going to find some more shoe boxes,' Alison says. 'Wish me luck!' And with that, she goes off, slinging her shoulder bag over her hip, with a tuning fork hanging out of it.

'You know what I do when it all gets a bit much –' And I can tell, Felix is feeling guilty and trying to be thoughtful, now.

'What's that?'

'A little yoga position called Salute to the Sun.'

'No thanks. Catherine used to do it. Ridiculous.'

And because Felix doesn't answer for a bit, I have a spare

moment for a memory of sorts, or at least a quick flash in my mind's eye, of Catherine in her yellow T-shirt and old tracksuit, doing her yoga in our bedroom on sunny Saturday mornings, while I made the toast for breakfast, downstairs.

'I'm going for a walk,' I say. There is now a lump in my throat like a marble.

'Fair enough,' Felix says.

I can see he doesn't know what to do with me. But then, I don't know what to do with me, either.

I head for the playing fields, which really belong to the 'big boys' school' as the children call it. It's across the road from us, but a gap in the fence still lets you in. It smells of worms, and mud, and mushrooms, as it always does, no matter what the weather's like, and you can see where half the kids have been smoking in the bushes – and probably doing other things in the bushes, as well.

I'm trying not to think of Catherine, but perhaps that's wrong. And I wonder if I'm safe to let go here, to let rip in the middle of the playing fields. Probably not.

I have the wrong shoes on for tramping around – black lace-up teacher shoes – and even moving sideways from one mound of bare earth to another doesn't stop mud coming up over the sides of them. And now there's another reason to turn back, too. I can see Tess Blake walking the other way. She's unmistakable, because she has that kind of wild, frizzy blonde hair that very few other human beings seem able to grow. It stands out in the sun like a big yellow halo. You'd know Tess Blake anywhere. Strange, pale blue eyes, and famously mad hair.

She waves energetically. So I smile – or rather, I over-smile.

'Mark!' she bounds up to me.

Tess is a Christian, and she works part-time as a teacher's aide at our school. Along with the hair, she sings with a very frightening Christian rock band, whose name is Faith Lift.

'Hi there,' I offer.

'Hello, Mark.'

I hope I don't strike Tess Blake as a man on the run at the moment. She's the kind of person who has antennae for that kind of thing. It's a kind of sick-nurse quality. Somewhere between Julie Andrews and your mother. It's a shame, because it gets in the way of her attractiveness. Something that's probably struck every male teacher in the school, at some point, whenever she's wandered into their class.

'It's not a bad day,' she says, looking up at the clouds.

What is it about Christians that makes me want to swear, violently? Part of me feels like screaming, 'Actually, Tess, the day is total bloody shit.' Instead, I smile back again. It's making my face ache.

'It's good to see you back at school,' she chirrups.

'Thanks.'

'It's what I did,' she explains, 'when my father died.'

'Right.'

'Although,' she adds, 'I'm still mourning him in a way.'

This is now officially ridiculous. I hardly know Tess – she helps with children much younger than my lot, and she's only in every Tuesday and Thursday or something – and we are standing in the middle of a field talking about her dead father.

'I'd love it if you could come to our gig tomorrow night,' she says.

'Oh, the band.'

'Faith Lift are playing a benefit gig. For Christian Aid. Felix and Alison are coming.'

'Oh, are they?'

They didn't tell me that. And frankly I'm shocked. Alison I could just about see going, but not Felix.

'I decided I'd invite some of the staff for a change,' Tess shrugs. 'Make an effort to get to know people better. It's not far from where you live, actually,' Tess enthuses. 'At the Pig's Head.'

I think she can now tell that I'm definitely not going to come. There may even be a look on my face that says I'd rather have my arm cut off than go and see Faith Lift at the Pig's Head in Clapham. Dire band, dire pub. And I don't care if it is near me. Or even for the little kiddies in Africa supported by Christian Aid, come to that.

'Anyway,' she waves a hand. 'If you're free. If you're in the mood.'

'Sure. Great. Thanks!'

I wait a fraction of a second to sort out which way she's heading, and then I stride purposefully and meaningfully the other way. Not quite in the opposite direction, because that would be rude, and she'd notice. But let's just say that where Tess Blake is concerned, I instinctively want to head elsewhere. And there's no way I'm going to watch frigging Faith Lift at the Pig's Head, Clapham, just because Catherine's died and people feel sorry for me, and there's nothing else in my life on a Saturday night any more.

five

I'm watching Faith Lift at the Pig's Head in Clapham. Their first song is called *I'm A Sponge*, if I'm hearing it correctly, and the singer – some irritatingly dark, tall and good-looking bloke with big Bugs Bunny teeth and a nicely ironed denim shirt – introduces it this way.

'Hi, we're Faith Lift, and I'm Peter. And this song is called *I'm A Sponge* because, when we fill up with faith, we're just like big sponges.' He coughs and hesitates, adding, 'Well, I know I was.' And then they begin.

I can't quite believe this, but Felix and Alison have both failed to show, the bastards. And there's nobody else from Rivett Street here, either. So I'm here, at the Pig's Head, on my own, watching Tess Blake with her big, blonde halo of hair (she sings and plays keyboards) and the mighty Peter, her fellow Christian, bang out some horrible sub-funk crap about Jesus and sponges, while the punters talk over the top of them, watch the football on Sky and smoke.

Of course, Faith Lift have got their fan base. It appears to be more attractive, dark-haired people with big teeth, probably related to Peter by the look of them, and a lot of Chinese students with backpacks and glasses. Who brings a backpack to a pub? There is a lot of over-enthusiastic nodding to the beat, too. Also tiny, imperceptible taps of the feet, a few embarrassingly feeble 'Whoaas!' and – I hope this isn't true, but I think it is – there is a woman in the corner in a cowboy hat clapping along to the music. Bloody Christians and their demented clapping. I'd forgotten all about that.

It's tempting to go home, even before the first song has finished. The house is dark and empty, and I'm torn between wanting to cry, and being unable to cry, every time I get into what used to be mine and Catherine's bed, but at least it's better than this crap. At home, I can watch television. Maybe I could even try to read a book. Whatever.

Then, suddenly, someone slaps me on the back. It is Felix Saddleton, pissed out of his mind.

'I've been scrubbed down!' he shouts in my ear. He's so drunk he can't even position his mouth correctly, so he ends up shouting past me, sending gin fumes straight into the face of a startled Chinese student.

'What?'

This is the trouble with the Pig's Head. It's so loud in here, it's just one long night of 'What?' basically, and I remember now why Catherine and I never came into the place.

'Mark! I've been scrubbed down and oiled by some very, very naughty and uninhibited boys in Pimlico! And I've been asked to join the Hair Bear Club!'

'What's the Hair Bears?' I yell back, motioning for us to move to the back of the pub, where at least I don't have to be shouted at. He stinks of drink.

'I'm a hairy man,' Felix leers at me, gesturing clumsily to somewhere that is either his back, or his arse. I really don't want to focus too hard on either.

'Felix, what are you on about?'

'I might not look hairy, but I'm secretly very, very hairy indeed,' he insists. 'A hairy beary! A hairy fairy!' Then he suddenly looks theatrically proud for a minute. 'We who are hirsute, are asked to join,' he says mysteriously, tapping the side of his nose. 'It's a cult. A cult at the secret gay sauna in Pimlico. And I tell you, Mark Buckle, it's faaaaabulous. Champagne. Spa baths. Bubbles. Soap' – To emphasise the point, Felix churns up imaginary bubbles with his hands – 'And,' he continues, 'there's a special section for all the hairiest of the Hair Bears. And we're the very naughtiest, naughtiest men of all!' he cackles, doing a little dance of glee in his overly tight trousers.

Then Alison arrives.

'Sorry I'm late everybody,' she pants, talking over the top of Felix and breathing hard.

Going up the stairs of the Pig's Head has obviously been too much for her. It's weird seeing Alison out of context, away from the staffroom. She's even got make-up on, which is frightening.

'You go away, Alison,' Felix slurs, pushing her away with his hand. 'You go away because you'll never understand, you *woman.*'

'Oh look, there's Tess!' Alison says, ignoring him and trying to make eye contact with the stage. It's ridiculous, really, watching her get this huge thrill from actually knowing someone in the band. Especially this band. With this song. In this pub. Not that she knows Tess any better than the rest of us.

'What it is,' Felix continues, drunkenly squeezing my arm, and I suppose he means his gay sauna club in Pimlico, 'is very healthy, very clean. Scandinavian healthy living for hairy homosexuals.'

'Yes. You said. In Pimlico,' I add helplessly. Felix is going to go cross-eyed and keel over sideways in a minute.

Felix suddenly starts talking behind his hand. 'You should come along, Mark. I bet you're hairy enough to get into our tub. No women, though,' Felix adds conspiratorially, giving Alison a nasty look. 'Just us very naughty, naughty well-oiled young men.'

'I'm flattered.' I say. 'Even though I'm not particularly hairy, Felix, I'm flattered.'

'There, you see,' Felix smiles triumphantly, and skips around me, making little butterfly motions with his hands. 'I knew you'd be flattered.' Except, of course, he can't say the word 'flattered'. In fact, he can't even pronounce anything beginning with f, s or d at the moment.

'I bet Alison's hairy,' he slurs, staring hard at her leaning up against the bar.

'I bet you're right, mate,' I reply.

'Oooh, I love it when you call me mate,' Felix smirks, mincing off to join her. And he really is mincing, too. Worse than Dick Emery ever minced. Any minute now, I think, he's going to be spotted by a bouncer. Or worse, some of the non-Christians in the crowd, some of the hard men of Clapham – well, violent 18-year-old thugs, anyway. The thought of dragging Felix away from a fight later does not appeal, and it's not something I think I'd be very good at, but I'm preparing myself for it anyway.

The song ends. And then Peter tells us, through his gigantic teeth, that a special guest is coming on now. A special guest with a saxophone. Oh please, God, anything but a bloody saxophone. In a minute they'll be shakin' and groovin' for the Lord, and I think I'll have to leave if that all starts.

'And on tambourine, keyboards and glockenspiel,' Peter spits into the microphone, 'Tess Blake!'

Of course she'd be on glockenspiel – she probably stole it from school. Some Christian she is.

But, judging by the slightly more excited 'Whooos!' this time, Tess has a few personal fans in the audience, mostly male, and I'm not surprised. She looks great. In fact, she looks amazing. When she comes out from behind her keyboards, it turns out that she's wearing something you might have remembered Kate Bush wearing once, in one of those videos that used to drive boys of a certain age wild in the late 70s. And she has a tan mark, where her bikini must have been last holidays. And now, like every other man in this audience, Christian or non-Christian, I find myself staring at it.

Alison wobbles back, with Felix in tow.

'Outrageously cheap wine, it was worth getting the taxi from Mummy's after all,' she says. Then she remembers how we all send her up when she calls her mother Mummy, and she stops. I suppose she's been cocooned with her family all afternoon, so they've been getting into the Mummy/Daddy thing, and she's just forgotten.

'Where's your hot date?' Felix slurs, giving her a sharp look.

'Where's your world-famous boyfriend, Charlie?'

'Oh, he's had to go to a wedding,' Alison says, not quite looking back at him. This is not surprising. Charlie is permanently at weddings. Or he's away in Spain. Or he's ill. Or he's skiing. Or doing other predictable upper-class things, like seeing to the hounds, or shooting clay pigeons, or going to the polo.

'I had to leave Pimlico because I ran out of money,' Felix confides in me, barking drunkenly in my ear.

'I can lend you some if you want to go back,' I say.

'No, no, no, dear boy,' Felix waves me away, sounding like Noel Coward, although it's all wrong because of the pissed Australian *Neighbours* accent. 'Besides which,' he gives me a worried look, 'just look at my fingers!'

He holds them up for inspection, and I suppose it's been raining out there as well, but his hands are definitely like prunes. Pink, soggy prunes.

'I sat in the spa with the naughty Hair Bears for hours and hours and hours,' he nudges me, giving me a bad wink. Then he repeats, as drunks always do, 'Just look at my fingers!' and waggles them around in the air, experimentally.

'Anyway, Charlie will be back on Sunday night, so that's all right,' Alison interrupts, as if she's just finishing a sentence – although this kind of information is something neither Felix nor I care about.

'What happened to you?' she says suddenly, staring at Felix's wrinkled hands, while she knocks back a glass of red wine.

'You're a woman and I can't tell you!' he pouts.

'You should fly to Morroco for that kind of thing,' Alison shouts, cheerfully. 'It's much cheaper and you won't get arrested. Very relaxed laws in Morocco.'

'There was lots of hair in the bath when we pulled that plug out,' Felix explains to me, solemnly.

Meanwhile, Faith Lift play on. It's The Monkees song, *I'm A Believer*, lifted conveniently for their cause. And I used to quite like it too – what a shame. I suppose Tess is doing an okay job on the keyboards, getting that authentic 60s sound, but Peter and his teeth are just woeful. Davy Jones, though he was English, never sounded this chronically English.

'Oooh, it's just like being in church!' Felix squeals, clapping his hands together and sending up the woman in the corner.

Alison lights a cigarette.

'Don't be like that about Tess,' she says, talking through the side of her mouth as the smoke wafts into my face. 'She's such a nice girl.'

And I suppose Tess Blake is a nice girl. Or she wouldn't have invited me here tonight. But then again, what the hell am I doing here? There is an unreality about all this, now. It's like being a tourist. Too foreign. I never go to this pub.

On Saturday nights, I would either be out with Catherine and some of her friends, or we'd be at home together with a video, or – very occasionally – I might go out and see a film with someone I know – but this situation, here, in the Pig's Head, with this awful band and this strange, pissed version of people I work with every day, is not normal. I feel like a strange person in a strange land, like I always do when I'm somewhere new. And it doesn't feel good.

'Let's get pissed,' Alison clinks her glass against mine. 'You need a drink.'

Felix is ahead of her, though, and having sloped back from the bar with one double gin and tonic, has already finished it, and is heading back to the bar to push his way through for more.

'I'm going to be like a little, truffling, hairy pig,' he tells us all, waving his finger in the air, ominously. 'Just watch me truffle through them all! Oink! Oink! Get out of my way, infidels of Clapham!'

And he does push his way through, keeping his head down and his elbows to the sides, although I can see by the annoyed looks he's getting from some of the crowd that I will, indeed, later be scraping him off a Clapham pavement.

The atrocious Faith Lift grind on through *I'm A Believer*.

'Strange lighting,' I hear myself saying to Alison. 'Isn't it.'

Each member of the band has a multicoloured light going around them, but also – bizarrely – through them. Tess has gone gold. Peter has gone an interesting mixture of purple, green and yellow. And the drummer and guitarist are various shades of blue. Alison's not listening, though. Or, at least, she doesn't understand what I'm saying.

Automatically, I look back to the mixing desk to see what, if anything, they are doing with the lights. It's certainly the most sophisticated set-up I've ever seen in a London pub.

'It could be lasers, I suppose,' I say to Alison, although she's still not listening. 'It's got that kind of effect.'

The band finishes ruining The Monkees, and then Peter takes over the keyboards for a while, while Tess moves to the front. She is wearing an amazing, tight white dress. It's almost *Sex and the City*, but not quite. Weird for a Christian. But then, there are so many modern variations on their religion – or indeed, any religion – that I've lost track. Just when you think you've got Catholics or Mormons or whatever sussed, they break their own rules again. So, I don't know, maybe this is allowed in her church these days – this undeniably sexy look.

'I say, young Tess has gone a bit saucy hasn't she,' Felix slurs, staring at her and coming back with more drinks. 'Lucky the parents of 2B aren't seeing this!'

'I'm going to sing this song for someone in the audience here tonight,' Tess explains, 'a friend of mine, who I work with, who knows what it is to lose someone.' Then she looks as if she's going to say something else, but doesn't, and the band launches into a song I thought I'd forgotten, but I haven't. *Never Tear Us Apart*. INXS.

'I used to know them in Sydney, you know,' Felix gabbles in my ear, waving his gin around.

'Shhh!' Alison hisses, cutting him off, 'she's doing the song for Mark.'

A beer is put in my hand. And vaguely, I'm aware that this may be the third or fourth pint, and maybe that's why I'm beginning to feel like this – but there are more colours, on the stage, suddenly. In fact, they seem to be timed to the music.

Two worlds collided, Tess sings, and a kind of blue light pulses through, and around her throat. *And they could never tear us apart* . . . Whereupon, she pauses for a fraction of a second, as the guitars stop too, and green light starts spinning around the bottom half of her body – almost to the point where you can't see the dress, or even Tess, any more. Weird. Every colour of the spectrum, much as I teach the kids at school, surrounding each member of the band in turn.

'Incredible lights,' I check with Felix. And although he nods, I can see that he can't see what I'm seeing. Like the green lights in the bedroom a few nights after Catherine died, this is a phenomenon meant for me. And don't ask me how I know that either, I just know.

I love your precious heart, Tess sings, doing it almost as well as Michael Hutchence did, and I can feel myself about to go into the cry/not cry zone again. An empty, exhausted dryness. Whatever it is, it's way beyond tears.

'She's singing this for you, you know, Mark,' Felix nods solemnly and drunkenly to himself, off in his own little world, the gin switching his mood from inane to serious in a second.

Suddenly, Alison starts sniffling. Worse, she wants me to notice her, so that I can somehow appreciate the fact that she's crying.

'Mark!' she mouths silently, with shiny wet eyes, as Tess sings her sad song. *Two worlds collided,* she sings up to the roof, as the blue light goes through her, and around her.

Then Alison gives a muffled squeak, like a rabbit who's been stepped on, and bolts to the loo, stuffing a tissue into her face.

'Tess is very good,' Felix notes, to nobody in particular. 'Very, very good, in fact. Wow. What a song, shweetie darling! What a song!'

I make a drinking motion to him with my hand, offering him another from the bar. It's irresponsible of me, because he's close to vomiting stage, but I need someone to get totally wasted with now, and it's not going to be Alison.

'I thought you'd never ask!' Felix shouts at me, giving me the two-finger signal that means he wants a double gin again, and then turning it into a wobbly thumbs-up sign.

On the way to the bar, I stop for a minute, near the front of the stage, finding a space. It's an old INXS song I haven't heard for years, but in my tired and semi-drunk state, it's enough to make my eyes sting with tears. And still, the coloured lights pulse around the band, but every time I look up to the ceiling, all I can see is the standard red spot, white spot and blue spot that every other pub band in the country – including us, in our heyday – has always had.

Finally, Tess finishes the song, with such total devotion to the lyrics that you can feel the people in the crowd – even the mug punters of South London – all standing still for it. The guitarist nearly screws it up with an overly dramatic finish, but at the end, there is an echo and a silence that I don't think the Pig's Head stage has ever seen or felt in its life.

And then there is screaming, from some woman. And clapping. Much clapping. The pulsating blue light around Tess's throat gets stronger, and now seems to be extending into the wall, where it passes through a mirror with a beer ad engraved on it, and into the bricks.

The bar is emptier, because everyone has been listening and nobody has been drinking. And I order, and make it a double for Felix, and another pint for me. Then I add a further pint, just in case it's too much hassle to get back to the bar, and throw in a packet of crisps for Alison. That should keep her happy. And that's probably about six pints for me now, which is great. I can walk back home anyway. Shwalk back home. Shwalk back shome.

Alison is out of the loo, now, still blowing her nose, with watery eyes.

'Are you okay?' she touches my arm. I nod.

'I'm just seeing things,' I yell, over the top of the next song. Peter is back in front of the microphone and the band is playing something I've never heard of now.

'Seeing things like what?' Alison yells back.

'See that light,' I point to where Tess was standing – but the light has gone, just when I was about to explain how it seemed to be penetrating the bricks, and the mirror with the beer advertisement on it.

'Do you want some fresh air?' Alison asks, touching my arm again.

'No I bloody don't want some fresh air,' I say, moving away from her. Alison has this quality – like a sponge herself, in fact – of getting way too soggy and drippy when she's had a few drinks. I do realise it's psychological compensation for the way she is the rest of the time, which is like Joyce Grenfell on acid, on a St Trinian's hockey tour of the home counties, but there's still no reason why I have to put up with it.

She goes off to pester Felix, and I find a stool to sit on, in

the dark, up the back. The reason it's empty is because someone's spilled a beer all over it, and then left two peanuts on top.
It's almost like pseudo dog crap, except it's food and drink. But
I sit in it anyway, happily perching in my jeans on the small
puddle, because I no longer care.

And I think about Tess – and look at her some more.

The lights have gone, whatever they were, but I've been left
with both a feeling and a physical sensation instead. They seem
old and long gone to me on the one hand, but also pleasantly,
excitingly familiar on the other.

And, as I'm downing the next pint, straight after the last one,
it comes to me. This is what I used to feel like, and be like,
before Catherine. And it's a physical and emotional blast of
energy that's sent me heading straight for many different girls,
at many different times in my life – sometimes for the wrong
reasons, sometimes for the right reasons, but always at the very
beginning.

I had it with Donna Roberts. I had it with Catherine's sister,
Veronica. And now, I have it with Tess Blake, the Christian.
Mad. Insane. Irrational.

I make a pathetic attempt to talk myself out of it. She loves
Jesus, Mark, not you. And anyway. Catherine's only just died. So
this is wrong, indecent, terrible. Isn't it, Mark? All of which
naturally makes it feel extremely right, of course.

And now, I catch myself thinking, I wouldn't mind another
beer actually. Aksherly. Akshoo-ally. Where's frigging Felix
when you need him?

Then, I notice something. Someone is standing next to my
right shoulder. I can feel their body heat. And they are very
close now. When I turn my head, though, there's nobody there.
Just a few flashes of light. White sparks, diamond twinkles, the
kind you get when you stand up from the bed too quickly and
see stars.

Then two things happen at once. My mobile phone blips,
and I see a text message from Veronica, to call her urgently. And
then it rings straight after that, and when I take it outside the
pub, I hear Catherine saying my name.

'Mark.'

Oh God. God help me. There's a truck going past, but it's

definitely her. And I no longer care that she is dead and I need to see a psychiatrist. Speak to me, speak to me, Catherine.

'Mark.'

And then the phone dies on me.

six

The hangover passes eventually. It takes right up until Sunday night to go completely, but with all kinds of well-worn tricks – the fingers down the throat when I get home, the children's anti-diarrhoea drink from the chemist (Felix's suggestion), the Bloody Mary, the McDonald's breakfast (Alison's suggestion) – it ultimately goes.

And then I am in the bath, at almost 1 a.m. on Monday morning, listening to the radio, when Catherine tries all over again. It begins, as it did in the Pig's Head, with the strong sensation that she is there – or someone is there, anyway – standing by my side, just by the edge of the bathtub. And then my eyes, closed until this point, suddenly have to open.

When I turn my head, half wanting to see, half not, there is a small cloud of electric, acid green light again. Fuzzy, almost neon. Like the green that was around Tess when she was singing. Like the green in our bedroom, when Catherine was sitting on the chair after the funeral. Through the green light, somewhere, I know Catherine will be there again, too, but it's still a shock when my mobile phone rings. It's in the pocket of my trousers, crumpled on the floor. If I stretch my arm out over the bath, I can probably find it. Do I want to find it? Not sure. No, hang on, I want to find it, Catherine, don't hang up. My arm passes straight through the green light.

'Mark.' It is Catherine's voice, on the telephone, and then it is gone. And I can't see her, but I have definitely, absolutely, undeniably just heard her. This is a fact. Somehow, thinking this comforts me. It is A Fact. A subjective experience, certainly, but something which I know to be true, just as I know I had baked beans on toast for dinner at 7 p.m., and that I have just been using a bar of white soap from The Body Shop with bits of porridge in it, and someone's car alarm just went off in the street outside. Anyone would accept these things as facts. The baked beans, the soap, the car alarm, the green light – and the voice. The phone rang, and it was very clearly her. No confusion there.

I can't see Catherine, then, like I did the first time in the bedroom, but it seems I can now hear her. And I can feel her. In the sense that, if you had blindfolded me when we were together, not that we ever did anything kinky like that, and if you had made her stand beside me, very close, this is exactly what it would have felt like.

And now, there is something else too. I can smell her. Same perfume. Unmistakeable. Heady, expensive, French. Give me a minute to think about it, Catherine, and I might even get the name of it. I bought it for her duty-free in Paris. It still cost a fortune, even then. I gave it to her once for Christmas, after she asked for it. Or am I imagining the smell? It could be this porridgy soap. But sniffing the air, and then practically snorting the air, I nearly pass out at the smell.

The next sentence is a thought, not a voice. A thought that is not generated by me, but placed there, with Catherine's accent, and her kind of words, although my ears register absolutely nothing in the air beside me.

'Joy!'

Of course. A perfume, strangely enough, called Joy. That's it. And I wouldn't have remembered the name of the perfume, not in a million years, so that thought clearly wasn't coming from me, then. So I'm neither remembering, nor making things up. I'm just receiving information. That much, anyway, is clear.

Then, suddenly, crouching forward in the bath water, I get a sense of urgency that's almost like an adrenaline rush. Not quite heart-thumping, speedy panic but very definitely an insane desire to do – what? Go to the mirror. Yup, that's it, go to the mirror.

Once again, I'm not thinking this, I'm not generating it, and I'm not hearing it. Nobody is talking to me, there's no volume. But it's like – what is it like, this feeling? A frog in a drawing I saw once, being connected up to some horrible experiment from the nineteenth century where they pushed a button and made its legs move. I'm that frog. I'm in the bath, and I'm being moved around, manipulated, practically pushed to do things, now.

Catherine and I used to hang around talking in the bathroom all the time. It's not as if I'm self-conscious about being naked. But it still feels vulnerable. So, with the green fuzzy light still in my peripheral vision, I find a towel. Getting out of the bath is complicated by the fact that I need to lean so far forward to get out – I have a fear of somehow treading in the green light, or breaking it up with my body, or somehow shattering the moment.

Then I see something new. Catherine's dressing gown is on the back of the door. And instantly, I know that's wrong. It's in a black plastic rubbish bag downstairs, in the hall cupboard. I folded it. I deliberately put it on the top of the pile, just in case I changed my mind and wanted it back again, for some reason. But somehow, once again with a sense of urgency, I know I'm supposed to put this dressing gown on now. Ridiculous. Laughable. It comes up to the top of my legs, where it used to go to her knees. And it's pink, with daisies embroidered on the pocket.

Then: 'Mirror!' one word, roaring at me out of a wind tunnel again.

Thus, I find myself standing in Catherine's pink dressing gown, staring stupidly at my face and shoulders in the mirror above the sink, at around twenty past one in the morning. And then she transplants herself onto my head. Just like that.

By concentrating hard, I can look at her – or what seems to be an imprint, in light, of her face – hovering over my head and shoulders. If I lose the thought, she goes. If I keep at it, she stays. And as she hovers across the top of my reflection in the glass, I can only think that it's like looking at one transparency being placed on top of another. Exactly like an overhead projector at school – except this is almost three-dimensional. Her face, over mine, certainly isn't flat.

I have a feeling, somewhere inside, that this may be a remarkable phenomenon that might never be repeated. The old science student in me is aware that it needs to be observed. And so I do, checking the fact that her face is colourless, sort of white-transparent, but also that there is some depth there – the hollows of her cheeks, for example, extend back further than mine in the mirror. I also notice that when I force myself to smile, she smiles too, over the top of me. When I relax my face, hers relaxes. The smell of her perfume is overpowering now. And the imprint, in light, of her body in a dressing gown, in the mirror, matches mine also in her dressing gown, almost exactly.

Catherine. As familiar as anything in my world, and now as shocking to me as a heart attack. Not that I've ever had one. But who knows. Maybe I'm having one now. Maybe I just died in my bath.

I start going acid green. Or rather, Catherine, over me, goes green. And I get the sense that she's trying, she's learning, she's experimenting. She's only just died, so it's early days yet. Is that the explanation? Is that the rational answer? And where did it come from, did I *think* that thought then, or did she send it to me?

I am staring so hard in the mirror, willing her to stay there, on top of my face, that my eyes start watering now. And I have been concentrating so intensely that I've forgotten to breathe. My legs are starting to get tired. My feet are starting to freeze on the bathroom floor.

'Hear you,' says Catherine's voice, in my left ear. But this is interesting. My lips didn't move. And neither did hers. And then something tells me enough is enough. This session is over. And there's no point in staying here, staring at this glimmer of her, in the mirror, any longer.

The light imprint of her on my face fades, and I am left staring at myself, tired, with dark circles under my eyes, and tear stains. What does she mean, hear you?

I exchange her dressing gown for my own tattered terry-towelling one, and head back to the bedroom where it's warm. Hear you. Replaying what I just heard, it doesn't make sense. Unless it was part of a sentence. What, hear you as in, 'I can hear you?' Or even, 'I'd like to hear you?' Does Catherine want me to talk to her?

Then I am almost knocked over by a huge, shuddering electric shock, from the top of my scalp down through my legs. Like the shivers you get when you hear a great song, but powered by a few thousand volts.

'It's okay, it's okay,' I tell the air in the empty bedroom. 'I get it. This is a yes, right?'

Another wave of electrifying chills, again and again, like a series of waves, going from my head to my feet. And so, at just after 2 a.m., judging by the alarm clock by the side of the bed, I start to talk, as she seems to want. Because, it seems, she really can hear.

And it's a relief. It's like breathing out after being suffocated. And although I'm talking to thin air, alone in this bedroom, the thought crosses my mind that, at least if I'm developing schizo-phrenia, I may as well get something out of it. I mean, I may as well get the full experience of having her back, before they cart me off to a psychiatrist.

'I haven't rung your sister back,' I begin, addressing the empty space in the bedroom, 'because I can't be bothered. I'm sorry.' And this is a good beginning. It's exactly what I would be saying to Catherine now, in the early hours of Monday morning, if she was here this weekend.

'It's just that Veronica does that urgent text message thing, and you know it's not urgent,' I continue. One of Catherine's old teddy bears, which I've saved and plonked on my side of the bed, stares balefully at me. What now? Will its eyes light up and spin round, like something out of a Spielberg film? Will its tiny pink teddy lips open and start speaking to me, in Catherine's voice?

Then I'm sniggering with stupid, tired laughter, and also

crying again, at the same time. And snot is coming out of my nose, but there are no tissues.

'I haven't shopped since you went,' I tell her. 'No tissues. In fact, no loo paper either. I suppose I'd better do something about that.'

Silence. Then the clock goes off – just like that. It pings out, into digital blackness. On the bedside table, the anglepoise lamp we bought from Habitat flickers, then goes brighter than normal, then flickers again. I was wrong. This is like a Spielberg film, suddenly. So I check the bear. But it's okay. His lips aren't moving yet.

'What it is,' I tell the wall, because it's the only thing I can talk to and focus on, 'is a kind of desperation.' And what I mean is, and what I hope Catherine will understand, if she can hear me, is my new desire for Tess Blake.

'I probably don't really fancy her at all, Catherine. And anyway, nothing would happen for months. Years. It's just that I'm needy. Extra needy at the moment. Just being a man, I suppose.' Then I realise how pathetic that sounds, and how she'd laugh at me, or shove a pillow in my face, if she was still around. So what can I expect now, a low-flying pillow, suddenly hurled around our bedroom, in poltergeist rage? But no, nothing. It's just my own, feeble, honest voice, now, alone in the bedroom.

The alarm clock switches back on, and starts flashing 12.00 which it always does when I've accidentally kicked the plug out of the wall, or even wrenched the cord out of the wall, in early morning irritation. Maybe that's it. I kicked the plug. Yeah, that'll do. How am I going to sleep otherwise? And I'm so tired, now. Really, really tired.

When I do finally pass out, though, it's to a dream which seems to star Catherine and God. In my dream (which is so real that it seems, well, *real*), Catherine is wearing her pink dressing gown again, the one with the daisy on the pocket. And, although God isn't actually there, in the sense that Charlton Heston isn't there with a beard and a robe, he's somehow around both of us. Or is it a he? I mean, that's the traditional expectation isn't it, but this presence surrounding Catherine and me is more like a force of nature, than something with a beard or a big nose.

'Of course, I know you don't believe in this,' Catherine points out, in the dream. 'You've never liked religion,' she goes on.

'Well, what about you?' I shoot back. We are both sitting in armchairs, for some reason. They are the armchairs from downstairs, but they have been moved to some sort of space like a field, or a meadow. It's sunny and very, very bright.

'This is all a thought form,' she sighs, anticipating my next question, waving a hand at the chairs, and the grass, and the sky. 'We create by thinking over here. I was surprised when I found out, but I've had a go – and I can do it too.'

'Well, you've done a good job,' I say. 'I mean, this is just like that place where we used to go camping sometimes, in Cornwall.'

'Shall I tell you what happened when I died?' she asks me.

And part of me thinks yes, fair enough, this is exactly what I'd imagine her wanting to do.

'Go on.'

'Well, I felt myself going out through the top of my head, if you can imagine that. As if there were two of me. One got stuck behind, and that was the one they said had died, in the back of the ambulance. The other one just moved, very quickly, into a garden. And my grandparents were there, both sets, and an uncle, and even some great-grandparents I'd forgotten about. And they took me into a nice room, where I could just rest.'

'And how did all these grandparents and uncles look?'

'Grandad Mac died when he was in his seventies, but he looked forty-five.'

'Right.'

'You can look how you like here.'

'And how do you look?'

'I've chosen to look like this now, because you're here. I thought this dressing gown would be good.'

'It is good.'

It is good, I think, except somewhere in the real world it's been packed into a rubbish bag, then mysteriously moved itself to the back of the bathroom door.

'Catherine, can I tell you something?'

'Yes.'

'Normally, in a dream, when I'm conscious of the fact that I'm dreaming, I wake up. But I haven't woken up yet.'

'Well you're not dreaming, exactly. Does that explain it?'

'When you died,' I manage to say at last, 'was it bad?'

'It hurt a bit. Not much. I left my body pretty quickly.'

Catherine wrinkles her nose in my dream, in a way I had almost forgotten.

'Shit, Catherine. And is this heaven? Where we are?'

'Well, kind of. Not the way you think of it.'

'Well, where are we, then?'

'That was my first question. It's one space. Among many spaces. Does that make sense? There's no up and down here, no gravity, no time. So they all sort of weave around each other.'

'But when you're in this field, that's all you can see.'

'Right.'

'I can't believe I'm having this conversation, Catherine.'

And she laughs at this, and I can feel her laugh go through my body. It's the best feeling I've had since she died. Better than sex. Better than anything I could invent.

Catherine turns her head a little, and smiles. She is surrounded by a changing field of light, I notice. Some of it is in blobs, while the rest of it moves around her head and shoulders like water.

'I think about our argument all the time,' I say. 'When I made you cut your legs when you were shaving.'

'I know you do. I've been – sort of visiting you – when you've been crying about it. At night. Don't think about it, Mark. It's not important.'

'If you say so.'

And she laughs again, and I feel it going up through my chest and into my shoulders.

'You know we sent Tess to you,' she says.

'Who's we?'

'All of us here. Since I died, a decision has been made. We want you to get to know her better.'

'Catherine, this is driving me insane. This "we" stuff, and this pseudo-heaven stuff. It's not you. I mean, what do you mean, when you talk about "we"?'

'Feel it,' she says. 'Just feel the feeling of where I am for a minute. It's better than any explanation I can come up with.'

And then the armchair seems to take me, in its velvet arms, and I sink into love. What love? Every kind of love. We had a dog called Beano, who used to follow me everywhere when I was a kid, and it used to put its paws around my neck and chase cricket balls for me. Part of the feeling is Beano love, now. And then there's something else. Maybe grandmother love, from long-gone childhood Christmases. And Catherine love, of course. And then, much more, even beyond that. I can only think, I took acid once, at teacher training college, and it was never like this.

'I want you back,' I finally tell Catherine, after the love has taken me over.

'But I'm here now. I can't go back.'

'With God. Bloody God, I suppose – is that who's got you now?'

She laughs again, and gets up from her armchair.

'Don't go!'

'I'll be back soon. You'll hear from Tess tomorrow. She wants you to go to a party where everyone has to dress as Elvis. And ring my sister back. She's pissed off with you, you haven't replied to her text.'

When I wake up, the alarm clock is still flashing 12.00 in its tiny electronic-brained way, and I have no idea what time it is, until I ring the speaking clock. A voice, which sounds vaguely like it could be one of Alison's strange upper-class relatives, informs me that at the third stroke, it will be 10.18 and twenty seconds.

What is left in my brain feels like one of those dreams you usually have after too much red wine and pizza. A party where everyone has to go like Elvis. A strange, frustrating, dream argument. Armchairs in a field. Strange colours and lights. A feeling of love.

I ring up the school and tell them I'll be in after lunch. Then I check my mobile phone and see another text from Veronica.

R U OK? I'M WORRIED! it says. Which means, she's not worried about me at all, but this is a good way of nagging me to get back to her.

After I make a cup of instant coffee in the kitchen, I finally ring Veronica, at work.

'Has your phone been switched off all weekend?' she asks.

'Sorry.'

'Don't worry, you're a man, they're all hopeless at returning calls,' she says, the bile rising, as it always does.

'Veronica, lay off. I've had a lost weekend, all right? Drunk too much. All that. I just slept through the alarm.'

'Well, it's really hard to talk about this now,' she says, through gritted teeth, 'because I'm at work, but I really need you to know something.'

'What?'

'For God's sake, it's so hard to talk to you, Mark, but it's about Catherine.'

'What?'

'I saw her in my kitchen on Saturday night.'

'Did you?'

A pause. 'Take this seriously.'

'Don't be so bloody paranoid, I am taking it seriously.'

'She came to tell me she was all right, Mark.'

'Right.'

'See,' she says triumphantly, 'I knew it was a risk, texting you that message.'

'No, no. Veronica. You've got it all wrong.'

'You don't believe me.'

'I didn't say anything, okay!'

'Anyway,' she sighs heavily, and I can hear her hurrying up the call because her boss is wandering around. 'Just in case you're worried, she's okay, and so that's that.' And then she hangs up.

Switching on the TV, I see the giant baby in the sun, on *Teletubbies*. More heaven stuff. Or some kiddy TV person's idea of heaven. And then, like some kind of cosmic conspiracy, two Jehovah's Witnesses in blue suits knock on my door, just after 11 a.m.

'Bugger off, God,' I say to the sky, after I tell them to bugger off too, through the letterbox.

Because, at the end of the day, I don't believe in him. In her. In it. I mean, very convincing dream and all that, Catherine, and nice try with the love thing in the armchair, but I just don't believe. And why don't I believe? Because, on page 18 of the paper, under World News, there is a story about two Catholic nuns, who have been found guilty of helping some soldiers in Rwanda butcher and burn local people alive – people who had fled to the convent for safety and shelter. The nuns gave the soldiers the keys to the petrol shed, apparently. Yet, despite this, I suppose they'll go to heaven – it's in their contract, isn't it?

And on another page of the newspaper, there's more stupid crap going on in Northern Ireland. And the Middle East. All in the name of God and presumably some belief in heaven's rewards – although whose God and whose heaven they're slaughtering each other for, I'm not quite sure. And then, at the back of the paper, there's some writing vicar, some preacher in print, who I've never actually bothered to read before, jammed next to the crossword, with his thought for the day – just to nauseate me even more.

His thought for the day is from the Bible, and it makes no sense – but then, nothing in the Bible ever has, to me. The scribbling vicar is doing his column this week about the bereaved, too – which is me. Not that it brings me any comfort at all. No help at all, then, from God's man on earth. So – two fingers up in the air to you, God. Judging by today's newspaper, it's just business as usual. Killing and slaughtering, preaching and lecturing. Utter crap.

Yet, when I finally make it into school after lunch, the first person I run into is Tess Blake, walking across the car park, carrying a white Elvis Presley suit, circa 1973, draped across her arm. And part of me thinks, well of course I'm running into Tess Blake in the car park, and she's off to an Elvis party. Because that really was Catherine in the dream, right? And any minute now I'll be getting my invitation to turn up next Saturday night somewhere with a copy of *Heartbreak Hotel* under my arm, and false sideburns and a black wig.

Tess looks incredible today. She is in a short kilt thing, and high boots, like some kind of 1960s female spy. And her voice is slightly throatier and huskier than usual, maybe from the singing.

'Faith Lift are playing at a party next Saturday night,' she says, pushing her frizzy hair out of her eyes. 'I'd love it if you can all come. You, and Felix and Alison. It's an Elvis night. So we're doing all Elvis covers for a change.'

'Thanks. I'll let them know. Though I can't imagine Alison participating, to be quite honest with you.'

'I hope it wasn't too much,' she says, looking embarrassed. 'With the song, and all, the other night. You left the pub before I had a chance to explain it to you.'

'No. I mean –' And I wave my hand. I can't speak. What am I going to say? That the song made Alison burst into tears? That I sat on a bar stool in a puddle of peanuts, and practically fell in love with Tess Blake on the spot in a drunken, lustful stupor? That the song she dedicated to me, probably meant more to me than every hymn at Catherine's funeral put together?

So I say nothing. But I notice the little gold cross around Tess's neck, and she catches me looking at it.

'Everyone thinks I want to convert them,' she says, reading my mind. And for a moment she even manages to look annoyed, through her curtain of blonde, frizzy hair. It's like looking at a cheesed-off angel.

'No, no.'

'It's a drag. Pushy Christians are a pain. I'm not like that.'

'So where's the party?' I ask, changing the subject.

It's miles away, on the other side of London, in Richmond of all places. A total tube nightmare.

'Great,' I hear myself saying, though as with so many of these things, part of me knows I'm probably not going at all. And all the time, Tess Blake just stands there, and smiles.

seven

Sanity, I am happy to say, returns the next day, and as the Head has given me time off for delayed bereavement-related shock and associated problems, I make an appointment to see our local doctor. So far, Dr Smita Patel has only seen me for a sore throat, an embarrassing case of ringworm and some weird stomach thing everyone at school caught last winter – but she may as well see me for mental illness, as well.

'How many voices are you hearing?' she says, taking notes on her pad – which, like all doctor's stationery, has some big pharmaceutical company logo printed on the bottom.

In fact, if you look at Dr Patel's desk, here in this dingy surgery in South London, pretty much everything is sponsored. The pens, which advertise an anti-depressant. The paperweight, which has something to do with women's contraceptives. Even the computer has a little rubber cartoon condom man dancing and waving a merry gloved hand, on top of it. The only thing that doesn't have a logo on it is the framed photograph of Dr Patel's children, laughing and playing on a swing, framed on her desk.

'I only hear Catherine's voice, nobody else,' I tell her. She nods, dangling one shoe off her foot. I like Dr Patel. She's always seemed more human to me than other doctors I've seen. Fiddling with her earring, she continues to ask me questions. How am I sleeping? Do I feel threatened or manipulated when Catherine talks to me?

'Well, no more than I did when she was alive,' I make a weak joke. Dr Patel smiles, and continues. What does Catherine say, when she talks to me? Do I hear it in my head, or do I really hear it? How do I feel about the other teachers at school, at the moment, about the children?

'There's a particularly foul boy called Scott O'Grady, who farts all the time, but otherwise everything's fine,' I tell her.

'What else are you experiencing?' she asks, carefully.

'I saw her face in the mirror. Catherine's face. It went over mine. And I see green lights. In fact, the other night I saw heaps of coloured lights. Oh, and I smelled her perfume.'

'Okay. Fine.'

And I can tell this news isn't fine. But she lets it go, and keeps on scribbling.

There's a horrible smell of sick drifting in from the surgery next door, and I wonder what's going on. It unnerves me for a minute, too, so that I almost think Dr Patel might be changing her mind and recommending a psychiatric examination.

Images of mental hospitals zip through my head. *One Flew Over The Cuckoo's Nest*. White coats. Jack Nicholson. Nasty night nurses. Maybe I shouldn't have told her about the face in the mirror.

'In India,' Dr Patel says at last, 'what you describe is not unusual.'

'Thank God for that.'

'In fact, I've heard about things in my father's old village, which would get me examined,' she giggles.

'Like what?'

'Dust appearing in a man's hands. Dust that heals people of wounds, cures them. There is a man called Sai Baba in India who is said to have these powers.'

'Wow.'

Automatically, I don't believe her. But I listen politely anyway.

'I have heard of a necklace appearing around a woman's neck, just like that.' Dr Patel snaps her fingers. 'And I have heard of the future being foretold to the living, by the dead. All kinds of things,' she shrugs, with an apologetic smile.

'Are you sure?' This sounds rude, but I need to know – is she sure?

'You could say it's a way of life where I come from.'

'I've always wanted to go to India,' I say, politely. 'Or anyway, Catherine did, and I was going to be her baggage handler. She was the one who used to get the discounts, you see. At the travel agency.'

'You need to talk more about your wife. Let it all out,' Dr Patel says, dangling her shoe again. I'm glad to see that the sick smell from next door has been replaced with disinfectant instead.

'She was my girlfriend, actually. We never married.'

'Talk about it anyway,' Dr Patel recommends. 'Men are not very good at this sort of thing, they bottle things up . . .'

There she goes again. Just like a member of the Veronica Army. Making asssumptions.

'Do you have a good friend you can talk to?' she asks.

I nod. But, of course I don't. There's Alan from university, who's had two children and plays golf, and has become very boring, and there's a few band people from the old days, and there's the King of the Hair Bears himself, Felix Saddleton, the hirsute toast of the Pimlico gay sauna scene, but that's pretty much it these days.

'No family members you can confide in?' she says, anticipating a no.

'My parents think I'm cracked already. This would take it beyond the point of no return.'

'I think you're normal, Mark,' Dr Patel sums up at last. 'You are not exhibiting anything other than a lack of sleep, and mild stress.'

Then she scribbles a name on a notepad.

'This ends our session as patient and doctor. But I am only a human being, and you are too. This man is a very good medium, not far from you. My girlfriends all go to him. They go to get their fortunes told –' Dr Patel gives a glimmer of a smile. 'But I think you should go to find out about your girl-friend. And don't tell anyone I gave you his number, or I'll be struck off!'

Then she gives a shy giggle, tweaks her shoe back on, and that's it. Over. I am officially not mad, but also, in a way, I am still entirely mad. When I get home, I ring the medium. His name is, comfortingly enough, John Smith. And I like a man who's named after a good old-fashioned English beer. Especially if he's in the business of talking to dead people. It's reassuring, somehow.

When I get through to John Smith, though – or rather his wife, who seems to act as his secretary – it turns out there's a waiting list.

'I'm very sorry about that,' she says. 'He can fit you in next year, if that's okay.'

Next year? She's saying it like it's routine.

'He was on television you see, there was a programme about him, so we had a lot of calls. Who sent you?'

'Dr Smita Patel.'

'I don't know her,' Mrs Smith says, sounding apologetic.

'My girlfriend was killed by a car,' I suddenly hear myself saying.

'I'm sorry, love.'

'She's talking to me. Weird things keep happening. That's why I saw the doctor.'

'Yes, love. Oh, hang on a sec.'

The phone clunks down on the table, and I can then hear a muffled man's voice in the background.

'Hello, this is John Smith,' the voice says as the phone is picked up again. 'Are you Mark?'

'Yes.'

'And did your girlfriend pass suddenly?'

'Yes.'

'Okay. She's saying tofu or something, you never liked tofu.'

'No.'

What the hell is he talking about now?

'I'm getting nausea, now,' John Smith says, 'a terrible feeling, like I want to be sick. A tofu casserole.'

'It was our first date,' I say automatically, as the memory surfaces.

'Well, there you go, that's your survival evidence for you,' the medium says. 'Sorry – my wife is calling me away again. I just had your girlfriend in here this morning, though, bothering me.'

'That sounds like Catherine.'

'Quite a good communicator,' he goes on, 'you should have some luck there. And I'm sorry, I can't see you now, Mark, but at least we've managed to have this chat. Look after yourself. God bless you. Love and light. Nice perfume she's wearing by the way.' And he's off again.

Mrs Smith asks me if I want to make an appointment for next year. I say no. I can smell the perfume now too. Joy – again.

'You take that seriously about the tofu casserole, though,' she says, rambling on about her husband's appointment book. 'John's been looking green in the face with it, the last five minutes.'

'I will.'

What does he mean, survival evidence? What sort of technical term is that? My mind flicks back to the tofu incident. It's impossible to forget. We'd gone on a first official date, after all the years of knowing each other, to some stupidly trendy restaurant in Camden, and Catherine had ordered dishes to share, including this blobby white thing with brown sludge all over it, which turned out to be tofu casserole. I'd been so nervous about our first proper date together that I'd drunk too much riesling. And I threw up, on the pavement, outside the restaurant, just as she was hailing a cab. She laughed, I basically wanted the Camden earth to swallow me up. Eventually it became one of those private jokes that nobody else understands. And – here's the thing – I don't think anybody else knows about it, either. Certainly not John Smith. So how could he know, unless he was talking to Catherine?

The perfume smell goes. Then I finally decide to do something about Veronica, and ring her.

She's in a wine bar, when I call, on her mobile phone, and she doesn't sound cooperative. From her tight, strained voice, it sounds as if Veronica is out with her no-hoper boyfriend, enduring another night in their bad relationship.

'Maybe I should ring you later,' I say, 'at a better time.'

'God, first I can't get you to call back, then I can't get you off the bloody phone!' she shoots back. And I can tell she's saying it for her boyfriend's benefit, as well as mine. Her boyfriend's never liked me, and sometimes Veronica plays a little game where they both take sides against me – her attacking, him listening.

'Can you take the phone outside the bar?' I persist.

There is much mumbling, after this, with her hand over the receiver. Then, a few seconds later, she comes back to me, walking as she talks.

'The whole reason I left that urgent message on Saturday night, Mark, you stupid arsehole, was because it was urgent. And I didn't tell you the whole story about Catherine the other morning, either.'

'Hang on. Slow down a minute. What, in the kitchen?'

'Yes, in my kitchen, on Saturday night. I couldn't sleep' – and I can hear Veronica is almost gabbling now – 'I couldn't sleep, so I got up to make a cup of tea, and then she was standing there –'

'What was she wearing?'

'Oh, for God's sake.'

'For the last time, Veronica, I am not being funny. I believe you. I believe you!'

There's a pause, while she gets herself together again.

'Her dressing gown I got her for her birthday. From Next.'

'Yeah, the pink dressing gown with the daisy on the front.'

'What worries me most, Mark, and the reason I tried to get you, was – she knows now.'

'Knows what now?'

'About us.'

And hearing that from Veronica, after all this time, is like receiving a kick in the stomach.

'How could she know?' I hear myself saying, stupidly, even though I know exactly what she's talking about.

'She bloody told me,' Veronica says. 'And she said' – Veronica is holding back on crying now – 'she understands why we did it, and she's forgiven me.'

'But not me. She's not forgiven me. Is that right?'

'Well, I don't know!' she practically yells into the phone. 'Why don't you ask her?'

In the end, I hang up. Veronica angry, which is five thousand times scarier than her usual faintly pissed-off temperament, is impossible to deal with. It does give me something to think about, though. Or not think about. Or not sleep about, or something.

Because, as Veronica has just reminded me – and the entire wine bar where she's calling from – we did, in fact, have sex about a year ago. Behind Catherine's back. When she went away for the weekend. And we did it in our bed. And now, it seems, Catherine has finally found out about it, in her velvet armchair in the meadow, somewhere in the heaven that isn't really heaven.

eight

So, why did I end up betraying Catherine? Why does anyone betray anyone? Because it wasn't going very well. Because Catherine and I were bored, and fed up with each other. Because the sex had become perfunctory, and that to me seemed proof that there was something really wrong.

Ultimately, it all happened because Veronica was having problems in her own life, and also – I would say this was the main reason – because we were blind drunk. We had set out to get that way, and it had happened quicker than we thought, and on an empty stomach, too. And the rest is history.

It's a blur now – I can't even remember if we got any real enjoyment out of it, apart from the illicit thrill of doing something wrong – but it began, as these things often do, with some playful, stupid remark from Veronica about the way my head was shaved.

Which resulted in her rubbing it, to see what it felt like. Which resulted in me grabbing her, in mock retaliation. She bit me. I knocked a bottle of vodka over. Kick, giggle, squeal is what I mostly remember, and I'm ashamed to say, most of it was coming from me. Like one of the kids from the big boys' school down the road, mucking around in the bushes. Or even like Felix in his Pimlico spa bath.

The problem with never, ever sleeping with someone is that the mystery is always there. The question mark is always there, too, like the riddle of the Sphinx, or – if you read Tintin, which I occasionally do – *The Secret of the Unicorn*. What would it be like? What it would actually be like, to really be with this person you know so well, this person who you've snogged, but never quite gone to the edge of the abyss with?

So many years of lying around in the Canterbury flat in the late 80s, with the carriage lamps out the front, mucking around on the carpet with Veronica, drinking cheap wine, occasionally snogging, and listening to Depeche Mode finally got up and bit me, I suppose. When she offered to bed me – as she practically did, twelve months ago – it seemed almost like picking up where we hadn't left off. So I had no resistance.

It seemed safe, because we both knew it couldn't go anywhere, after this one afternoon. What were we going to do, ruin Catherine's life by running off to have ten strapping babies together and a big white wedding? It seemed to have – I don't know – built-in obsolescence, and that let me off the hook.

It almost seemed adult, and responsible, too, because she had a packet of condoms in her handbag. And it even seemed emotionally right, and appropriate – because we were both on some sentimental, drunken nostalgia trip into our extreme youth, deliberately playing the dustiest Cure singles and Siouxsie and The Banshees albums we could find. And, if you really must know, she took my hand and led me up the stairs. Like a zookeeper taking a chimp for a bath. And yeah, I went quietly.

Of course, this is no moral or ethical argument whatsoever. In fact, even I know it's bullshit, and I, Mark Buckle, am the king of self-deception. But there was a definite sense of delayed inevitability when Veronica and I finally crawled into bed together, in this house, just over a year ago.

It was almost as if 1985, or whatever year it was that Veronica and I *hadn't* had sex – had suddenly rolled into the start of this new century, and nothing had changed, except we were now ready to go boldly where we'd both been too cowardly to ever go before.

Within that perceived jump in time, my new life with Catherine simply didn't exist. Against the background of The Cure singing *Let's Go To Bed*, not to mention half a bottle of Absolut lemon vodka, it seemed like merely a blip in history. Mine and Veronica's history, of course.

'We've shared a lot,' is one of the things Veronica said that afternoon, once we finally stopped rolling around like idiots and biting each other in the neck. And what she said almost made it seem right, too. Even, morally right.

And there's more, I suppose. Around the same time, when Catherine went away on a travel agency junket to Frankfurt – and she hadn't wanted to take me because I was being a pain in the arse – I also suspected her of wanting someone else. Or at least looking around. So, the thought was there. *This isn't going very well, is it? I think she's going off me.*

And how did I know she was having doubts about me? No hard evidence, really. Just a bit of boredom and irritation between us, going on for weeks at a time, that ultimately led to her confessing that the guy at the video shop had slipped his phone number into one of her videos. And she used to talk a lot about some guy at her work. Some man with a stupid name, like Gideon, or Griffin, or something, who did all the marketing for Virgin, who she was filled with admiration for.

When you've lived with each other for a while, you develop antennae for things like that. You learn to detect the difference between merely rambling on about work colleagues, and talking almost compulsively, longingly, about them. So – I was entirely justified then, in sleeping with Catherine's sister. Yeah, *right*.

As for Veronica, I really don't know what was motivating her. Maybe jealousy – because, after all, Catherine and I had bought a place together, and her own life hadn't ever got sorted, by that stage.

I don't think Veronica was in love with me or anything. I'm fairly sure of that. And to be honest, why would you be? Mark Buckle, thirtysomething teacher, bald, unlikely to be promoted anytime soon, miserable bastard on winter mornings, pathetic desire to play, and replay, songs from his lost youth, cynic, smoker, inveterate bad TV watcher, sexual deviant.

That last one is a joke, of course. One thing I do remember about going to bed with Veronica, is the way she suddenly sat up, leaned on one elbow and stared at me, hours after it was over and said, 'God, you are conservative aren't you?'

To which I replied jokily, 'What, you wanted pythons and handcuffs?'

But maybe that's just me, I don't know. Having the kind of romp with her that people in senior citizens' homes might enjoy with each other – perhaps after their evening cocoa – might have been my way of minimising the sinfulness of the betrayal. Or maybe I was just too pissed, I can't really remember what I was thinking now. Sex is so often like that, too. I mean, of all the five million times that you've ever done it in your life, can you remember even more than one per cent of it? It's like trying to remember all the food you've ever eaten.

I do recall the way Veronica's remark about being conservative made me wince, though. Once again, game, set and match to Ms Roden, I thought. A lazy afternoon of drunken adultery with her, and all I can come up with is old-man's sex, in her opinion. As opposed to whatever high-level erotic escapades she'd been through with the singer in The Voodoo Blitz or any other of the crazed goths, drug addicts, foreign language students and convicted criminals she's slept with since then.

Veronica. Just like the Elvis Costello song. What will she be like when she's in an old people's home herself? It was the last thing on my mind when she was throwing her bra off the bottom of the bed, onto her own sister's laundry basket. But now I find myself thinking about it. What on earth does the future hold for Veronica Roden?

And I also wonder, who was the worst criminal that day? Was it me, for going off with Catherine's own flesh and blood (taking the easiest, laziest option as always) or was it Veronica, for actually encouraging it? Who knows – and this is a horrible thought – maybe she even set it up. Maybe she had even planned it for months.

And now Catherine knows, at last. Or seems to, according to

Veronica. And it's always been in the back of my mind, I suppose, since Catherine's been appearing and disappearing, in my dreams, in our bathroom, and in our bedroom. Lucky for her she's in the velvet armchairs in the meadow. No doubt Veronica and I – or one of us anyway – will be going straight to hell for this. Which reminds me. I must ask Catherine about hell sometime.

'Can you hear me, Catherine?' I ask the empty air in the living room. It's gone dark since I've been thinking about all this, and the winds started to blow. But there's nothing. No shivers from head to foot, no green lights, no mobile phone ringing with her voice on the other end.

I knew I had to cry properly sometime, and I do. And I'm still crying when it's gone pitch black outside, and even the moon is beginning to show. And it's one of those serial cries, where you aren't just losing it because of the matter at hand, you chuck in everything else as well.

The time my Dad died for eighty-eight seconds in the hospital, and how he's too worried to tell my mum. The day I broke Noel Oliver's nose at the Dymchurch Caravan Park, and Veronica called me a bloody racist little bastard. The day England drew with Poland in 1973, when my father was in tears too. All those things. It's basically all coming out, through my eyes, and my nose. And no, I still haven't bought any tissues.

nine

'Look what's just been deposited in my pigeonhole,' Felix Saddleton says gloomily, a few days later, when I stagger into the staffroom for lunch. I got to school late again, but once again, they covered for me. I hate to be cynical – although I am, by nature – but this bereavement thing is resulting in the best treatment I've ever had from the school in my entire life.

'It's a note from the Head,' I say, looking at Felix's letter. I'd know that pale blue writing paper anywhere. He hasn't opened the envelope yet.

'Yes,' Felix sighs, 'Frightening object, isn't it? You know what, Mark? I think I've been seen.'

What he means is, he's been seen carrying on like a drooling madman at the Pig's Head the other Saturday night, camping it up like John Inman in *Are You Being Served?* and generally pissing off half the bar staff.

'Poor you,' Alison says, giving him a quick scalp massage with her fingernails.

'I'm not sure I want her hands in my hair,' Felix mutters under his breath as she gets up from her chair to make a cup of Earl Grey.

He opens the note from the Head. And what I think, but don't tell him, is that it could be even worse than one of the parents spotting him at the pub. He may, in fact, have been floating around with one of the said parents in the hairy spa bath in Pimlico – probably without realising it.

'Oh woe, oh unhappy day,' Felix says, scanning the letter, and his face drops.

'What? What?' Alison asks breathlessly, wobbling back from the sink with her cup of tea.

'I have to coach the frigging football!' he says, his voice cracking.

If this was an American sitcom, I suppose we'd all be laughing in a kind of 'Ba ha ha ha! He's only been asked to coach the football!' fashion at this, like some old re-run audience for *M*A*S*H*. But we don't laugh. And why don't we laugh? Because we are teachers, and we know what it is to coach the frigging football. The Head couldn't have given him worse news in his pigeonhole if he'd been trying to sack him.

I suppose there are millions of parents, all over the football-playing world, who never really think about the process involved to get their little wunderkinds to that magical stage when they start kicking a ball into the net, instead of into each other's faces. But let me tell you, I know that process – in fact, for several long, coaching seasons, I've been that process, single-handedly – and it's pure torture.

Felix knows it too.

'Aaargh!' he puts his head in his hands, and both Alison and I notice at the same time, that his little fingernail is painted with pink glitter.

'Aaargh! Getting up at six o'clock on Saturday mornings! Sacrificing my body to the freezing cold and dark on Thursday nights!'

'You poor sod,' Alison tuts.

'Oh, it's not so bad,' I interrupt him. 'Think about it, Felix. You could be coaching the next David Beckham without knowing it.'

'But I don't even know what football is!' he counters, with a shriek like a mandrake being uprooted from the earth. 'I didn't even know it was called football until six months ago, I thought it was supposed to be called soccer!'

Felix, being Australian, doesn't know much.

I light a cigarette and think about the situation for a moment. 'There are two possibilities here,' I say.

'You'll do it? You'll swap with me? You'll make that sacrifice?' Felix counters. 'Oh please,' he gabbles, 'I'll do anything. I'll clean out your goldfish tank. I'll wipe down your glockenspiels. What do you want? Do you want money? Hard drugs?'

'Nah. Sorry. No deal. Been there, coached that. But I tell you what, I think this football thing and this Pimlico Hair Bear thing might be connected, Felix.'

'How? How?'

'The Head's obviously heard something. Or seen something.'

'Yes,' says Alison, shifting herself around in the chair and borrowing my lighter. 'You have been camping it up a bit lately, Felix. Do admit.'

'So you think the Head is trying to make me butch,' Felix shakes his head sadly. 'I knew it.' He looks down at his clothes for a second. 'All this tweed, all this hearty Harris Tweed from the Oxfam shop I find to wear, and it's still not enough for him. What does he want from me? A pipe? A deep, booming laugh? A hip flask and a spell in the army?'

'On the contrary,' Alison says, lighting up her Silk Cut, 'if we are to play devil's advocate in this situation, then it may well be that Felix is quite acceptable to the Head, Mark. In fact, knowing the Head as I do –' Felix and I both look at each other, noting the admission of past intimacy. 'Well,' Alison continues, 'it may be that there is no question about Felix's sexual preferences at all. In fact, it may be that he is the Head's golden boy . . .'

'Mamma mia!' Felix interjects, 'imagine that! And me so young!'

'And,' Alison continues smoothly, ignoring his histrionics, 'the Head may well be grooming you for promotion, Felix. As we all know, coaching Rivett Street Junior at football is the very first step.'

'Yeah, well, it did sod all for me,' I moan, picking up *The Guardian*'s jobs section. Why are all the teaching jobs in London always on exactly the same lousy salary?

Felix shakes his head again. 'This is a very serious letter, you know,' he says, handing it straight to me. 'I really think there can be no escape.'

'Nowhere to run, nowhere to hide, baby,' Alison says, in one of her annoying silly voices. 'Oh, poor you.'

I read it. It's a typical letter from the Head, in that his crazed, illiterate, loopy signature takes up half the page, and the rest of it is full of spelling mistakes. It's polite, but it's also – as Felix correctly identifies – serious. In other words, if Felix doesn't front up at the practice pitch next Thursday night, having personally washed all the team shirts himself from last season, there will be trouble.

'It's because I created such pandemonium with the tooth-brushes during Teeth,' he says, leaning his entire body out of the window so he can exhale his cigarette. 'That was my crime, and now I must pay. Oh, God, that I had never been distracted by the charms of spunky School Dentist!'

Alison demurs.

'That might just be it after all,' she says. 'A sort of mix between grooming you for promotion, trying to make you more butch, and punishing you for sending Tiffany Whittaker home with Kelvin O'Reilly's dirty old Thomas the Tank Engine toothbrush, or whatever it was.'

'But what you don't get, what you don't seem to com-prehend, what you both don't seem to *realise*,' Felix says, waving his hands around, 'is that I don't know a damn thing about the stupid game!'

'What's to know?' Alison dismisses him airily. 'Basically, you've got about five main mascots. There are others, but you won't need to know about all of them. First of all, there's Freddie the Fox. He's Halifax. Then you've got Barclay the Bluebird. He's Cardiff. At Rochdale they've got Desmond the Dragon. And at Swansea they have Cyril the Swan.'

'It's big fluffy animals with absolutely acres of agonisingly awful and appalling alliteration in their names,' I explain to Felix, who is clearly not understanding a word of what she is saying.

'So that's it,' Alison says, sounding pleased with herself for remembering everything. 'They go on, they try to kick a goal, nothing happens, it's very boring, everyone eats hot dogs, they have a bath together in the nude afterwards – you'll like that bit, Felix – then, the big fluffy animals beat each other up on the pitch, and everyone goes home.' Felix's mouth hangs open for a second, and then he sniggers, coughing the cigarette smoke out.

'No, really, Felix,' I stop him for a moment. 'This is no laughing matter. To be fair, the mascots in professional, league-level English football can do a lot of damage. This is something you have to know, if you're going to talk to the children about their sport. You need to be sensitive to the politics of the game.'

He looks at me for a minute.

'You're being English. I'm Australian and you're taking advantage of me, and you're having a little silly pommy joke with me, now. Aren't you?'

'Without a word of a lie, Felix,' I continue, 'in 1998, Wolfie of Wolverhampton Wanderers was involved in an incident – quite a serious incident – with Bristol City's pig. Percy, or Porky, or Pinky, or Perky, or something like that. Anyway. It began with P. And the following year, there was another incident – with Baggie Bird from West Bromwich.'

'And not only that, two years ago Cyril the Swan was fined a thousand quid and banned from the touchline,' Alison adds breathlessly.

'Why?' Felix asks.

'Single-handed pitch invasion,' I fill him in. 'He just flapped in on the ground by himself and went psychotic.'

'And don't forget Freddie the Fox, who weed on Rochdale's goalpost,' Alison interrupts.

'And what happened?' Felix asks, looking amazed.

'Desmond the Dragon from Rochdale cut his head off with a chainsaw,' Alison finishes.

'No, he didn't,' I contradict her. But Felix is now looking very worried. Satisfyingly worried, you might say, if the looks on the other teachers' faces round here are anything to go by. He has, after all, been highly annoying lately. And they're enjoying his very public turmoil.

Later that day, I check into the staffroom to pick up my coat, and find Felix buried in a football annual he's either borrowed or stolen from the school library. Judging by the terrifying perms on the front cover, it's an old one too. And, as always with our old library books, there are suspicious dirty green smears all over the front and back cover.

'Oh, God, listen to this,' Felix reads aloud from his annual. 'The Chinese used to play with a stone football. To make their leg muscles stronger for war.'

'It's only what they do at Man United,' I say, but there's really no point doing the jokey English pub football thing with Felix.

'You know my greatest problem, Mark?' Felix says, with round, frightened, slightly widened eyes, as I head for the door.

'What's that?

'Football in this country isn't a sport at all, it's a sacred religion. Or a cult. And I'm being asked to become the high priest of a horrible' – he spits the word out – '*sport* I don't even understand!'

'You'll come to believe, mate,' I say. 'We'll make a believer out of you. The England-West Germany game, 1966. They think it's all over. Kenneth Wolstenholme. Get it out on video. That'll do it.'

And I leave him to it.

t e n

A few days later, I manage to crawl home, take the phone off the hook, open a can of lager and think about Veronica and Catherine, properly. The alarm clock is no longer flashing 12.00 in the bedroom, the green light has disappeared from the house, and the David Bowie cat is behaving itself, so there's even a chance I might have some peace and quiet to go over things, at last.

After the Veronica conservative old-man sex episode, I suppose I had a slight fear that Catherine would find out about us, and that there would be a scene – even a real Roden family showdown, which would have meant the end for us, and the mortgage on this house.

As the months went by though, and nothing went wrong – Veronica didn't go barking mad and confess all, Catherine didn't find any evidence, like a vodka bottle cap, or a condom under the bed – I relaxed. I let it go. And I forgot all about it.

The afternoon of betrayal with Veronica Roden became just another thing in my life, small and troublesome, but not important enough to really bother me much. Like being passed over for promotion, never getting anywhere with The Bottom Line, never becoming a rock star, having a crap break-up with Donna Roberts – all those things – it became a dot on the landscape of my imperfect life.

But now, it appears, Catherine does want to have it out. From wherever she is. And John Smith, the man with the name like a beer, is on the telephone now, telling me all about it. He rings late, well after 10 p.m., just as I'm about to go to bed.

'Your girlfriend has been at me again,' he says. 'I'm trying to go to sleep and she's in my ear all the time. Can you take this call? I know it's late.'

'I'm sorry she's been pestering you,' I say, feeling ridiculous.

'Catherine's using me, because she can't get through to you.'

'Well, why can't she get through to me?'

I'm sitting in one of the velvet armchairs Catherine dreamed up for her sunny meadow. Except this is the real thing, and it's freezing outside. Someone's dustbin lid is blowing along the pavement, and the people who occasionally rush past my living room window late at night, from the pub, have their heads down and their collars up.

'Catherine has only been over a short time,' John Smith explains. It's as if he's telling me she's gone to Paris on Eurostar.

'So does that make it harder for her to speak to me?'

'She's still getting used to it. And by the way, your vibration is too heavy for her.'

And what the hell does that mean?

'Um, John,' I begin, 'I'm accepting everything you say, because after all, you're the expert, and I'm on new ground here, but – can you explain it another way to me?' And as I say this, I find myself talking like a teacher again – and with all this talk of vibrations, thoughts of Alison's tuning fork lesons with 4B come to mind too.

'You eat a lot of meat.'

Yes, Mum's endless Tupperware containers full of spaghetti bolognaise.

'That slows down your vibration, and makes it thick and muddy, like concrete. Because you're carrying the fear and pain vibration of the animals, at their point of death in the abbatoir.

So Catherine has trouble tuning in.'

'Oh. Right.'

'And, you've got a lot on your mind as well,' John Smith continues. 'That's not helping communication either. You don't sleep well, Mark. You are full of anxiety. You are full of guilt. And also, when she tries to get through, you're naturally full of emotion. To her, that vibration is like swimming through wet cement, you understand? Your state of mind affects your energy field. For Catherine, trying to have a sensible conversation with you in the middle of all that disturbance is like trying to talk in the middle of a hurricane.'

'It distorts?'

'Yes, it distorts,' John Smith goes on. 'When they try to get through to us, they have to lower their vibration because we are physical matter. It's like us going scuba diving and having to get an oxygen tank. So do you understand that?' He asks again, like a man who is fairly sure I'm understanding very little.

'Maybe. Not really. So what is she – they – made up of now? Is it light? Is it colour? Is it electricity?'

I have been thinking about all these things lately, ever since the mirror incident, and the way my body goes hot – or shiveringly cold – when she is around me.

John Smith sighs the sigh of a man who is always being interrogated, but seldom understood.

'I don't want to change the subject, Mark, but how about this. If I tell you how to make contact with her – properly – will you do it?'

'I'll try. I mean, better than having her make your life hell,' I attempt to joke.

Outside, the cat with the David Bowie eyes is pressing itself against the window, trying to get in. And I can smell her perfume. Joy. Not cooking smells from the kitchen, not the carpet shampoo I squirted over the rug this morning, but the unmistakeable smell of her favourite perfume.

'You need to go into meditation in order to talk to her,' John Smith says.

'Is that what you do?' I have an absurd mental picture of some fat, red-cheeked old bloke from Balham in the lotus position, and I let it go quickly – in case John Smith is also reading my mind and feeling insulted. To tell you the truth, I'm a bit nervous about John Smith.

'Meditating is something your girlfriend says you know how to do,' he says.

'Is she telling you that now?'

'My guide is telling me. She's talking to my guide.'

Like a party line. Right.

'Well, yeah,' I tell John, listening patiently on the other end of the phone. 'Catherine did make me go to her yoga class once. And they made us sit on the floor, and turned the lights out and lit candles, and – I fell asleep, if you must know.'

The medium laughs.

Yes, it's all coming back to me now. Our meditation session. And her yoga class, with all the demented New Agers who wrote me notes on recycled paper after she'd died, and told me about her higher self and her karma.

'In that meditative state, your vibrations are raised,' John Smith tells me, interrupting my train of thought, 'So she'll be able to get through.'

Then I think of something else, while the cat is going crazy outside the window.

'How is she moving the objects?'

'It's happening in your house?'

'A dressing gown. A Post-it note stuck on my back. How is she ringing me up on the mobile? And what about the cat? Why is the cat going mental? Is she – I dunno – inside the cat?'

John Smith excuses himself for a minute, and comes back to the phone.

'I'm very sorry, Mark, but I have to call it a day. We're all very tired here.'

The presence of his wife/secretary Mrs Smith is felt, but not seen.

'Can I ask you something else, though, just before you go?' I interrupt him.

'Yes.' He sounds distracted, but he's with me. 'Yes.'

'Assuming that I suspend my disbelief, which I've been doing since the day she died, assuming that I'm willing to go along with all this – nuttiness – around me . . .'

'Yes.'

'What's the point? I mean – this doesn't happen to everyone else I know who's lost someone. So. Why me? Why her?'

'You just happen to be a good receiver, Mark.'

'What, like a radio?'

'Yes. It may surprise you to hear this, but you can pick up signals from the spirit world that most people miss. And she's taking advantage of that.'

'Any other reason?'

'She has a reason to want to communicate with you now. Put it that way. She died suddenly. And things weren't always good between you. So she has things to say. Plus –' He breaks off.

'What?'

'You're not going to like this, Mark,' he laughs, 'but you share several past life debts together. Catherine's only just found this out. Now, she wants to explain it to you, too.'

Then his wife interrupts.

'John!' I hear his wife squeal. And he almost ends the call. But not before I notice that the cat at the window is now surrounded by birds. Cats and birds, all going crazy, all trying to get in. It's dark. Pitch black. Aren't the birds supposed to be in their nests?

John Smith talks very fast now.

'You teach science (how did he know that?) and you're a natural sceptic, which is fine. But let me tell you this, Mark. If the next four things I tell you are right, can you accept that the fifth and sixth things I tell you are right?'

'Yup. I dunno. It's not very scientific. But – maybe. Try me.'

'You had a fight once, over a red plastic heart that came apart, then went back together. You knew a girl whose name was D. You knew a girl whose name was V. Your mother's nickname is Chops.'

There's a pause, from my end, not his.

'Mark?'

'Yes, John.'

My jaw, as Felix often says, is on the floor.

'I have to go. I'm sorry.'

And the amazing John Smith does, with his wife still sounding worried, and nagging him in the background.

'No, hang on,' I hear myself stopping him. 'What were the fifth and sixth things?'

'You and she will be back together again one day. After you pass over.'

'Me and Catherine?'

Funny, really, the way that makes my heart leap twenty feet in the air with dim hope.

'Yes. And the sixth thing is, someone beginning with T. She's very important.'

'Tess?'

'Yes. Her. Mark, I've really got to go.'

I do the right thing, let the poor, tired John Smith and Mrs Smith get off the phone and to bed, then I go into the kitchen to put tea in the microwave. That's how lazy I've become, since Catherine died. Ninety seconds of hot water and a bag in a mug, spinning round on a plate. And it's the same mug from the last twenty-seven times I've done this too, because I can never be bothered to wash it up. Meanwhile, the microwave is flashing one word. It's made up of green digits, but it's still there. HELLO.

I turn my back on it immediately, without even looking back to check that the HELLO is still there, and take the tea up to the bedroom, which is no safer than the kitchen or the bathroom these days, but at least it's the warmest room in the house. And I can't see the cat or the mad sparrows and starlings being able to shin up the drainpipe there.

I have to be honest with myself. Being English and polite, as I am, I am somewhat embarrassed about the fact that John Smith – a very busy man, who, let's face it, charges one hundred pounds for his services, and has been on television, as his wife told me – is being pestered by Catherine day and night. And that I'm not paying. So, for John Smith's sake, anyway, or at least for the harassed Mrs Smith's sake, maybe I should do what he asks. And get Catherine to use a different telephone exchange, namely me. Which means – oh God, no, not that – meditating. Dimming the lights. Finding a candle. Crossing my legs. Breathing. Being, and looking, ridiculous.

It may, however, be worth it. Especially if I need to talk about Tess. Or being together again. Or anything else to do with John Smith's facts five and six, following facts one, two, three and four – which, frankly, just about made me drop the phone.

I finish the tea, go downstairs again, switch on the TV, flick through the channels, switch it off, and make another cup and take it back to the armchair. The cat has given up and gone next door, by the look of it. Taking the birds with it.

School was hell today. Or, as Felix Saddleton would say, 'A dreadful abyss of despair, snot, recorder spit and Harry Potter-fuelled insanity.' Scott O'Grady punched one of the girls in the buttock – a first, even for him – and we had the parents round, as well as ongoing scenes in the Head's office.

Meditate? Yeah, right. But I light a candle anyway.

Somehow, though, sitting in the wing-backed armchair, with the fat velvet cushions holding me up, the leg-crossing thing seems simpler. Better than trying it on a hard wooden floor in some place in Brixton, with a bunch of women in tracksuits. Then I get up and close the curtains. Because, basically, if anyone sees me doing this, I'm finished.

If you don't try to do it like Gandhi, it's actually possible to meditate, of course. And that means not forcing one foot under the other leg, suffering pins and needles and shooting pains in the knee. If you cheat it with the cushions, sort of half crossing your legs, I discover that it's even reasonably comfortable. I half-close my eyes. This is what they did in the yoga class, after all.

And what else? Oh yes. The white light. That's what the woman told us. You suck it in through your head, which is patently impossible as we all know, then you force it through your eyebrows, your neck, down through your gullet, through your heart chakra – funny how I remember that bit – and then (oh, how we glossed over this bit in yoga class) through your bum, and somehow it ends up going into the earth.

Through my half-open eyes, I see the David Bowie cat, sitting on the window ledge, and staring at me through the gap in the curtains. It is glowing white. I shut my eyes. Perhaps, like going to the dentist, or having your balls checked by Dr Patel, this is something that has to be endured, got over with quickly, and then finished. I imagine the white light. I pull it through my head. I'm being distracted by the cat again, banging against the window, but I keep pulling anyway. Throat, chest, heart chakra – whatever that is – I keep going, and going, until something odd happens.

I am no longer here. The inside of my head has gone three-dimensional. I have a head like Dr Who's tardis in fact. It's spacious. Roomy.

'Hello,' Catherine says. She's changed her clothes, I notice. No longer the pink dressing gown, but a pair of jeans, and a red T-shirt I remember very well, from a camping trip we once took.

We are in a garden that reminds me of Tuscany. There is, after all, a terracotta flower pot, and a big white house with a brown roof. A Tuscan villa, perhaps? Catherine was always going on about them, nagging me to take her on a holiday in one, but I never did.

It's warm here now, wherever we are. There are olive trees. But of course, the joke is, she's the one who's been to Tuscany – and I never have. So this is my first trip.

'We need to talk about my sister,' Catherine says.

I'd forgotten that about her – that she always called Veronica 'my sister' instead of her proper name.

Out of interest, before Catherine can say anything else, I look down to see what I'm wearing in this Tuscan paradise. The same clothes I had on, before I sat cross-legged in the armchair? Yes. Well. That's a relief, then.

'Which part about your sister?' I ask her, and she answers me immediately.

'When I died, I saw a replay of you doing it. I mean, not the sex bit – that would have been too much. But they showed me you and Veronica playing the Cure records, and you saying something about her wanting a python and handcuffs.'

To her credit, Catherine almost manages to smile at that bit.

'This is weird,' I interrupt, 'because I know that I'm just going along with this – this dream sequence, or this altered meditative state, or whatever it is – but at the same time, it just keeps happening anyway. I mean, it's going on regardless of whatever I'm doubting, or thinking.'

Catherine gives me a look, and gets back to the point. That reaction of hers also has a ring of familiarity about it, I have to say.

'When I saw you and Veronica together, I could see straight through to your heart as well,' she says.

'And what does that mean? Catherine, you never used to talk like this.'

'Yes I did. Well, not to you. But in my own mind. Believe me, Mark, that's pretty much how I used to see life.'

'Yeah, yeah, and I never did, because I'm an insensitive wanker, and that's why we used to fight all the time. Catherine, I think we've done all this. I mean, we've been through it.'

She smiles again.

'Anyway,' I give in, 'so you saw through to my heart. And Veronica's as well? So what did you see?'

I become aware, suddenly, of something odd happening in the background of the Tuscan villa. A dog has just trotted past with a cat. A highly unusual sight. Even more unusual, it's my old dog. Beano. And Beano used to hate cats. Plus, of course, he's dead. Like Catherine, he was killed by a car.

'I saw that you were hurt during the time with my sister,' Catherine says, 'because you thought I didn't love you any more. And I saw that you were jealous and insecure. And you were confused.'

'And drunk. Don't forget that part.'

'I saw that my sister hated herself, both before and afterwards. She thought that it would make her stronger, proving to herself that you wanted her more than me, but at the end, she only felt weaker in her life. That is why she is so unhappy now. That's why I had to go and see her the other day, to try to tell her I'd forgiven her.'

I say nothing, and look at Beano, the long-lost Beano, sauntering past with the cat again. I suppose it will turn out to be some cat he once killed.

'Yes it is.'

'What?'

Catherine smiles. 'It is the cat he killed. He didn't mean to. It was when he was a puppy and the cat was a kitten, and he didn't know what he was doing.'

'Catherine?'

She smiles again.

'Can we just take it slowly? Can we just take it very, very

slowly? I mean, these dead dogs and cats, and this imaginary Tuscan villa, and Veronica and everything. It's too much. Okay? I mean, I have a head that's about to –' And I make a gesture that looks like a head about to explode, which is pretty much how I feel.

Catherine nods at this, and for some reason I suddenly feel very clear about everything. Very calm. Very relaxed.

'Are you doing this?' I try to take her to task.

'Yes, I'm altering your mood. Calming you down.'

'Well, don't.'

'I used to rub your shoulders sometimes, when you were stressed out,' she says. 'This is the same. I'll stop if you like.'

But no, I don't want her to stop.

'Let me give it to you from my side,' I say at last, noticing the way there are shadows on the grass ahead of us, even though I can't see the sun. 'You die, Catherine. You go off one night, you die, and that's it. It's horrible. I see your body in the hospital. You've got bruises all over you. You don't look like you. Then I go to the funeral –'

'You wore the black jacket you used to wear with the band, on stage. The Bottom Line. Because you had nothing else to wear,' she smiles.

'And you're even interrupting me, the way you used to do when you were alive!'

'Sorry,' she shuts up.

'I saw you in the coffin, I saw you go into the cremation oven thing. But the whole time this death of yours is going on, you were still talking to me. And I could see you as well. I mean –'

I take a deep breath.

'Okay, okay,' Catherine soothes me, as she used to do in the old days, before we had problems. 'I'm with you. Just keep talking to me.'

'Well,' I oblige and keep talking to her, 'what I want to know is – why? I mean, this doesn't happen to other people. Why is it happening to me? Why is it happening to you? I don't want to know about Beano, or past lives, or all that stuff John Smith was telling me, or any of it. I just want, in words of one syllable, the truth about us.'

Catherine smiles again. Her arm is linked through mine

now, and it's real – as real as anything else, in fact. I'd forgotten about that, with her and me. We used to walk down the street to get the paper, sometimes, with our arms hooked up. I don't suppose we did it once, the six months before she was killed. But now, it feels fantastic.

'Okay, I'll tell you the truth about us,' Catherine says.

'Right.'

'What I've been told over here is, we've always had relationships. In other lives. I never knew until I came over here. You and I have always been together. Sometimes I've been a man. Sometimes you've been a woman. And we've always loved each other and always hurt each other.'

'Well, how come I don't remember any of these other lives then?'

'Because birth is a kind of forgetting. But the first time you saw me, you thought I was familiar. Didn't you? I mean, it was something we talked about once.'

'Dunno. Okay. Maybe. But – oh God. I can't talk to you about this stuff.'

I can feel myself becoming anxious again. Even angry, that since her death, Catherine is suddenly seeing the world in a way that I can't relate to – in a way that makes no sense to me. Then, instantly, a wave of warmth goes through my body, and the tightness in my jaw, and in the front of my head, melts away.

The thought occurs to me that I am now feeling more relaxed, more comfortable and more peaceful than I have for months. Part of me knows that I am cross-legged and fast asleep in an armchair in a house in South London, but the other part of me couldn't care less. It's Tuscany. It's warm. The hyacinths are better than any hyacinths I've ever seen anywhere. They're a bright, incredible blue and they smell of her – of Catherine. Of her Joy – and her joy, as well. I feel great.

'Catherine. I'm feeling very good. Consequently, I'm feeling manipulated.'

'Don't be. Just relax,' she smiles.

In this strange sunny Tuscan garden, feelings seem amplified. So when I next catch her eye, and register my sudden longing for her, it almost knocks me off my feet.

101

'I feel like that too, sometimes,' she says. 'But I also feel sad about you.'

'Because of what happened with Veronica?'

'Because we were given a chance to sort things out, while I was alive, and we never did. We had a chance to even out the balance sheet between us and we never did it.'

'What balance sheet?'

'Sometimes I've trusted you, and you've let me down. Sometimes you've made commitments to me, and I've betrayed you. Over and over again, it seems.'

'What, in other lives?'

'Yes.'

'Catherine, you never used to believe this crap.'

'Sorry, Mark, it's the way it is.'

'So why did you die?' I say, surprising myself even as I ask the question.

She shakes her head. 'You're the one saying, keep it simple.'

'Okay. Let's just stick to you and me, then.'

'Good.'

'Although it's hard, when I've just had that guy John Smith in my ear.'

'I was telling him all that tonight,' Catherine admits. 'About the plastic love heart badge from the *Jackie* magazine, and Donna. He was great. I knew he'd ring you.'

'And it's easier now, isn't it, for you to get through and talk? Now that I'm meditating?'

'Seamless,' Catherine says. And this is such a Catherine word to use, that now, more than ever, I know she is really here with me again.

'Well, I must meditate more often,' I tell her. 'I must twist myself into impossible positions in the chair a great deal more often –' and she laughs.

'You must,' Catherine picks up my mood, then gets serious again. 'Think of meditation as a phone line.'

'What state are you in, then?' I ask her. 'Are you meditating now?'

'I just am. I'm here, where I am.'

'Do you have any sense of time?'

'Good question,' she shoots back. 'No.'

'Do you know how long it is since you died?'

'No.'

'So it's true then, according to you – about the reincarnation thing. Half the world's religions got it right.'

'Well, it's a bit more complicated than that, but – yes.'

Just like that. Yes.

Catherine points to the landscape beyond the garden wall, where we're sitting, and suddenly I can see all kinds of animals and people. Peacocks, and horses, and people wearing natty little suits and hats from the 50s, and someone who looks like a famous, long-dead footballer in big, baggy shorts – and Buddhist monks, and Chinese mandarins with long beards. And then I see my grandmother, too. She died of cancer. She looks great – she looks young, too. About twenty-five. I'd forgotten that brown flowery dress she always wore.

'Your grandmother has been helping me a lot,' Catherine explains. 'She was one of the people who met me when I came over.'

'She had a lot of common sense,' I say.

'She still does.'

And I look over the wall and see my grandmother waving.

Something occurs to me. Some long-forgotten piece of logic, from a pub argument.

'There are more people alive on the earth now than were ever alive thousands of years ago,' I say. 'So how does that work? How do you create billions of people from what used to be millions of people?'

'You won't believe me if I tell you,' she says.

'Okay. Stop there. I won't.'

'And you're angry.'

'Yes, all right, and I'm disturbing my energy field or something.'

I try to calm down. But I can feel myself slipping back. I'm aware of the cat at the window, staring at me through the curtains. The candle has burned down to half its length. And it's starting to rain – amazingly, I didn't hear it.

I try Catherine again.

'Are you coming back to me, again, before I die? Will I run into some one-year-old toddler in the street and realise it's you?'

But my eyes are open, and nobody is listening, and the Tuscan landscape has gone.

'Well, if you don't come back immediately, when will we be together again?' I ask. 'When am I supposed to die and be with you?'

Nothing. Just the cat with the mad eyes.

'This is all like a very, very bad TV show from the 1960s,' I tell the cat, as it bangs against the window in the rain. 'Early *Star Trek* crossed with *Randall and Hopkirk (Deceased)*. Or *The Ghost and Mrs Muir*.'

I give in, and open the door to let it in, and it rushes between my legs. I don't like cats. Catherine did. But who am I to have the RSPCA on my back at this time of night? I take it in, and shut the door.

eleven

I've never really liked Elvis Presley. In fact, I've always found him deeply naff, so I can't really find much enthusiasm for my costume. I am, of course, going to the party to see Faith Lift after all – or more precisely, Tess Blake – halfway across London, into the expensive wilderness of Richmond, with Felix Saddleton in tow. Alison isn't coming, because Charlie has the flu – the mythical Charlie – and she has to look after him.

'Poor old Charlie,' Felix observes as we sit side-by-side on the tube, rattling away from Victoria on the District Line. 'I swear, Alison lives and dies for that man. And –' he gives me a leering sideways glance, 'some day, Mark, we may even get to see him. Sickly young creature that he is.'

Felix is wearing a black shirt, black pants, which threaten to cut off even his circulation, and a black Elvis wig. We have both burned the cork from our shared bottle of cheap red wine, using Felix's cigarette lighter, and made pretend sideburns on our faces, though with me, it's pointless, because I couldn't be arsed to get a wig, so I basically have a shaved head, and two black marks going down my cheeks.

I look not so much like Elvis, more like someone who's escaped from prison, possibly in an *Eastenders* episode, then slept on a pavement all night.

'We'll share the glasses,' Felix offers. 'I'll wear them until midnight, then you can have them.'

He's bought a classic, mid-70s pair of bug-eyed sunglasses, covering half his face.

And I suddenly realise, from the way everyone isn't looking at us now, that a lot of people in our train carriage think we're a couple. And Felix, of course, is making the most of it.

'Let me just do this,' he says, fussing around with my collar and turning it up.

'Sod off.'

'No, come on sweetie, let me just turn this up.'

'SOD OFF.'

We finish the rest of the train journey in silence, with our fellow passengers discreetly looking the other way, or studiedly reading old bits of *Metro*.

When Felix and I finally reach the party, after hours of forgettable stations, and the world's most expensive taxi, an amazing woman in a mini skirt and an enormous black wig lets us in at the front door. It's a posh house, and this is a posh American hostess. The kind of woman you never see anywhere between Balham and Brixton on a weekday. And for a moment, I do wonder if we've found the right address. But then –

'Tess. What can I say?' Felix exclaims, shaking the beautiful, posh woman's hand.

The frizzy blonde hair has gone, and so have the teacher's clothes. And Tess is doing Priscilla Presley, of course, but she's doing it in a way that even Priscilla never quite managed. I mean, Elvis would be revolving at 45rpm in his grave.

'Come in and I'll get you some glasses,' Tess says, taking the bottle of wine, and kissing Felix on the cheek first – or kissing the air around his face, because of her pink lipstick – and then doing the same to me. When she does it to me, despite my best intentions, I feel like I'm ten years old.

Immediately, two old songs from my album collection spring

into my head. The Buzzcocks' *Ever Fallen In Love With Someone (You Shouldn't Have Fallen In Love With)* and, naturally, *I Want The One I Can't Have*, by The Smiths.

Other people have original, proper thought processes and feelings about women. I have songs. Annoyingly, I also know these two songs will now be in my head for the rest of the week, the month, the year. I want the one I can't have, as Morrissey once noted, and it's driving me mad.

The song lyrics are all wrong, of course. I don't feel that strongly about Tess Blake. But still, the songs go round my head anyway, as we weave our way through the crowd following Tess in her white Priscilla Presley suit.

There's a man hanging around Tess, now, somewhere in the background, who I remember seeing at the Faith Lift gig the other night. I didn't like the look of him then, and I don't like it now. He's got curly hair, and some kind of necklace thing around his neck. And he's looking at Tess as if she belongs to him. He's also wearing the kind of designer surf gear, even in these low temperatures, that I could never afford, in a million years.

Suddenly, Felix spots someone he automatically suspects is gay, and single, and eligible, and starts jabbing me in the ribs.

'Conquest! conquest!' he hisses in my ear.

'Shut up,' I hiss back.

Fortunately, Tess is now looking for glasses in the kitchen cupboard and she can't hear anything Felix is saying.

'What makes you think that bloke over there is playing for your team?' I demand, once Felix has stopped hissing and jumping up and down.

'Very tight pants and a very big pout.'

'Yeah, but he's come as Elvis Presley circa *Burning Love*. Everyone in this room looks like that.'

Felix picks up the cue, ignores the rest of my advice, and immediately wanders over to talk to the potential Conquest, singing the song in a deep, booming voice as he goes. I suppose he's trying to be irresistible. Or something.

'Oh well,' Tess says, when she finally emerges with three plastic cups of red wine from the kitchen. The curly-haired idiot with the necklace, I notice, has found someone else to talk to.

'Shall I interrupt him or not?' Tess asks, looking at Felix across the room.

Saddleton is swigging champagne now, straight from the bottle, as the man with the jewellery and the eye make-up holds the other end. So maybe he was right after all. Or maybe the other guy is just a clueless Christian – it looks like there are a few of them around tonight – and he just thinks Felix has found the Lord, or something, and they're sharing the moment.

'I'll have it,' I say, grabbing the third plastic cup from Tess, so I now have one cup of cheap red wine in each hand. A class act, to be sure.

'Don't have too much to drink,' Tess says kindly, then the necklace man gives her some kind of look, or signal – and I immediately feel her attention flickering. It's something you just know, or feel, basically, and although I haven't felt it for years – because with Catherine, I was never put in this position with women at parties – I immediately want to move away, before she starts making excuses.

'I'll go and circulate,' I say.

'No, no.'

'No, really,' I take both the plastic cups, one in each hand. 'It's good for me. I should try harder at parties. I'm not sociable enough. Catherine always said that.'

And there, I've played the Catherine card, the sympathy card, but maybe that's the kind of desperate and pathetic man that I have become. Mark miserable Buckle – so crap, he'll try anything to keep a woman in a mini skirt and thigh-high boots talking to him, for as long as possible. Even using his dead girlfriend in conversation.

'Actually, there are some interesting people here,' Tess lobs back, staring at me wide-eyed through her false Priscilla eyelashes.

And that's it really. She waves a couple of her friends over – two women, both unwisely dressed as Elvis in his fat period – and I'm now unofficially out of her orbit. Just like that.

'I'm Tina,' says one of the women, shaking my hand. I mean – who shakes hands any more, except at job interviews?

'I'm Pam,' says the other one, and gives me a big, single smile.

'Do you go to Crosslink?' they both ask, virtually at the same time.

'Maybe I would if I knew what it was,' I say, knocking back the first plastic cupful of red wine. 'Is it a gym?'

Much laughter from Pam and Tina – so much laughter, in fact, that their Elvis jowls both start wobbling at the same time too.

'No, it's our church group!' Tina yells, waving her bottle of mineral water around in the air as if this is the most spectacularly funny conversation she's ever had in her entire life.

'Oh, right.'

'Tess goes to Crosslink,' Pam continues, as if this is going to make it all right, somehow. Or acceptable. I think she's just realised I am Not Of The Faith.

'I'm sure she does,' I say, taking another slug of red wine.

I can see Tess now, standing on tiptoe and saying something into the necklace guy's ear. Who the hell is he?

'Who's that bloke talking to Tess?' I ask Pam and Tina, sounding as if I couldn't care less.

'Robin,' Pam offers.

'So is he in Crosslink?' I persist.

'Robin's in everything,' they say, almost in unison again.

And that leaves me wondering about lots of things, as I make my excuses, and drift, inevitably, into the back garden. If Robin is in everything, then does that mean he is also a member of some gigantic, global, Christian ping-pong playing collective? Is the mysterious Robin in another band, something like Faith Lift, but even more horrible?

And if he's in everything, in Pam and Tina's tiny little world, does that mean he coaches a swimming class for whales who've lost their flippers, and volunteers for singalongs on youth camps, and paints the ceiling of St Paul's Cathedral on Sunday mornings? Does he lead his local village on the Easter egg hunt every April, does he teach starving children in Africa how to knit?

It's freezing in the garden, unusually cold for the tail-end of what's been a non-existent summer, but someone has lit a huge camp fire – of course. I mean, the camp fire is virtually a Christian institution. Not so much a way to cook sausages, more a registered trademark of the breed.

'I really like your outfit,' says a Chinese student with a back-pack. I think he was at the pub the other night, too.

I'm not sure what to say back. It is, after all, patently a crap Elvis outfit. And he isn't wearing an Elvis outfit at all, so I can hardly repeat the compliment.

'That's a very good backpack,' I hear myself saying. 'Sturdy.'

Then we stand around looking mindlessly at the camp fire for a while, until a small miracle occurs.

It is Tess Blake's hand on my arm.

'Sorry,' she says. 'I didn't mean to desert you. I forgot. You don't know many people here.'

'Oh no,' I wave her aside. But after that, there's really no point in denying it, because she's right. In fact, never mind the party, you could say I don't know many people full stop.

'That was my friend, Robin,' she explains, nodding back at the house.

'Yeah, I saw him the other night.'

'He works for a bank – and she names the bank, one of those huge multinational things that don't exist on the high street at all, least of all in my part of London, just in the front pages of *The Wall Street Journal*.

'Robin and I do a course called Crosslink together,' she says. 'In Clapham.'

'Right.'

'You should come along.'

'I don't think so.'

And I can't even look at her, now. Is this what it's all been about? The batted eyelashes and the specially dedicated songs? I mean, I thought those short skirts and high heels she's been wearing were for my benefit. Or something.

'Tess, I know you mean well, but –' In the end I just shake my head, because there's nothing more I can say. To go on would mean I might be in danger of losing it, and she doesn't really deserve that. Instead, I just keep drinking from both plastic cups in turn. It seems best, really.

'No, that' s cool,' she says, 'that's cool.'

I can see her face in the flames from the fire, and she looks worried. Perhaps the most worried I've ever seen her.

'It's in your course, though, isn't it?' I ask. 'I read about it somewhere. You've got to spread the word of the Lord and convert people. Spread the Good News.'

I can barely keep the disgust out of my voice, I suppose, because I suddenly see her wince.

'Do you want some water?' She's looking at my two hands, now, holding my two plastic cups, and no doubt, my wine-stained teeth as well. It's that kind of red wine.

'No,' I hear myself saying to the camp fire, 'I don't want some frigging water.'

Partly because of John Smith's phone calls, partly because of Catherine, and partly because of the night on the soaking bar stool at the Pig's Head, I now feel more than disappointed. I feel outraged. And if I stand here any longer, next to this woman – this woman who is not on a mission of love for me, or even lust, but on a mission for the Lord – I think I might do some serious verbal damage.

In the end, I do the only thing I can, under the circumstances. I chuck the two empty plastic cups into the fire, and walk straight through the kitchen, through the corridor, past Felix still gyrating with the Elvis lookalike in front of the stereo, to *Blue Suede Shoes*, and out into the front garden. It's bloody freezing.

There's a park across the road. And I think, I'll probably get mugged there, but what the hell. I'm past caring.

Apart from two young kids having a fag and swinging on the gates, though, there's no sign of life in the park at all. Just an ominously dark sky, and a few dodgy, flickering street lamps and endless amounts of trees.

I walk far enough to lose the sound of Elvis blaring from the open front door of the house, and far enough to have to squint to see the light from the front windows, and then I sit down. On a pile of rotting leaves and wet grass as it turns out. This is becoming a habit, sitting in piles of crap on a Saturday night.

Tess Blake. What was I thinking? She has turned me off from the waist down, purely by turning me off from the head up. I told Catherine I was needy, and I was. And maybe that's it. Nothing more complicated than that. An empty bed, nobody to talk to – except someone who fades in and out of my dreams – and some kind of delayed, shock reaction. The more I analyse it, even under the influence of that cheap and poisonous red wine, the more the Tess Blake thing will make sense to me. If I stick at it, anyway.

Tess is meant for the necklace man, who is in everything, the posh Christian banker in the designer surf gear, Robin, and I am meant for nobody.

I don't care what Catherine says – even if she has been convincing so far. Because, sitting here in this freezing park, with a wet arse, and fluorescent street lights in my face, life suddenly seems very real. All the unreal things since Catherine died – the mad promises about our life together in some unlikely reincarnated future, the Tuscan fields, the transported armchairs, the weird John Smith stuff about the six facts – is diminishing by the minute.

I am flesh and blood, and Tess is flesh and blood, and if I'm going to be brutally honest here, I wanted her for five seconds, and now I don't. I thought she wanted me, too. And she doesn't. She just wants to convert me. Or she feels sorry for me. I'm not even rated as a sympathy bonk, me. I'm just a sympathy conversion to the church.

And I get the thing about the invitation to her band, at the pub. And this party. She basically thinks I'm sitting at home alone on Saturday nights crying since Catherine died – which I'm bloody not, thankyou very much – or at least, I'm not crying any more. And she's sorry for me. And she wants to bring me out of myself, or something. No more than that.

No doubt Tess has had a quiet word to Felix about me, as well. No wonder he's been following me around like a faithful hound. And I suppose Tess has been talking discreetly to Alison, too. No wonder she's been making me constant mugs of her horrible Earl Grey tea.

As I get up and tramp on through the leaves, it occurs to me that the Tess Blake semi-crush has been nothing more than a fantastic piece of self-deception, and that's not something new in my life, either.

I mean, come on. Tess Blake? Christian. Teacher's aide, that most put-upon of species. Nice woman. Crosslink person. Singer. Ping-pong player, no doubt. Possibly the last female on earth, or at least in South London, to jump into Catherine's parking space now, outside our front door, and certainly the last woman to replace her on the empty side of the bed – at least, not while the sympathy cards are still thudding into my letterbox.

I can see Donna Roberts there, in both those spaces – the car slot, and the bed slot – but not Tess. And for my part, I'm not sure I like myself for even having contemplated it. Not for one minute.

I move over to the concrete footpath, because even I can't take much more wet grass soaking through my white plimsolls (the Elvis shoe compromise), and I walk over to the other side of the park.

It looks like there's an all-night supermarket over there, or something, so maybe I can get some more booze, buy some fags, and something to eat, and then come back and tell Felix I'm going home. He seemed happy enough on the dance floor, anyway. Bloody Saddleton. Life's just one long spa bath for him.

As I plough down the footpath, I wonder about Robin and Tess. Do they have sex together? Do they actually do it? And if so, do they do it the same way everyone else does it? Then, it occurs to me that I know less about Christians than almost anything else in the world.

You could push me onto a TV quiz show tomorrow, and ask me questions about anything from the offside rule to Duran Duran, from the Weimar Republic to the second law of thermodynamics, and I could wing it. But ask me about Crosslink, or the New Testament, or any of it, and I'm off the show. Out of the game.

I don't care if there are three million Christians wandering around London, or whatever that statistic is. None of us know a damn thing about them. Even if they are blonde and gorgeous, and they walk around in mini skirts dressed as Priscilla Presley.

The birds are going crazy again, around my head. And in the dark, I can't even see what they are. Sparrows? Misguided pigeons a very long way from Trafalgar Square? Perhaps it's nothing to do with the Catherine weirdness at all. For all I know, I'll pick up the paper tomorrow and read about some strange new example of morphic resonance, where all the birds are going apeshit after dark, together.

So. Tess Blake. Tess Blake. A potentially bad mistake, narrowly avoided. And in any case, I have to admit, I'm not really sure where it would have taken us. Like Veronica all over again – a definitely impossible, possibility.

Tess Blake is nothing that would last. Nothing that could last. Why? Because it's just not right. In fact, in capital letters, It's Just Not Right. For all kinds of reasons.

Realistically, nothing that could happen between Tess and me, would be anything more than a night of confusion now and – later on – horrible embarrassment for her, and essentially, a night of drunken stupor and sheer physical relief for me. None of which is particularly nice to think about, and none of which makes me feel particularly proud of myself. It's basically Veronica all over again, and after all Catherine's done for me, too.

And then I hear her running over the wet grass, in her ridiculous Priscilla Presley outfit. Tess Blake. The Queen of the Crosslink jungle.

She's holding her big, black wig on with one hand, and keeping her skirt together with the other. It's hard to know where to look.

'The birds!' she half-laughs, with that dreadful fake jokey sound you try on, when you're trying to break the ice. Though in our case, after that scene in the garden, the ice is Antarctic-thick.

She points to the half-dozen flapping starlings, or jackdaws, or whatever they are, flying in and out of the shadows.

'You get used to it,' I tell her. And for a second, I almost contemplate telling her everything. The armchairs in the garden, Catherine's face in the mirror – everything.

'What's going on, Mark?'

Tess looks so funny now with her black eye make-up half off her face, and her ridiculously short skirt, and her knobbly knees, that I half want to kiss her right here, right now.

But that's typical of me. I talk myself out of something, and five seconds later, that makes me want to reverse – fast – and talk myself back in again. Especially after cheap red wine.

'I'm in no fit state to drink, or go to a party, or do anything else,' I say, blankly, by way of apology for the camp fire thing. And this is possibly the truth. Although it hasn't occured to me until now.

'I didn't want you to think I'm only here for you, because I want to convert you,' Tess says breathlessly.

Instantly, the desire to kiss her vanishes again. It's like being warmed up nicely in front of a log fire, then having a ton of ice cubes dropped down your trousers. I sound angry, because she's just turned me off again, but I can't help it.

'Tess. Please. Talk English, at least. What is that crap – "I'm here for you?"'

'You can be angry, I don't mind, I can take it,' Tess says, all in a rush.

'Very noble.'

We look away from each other, and up to the sky, and the birds, and the lights. There's really nowhere else to look at this moment.

Then –

'I like you,' she says at last.

'Well good. I like you too.'

'Now you're being patronising,' she says.

'That's not very Christian of you. That's not very Crosslink.'

'I'm sorry,' Tess says, her big, blue, black-lashed eyes blinking in the light.

Then, another long pause while we both don't look at each other.

'I'm a virgin,' she says, finally.

What?

'I'm a virgin,' Tess says, as if I didn't hear and understand it the first time. 'I thought I should explain that to you.'

I look at her for a minute. And all I can think of is, all those awful jokes you hear about the last virgin left in London.

'And,' Tess says, 'I know Catherine hasn't been dead long.'

'Not long at all,' I say, adding it up in my head for the first time.

'Exactly.'

Tess wipes away some of her false eyelashes, which are falling off on her cheek, and looks suddenly old and tired, rather than a 60s sex kitten with a cross around her neck.

'I'm a bit pissed,' she sniffs. 'And I'm trying to explain something to you here, and I'm not even sure what I really mean.'

'Isn't getting pissed against the Crosslink rules?'

'Yes. I mean – everything is against the rules for me at the moment. If you must know.'

'Right.'

I look at her, and decide to push it.

'And what's all that with Robin?'

'Oh, he wants to get serious with me, and I don't. It's been going on for years –' she waves a hand dismissively, and I suddenly notice the birds have finally scarpered back into the trees.

'This is not a normal conversation and we should both be in bed,' I hear myself saying. Then I correct the sentence. 'In bed. Separately. In our own beds.'

'Of course.' Despite herself, Tess smiles. And stops looking tired, and suddenly looks unspeakably lovely.

'You've had a few drinks and you're not used to it,' I tell her.

'Yup.'

'I'm half dead from lack of sleep, stress, grief, total madness,' I go on.

'And that red wine,' Tess adds.

'Exactly.'

'I finished the bottle for you,' she says. 'Which is why I feel a bit – I dunno.'

I want to hold her hand. Why do I want to hold her hand? That'll be the next song going round my head, a Beatles song. Instead of an honest thought or emotion.

'Felix is having a good time,' Tess says, turning to go back to the house, and staring up at me all at the same time.

'And that's okay by you lot, is it? Felix Saddleton doing the wild thing in the corner?'

'What do you mean?'

And as I check Tess's eyes, with their big, black spidery lashes, it occurs to me that she really doesn't know. That she's genuinely, hopelessly, clueless.

'He's gay.'

Tess stops and pulls at her wig, dragging it back over the other side of her head.

'Well, I knew that.'

'No, you didn't.'

'Okay. I didn't. But now you say it, it all makes sense. I mean, it sort of adds up about him.'

'And tell me something,' I hear myself saying, 'what does good old Bible-bashing Crosslink say about people like Felix Saddleton, then? I mean, is it off to the monastery with him in the morning? What about this football team at school he's got to coach? Would you ban him from the pitch on the first day, or just try to convert him to heterosexuality before he can even get permission to throw the children the ball?'

'I don't know what you're talking about.'

Tess is walking very fast now, and it's beginning to rain.

'Come on. I know a bit about this Crosslink thing. Big questions of life and death. The new Christianity revival thing. Everyone's doing it. And this is a big question, isn't it? About the suitability, or unsuitability, of Felix Saddleton? So how come you don't have an answer? I mean, come on Tess. Is he less than human, because he has sex with other men?'

And then Tess walks away from me, very straight and very fast, her heels clicking across the wet grass in the Priscilla Presley boots, and although I can't hear her crying, I know, without a shadow of a doubt, that I have made her cry.

What is it that Veronica Roden constantly says about me? In fact, what has she always said about me, ever since I was a nine-year-old twerp at the Dymchurch Caravan Park? Exactly. Those two words – bastard and arsehole. And, in one magnificent display of pissed – and pissed-off – frustration and anger, I have managed to become both of those things, at the same time.

The rain goes on, and I let Tess go, watching her stumble occasionally in her Priscilla Presley boots as she makes for the safety of the big, warm, lit-up house on the other side of the park.

'Go away,' I say to the thin air, before Catherine can even think about making an appearance. I mean, the stage is set, really. It's dark. I'm alone. There's nobody to see us. I'd say this moment was just about perfect for a waft of Joy, or a strange green light around the trees, or a sudden ring tone on my mobile phone.

There is nothing, though. Not in the park, not on the way home in the mini-cab that costs me nearly thirty quid, not in the kitchen when I pour myself a jug of water, and not even in our bed, when I finally pass out at about 2 a.m. And you know the worst thing? I'm starting to both expect it, and to miss it, all at the same time.

twelve

Of course it was a sex thing, the Tess Blake thing, and so a few weeks later, I find myself doing something I haven't done since I was wearing short pants at Dymchurch Caravan Park. Something that makes me feel a bit self-conscious, and embarrassed, but nevertheless, something that I genuinely hope will help offload some of the physical tension.

I start going swimming.

It's my father who puts me onto it. Not (naturally) because we have a frank and uninhibited discussion about my libido, and the effects of good healthy exercise and cold water upon the aforementioned libido – but mainly because he gives me his membership card for Oak Street Baths.

Oak Street Baths are about three miles from my house, and I figure that the brisk walk required to get me there should also help – along with the swim in the freezing cold water, of course.

Does this happen to anybody else, I wonder? Does anybody

else get a phone call to say that their girlfriend is dead, and go to the hospital and identify the body, and make it through the funeral, and deal with the will – only to wake up in lust with someone new, a few weeks down the track? Particularly, and very specifically, a virgin who is also a member of a Christian rock band, not to mention a church group?

One of the things I am beginning to discover about death is that it forces you into a very private club, with one member – you. I know people who've had people die on them, of course. There's Alan, the bloke who was once my friend, but then had kids, became boring and started playing golf. He had a girlfriend die in some terrible bus crash in Portugal, when we were both at college. But I can hardly ring up Alan now, and ask him if the immediate after-effects of his girlfriend's death included an inappropriate longing for someone else, straight afterwards.

Oak Street Baths have a vaguely disturbing smell at the front desk, locker key part – it makes me think of athlete's foot in the showers, or small children, possibly from our school, peeing in the water. Nevertheless, my father has given me his membership card, so it only costs me 50p if I can manage to rush in through the turnstile before the bored bloke at reception can take a closer look at the name on the card.

It soon occurs to me that this might be where all the single people in South London go. Or all the lonely people, perhaps. Not that my dad would ever have noticed, of course. But in the men's change rooms at least, there's an air of expectancy. Men – of all ages, shapes and sizes – rushing through the footbath (perhaps that's the source of the smell) and into the big, under-cover pool area, where there are women, once again of all ages, shapes and sizes, ploughing up and down the lanes, occasionally crashing into the blue plastic ropes.

I don't think I've ever consciously been to a pick-up joint, but as I wander over to the wooden benches and make a space for my towel, it occurs to me that this might be it. A woman, about my age, but with a tight rubber bathing cap on that makes her look like an alien life form, winks at me. She has a gold tooth. She has also decided to move her towel up a bit. As I arrived, she was a few metres away. Now, mysteriously, my spot has suddenly become the hot spot. The desirable towel-placing spot. Another woman has also followed suit, and now I find myself being surrounded by other towels, and the available bench space slowly diminishes in front of me.

I try to be polite. This is my first time at Oak Street Baths, after all, and I'm willing to try. So when the woman, who looks like an alien with a gold tooth, says 'The water's nice and warm today,' I make a noise that sounds like it might be 'Mmmm' in agreement, except it comes out all wrong, possibly because I've been listening to Felix Saddleton too much, and I sound ridiculously camp, like Kenneth Williams in a film that's possibly called 'Carry On Up The Deep End'.

The woman looks momentarily disappointed, and moves away, flicking her towel over her shoulder. Thank God. But, on the way to the ladder in the shallow end, there is another obstacle. This one is big and has tattooed shoulders. He has a shaven head, like me. And he has enormous feet, like a dinosaur. And jewellery. Loads of jewellery.

He looks at the plastic clock at the end of the baths, and then looks at me, then back at the clock. I get the impression that this is some kind of common Oak Street Baths ritual – a silent bet, made between consenting male swimmers, that the race is on.

But if I race him, and frankly I don't want to, because, let's face it, I might die of heart failure, it occurs to me that this is something I might have to ask Felix Saddleton about. Because, if I'm not careful, I'll be getting into very deep water indeed. Put it this way – the tattooed man has a Pimlico feeling about him, and that's almost enough to make me go all the way back up the ladder again, and straight out of the pool.

The water isn't too bad, although as I let myself in, a long-forgotten childhood impulse to go 'Aaargh!' and then immediately submerge myself, has to be suppressed. I am swimming, for the first time in decades, in a pair of trunks that have suddenly become embarrassingly transparent in the water, and I feel about nine years old, as I once did on holiday with Catherine, all those years ago. And now Gold Tooth Woman is looking at my trunks, too, I notice. So maybe a spot of submergence isn't such a bad idea.

I push myself down under the water, eyes stinging as I expected – although it's also worse than I expected, really scorching – and swim forward, away from all the blurry fleshy things I can see below, all of which threaten to be people's legs, and particularly the legs of those who have some desire to place their towel next to mine, or to race me against the clock.

When I finally surface, gasping like an idiot, I manage a front crawl, head swinging from side to side, mouth open. Not because I've forgotten how you do it, I hasten to add. It's just that I'm not putting my mouth in that water and breathing in other people's sweat and stuff. No way. Not with the tattooed man in there as well.

Because I'm a slow swimmer – in fact, practically a water-walker – as I waggle my way from side to side, lurching up the lanes, and being overtaken, even by the very oldest and fattest people, I notice that while most of the pool is empty, the benches around the sides are bursting at the seams. My eyes are stinging, and my vision's not great, but even from here, I can see people exhibiting all the strange body language you might expect to see in a wine bar. Or some kind of speed-dating situation.

Alison has told me all about speed dating. All her single friends in Chelsea are doing it, she says. In her friends' case, they basically front up to somewhere off Sloane Street, pay hundreds of quid for a lot of lethal, very old French wine, and shoot off questions to each other. Alison explained it this way:

'Well, you might look at your date and say, labrador, Mark.'

'Labrador?'

'Just a quick question. Although people talk so fast now, at these speed-dating things, that they don't even have to say the whole sentence. You just use key words instead. Like labrador. As in, do you have a labrador, and do you like labradors?'

'Right.'

'And then you might go, Church of England, Wimbledon, Strawberries and Cream, Provence, a little bit of blow now and then, Veuve Clicquot and The Gypsy Kings.'

Shortly after this, Alison asked me if I would be interested in speed dating. One day. Not right now, because I was still – you know, getting over things – but if I ever wanted to try it, when I was ready, I only had to ask.

Alison is the only teacher at the school who *talks in italics*. The kids imitate her squashed-down-posh voice sometimes, as they also imitate Felix.

Both Felix and I suspect that far from merely having friends who speed date, Alison is actually a full-time participant herself. But she's all right, Alison, in her own irritating, bumbling, embarrassing way. She's not a bad person, and possibly even quite a good person, and I don't wish her any ill.

Now that I am single too, I find myself almost wishing she could find the man of her dreams – not the mythical Charlie, but the man who will lean across a speed-dating table in a Chelsea restaurant and say the magic words: Labrador, Church of England, Wimbledon, Strawberries and Cream, Provence, and all the rest of it. Even The Gypsy Kings, and the small, occasional quantities of cocaine.

I keep swimming, mindlessly. The exercise has achieved what I set out to do, namely, to completely suppress my libido, but not for the reasons I imagined. It's got nothing to do with cold water, and nothing to do with the physical exertion, either. Instead, it's the sight of all those women in goggles and yellowing rubber caps that used to be white, flailing around and spitting, and choking on the chlorine, and lounging around on the benches, checking out all the available men.

I didn't know about the Oak Street Baths scene. I didn't know about all this, just a few miles away from the house. I suppose Dad joined because of his heart – after he came out of hospital. The people here have also joined on account of their hearts, it seems, and for different reasons, but I can't see much hope for them in this place.

After the obligatory ten laps, I find a spot in the water where both my feet will actually touch the bottom, and half-walk, half-swim towards the ladder in the shallow end. There is no sign of the woman with the gold tooth, nor the man with the tattoo and the strange look in his eye.

Somehow, I can't help thinking that Felix Saddleton's alternative, all that rampant romping with hairy men in the spa baths of Pimlico, must be more fun. Less repressed. Less desperate, somehow, than this weird scene now being played out in front of me.

I make my way into the men's change rooms, avoiding every eye, to the point where I almost fall off the side of the pool and crash my head on the cement. Then I wade through the footbath, and find my locker. It's number 13. Unlucky for some.

I am never coming back here again, even if I do have my father's magic discount card. I'd rather take drugs. Some kind of anti-Viagra perhaps. Maybe Dr Smita Patel can recommend something. Doesn't the army give their men some kind of drug, to suppress all their natural urges?

When I finally stagger home, eyes stinging and bloodshot, skin dry and wet in the freezing wind, I pick up the phone and call Dad, to tell him he can have his membership card back. Instead, though, it is my mother who answers – he's gone out with his darts team apparently – and she wants to talk, which she does, on and on.

'How was the swim?' she asks me.

'Not great.'

'Oh. Your father says the water's very warm.'

'Has he ever noticed anything else about the place?'

'Why?'

'It's a pick-up joint.'

'Oh God, not your father!'

And my mother laughs hard at this, to the point where she's almost snorting. This is one of my father's favourite things about my mother – this tendency to forget herself, and lapse into pig sounds, when she's amused.

A few minutes later, she calms down and blows her nose.

'Would you like to come round for dinner tonight? We're having spaghetti bolognaise.'

And what do I say to that? No I can't, Mum? Because John Smith told me meat was ruining my vibrations?

'Great.'

'Oh good. I suppose you've run out of the other lot I gave you.'

'Yeah.'

'Is everything okay, then?'

'Yeah.'

No, Mum, I just spent the other Saturday night in a park, sitting on a pile of wet leaves, and made a perfectly okay woman cry. A Christian woman, who I also want to sleep with. Who also happens to be a virgin. Maybe even a 35-year-old virgin.

We talk about the Rodens for a minute. Mum is worried about Catherine's parents, particularly her father, who has always been ill, off and on, and, to her, seems the most vulnerable in the family.

'No, Mum. He's fine.'

'Have you spoken to him?'

'Veronica says he's fine.'

'But she wouldn't know. Would she?'

And again, I think, I could talk to my mother for at least three hours now, about Veronica Roden, and the things she does, and doesn't, know about life. But the David Bowie cat is back now, banging against the window, as it doesn't seem to know the meaning of the magic phrase 'Bugger off'.

'I think I've got to go,' I tell her.

'See you for dinner then,' she finishes the call.

'Great.'

Yeah, really great. Welcome to life as a widower, and I never even got married. Spag bol, smelly swimming pools, and the prospect of speed dating with Sloane Rangers.

Great.

thirteen

The following Friday, Felix Saddleton asks me to watch football videos at his place. He issues the invitation very loudly and flamboyantly, in the staffroom, so that I am sure every other teacher in the place thinks that it's some kind of date, and that Felix is successfully beginning to convert me to a life of uninhibited man-shagging.

'How would you like to sit on the sofa with me and watch a lot of grown men playing with balls?' is how he puts it, and the rustling of all the copies of *The Guardian* in the staffroom, suddenly stops, and you can hear people coughing over the top of Radio Four.

I couldn't care less what anyone else in this school thinks, though. And in fact, I have nothing to do this weekend – except sit around at home, and worry about Tess, and worry about Catherine, and worry about myself, and even worry about Veronica. So I accept his offer. In fact, I even accept with enthusiasm. Besides, how's Felix going to learn about football if he doesn't learn it from an expert?

On Sunday evening, then, I find myself perched on the edge of Felix Saddleton's Ikea sofa – I'd know that strange Swedish shape and those pointy castors anywhere, because I've screwed similar things together a million times – eating peanuts from his Ikea bowls, and trying to keep my feet off his Ikea coffee table.

There is some arty poster on the wall, and a lot of different men's aftershaves in the bathroom, all stacked up together in a neat row. It feels very strange. I've never known anyone who's lived like this. And he's got candles lit as well. He's possibly the only man I've ever met who owns a candle.

He also has a snowdome of the Sydney Opera House, and a silver-framed poster advertising something calling itself The Sydney Gay and Lesbian Mardi Gras, which sounds like the event I'd least like to attend, some time soon.

'Are you going to tell me about the offside rule now?' Felix asks, as we watch a vintage Beckham shot going into the back of the net.

'No.'

'And why do you keep shouting at the television whenever we watch a match? Should I be doing that as well?'

'One day, Felix, you might not even have to ask.'

'But this offside rule – why won't you tell me?' And Felix gives a little Elvis Presley pout. 'Everyone at school keeps telling me it's the most important thing!'

'Felix, you haven't even worked out what a wing back does yet. How the hell am I going to explain offside to you?'

'No, but I think KFC definitely make the best wing backs, since you ask.' Felix makes a crap joke, and munches on a handful of cashew nuts.

Felix continues to pick all the cashews out of the bowl, leaving me with the peanuts, while we watch Beckham being Beckham for a few more minutes.

'When did the Head tell you that you have to start with the team?' I ask him.

'In two weeks,' he says, sounding depressed.

'Have you got anyone else helping you, apart from me?'

'No.'

'Are you reading any books, or anything?'

'Only that old *Scorcher* annual,' he says, throwing a glance in the direction of the football book with Kevin Keegan on the front, that he's stolen from the school library.

'Right. Shit. Do you know about extra time, yet?'

'No. Extra time for what?'

'Do you know about fouls?'

'No.'

'Goal kicks?'

'No.'

'Corners?'

'Mark, it sounds like we're talking about making the bed,' Felix sighs.

In the end, we take the football videos back to the shop, and swap them for *The Sound Of Music*, which Felix desperately wants to see, and I give in to. I'll fall asleep on his sofa anyway, so it doesn't really matter, I guess.

The man in the video shop is the same man who stuck his phone number on a piece of paper, into Catherine's video box once. And by the look on his face, he remembers me too. I wonder if he's heard that she's dead? I push the thought away.

'Why don't you just run through the offside rule with me quickly, when we get home?'

Felix suggests, picking up more nuts and chocolate at the front counter.

'No.'

'But why? Why is it such a taboo? Mark, what is it people aren't telling me in this country?'

'I can't explain.'

'No, please.' Felix is now practically fizzing with frustration, like human Fanta.

'The offside rule,' I explain, 'has destroyed healthy marriages, split families, devasted friendships and completely crushed grown men who are better informed, and probably better men, than you and I. Now, why would I even want to go there? Especially if you don't know what a frigging wingback is!'

'And can you tell me something else about soccer?'

'Football.'

'Sorry, football. When they interview the players after the game, on TV, why do they use that weird past tense?'

'What do you mean?'

'Instead of saying someone knocked in a great cross, they say he *has* knocked in a great cross. You know. "Well, Beckham has knocked in a great cross and I've got in there and lobbed it in." That kind of thing. I mean, I teach English. You know? I find it very confusing.'

In the end, Felix shuts up, thank God, but he buys so many crisps, and giant bars of Toblerone, and packets of Maltesers, that I end up having to hold his copy of *The Sound Of Music* for him, and walk home with it under my arm. It's embarrassing, of course, being seen like this, particularly as Felix is swinging his arms as he walks beside me, trilling the song about being sixteen, going on seventeen – but then, it can't be any more embarrassing than anything else that's happened to me in the past month.

As I predict, I manage to sit through the alpine introduction to *The Sound Of Music*, before falling asleep on his sofa, and I am still there, at three o'clock in the morning, when Felix pads into the kitchen in his dressing gown, for a glass of water.

I wake with his long, bony finger prodding me in the shoulder.

'Mark.'

And I suppose this would scare the living crap out of any other man, this scenario with Felix in his silk dressing gown, a few inches away from my face, reeking of aftershave, but there have been so many more terrifying things in my life lately that I'm almost immune.

'Mark, I think I understand soccer!'

'What? Stop calling it soccer.'

Felix switches on the lamp, next to the sofa.

'I had a revelatory dream!' he whispers. 'An amazingly revelatory dream!'

'You don't need to whisper, I'm awake now.'

'An amazingly good-looking and spunky football player in big old-fashioned shorts came to me in my dream and told me everything!'

'Right.'

'Could it have been Sir Stanley Matthews? Or Dixie Dean?' Felix asks, excitedly.

'Frankly, no. Felix, it's –' I look at my watch and curse, then fall back on the cushions.

'I know about throw-ins now! I understand!' he hisses.

'Yeah. Brilliant.'

'Can I show you the offside rule?' he gabbles, searching around excitedly for the bowl of peanuts, and our empty beer cans, as demonstration tools.

'No, not at this time of night.'

'Oh.' And Felix sounds so genuinely disappointed now, that I even think the miracle may have occurred. The Felix Saddleton football conversion may actually be underway, in fact. This was, without any doubt, a man who went to bed not knowing what a foul was. Now, he appears to have woken up, longing – practically salivating – to explain the offside rule to me.

'Just go away, please,' I tell him. 'Please, please, please just go away.'

'Oh. Okay,' he whispers, and pads back to bed.

When I roll over and try to fall asleep again, I discover a peanut in my ear, and the video case for *The Sound Of Music* jabbing into my leg. But I manage to ignore both these irritations, and pass out anyway. I'll say that much for Felix's flat. What with the candles, and the incense, and the mood lighting and everything else, it has a genuinely soporific effect.

A few days later, Felix and I are going over the offside rule again – which, to my amazement, he now seems to understand better, and explain better, than most school football coaches I've met – when Alison interrupts us.

'Got a cigarette?' she asks, striding into the staffroom.

'You had a full packet of Silk Cut this morning,' Felix accuses her.

'I just want one of yours, please,' she says lamely.

Handing her one of his cigarettes, Felix gives her a look.

'What is it?' he says suspiciously. 'Come on, spit it out, you're not here for my fags, what do you want?'

And then, with a barely concealed smile of triumph, Alison tells us her gossip. Tess Blake is leaving the school. She's just heard she's been accepted into a scholarship teaching scheme, with some Christian school in New York, in a really rough part of the Bronx, where they try to bring Jesus into the lives of crack-smoking, knife-wielding ten year olds. And consequently, she won't be with us past Friday.

'She's having a leaving do, and she asked me if you both wanted to come along,' Alison says breathlessly.

'Well,' Felix replies, 'this is sudden.'

Then both Felix and Alison turn and look at me.

'What?' I say.

They keep looking.

'What?'

In the end, I give up. There is a pattern of behaviour at Rivett Street Junior School, which has been in existence for many years, which basically consists of surreptitious gossip, hidden agendas, meaningful silences and horrendous hearsay. And I'm now being reminded of this fact, and worse, I have a suspicion that for the past few weeks, it's all been applied to me.

'Tess will love it in the States,' I say at last. 'Ideal for her.'

'She'll be very disappointed if you don't come to her leaving drinks,' Alison says, pointedly.

And what does that mean? Have Tess and Alison been talking about the possibility that I might refuse to go? Has this been the subject of hot debate, by email, between Felix Saddleton, Alison, Tess and the rest of the school, including the Head, and even Blount the schoolkeeper, and possibly his alsatian too?

'Why wouldn't I be at her party?' I say at last. Which is, in its own way, a trap. Because now I'll have to front up, of course, and see Robin the Christian banker with the necklace, probably with his tongue halfway down her throat, and the two jolly girls from Crosslink, and no doubt the Chinese students with the backpacks. And I'll have to kiss Tess Blake goodbye or something, and then the whole game will be up. My one attempt at swimming, incidentally, hasn't cured the Tess lust problem.

'Tess is going to move over there with her friend,' Alison informs me.

'Well, that's great,' I say. The irritation factor with Alison is now at rubber band-twanging stage. And if she's not careful, I may strike her. Or something.

What friend? I suppose she means Robin. But I'm not going to ask, either. Why give Alison that satisfaction?

'I'm going to miss our nice teacher's aide,' Felix sighs, dramatically, leaning half his body out of the window so he can breathe out the cigarette smoke like Greta Garbo.

'Anyway,' I say at last, 'we were just going over some football stuff, Alison. So we'd probably better get back to it.'

'Okay,' she submits, 'okay, okay. Not going to interrupt boys' talk.'

And with that, she waddles off in her strange Harrods shoes to make herself another cup of Earl Grey tea, leaving Felix to crap on endlessly about Franz Beckenbauer and Nobby Stiles ('Oh, but how cruel Mother Nature was to that man, despite his great talent!') and leaving me to stare out of the window. Felix on football is more than I can stand, at the moment.

So – Tess Blake in New York. I suppose she thinks she'll be like Michelle Pfeiffer in that film, the one where she gets to perform miracles in front of the blackboard, changing young urban lives.

Or perhaps she sees herself as a kind of female Sir, in *To Sir, With Love*. I wonder if the little kids in the Bronx really do carry flick-knives to school, the way you always hear about on television? I can't imagine Tess dealing with that, somehow.

And then, as Felix blithely runs through his masterplans for Rivett Street Junior School FC, something else occurs to me. If Tess Blake is going to America with Robin the necklace man, then maybe her virginity is all off. Or, alternatively, maybe it's all still on, but she's going to give in and get married to him after all. Weather's nice for a white wedding, and all that kind of thing.

'Mark,' Felix prods me.

'Yeah?'

'Mark, what do you think about making the team do keepie-uppie before school? Just half an hour of practice? Do you think the parents would agree?'

He is, of course, talking about small boys bouncing footballs on their knees, but if we're going to talk about keepie-uppie, the only thing I can think of is the way Tess hasn't kept up anything, at least since our talk at the party. And for my part, I certainly can't keep up with her, either. I mean, can someone – dead or alive, it doesn't really matter any more – tell me what's going on?

fourteen

A few days later, something amazing – at least by Rivett Street Junior standards – occurs. Alison walks into the staffroom with the Head, who is holding her hand and, later, kisses her – properly – in full view of all the staff.

The Head, as we call him – his name is Tony McSheedy, but nobody bothers with that – is much shorter than Alison, and a great deal thinner, so it's an odd sight anyway, but in the circumstances, it may even be the oddest thing, among many odd things, that has happened in this school since the late 1940s. And that includes the school alsatian trying to mount one of the children during assembly, or the day Scott O'Grady tried to stick a biro up a guinea pig.

'So what happened to Charlie?' Felix hisses at me over the tea urn, when the Head and Alison have finally finished their cups of her Earl Grey, smoked her Silk Cut and left. 'I mean,' he whispers, above the radio, 'it's like one of those things where Prince Charles goes poncing off to a ball with Camilla, so that everyone will know they've gone public.'

'And –' Felix goes on, 'who amongst us knew that the Head smoked? Now, isn't that alarming news!' He now sounds genuinely panicked. 'I mean, Mark, let's face it, he never smoked before. In fact, I was always being lectured about it.' He flaps his hands up and down. 'Aaargh, what's going on? What in the name of frigging sanity is going on?'

I don't know either. But I know it's probably a good thing. Alison is not one of those women who really suit the single life, and despite the endless stories about Charlie, that perpetually busy, sickly and ski-mad creature, everyone round here knows she's been by herself forever.

'Or,' as Felix challenges me later, when we are settling back at his flat, watching an old Argentina video, 'has she been shagging the Head the entire time and not telling us?'

It seems odd to have to talk to another man in front of the football, but I suppose I should be polite. This is, after all, Felix's flat, and his television too. And he paid for the video.

'I doubt they've been shagging,' I tell him, not taking my eyes off the screen. 'I think it's a new thing. I think she's just finally crumbled, and given into him, after years of resistance.'

'So,' Felix persists, 'they were at it when she took the job here, but then it stopped, and now it's started again. Is that what you think?'

'No, I think you should shut up and watch the bloody game,' I reply, pointing out that something interesting is about to happen with Maradona. 'I mean, talk about keepie-uppie, Felix,' I tell him, 'this bloke here is the King of Keepie-Uppie. And you're not even watching.'

'I don't know what Alison's got in common with the Head,' Felix sighs, opening a beer can and getting it wrong, so the ring-pull stays stuck in the top. 'And it really worries me.'

'Jesus!' I yell.

'What?' Felix begs me. 'What? What happened?'

And I can only point at the screen, wordlessly, as something that shouldn't be going on in midfield is now definitely going on.

'Jesus!' Felix joins in, copying me. Sometimes, I think, he's just not taking any of this seriously.

'Alison once told me she was looking for a man who liked

strawberries, cocaine and labradors,' I inform Felix, when things on the screen start to calm down and get a bit boring again.

'So the Head is on Class A drugs? I knew it!'

'No, but he's on labradors. He's definitely got a labrador. It's just you never see it, it stays hiding in the back of his car, because of Blount's alsatian.'

'Ah, yes,' Felix gives me a knowing look, as the Argentinians devastate the defence on the TV. 'A strangely territorial animal. I don't blame the Head's labrador for staying away. It cocks its leg, you know, on the lollipop lady sometimes. She gets very upset.'

We both watch the TV, open-mouthed, as Maradona goes in for the kill.

'So tell me about Tess,' Felix says, after a bit.

'Nothing to tell.'

'You know, I went home with that chap the other night. That chap from the party.'

'The Elvis bloke?'

'Well, they were all Elvis blokes, Mark, but I know what you mean. Anyway. He looked exactly like Rupert Everett when he took his wig off. So, I don't need to tell you, we both drank freely from the Cup of Adonis.'

'Oh, well. Never mind. Nice guy?'

I mean, I'm trying here, but Maradona is in the action replay now, and quite frankly, I have no idea what's *de rigueur* in the world of post-coital gay bloke chat, as far as Felix is concerned.

'My friend told me a bit about Tess,' Felix says, staring hard at me to see if I'll react.

'Like, what?' I make my face go blank, and stare at Maradona's flashing feet for a few minutes.

'She's a virgin.'

'Yeah, well, I knew that.'

'I mean,' Felix says, 'My God, weren't you shocked? Ooooh! –' He suddenly gets up from his couch and claps his hands together, as the Argentinian goalkeeper does the impossible. 'Nice save, big boy!'

'A word of advice, Felix,' I tell him, as the game goes back to a replay, 'never do that, or say that, in that particular voice, during a real game, or you will be killed. Killed by a large group

135

of men. Men who piss on the terraces, because they're too hard to use the toilets.'

'Anyway,' Felix says, reaching for more food because he's given up on the beer. 'I can see you don't want to talk about Tess, so I'm not going to push it.'

'Good. Because there's nothing to talk about.'

Then, suddenly, Felix goes quiet for a while, and all we can hear is the tinny roar of the crowd as Argentina starts to finish off the game.

'I miss her,' he says. And I know he means Catherine.

When I take my eyes off the TV, and look at him again, he is in tears.

'Oh no.' I shake my head at him.

'Don't be angry with me,' Felix says.

'I'm not.'

'I just miss her. I haven't really thought about it until now. Sorry.'

And with that we watch Argentina play on for a few more minutes, and I find there is suddenly a lump in my throat too, that means I have to look the other way.

It's a relief, for both Felix and me, when Alison suddenly and unexpectedly rings the front door buzzer.

'Yoo hoo!' she yells, through the electronic security system.

This means, without a doubt, that all good things – like Maradona on the telly – will suddenly have to come to an end. However, it also means we don't have to talk about Catherine – and I know, inexorably, that's where the conversation was heading.

So while Felix goes downstairs to answer the door, I squeeze a few more seconds out of the game, punch the off switch on the remote, and prepare myself for – I don't know what. I mean, is the Head with her tonight? Is Alison dropping in unannounced with Tony McSheedy holding her hand?

Much to my relief, and Felix's too, it's just Alison by herself. She has, however, come with a big box of chocolates.

'Mummy sent them,' she explains, then she remembers about not being allowed to use the Mummy word, and shuts up.

We all settle down in the strange Ikea chairs.

'Your mother sent you chocolates because you're shagging the Head?' Felix says, offering her a beer.

Alison screams with laughter, and then stops, with a chocolate halfway up to her mouth, looking embarrassed.

'Well,' I begin where Felix has left off. 'Are you shagging him, Alison? Are you indulging yourselves in the kinds of vulgar excess we imagine? I mean, not that it's any of our business.'

'His separation came through,' she says simply. And that's a shock to everyone. Not that we ever think about the Head's marital situation, of course.

'Tony's very relieved that his ex-wife has finally seen sense,' she adds, pouring her beer demurely into a glass, while Felix and I continue to drink out of the can.

'I'm not sure I can deal with this Tony thing,' Felix says, crossing, then uncrossing his legs. 'I mean, he's forever telling us all to call him Tony, but it's like – I don't know – having Satan saying, "Call me Trevor".'

Alison looks worried by this.

'Not that I hate him or anything,' Felix says hurriedly, 'or I think he's the devil. Although some people at school obviously do think he's Satan, because of his handwriting.'

'What?' Alison looks puzzled.

'I don't know, he writes letters like he's got cloven hooves instead of hands, or something,' Felix finishes, before giving up and going back to his beer.

There's a long silence while Alison tries to work out what he means.

'But anyway,' Felix continues, 'don't tell him anything about me, basically. Or anything about Pimlico. That's what I'm trying to say. And for God's sake, don't tell him the thing I just said about the cloven hooves, either.'

Alison smirks, and lights a cigarette.

'I am the soul of discretion,' she says.

'Well, you must be,' I tell her, 'if you've managed to keep this Head thing a secret for all this time.'

'Charlie was very upset,' Alison informs us, and Felix looks the other way, swallowing hard.

'Poor bastard,' I offer. 'You've finally dumped him, after all these years.'

'Oh, Charlie's going to be all right. He'll survive,' Alison says, shaking her head from side to side, as if she's talking about one of her smelly dogs going to the vet.

Felix and I give each other a look, man to man – or as man to man as we're ever going to get – and go back to the game on the television.

fifteen

As Friday, the day of Tess's leaving party, draws closer, I find myself thinking more about Catherine. It's partly because – as I realise, when I'm shaving – there's been a total absence of her lately. No harassed calls from John Smith, acting as a go-between. No microwave ovens flashing HELLO. No birds going crazy, no perfume in the air. And I haven't even felt the urge to sit cross-legged in the armchair and make contact in her strange, sunny Tuscan garden.

Is she really dead then, now? Is this it? The thought occurs to me, with strange suddenness, as I'm marking 4B's science projects, on Wednesday night at home. We've been doing the animal kingdom this week, which means I have a whole load of stuff about flatworms and tapeworms to look at, which, when you think about the amount of worms carried in the instestines of the children at Rivett Street Junior, amounts to first-hand reportage.

Because I don't want to look at any more crayon drawings of molluscs, or even the children's sad attempts to draw protozoa, I go up to the bedroom instead, and lie flat on Catherine's side of the mattress, something which I've thus far banned myself from doing.

It seems like years since she died. Time has distorted. And shock, I suppose, has blurred everything. If I had any common sense, I would have switched doctors, and asked for real help by now. Dr Patel is nice enough, but she's not quick enough with the drugs – she never has been – and that's probably what I've needed, all along. Prozac, or something, would numb the pain. And make the loneliness seem less, well, lonely.

With Catherine, I never felt alone. All the years that we were together, she filled up so much space in my life, that I had the illusion I was surrounded. Now that she is gone, there is almost nobody. How did that happen? I have parents, which is more than a lot of people have, and they are good parents, but that's not the answer. And I have school, and I suppose I have Felix, for some strange reason. Saddleton has, indeed, tapewormed his way into my life, in a way that would have seemed impossible a year ago.

That's got a lot to do with Catherine as well, though. She knew him in Australia, and knew him well enough here, for him to send the biggest wreath of all to her funeral. So having him around, even under the guise of initiating him into the world of football coaching, is a bit like having her in my life too.

I have kept one or two things of Catherine's under the bed. They normally stood on her bedside chest of drawers. A tube of her lip stuff, which still has the taste and smell of her mouth on it, so I can't let it go, and a photo of her and me, camping, holding up mugs of tea and grinning like idiots.

That was taken early on, that picture. Not so long after the tofu dinner in Camden.

I'm falling asleep now. I shouldn't, because that means I'll have to get up at the crack of dawn tomorrow, and finish the marking. So I feel myself fighting it off, then giving in, then fighting it again.

'Mark.'

Suddenly, Catherine is saying my name. I open my eyes, and see nothing, and nobody – just the tube of her lip stuff, a few inches away from my face, on the sheets. Then it occurs to me – I must have dozed off after all, and just woken up, not because she said my name, but because she has also been throwing the stick of lip balm at my face.

'Catherine?'

Nothing. Try again.

'Catherine? What?'

She must be swimming through concrete to get to me. Wading through wet cement. Shouting into a hurricane. I've been eating a lot of meat lately. Not meditating. Worrying too much. Getting thick vibrations, as opposed to good vibrations. All those things that John Smith told me not to do.

I pull myself up on my elbows, and, yawning despite myself, I manage to cross my legs and assume the position. Sort of. If you can call it a position, when I'm also sliding down the wall from exhaustion.

'Love you,' Catherine says. And although my eyes are closed now, the inner space seems to have opened up again, and any minute now, I know the light will follow, and I will see her, in the pink dressing gown that Veronica bought her.

Instead, though I peer into the blackness for ages, I see nothing at all. Just a quick impression of her face, flashing into my mind, then disappearing again, just as quickly. So I'm still in darkness. A kind of velvety, roomy darkness – but, that's all there is.

'Hear you,' Catherine says. But that's okay, I know what that means – we've done that bit before – so I open my eyes and start talking.

'Okay. Okay. If you can hear me, then – um. I don't know. Catherine. Are you there? Are you okay?'

No reply now. Just thin air, and this over-familiar bedroom, and the end of the bed.

The thing is, I remind myself, to talk to her as if she were still here. As if it were just another night at home, and we hadn't seen each other for ages.

So –

'I've been seeing a bit of Felix,' I hear myself saying, 'because the Head's given him the football team to look after. So I'm helping him. Kind of.'

No reply. Total silence, except for the traffic outside.

'Tess is going to America with that guy,' I continue, forcing myself to go on. 'So I don't know what you were on about, really. I don't know what John Smith was on about. I mean, nothing's going to happen.'

Then, like wind roaring through a tunnel, I get Catherine, all in a rush.

'Noel Oliver.'

What?

'Noel Oliver. Donna's pregnant.'

'Catherine?'

But, as quickly as it blasted through the room, the rushing sound of her voice has gone. Or was it sound at all? Something like – I dunno. The illusion of sound. The suggestion of volume, and tone.

When I close my eyes again, the three-dimensional darkness has gone, and everything is flat and black in front of my eyes. I yawn, stave it off, then yawn again. Donna is pregnant. Noel Oliver. What? Donna is pregnant by Noel, or is it Donna Roberts and Noel Oliver separately, that I have to think about? Maybe the pregnancy part of the sentence got mixed up, and it's Noel who's having a baby. The thing is, you see, I can't imagine Donna ever being a mother.

'Catherine, you're going to have to come back and tell me more,' I tell the walls. But, even though I wait for ten minutes, twenty minutes, I don't know how long, there is no more of her to talk to.

Suddenly, my mobile phone rings. Thank God. And I snatch it up, expecting to hear her voice again – I'll concentrate, Catherine, I'll do anything – but instead, it is John Smith.

'I'm sorry to ring you so late,' he explains.

'No. Don't be sorry. Have you got her?' I realise I sound frantic, but it can't be helped.

'Have you?' he asks me, in return.

'I had her. It's as if she can't get through any more, though. Look, I think I need to see you. And I know you've got a waiting list, but what if someone drops out? Can I drop myself in?'

'Never mind that.'

'I'll pay you. Whatever it is you charge, that's fine.'

'There's nothing to pay,' says the patient voice from Balham, on the other end of the phone. 'And this won't take up too much of your time.'

'Right.'

'So are you listening? Can you take all this in?'

'Yep.'

I sit back on the pillows, my back against the wall, and I wait.

'First things first,' John Smith begins. 'And quite honestly, Mark, this is the last time I'm ever going to do this for you. You know, from now on, Catherine will be with you less. When she does visit you, over the next few years, you are unlikely to hear her, or see her, quite as powerfully.'

'Why?'

'Because she was closer to the earth plane a few weeks ago, and now she has adjusted. Her vibration has become finer, and lighter. She's not drawing herself down so closely to your level.'

'Right.'

Clear as mud, sadly, still clear as mud.

'You'll still smell her perfume from time to time,' John Smith explains. 'Or you might hear a song on the radio, sometimes, and have a feeling –'

'Oh, that's happening already.'

And it is. The number of times I've heard INXS doing *Never Tear Us Apart* lately on the radio, and in shops, is statistically ridiculous. I've heard it more times in four weeks than I have in four years.

'Catherine just said someone I knew was pregnant,' I hear myself telling him. 'It was like her voice, coming through a wind tunnel. It was about someone having a baby, definitely.'

'Well, you must take that further,' John Smith says. 'You need to find out.'

'And she said the name of a guy I haven't seen for about thirty years. I mean, is it him? Is he the father?'

There is a pause, while John Smith seems to concentrate. Then finally, he comes back to me.

'I don't think those names are connected,' he reassures me. 'But they are both important. Catherine is trying to help you, Mark. It might be wise to follow it up.'

Then Mrs Smith comes to the phone and asks her husband

who he's talking to. Any minute now, I think, I'm going to lose him again. And that means no sleep, and too many unanswered questions, at least for me, between now and tomorrow morning.

'Okay. Fine. I'll do it,' I say, as he makes his apologies.

'Look, Mark, before I go, will you promise me something?'

'What?'

'Really say goodbye to your girlfriend. Do it properly. You're more powerful, energetically, than you realise. In many ways, you're a natural medium yourself. And your energy is keeping her here.'

And with that, John Smith hangs up the phone.

The clock says 11.20, even though it feels much later. And I'll have to be up in six hours, marking tapeworm assignments. Despite John Smith's verdict on my amazing abilities, I feel about as energetically powerful as a lump of lard.

I do know something, though. If I logically accept everything else from the last few months – which, despite everything I've ever believed, I have to – then Donna Roberts is pregnant. And Catherine wants me to find her. And when that's done, I'll tackle Noel Oliver, though I have no idea why.

I ring Donna's number, without even knowing how I'm going to start, or what I'm going to say, and she picks up the phone immediately, just as my stomach gives a huge lurch.

'Oh, hello Mark.' She sounds drunk, or stoned. But at least she sounds pleased to hear from me.

'Donna. I can't tell you why I'm asking this, but just tell me anyway. Are you okay?'

A pause.

'Yeah. Why?'

'I mean, are you ill or anything?'

She laughs.

'Oh, screw you, Mark, stop playing games. What are you up to?'

'Nothing. I just had – I don't know, someone told me you might have been ill. Or, I dunno. Even pregnant.'

'Bullshit. Nobody told you. You don't even know anyone who knows me. Not any more.'

'Well, that's okay then.'

Another awkward pause. What else is there to say?

'So, what else have you been up to?' I ask, in a ridiculously chirpy voice.

She laughs again.

'No, I'm not pregnant, you idiot. Why don't you come round?'

'No, really Donna. It's late.'

'You know you want to.'

'I don't want to. Honestly, I don't. I was just worried, that's all.'

'Worried about me? What a piece of shit.'

There's the sound of a male voice in the background, after that, and I wonder who she's in bed with, and how he can put up with this kind of phone conversation happening in their bedroom, at this hour of night. Maybe it's just part of life with Donna, by now, and he's used to it. I mean, what would happen if I came round now – would he just sit in the cupboard all night?

'I don't know why you're really calling, Mark, but whatever it is, oh hang on –' She breaks off the phone for a minute and talks to the deep voice, before coming back.

'I don't owe you any money, do I?'

'No.'

'Oh. Good. Cos I thought that might be why you're ringing. I mean, I'm definitely not having a baby, and I'm not ill. In fact, I feel radiantly healthy' – she gives a short laugh – 'So, you must be ringing about something.'

'Sorry. I'll go then,' I tell her. 'I must have got it wrong.'

I don't want to be on the other end of this phone any more, trying to be polite to this girl I used to sleep with, and even used to be in love with, such a long time ago.

'You're so much in your own little world, Mark,' Donna whines. 'Aren't you?'

'Goodnight, Donna.'

A dangerous pause.

'Well, screw you, then.'

She hangs on after that, waiting for me to be the first to hang up, but I'm so furious now that I chuck the mobile halfway across the room. What was it someone called her once, in a pub, when I was there? An evil cow from the planet Evil Cow. It was some guy who'd had a bad time with her, from memory, or someone whose car she'd crashed. In those days, Donna was always crashing other people's cars.

I sit up in bed, with my back against the wall, and switch both the lamps on, and I stay that way, churning and thinking, and remembering and occasionally swearing at the walls, and at Catherine for getting it wrong, until the alarm clock turns over to 6.00, and I force myself to go downstairs and mark the worm projects.

A more sane and reasonable man than I would just go back to bed at this point, and call the Head – who after all, couldn't care less about me, because he is currently obsessed with Alison – and make excuses, and have the rest of the day off.

I'm not that man, though, and I'm beginning to think that any notion I had about my own normality was just the biggest and best illusion of all. Especially now.

All the more reason, then, with this new-found acceptance of my own lack of normality, to stride into the staffroom a few hours later, right on 8.30 a.m., and see Tess Blake reading the paper, and go up to her, and shout in her face. Which, of course, is exactly what I do.

Nobody else is around. So, as Donna Roberts would say, screw it. Screw her.

'So are you getting married, then?'

I mean, I've sorted the facts out with one woman, why not all the rest of them, too?

'What?'

Tess's eyes are wide, and very blue, and scared-looking, under her curtain of hair.

'Just give me the real story. Are you marrying him?'

'Sit down. Calm down. Mark – are you okay?'

'No, I'm not okay. But I haven't got any time to lose, you know, because my girlfriend's dead. That has sunk in with you, hasn't it?'

Tess bites her lip and looks at me, then gets up and locks the staffroom door, and comes back.

'Say it quietly, say it quietly,' she half-whispers.

'When are you coming back?'

'From New York? I don't know. I'm not sure.'

'So, maybe never.'

'I'm not getting married to Robin,' Tess tells me, at last. Then she gets up and makes us both a cup of tea, taking a long time to fill the kettle at the tap, and find the teabags, and pour in the milk. Maybe she's locked me in, I think, so she can call the cops. Call the loony bin. Whatever.

'Tess?' I call halfway across the staffroom, while she potters round with the cups, and it feels like she's miles away.

She half-smiles back, looking like a woman who's just resigned herself to putting up with me.

'I've been up all night, you know. And half this morning, giving marks out of twenty for a bunch of tapeworm drawings.'

'And not only that, obviously,' Tess says, coming over with the tea, after she stirs everything very slowly, round and round. 'You look whacked.'

I look at her for a moment.

'Um. When your father died, did he ever talk to you?'

And Tess looks genuinely surprised at this, as if it's the last thing she ever expected to hear me say – which it probably is – but she finishes her first mouthful of tea anyway, and manages not to spit it out.

'He still does talk to me sometimes. Sort of in my head. When I pray, usually. Why?'

'Catherine's been talking to me. I've also seen her. And she's been moving stuff around. And I'm not even praying, you know? And that song you sang for me, that INXS song. I keep hearing it all over the bloody radio.'

'Okay.'

'No, it's not okay. And I'm now getting messages from beyond that tell me to ring up ex-girlfriends who are having babies, only to find that they're not.'

'Right.'

I wait a minute, then look at her again. Why, of all the women in this place, in this city, does she have to be the one I want? And why now, after everything I've been through with Catherine?

'God. My fucking life, Tess.'

'No,' she puts her hand on my arm, where it stays. 'No, it's a good life, Mark. I know it's painful at the moment, but it's a good life.'

'Don't Crosslink me.'

'I'm not. This is me,' she says, and takes her hand away.

I put it back.

'My girlfriend died in a car crash, getting out of the way of a dog,' I tell her. And I realise I'm crying now. Crying all over her, the tatty chairs, my sleeve, the tea. And I still don't have any tissues. I still haven't been to the supermarket.

'I know, I know,' Tess says.

'And you're fucking off to New York, all of a sudden.'

'Mark. Stop it.'

'Thankyou, God. Thankyou very fucking much. I mean, Jesus Christ, Tess, don't you wonder that I don't believe in anything, Tess? It's all just –'

I choke on my own throat at this point.

'It's all just so completely fucked.'

I look at her, and realise I have made her upset again, now.

'You need to sort a few things out,' she says, finally, slamming her mug down. And I realise her voice is tight, and that she's angry – at long, last. Oh, miracle of miracles, put out the flags, Tess Blake is angry, and it's happening on school time, too.

I finally feel myself calming down, as she goes redder and redder in the face.

'Sort it out,' she says again, in a tight voice. 'It's more than just Catherine dying.'

'Is it?'

Well, is it? Does Tess know about this, does she have some kind of proof? Because, to be honest, all the time since Donna Roberts left me, all the time since I slept with Veronica, maybe even since I smashed Noel Oliver in the face and broke his bloody nose – literally his bloody nose – part of me has been wondering the same thing, myself. Perhaps it's more than just one event, perhaps it's really me. Maybe Catherine was just the thing that plugged all the gaps, in myself, and my life. And now she's gone, I'm nowhere.

After this, I do what any normal man would do, under the circumstances. When Tess has finally recovered herself, and said a polite goodbye in the middle of the staffroom – it seems impossible, now, that I should go to her farewell party – I find a telephone. And I ring Directory Enquiries, and I go looking for Noel Oliver.

As I do so, I see Tess walking past the windows, across the playground, and back to her classroom, and I wave a hand, although she'll never see me in a million years. So long, Tess. And it's better this way, really. Leaving her to it with Robin, and her Bible, and the knife-wielding children of New York City.

What Catherine said to me in the early hours of this morning, in her wind-tunnel voice doesn't make sense. Not at all. Donna Roberts is definitely not pregnant – and frankly, I doubt it will ever happen. But, I have to ring Noel Oliver now. In fact, it's the only thing I feel like doing. And it's not for Catherine, or because of the karma or anything else, it's for me.

sixteen

I have no success with Noel Oliver. I don't know why I thought I would. I try everything I can think of, including a quick call to Veronica, who can't quite believe what she's hearing – that I want to look him up, about three decades later – but there's no way around it. Noel has just vanished. And even his parents don't seem to exist. He's probably even left the country, I think. Gone back to Kingston or something, where the weather's better, or just found a new life somewhere a lot more interesting than Dymchurch.

'Why do you suddenly want to talk to him now, after all this time?' Veronica says, sounding doubtful, when I call her.

'I'm taking stock.'

'Oh, really?' she says, so sarcastically that it makes me want to take the phone away from my ear.

'Don't be like that. I just need to talk to him, that's all. Catch up.'

'You broke his nose.'

'Yeah, well I know that.'

'He spoke with a funny voice after that' – Veronica makes a sort of tight, snuffling sound, as if she's holding her nose on the other end of the phone for my benefit, which I guess she is.

'You never told me that before,' I interrupt her, 'about Noel Oliver's voice.'

'Well, I saw him years ago, when the band was playing in some place in Margate. He said he'd seen my photo in the paper, and he thought he'd come along. See if I'd changed. Which of course –' Veronica gives a curt laugh, 'I had.'

'And?'

'He talked funny. And he was a bit stoned. That's all I remember, really.'

'Oh.'

All of which, naturally, makes me want to find Noel Oliver even more than I do already, and do something – anything. Give him my house. Stick my face in front of a brick, and ask him to just shove it in. The thought of him going through life with a funny voice, because of me, is more than I can stand.

Felix Saddleton thinks I'm being ridiculous.

'You were a kid,' he says as we sit in the staffroom, him leaning out of the window and smoking, me looking for better jobs, in the paper, that don't exist.

'I owe it to him. I have this vision of Noel having a ruined life.'

'Well, don't succumb to the vision, then,' Felix tuts. 'There are children – evil, malevolent little children – here, right now, at this very school, who do far worse things to each other than that.'

'No, there aren't.'

'Scott O'Grady,' Felix says triumphantly.

'Well all right then.'

Felix names the little girl Scott punched in the buttock the other day. Then he refers to the guinea pig. The guinea pig is called Lucky, as it happens. Though Felix always insists that its name should be changed to Unbelievably Lucky.

'Yeah, but that's Scott O'Grady for you,' I tell him, putting the newspaper down. 'He's in a category all by himself.'

And we both know this is wrong, this character assassination of a small boy, and that there are enough notes on his useless parents in the files to make us perfectly aware of the reasons for his dysfunctional behaviour with small animals – but still, we do it. The staffroom at Rivett Street has three rituals – lunchtime programmes on Radio 4, a new packet of shortbread biscuits every Monday, and en masse loathing of Scott O'Grady.

'I just think you're over-reacting to this childhood guilt thing, sweetie,' Felix yawns, stretching back in his chair. 'That's all. I mean, we all make mistakes. Especially at that age.'

Things have now reached the stage where Felix Saddleton calls me sweetie publicly, in the staffroom, and neither I, nor anyone else, actually notices. Perhaps it's the shock of Alison and the Head holding hands near the tea urn. It's blown everything else out of the water.

Maybe it's just the lack of Tess around the place, too. That's also having an effect on the way we all behave, sending us spinning out of our normal staffroom orbits. Because she's already gone, after all, flown out to JFK from Gatwick, and they're already talking about a new teacher's aide – some guy from Manchester – who's being shipped in to take her place. Nothing feels the same round here any more. And so, it seems, Felix can call me sweetie as much as he likes.

A few days after this, I find Noel. Almost. It seems that Noel Oliver is no longer called Noel Oliver. He has changed his name to Noel D. Jupiter. No wonder they couldn't find him at Directory Enquiries.

It is Veronica, in the end, who tracks him down. She asked a friend of a friend of someone in her old band, The Voodoo Blitz, who remembered Noel leaving home and going to London, to have an operation on his voice, and then marrying some weird New Age woman, and changing his name to Jupiter.

. I wonder what the D stands for? Maybe it's Dolphin. Noel Dolphin Jupiter, a man who was once a perfectly normal little boy – until I got to him, anyway. After which, he lost the plot, forgot all about supporting the West Indies in cricket and got into New Age nuttiness.

Noel D. Jupiter lives in a house in Forest Gate, with a rainbow painted on the front door, and a pram out the front, with a mobile hanging off it, made up of all the stars and planets. When he opens the door, I half expect someone with an afro, dreadlocked into a ponytail, maybe with some kind of tie-dyed T-shirt on. So it is, in fact, an interesting experience when Noel D. Jupiter opens the door, fulfilling my prediction exactly.

He hugs me. And his arms stay around me for a long time. He smells like his own branch of The Body Shop.

'Come in, come in, I had a dream about you,' Noel beckons me up the corridor of his house, past even more prams, and piles of books which all seem to be about massage, and crap paintings of unicorns, all signed N.D.J.

There is also, inevitably, the distinctive smell of spicy vegetable curry, the kind that's bright yellow, wafting from the kitchen. I mean, do people like Noel ever manage to actually get their teeth around a big, juicy steak?

A little girl with very few teeth waddles past us, waving her pants in the air.

'You'll have to forgive Marigold,' the new Noel Oliver tells me. 'She's an Aries. They're very demonstrative.'

I now steel myself to meet Mrs Noel D. Jupiter, and once again, it's pretty much what I expected. She's nice enough – and she even has a normal name, Ruth – and she's in distracted earth-mother mode, fussing over a little boy in a high chair, shovelling mashed banana into his mouth, while an unusually tall and plump teenage girl loiters in the background, looking bored.

'Ruth was married before,' Noel tells me later, when we are out of the smelly vegetarian earth-mother kitchen, and safely inside the pub on the corner. 'So I became a step-dad when I was 21, to a kid who was already half my age. And that was her.'

'Was that all right?' I ask him, thinking of the blank-faced, enormously tall girl from the kitchen.

'Everything is always all right,' Noel smiles broadly. His voice, I notice, is not what Veronica hinted at all. It's clear as a bell. Clearer than mine, in fact. So what was all that about?

'Let's have a couple of pints,' Noel says. As he gets up to the bar, waving my offer of money aside, I try to remember what Noel looked like as a child. What was he like, that irritating little dickhead, with his ridiculous *Jackie* magazine for Catherine, and his habit of hitting me in the back?

My memory fools me, and sends up a picture of the young Michael Jackson instead. But that's nothing like Noel. Whatever, or whoever, he was then, I am finding the twenty-first century version far too distracting now, to even think about making a comparison.

Noel comes back with the beer, grinning broadly.

'I've been recognised,' he says.

'Oh yes?'

'I've got myself a horoscope column, in the local rag. They started putting my picture up a few months ago, to see what the reaction was.'

'Great!' I say brightly.

'You'd be amazed how many people read it,' he says, sounding genuinely and modestly amazed himself, and shaking his dreadlocked head from side to side.

'Um, you're probably wondering why I'm here,' I start to say, like a pillock.

Noel laughs. 'No idea.'

'Catherine died.'

'Oh shit.'

His face drops, and in a minute, his eyes fill with tears.

'It's okay,' I manage.

'I remember that girl,' he says at last. 'I was so in love with her, that girl.'

'I broke your nose,' I struggle to say, after enough beer has gone down my throat.

'You did.'

'It's good, actually,' I find myself feeling newly enthused. 'Because I had this idea that it might have had some big effect on you. And I can see it hasn't. I mean, you look sorted to me.'

'Right.'

Noel D. Jupiter – he still hasn't told me what the D stands for – lowers his head, and looks up at me, in a shy, half-smiling, half-serious way, and suddenly I do remember the boy I used to fight, from Dymchurch Caravan Park. It's an old, long-gone familiar look, but I can place it instantly.

'My wife healed me,' Noel says finally, touching his face.

'Really?'

'She's a reiki healer,' Noel says, as if this needs no further explanation.

I suppose, in the world he now lives in, it doesn't. But I'm still not sure how I should react. And what does he mean, she healed him?

Noel gulps down his beer.

'I had problems for a few years,' he says, 'and who's to say it wasn't just the way my nasal passages worked. I dunno. But I couldn't talk properly – I used to get bad colds, lots of congestion. Because of the voice, that made me stand out.'

Oh, God.

'Right,' I say breezily, hoping that there's no more to this story, but already knowing there is.

'I got my head kicked in one night, in Margate. For lots of reasons. They didn't like me, you know? The way I talked, the way I walked, the way I looked.'

'How did you look?'

'You remember me being into *The Goodies*, right? The TV show?'

'Um. No. But anyway, I can see that you would have been. I mean, we all were.'

'Well, it was this stupid,' Noel tells me, 'I found this old *Goodies* T-shirt in a jumble sale. Just out of Margate. And I thought it was really funny, because it was only a quid, and it had the three of them on the front, on that freaky bike.'

'The bike with three seats.'

'Anyway,' Noel smiles, lulling me into a false sense of security as we share this sense of fleeting, mid-70s, TV-inspired solidarity. 'Anyway, Mark, it wasn't the place or time to be wearing that kind of thing. So I got my face kicked in. By the local branch of the National Front. All in their Doc Martens.'

'Oh. Shit.'

'Yeah, right,' Noel gives me his shy, half-smiling look again, up from under his beer glass. 'And they nutted me, too.'

He then tells me about how he's still got his *Goodies* T-shirt anyway, even if it has got bloodstains still on it, and how his eldest daughter now wants to wear it, because the 70s are all

155

ironic and fashionable again, and he tells me how Ruth healed him from head to foot.

'She got trained by a guy from Japan. The real thing. They transfer the energy to you, and they teach you these different ways of holding your hands.' He shakes his head.

'It's amazing.'

'And what happened?'

'End of story. She healed me. I married her.'

'And then you started doing horoscopes?'

'I started doing everything,' Noel D. Jupiter tells me, and starts to laugh.

I wonder, despite myself, what this might mean. Wizardry? Turning himself into an owl? Levitating across Forest Gate high street?

'The D in my name is for DIY,' Noel tells me. 'So when I want money, I don't go out and earn it, I manifest it. I do it myself, you know?'

'Right.'

'I do some feng shui on the house, put the energy into my money corner and –' he snaps his fingers.

'Right.'

I worry that my face is giving me away, at this point, but I keep on nodding anyway. Nodding, like a stupid nodding dog.

'I use crystals a lot,' Noel tells me. 'Are you into crystals at all?'

And I have to think about this for a minute.

'Actually, I do know something about them.'

'Yeah? Good. Well, you'll know what I'm talking about then.'

We finish our beers and look at each other. Man to man. Boy to boy. Non-believer to believer.

'I teach at a school in South London,' I explain, and I can already see I'm letting Noel down. 'We grow crystals, in jam jars. It's part of a unit that we do.'

'Cool!' says Noel D. Jupiter kindly. 'And what else?'

'Oh, we do tapeworms. Amoeba. Actually, we do something your kids might enjoy. It's called Outer Space Dancing.'

As I expected, this gets the right reaction. And then Noel's face goes still and quiet again.

'You're sorting out your life,' he says suddenly, although we haven't been discussing it. He gives me a long, cautious look. 'Is it feeling any better yet, Mark?'

'Um. A bit.'

'Since meeting me, do you feel better?'

'A bit of both. Better and worse. Do you want another beer?'

And as I go back to the bar to fetch two more pints, I think about what I can say to Noel D. Jupiter, the man who does a bit of everything, the man who believes that crystals can do things that I, frankly, think are ludicrous.

The man who got his head kicked in by a bunch of racist thugs in Margate, because he talked funny – because of me – and because he had a bent nose, and because he had the temerity to wear a *Goodies* T-shirt.

When I come back, I try to change the subject, back to schools, and education, and I try to involve Noel in a joint moaning session about government funding – but he's having none of it.

'You know something?' he says.

'What's that?'

'Look. I'm a bit psychic, right? I have to admit it. And I can see that your aura is full of holes.'

'Wow.' I take a gulp of beer. 'Should I be worried? I mean, what do you do for that, exactly?'

Noel laughs at me.

'You don't believe in anything, Mark. I mean – do you?'

'No. Actually, yes. That's not fair. I do.'

'No, come on,' Noel insists. 'I've got people like you at Marigold's school. They've done the whole science, maths bit. And I don't know what it is they teach them at those places, but they don't believe in anything, man.'

Then he stops and thinks for a minute.

'I don't mean that in a negative way,' he says kindly.

'But is it better to believe in everything?' I ask him, and nobody in particular, all at the same time. 'I mean, do you really think it's better to believe – without discrimination, without any kind of questioning?'

Noel D. Jupiter smiles.

'Yes,' he says. 'Yes, it is. I think it is. Besides, that's the whole point of it. It's faith. Innit?'

'Well, if you say so.' I make a gesture with my hand, in a jokey kind of way, but Noel is looking at me as if he's deadly serious.

'You've been got at,' he says again, shaking his head, and peering at what seems to be my left shoulder. 'Your aura is really bad.' He looks at me. 'Has she been back?'

'Who?'

'Little Catherine.'

'Not so little now,' I start to joke, then realise I'm using the wrong tense. It happens, every so often.

Noel leans back in his chair. He looks like a man who barely knows how to use a chair, and I suspect it's true – he probably spends most of his time cross-legged on the floor, in that complicated Gandhi meditation position I never could master, and never will.

'I've got a spirit guide,' Noel says.

'Have you?'

'He's talking to your spirit guide at the moment,' Noel goes on, cocking an ear.

'And?'

I suppose I'm almost used to this now, after all those phone conversations with John Smith.

'No, I can't quite get it,' Noel frowns, as if he's just lost Radio 1 in a thunderstorm.

I get on with the beer, and take another look at Noel D. Jupiter. He doesn't seem all that mad. He doesn't seem deluded, or dope-affected, or any of those other things I've come to associate with people who say they charge crystals – like they're charging video cameras, for God's sake – and people who hug you for too long, and talk about feng shui, and where to put your pot plants to make lots of money, without actually having to go to work.

'Anyway,' says Noel, 'I'm sure it's all part of the plan.'

'What is?'

'This –' Noel vaguely waves a hand in the air. 'Catherine. Your life. You finding me again. All that.'

'Oh yes. The plan.'

'Don't you believe in the plan?'

I take another gulp of beer.

'Why would I believe in a plan, Noel? I mean, look at my life. Look at my bloody life.'

'My spirit guide is laughing now,' Noel D. Jupiter says, cocking his head again.

'Yeah, well, I can't hear him. Tell him to come back later,' I say.

'You and me have many lives together, you know,' Noel says, after checking to see how I'm going to take this new, alarming piece of news. I suppose from the bleary-eyed, beery-eyed look on my face, it appears that I can take almost anything at the moment.

'How do you know we have many lives together?' I shoot back.

'I was regressed a few years ago. I wanted to find out who mattered in my life. You know? Even people who I thought didn't matter at all. People like you, who I'd forgotten about.'

Noel tucks his dreadlocks behind his ears, where they immediately spring out again, and he's beginning to irritate me now, this grown-up version of the boy from Dymchurch Caravan Park. For different reasons, of course, but the feeling is the same.

'We've done a few things together, I saw them when I was being regressed,' Noel says, staring into his beer.

'And why does that matter?'

'Because you've just fixed it. You coming over. I mean, you haven't said much. But it's more in your intention. And I do feel that intention.'

'Do you?'

Noel looks at me for a minute.

'Did Catherine tell you to come and see me?'

'No,' I lie.

'Anyway,' finishes Noel, 'my guide says you're on the way to fixing it now. By making the effort to apologise. For what you did when you were a kid. So we've got the all-clear from the higher power. Good.'

I look at him.

'But I haven't really apologised.'

'Don't have to,' Noel grins, 'spare yourself the embarrassment.' He hits his chest with one hand. 'The sentiment's there, all right? That's all I care about.'

I look around me at this point, to see if there are any other, normal, plain English-speaking individuals in this pub, people who might be currently avoiding us, our entire conversation and our table.

There is only the barmaid, though. And with her thrice-pierced ear, the Chinese tattoo on her wrist and her constant stream of whining, insidious, acid jazz, it's probably a safe bet that Noel's conversation seems no more unusual to her than the flushing sound of the ladies' toilets, down the pub stairs.

Eventually, after another beer – in which we get on safe ground and discuss this year's Ashes Test – Noel and I walk back to his house together, where he says a friend with a mini-cab will pick me up and take me home, at no charge.

'Are you sure?' It must be a huge cab fare.

I start to put my jacket on.

'Well,' confesses Noel. 'He won't actually be here for a while. I haven't manifested it yet.'

'Right.'

And now what? Do I take my jacket off again, until the manifesting commences? Do we all sit cross-legged on the floor, me and Ruth, and the kids, while Noel shuts his eyes, and Marigold wanders round without any pants on, making noises like Bill and Ben, which is what she seems keen on doing at the moment?

Fortunately, though, Ruth comes to the rescue. Not with reiki, but with an undeniable streak of common sense.

'I rang him up when you were at the pub,' she says, smiling at me. 'And he's on the way with the car now. He said he'd be happy to do it.'

And I think, she's already picked me for a true non-believer, and no mistake – despite Noel's endless optimism.

'I'm going to do a little ritual for you tonight,' Noel smiles at me. 'Keep the good karma going.'

Well, what can I say?

'Thanks,' I mumble, with as much sincerity as I can fake, shaking him by the hand at the front door, trying to avert an oncoming hug.

But it's no good. As Noel's mate with the mini-cab arrives – and judging by the weird dangling things on the mirror, I can tell it's definitely a friend of his – he practically takes me in his arms and suffocates me.

'I love you for doing this,' says Noel D. Jupiter, the astrologer formerly known as Noel Oliver, the man who got his nuts kicked in by the National Front, and then got healed by his wife.

'It's a pleasure,' I say, sounding very English, and very much like the Head, all of a sudden. I mean, what past lives did we share together, exactly? Was he Cleopatra and was I Marc Antony?

'You take care now,' Noel grins and waves, as I leap into the mini-cab, to get away from his boa-constrictor hug, and practically brain myself on the dangling mirror objects.

'Bye!' I shout, like an idiot, through the closed window.

'And don't forget about Tess!' Noel yells, as the engine starts up.

What?

'Forget about who?' I yell back.

But Noel is back indoors now, with his various children tagging along behind him. They've all come out to wave me off, which is strangely touching. I mean, who does that any more, with a total stranger?

I relax into the front seat of the mini-cab, or try to, anyway, with house music going doof-doof-doof through the speakers.

'He's good,' the driver informs me, looking at Noel as we pull away, ready for the long trip back to South London.

'Is he?'

I hear myself asking a question again, for the ninety-ninth time today. Mainly because people keep confronting me with statements for which there is no polite answer.

'I got my own business because of him,' the driver tells me. 'He did my midheaven.'

'Did he?' I ask, trying to stop the conversation right there, before too many crystals manage to weave their way in.

'His wife's good, too,' Noel's mini-cab man informs me.

'She's a healer, isn't she?'

'She cured my sinus,' he touches his nose.

'Yes, well she cured Noel's sinus as well, so it must be –' My voice trails off, as the mini-cab man hits the accelerator.

It must be – what? Frankly, I have no bloody idea. But Noel D. Jupiter called out Tess's name as we made our farewells just now, and of all the names he could have invented, got wrong, made up, or even traced through a private detective agency, that one would never, ever have come up. And how do I know this *a priori*, objective fact? Because, as far as I know, I never, ever talk about Tess Blake, to anyone. And why would I?

seventeen

It's my own fault, of course, but Donna Roberts eventually rings me back. And back. And back, until I think about changing my number. It wouldn't be the first time I've had to organise a different phone number, either.

'Hello cutie,' she calls down the phone, while I'm at home one night, watching a football video that Felix has lent me. I get all Felix's cast-offs these days, and it shows – as certain people in the staffroom have observed, I'm becoming a football bore – and so, in a more flamboyant way, is he.

'Donna. Hi. Let me turn the sound down,' I say, reaching for the remote, then I think better of it, and leave it turned up. Man United versus Liverpool. I'm not muting this, especially not for Donna bloody Roberts.

'I want to come round,' she says, sounding suddenly serious. 'Mark, please let me come round.'

'Oh God, I don't know, Donna.'

'Why not?'

'The place is a mess. I'm really tired. I've been teaching. And

I had to help someone coach the football as well. It's been a long day.'

She thinks about this for a moment, and I hear her sighing – a long, hard sigh.

'I've been waitressing all day,' she tells me. 'And this place looks like a bomb's hit it too, with Pete under most of the rubble, so don't give me any shit about your excuses. We have to see each other.'

We do?

Pete, who she's finally named for me, must be the man who has to listen to her abusive, night-time conversations with her ex-boyfriends – like me – while they're sitting up in bed in their pyjamas. Or, he might be sitting up in bed in his pyjamas. Donna doesn't wear anything from memory, just a G-string.

'Don't give me any shit,' she repeats, as I tear my attention away from the TV.

'We can meet at your cafe or something,' I hear myself saying, just to get rid of her. Because, in many ways, it's easier than changing my phone number. And putting a block on my email. And all the other ways she now knows how to get hold of me.

'Oh, I'd like that,' she says, in a silly, cooing voice. 'I'd like that, if you came over.'

'I know where it is, don't I. It's that one in Kentish Town, that burned down, and then became a pizza parlour.'

'Yeah, and now it's an outlet for salmonella,' Donna drawls.

For a moment, there is silence as we both remember the last time we talked about this new waitressing job of hers – it was the time, just after Catherine died, when Donna rang up demanding to go to the funeral, and she was telling me about losing her job in the second-hand bookshop, and still having eczema, and a dozen more things I couldn't really care less about.

It was, however, also the call where we felt it – that nameless buzz. I suppose someone like John Smith would call it a good vibration, or something. Whatever it was, though, I have to forget about it. In any case, I'm sure it's just like Pavlov's dogs. They salivated at the sound of a bell. I still react – though God knows why – to the sound of Donna's voice. Or rather, parts of my body over which I have no control, react.

'How about after school tomorrow?' I ask her, already dreading this little meeting before it even happens.

'Fine. Whatever. I get a break around five so why don't you come around then?'

And with that, I almost manage to end the call within five minutes – a record for a Donna Roberts phone conversation – just in time to turn the volume right up again, and catch Beckham putting one into the back of the net.

I have started something with Donna, so I have to finish it. I rang her up and tried to find out if she was having a baby, because Catherine said she was – and she wasn't – and now I have to suffer the consquences. I mean. God. What was Catherine thinking?

I think about Noel D. Jupiter for a moment, too. Catherine wanted me to see him – well, I assume she did, because her voice was coming out of a wind tunnel, and it was hard to tell – and I have seen him, not so much because Catherine wanted me to, but because I wanted to see him, on my own account.

Will the Donna Roberts experience be anything like the Noel D. Jupiter experience, then? I don't know. But I don't think I've had a coffee, or lunch, or anything else, with her, face-to-face, since I bought the house with Catherine. So maybe that should be fixed.

Noel has already rung me up, of course, since our afternoon in the pub. He's invited me to a party, next weekend. I might even go. I don't know. When he rang, he said he didn't want to lose touch with me, now that we'd finally found each other. I'd probably say the same thing, of course, but in a different, less mushy, way.

It's good to have bits of your past around you, and in my case, there are less and less of them these days. Very little of my childhood or my adolescence remains. Veronica can't and won't talk to me, for obvious reasons. I haven't seen the various members of The Bottom Line since the day we broke up. And Catherine is gone. Definitely gone, now, too.

Just after four, the following day, I make the long trek from the school gates by bus, changing to the tube, and finally getting off the train at Kentish Town Station. Then, I wander up the street to find Donna's cafe. She's sitting in the front window, wearing impossibly tight jeans and an apron, reading a magazine and having a cigarette.

When I walk in, she scrapes her chair back, so the only other customer in the place looks up, and then she gets up and kisses me hard on the mouth. It is, in fact, like the bottom of a budgie's cage in there.

'What a shit of a year you've had,' she says, and immediately tells the other waitress to get me a coffee, although I haven't asked for one. Then she adds a scone to the order, as if it's going to make my shit year any better.

I'm actually starving. I had no time to eat today because half the staff, including me, got involved in a Scott O'Grady incident, which centred on two older boys trying to force his head down the toilet, a female teacher having her shoes nicked and Blount being sent home with a migraine.

'I've got a new man, did I tell you?' Donna questions me, triumphantly. And I can tell she's watching me, to see how I'll react.

'Yes. Pete. Is that him?'

'He's a record producer,' she tells me. I wonder if this is the same man who used to hit her, because he was a record producer too, but really – I can't be bothered asking.

Her hair has changed, she's grown it longer, and she's also cut back on the make-up, which can only be a good thing.

'I'm doing a massage therapy course,' she says proudly, once again watching me to see how I'll react.

'And what, or who, do you massage once you qualify?' I ask, then realise I've just dropped myself in it.

'I could massage you if you like,' she laughs.

The waitress comes back with the coffee, and the lone scone. She bangs it down on the table as if she's very busy, although the other customer has gone, and the cafe is now empty. I suppose she resents being at Donna's beck and call. Or maybe she just resents Donna. Most women I know do.

'That was a funny phone call the other night,' she tells me.

'Yeah, I just heard something about you being in hospital,' I lie.

'Oh, come on.'

I realise that there is no point in, as Donna puts it, bull-shitting her. We spent too many years together, got way too intimate together, a hundred different ways together, and even my scant knowledge of anthropology and biology is enough to convince me that you can't get away with faking it. Not with someone you know that well.

'You really thought I was pregnant, didn't you?'

Donna is in full swing now. 'Pete's the most fantastic man I've ever had,' she yawns, flicking her cigarette ash into the saucer because the sulky waitress hasn't left an ashtray. I love the way she says she *had* him too. And I wonder, idly, if she used to tell people that she ever had me.

'Oh yeah, and why's Pete so fantastic?'

'Oh, don't be like that,' she teases me – or tries to tease me, anyway, because I'm having none of it.

Around us, the other waitress makes irritable, and irritating, clanking noises as she picks up dirty glasses and scoops up piles of plates with bits of egg all over them.

'Pete's probably going to be in LA next year, working on an album, so I said I might go with him,' she tosses her hair back.

'You like it there, don't you.'

'It's my town,' Donna says, not realising how stupid it looks to say this, as we sit in this dingy part of North London, in this typically crap English cafe, with the old luncheon voucher stickers on the window, and the naff radio station blaring out of the speakers.

I remember that LA was where one of her other boyfriends drowned. In a swimming pool. And I wonder how she can call it her town, after something like that has happened to her. Though the memory of this death in her life, a sudden tragedy, like Catherine's accident, does make me look at her differently. I know, after all, what it is like.

'I've had everything in my life,' Donna says, looking straight at me. 'I've had men throwing me down stairs, I've had junkies, I've had the lot.'

'You have. But, I mean, I already know this, Donna.'

There's a pause, then. After which Donna clears her throat, looks me straight in the eye, and drops her bombshell.

'You were the only one ever who got me pregnant, though.'

Hang on.

'I got you pregnant?'

Around us, the noisy waitress stops clanging, and starts eavesdropping.

'That's why I thought it was so weird, when you rang up the other night,' Donna tells me. 'I just thought, how bloody ironic. You of all people, asking me if I'm having a baby. I mean, no, I'm not. But I nearly did – once.'

'When did you get pregnant with me? When was it?'

Instinctively, I think she's lying about this. She's making this up, because the other thing – the mention of Pete, the glamorous record producer – didn't get the reaction she was hoping for.

'You thought you were so great,' she half-laughs, half-insults me, 'at pulling out.'

The eavesdropping waitress moves closer.

'Turn the radio up, Jill!' Donna yells, waving her away. We are, of course, listening to INXS playing *Never Tear Us Apart*. For the one hundredth time in my life this year.

'Why didn't you say anything to me?' I confront her, over the top of the music.

And I look at Donna now, properly, right into her eyes, to see what's there. But, because I know her so well, I can tell she's not lying at all. I wish she was, I wish this was a typical Donna stunt, but no – I think it might actually be the truth.

'You were with Catherine, at the time, or you thought you were. So that's why I couldn't tell you,' Donna says, lighting another cigarette. I'm definitely going to give up, I think, looking at her. It's a dirty habit.

'You should have told me, then. When it happened.'

'Why? You didn't give a shit.'

And then at last, Donna decides to fill in the gaps, putting all the details in place, bringing it all back for me.

'Remember when Catherine rang up her sister and she called you Frigging Mr Wobbly?'

'I remember.'

'You and Catherine had a fight about me. Then you came round to my place, in Shepherd's Bush, the house with the boiler that never worked, remember? And there was no food in the fridge, and we were starving, so we went out, and it was raining –'

'Yup.'

'And you had no money on your card, so we couldn't pay for the bill.'

I nod.

'And I made you do a runner, out of the restaurant, and I made you run miles down the street, until we got to the tube.'

I look at her. It is, in fact, all coming back. Including the sex, which happened later.

'Well, that was the night you got me pregnant,' Donna finishes. 'It had to be. I started feeling sick a few weeks later, and I didn't know why – I thought it was just a bug going round at work. And the doctor made me sit down and work it out, in his diary, and practically the only shag I'd had for the whole two months was you.'

'Right.'

'It was that night,' Donna shakes her head, 'and I even knew it at the time. I thought, "I bet I get pregnant now".'

'Why?'

'Because it would have made you come back to me. And I really wanted that. So, maybe, my body was just making it happen.'

'Oh, please.'

'See, you didn't know Catherine all that well, then,' Donna rattles on, ignoring me.

'You'd been with me longer. So maybe it was Mother Nature as well. It was time for us to have a baby. To bring us together.'

She says this triumphantly, now, wearing her little theory like a badge of honour. And that by itself is a bad thing, and a sad thing, because if I remember that night – and I do – the only thing in my head when I was with Donna, was Catherine. And the extremely ordinary sex that Donna and I had, on her flatmate's futon, with no sheets, in the Shepherd's Bush house, was just out of habit. That's all. A physical habit, like a dental check-up, or even checking the post.

'Are you angry I had the abortion?' she says. There, the dreaded word, out at last.

'I'm angry you're telling me now, in this place' – I look around the cafe.

'It's all right, we're closed in a minute,' she says.

I notice that the nosey waitress is getting her coat.

'It's okay,' Donna assures me, glancing at the woman, still in her apron, as she stands on a chair and turns the radio off. 'I told her the situation with us this morning, so she said she'd shut up early, leave us in peace.'

What situation with us?

'So – what did you tell her?'

'I told her you and I were going to have a talk.'

'So you didn't tell her about the abortion, then? Because, I'm just wondering, am I the last man in London to know?'

'Oh, don't be like that,' Donna pouts, and then she smiles. Her eyes crinkle up when she does this, and it's a smile that used to have a devastating effect on my mood, a long time ago, but it has absolutely no effect on me now.

'When you rang up and said you heard I was pregnant. Well' – Donna breaks off, and fiddles with her bracelet. 'That made Pete and me laugh. I mean, it ain't going to happen, you know? He's sterile for a start.'

'That's more information than I need to know, thanks.'

'But then, Pete and I had a big talk about it' – and here, she checks my face again, to how I feel about this – 'and we discussed me, you, and the whole Catherine thing, and the abortion, and it was actually Pete who made me give you the call, if you must know.'

'Right.'

'He said, life's too short to harbour secrets. You've got to clear the decks. And he's right. It is.'

I look at all the women going home from work now, walking past the windows of the cafe, heading for the tube. How many of them have had abortions? Because this is something that's never happened to me. Catherine never got pregnant. Veronica never got pregnant, that I'm sure of. None of my girlfriends have.

And whatever Donna might be sneering at now – my amazing, iron-willed withdrawal method – was only ever used on her. Mainly because she was too hopeless to remember to take the Pill, and too disorganised to buy condoms. None of the other women in my life have ever put me in that position. Literally.

'You didn't ever have condoms,' she says now, keeping pace with my thoughts, 'so you can't blame me.'

'Donna. You can't blame me for this either. You know?'

'Why not? Did you ever ask me about getting pregnant? No. You just did it.'

I'm angry now. Furiously angry, at this chain-smoking, teaspoon-tapping 37-year-old woman, with the endless amounts of silver rings on her fingers – including one I gave her – and the sneaky, secret history she's just thrown up in my face.

'You know what?' I say to her.

She shrugs.

'I didn't need to know this. Why are you telling me? It happened years ago. So, I didn't need to know this. Especially now.'

'Pete and I discussed it.'

'Screw Pete,' I say, taking the bait at last, and using Donna's favourite word into the bargain.

And, because she's pretty much got what she wanted, Donna relaxes, and sips at her coffee, and leans back in her seat.

Donna runs on jealousy. For whatever reason, it's the only thing she knows – and if it's not there, she'll try to make it happen – or convince herself that it's there, anyway. Catherine spotted it a long time before I did, and I kept on telling her to shut up – to my eternal shame. What Donna did with us was delicate, and careful, like weaving a spider's web, but it did us a lot of damage. All of which is coming back to me now, in this dingy cafe.

'The thing is,' Catherine once said, 'you and Donna are never actually brave enough to do anything with each other. You don't shag. You don't even touch each other. It's just this pseudo-friendship thing. This lovely, modern, platonic friendship you've got going on. You know – with me stuck in the middle of it. And I'm supposed to just put up with it.'

It made Catherine cry with frustration, once, and it made me lose my temper, and eventually it made her so ugly to me, that I did what she'd always feared, and I succumbed to Donna and her G-string and her flatmate's futon anyway.

And I think of her new boyfriend, Pete, suddenly, and

171

wonder how I could envy him on any level. Although, it's true – my life with Donna used to run on jealousy, aimed at either her outgoing, or her incoming, men.

'Move on,' Catherine said to me once, when I was at the peak of my Mr Wobbly behaviour, in the Frigging Mr Wobbly year. 'Move on, or get a life, or tell Donna to get a life, or something. It's over, Mark. Enough of the pseudo-friends crap.'

Donna has the life now, I think, as I remember Catherine talking about getting a life, and Catherine herself has nothing at all. It's enough to make you sick. Another fantastic display of brilliance from that incomparable organiser of lives, God, as copyrighted by Crosslink. Catherine is dead, and Donna is alive. Catherine was good, and also good for me. Just how good for me, I'm finding out more every day. And now she's gone into a cremation oven, and Donna is waitressing in North London and still driving herself, and other people, insane.

'When people die, it makes you look at your life,' Donna says suddenly, and I wonder what she means.

'How many weeks gone were you, when you had the abortion?' I ask her.

'Nothing. Four weeks. It's nothing,' she says.

I try to remember, from all the textbooks in the university library, when I was training to be a teacher, what a four-week-old embryo looks like.

I can't even face this coffee, now. It's got skin on the top, and there's a chip in the cup.

'What do you mean, when people die it makes you look at your life?' I ask her. 'I mean, who's died around you, lately?'

'Catherine.'

And I can't even look at Donna now. It's like that day when she rang up, whining and moaning, asking me to go and get pissed with her in the pub, then asking to go to the funeral, all in the same call.

'Is this all about you not being invited to the funeral?' I ask, at last. Donna, after all, always hated not getting her own way, and sooner or later, there was always some kind of retaliation. I know I rang up, in a fit of madness, and asked her if she was pregnant – but for her to come back to me now, with this news, this totally crap old news, has everything to do with revenge, and almost nothing to do with clearing the decks, as her genius boyfriend insists.

Of course, the elusive Pete may never have said anything about clearing the decks with me at all. For all I know, the soulful, deep and meaningful, late-night Pete-Donna conversation, after my call, never happened.

'I wanted to go to the funeral, because I wanted to say goodbye to Catherine and give her some flowers,' Donna says, lighting another cigarette. And then something bizarre happens. Before she can even get the cigarette up to her mouth, she starts to cry. And not even cry – howl.

I let her go on. And on. And then I find some tissues in my briefcase.

'I'm so fucking sorry,' Donna cries, blindly taking the tissues from my hand, and then just screwing them up in a ball, while her nose runs, and her eyes run, and everything runs. I give her time to speak. And then more time. And eventually I give up and go to the loo, and when I come back, I still have to wait.

The clock hands are moving on, though I have to squint to see them, and it's nearly six o'clock. Suddenly, part of me just wants to be normal. A normal bloke. Out of the world of women, and scrunched-up tissues, and abortions, and back to the football. With Felix Saddleton and his candles, even.

'I've been dreaming about Catherine since the funeral,' Donna says at last.

'What happens?'

'She talks to me.'

She looks at me curiously.

'Does she talk to you?'

And I am now at a precipice of trust, I suppose. Teetering on the edge with Donna Roberts, close to telling her more than any other person I have told anything to, so far. But – I don't. Call it long-forgotten instinct, but I don't.

I pull Donna up from the chair, even managing to take her hand – a little, snotty, wet paw – and my secret is safe.

'In the dreams, Catherine told me that I had to tell you about getting pregnant. I had to own up to you. So we could clear the decks. Sort it all out,' Donna says, still sounding dazed, as she gets to her feet. Her face is patchy, and red. And her eyes look sore, even in this light.

She's wearing high-heeled sandals and fishnets. Sandals and fishnets, in this weather.

'Maybe the dreams will stop, now you have.'

'And that's why I couldn't believe it, when you rang and asked me that question –'

Donna tries to go over the same old ground again, shaking her head at the wonder of it all, but my thoughts have already moved on, and I'm out of cigarettes now, and it's cold, and I want to go home.

Donna and I do something we've always been good at. We change the subject to something funny. In fact, if you want to know the reason we stayed together so long, it's probably no more complex than that. Ultimately it wasn't just the jealousy, nor the constant supply of G-string sex, nor the Mr Wobbly indecision. The fact is, when we tried, Donna and I could always make each other laugh.

We leave the cafe, and she double-locks the door, and I tell her about Lucky the guinea pig, and Scott O'Grady, and the biro, and it suddenly seems to take no time at all to get to the tube.

I'm not travelling back with her, though.

'You sure?' she says. People are staring now, because she looks like she's just been crying. God knows what I look like. As usual, probably the man who's responsible.

'I'll get the bus over the road,' I tell her, even though we both know this is the height of inconvenience and it will take me twice as long to get home.

'You'd like Pete,' Donna squeezes my arm, reaching up for a kiss. A last kiss, maybe? Perhaps it's about time. I don't think we've ever officially had one.

'Good luck,' I say, sounding like a teacher.

'I wish you and Catherine had got married,' Donna says quickly, then genuinely looks as if she regrets it. As if she finally thinks she's gone too far, for the first time in her life.

'I think it's bloody good that we didn't, if you must know. We fought like cat and dog.'

I give Donna an attempt at a smile after this, and give her a look that (I hope) will show her that I'm being as refreshingly cynical about life after Catherine, as I was when she was still alive.

Then I cross the road, dodging the rush-hour traffic, and I get on the bus and don't even look back at her, as she heads for the tube. I know she'll be trying to catch my eye, because this is what Donna is like – she never can say goodbye properly – but it's time for me to be back in my world, with my rules, not hers. It may be the only way I get through the rest of this week.

I wonder at Catherine's messages, and how much I missed, through the wind tunnel, while she was shouting into the hurricane of my wonky vibrations. What was the rest of the sentence about Noel Oliver? Was the information about Donna meant to be, she *was* pregnant? She's *sorry* she got pregnant? She's had her *last chance* to be pregnant? Some things you don't want to over-analyse, though. I lean my face against the bus window, watch the traffic, and go home.

eighteen

A few weeks after this, Felix and I discover that Alison is getting married to the Head. We find out on Thursday morning, when we reach into our pigeonholes expecting yet more memos about parent-teacher night, and find the invitations instead.

'Ding *dong!*' exclaims Felix, sounding suitably impressed as he opens the posh, expensive-looking envelope.

The invitation reveals a few things about Alison, and about Tony – we have to call him that now, I suppose – that I hadn't realised.

Alison's got a master's degree, for example (she managed to keep that quiet) because she is Miss Alison Dawson M.A., and her father was in the army, it seems, because he is Brig. Dawson.

The Head, on the other hand, has only got a B.A. Hons. which seems embarrassing for him. Alison's parents have an address that sounds like something right out of Beatrix Potter. Somewhere a hedgehog might live, perhaps, or a family of wild voles wearing pinnies and making strawberry jam.

Brig. and Mrs Phillip Dawson
The Old Cottage
Little Snapdragon Lane
Foxhole Pass
Winnie's Knuckle
Herts.

What the hell is Winnie's Knuckle? Alison's parents must be in charge of the invitations, too, because none of the Head's demonic, cloven-hoofed handwriting has been allowed, anywhere on the outside, or the inside, of the envelope.

'Engraved as well,' Felix says, inspecting his invitation closely, and lapsing into Australian for a minute. 'Cooee!'

'I shall expect lobster at the reception,' I say, in my best Lady Penelope from *Thunderbirds* voice, as we head across the car park, and over to The Hut, for our daily cigarette.

Sometimes, I think, just being around Saddleton is turning me camp.

Felix and I have cut our smoking back to one cigarette a day now, in a first attempt at giving up. We tell each other it's because we don't want to end up relying on the National Health when we've got lung cancer, but in actual fact, it's the thought of puffing away with Alison in the smoker's corner of the staffroom, that is turning us off. She is, after all, about to become Mrs Head.

'Blount's been invited to the wedding as well,' Felix says, chewing nicotine gum furiously.

'Even him?'

'Yes. And you know he's been killing the school pigeons and boiling them up in his evil hut kitchen, don't you?'

'Yeah?'

'I've seen him. He stuns them by turning up *The Archers* to full volume on his transistor, so they become incapable of movement, and then he sprays his Old Spice in their eyes and attacks them with his Swiss army knife. Then, he puts them in the pot with his Sainsbury's instant noodles.'

'Are you sure about this, Felix?'

'You doubt my word?' he protests. 'Listen, Mark. Remember Glenn Close with the rabbit in *Fatal Attraction*? It's the same.

It's Blount's own personal *Fatal Attraction*, except he wants pigeon soup at the end of it, not sex with a married man.'

We're picking up our coats, after this, when the bell has gone, when Alison appears at the end of the corridor, waving and smiling.

'Helloooo!' she trills, echoing her way across the lino.

Unlike most brides-to-be, Alison is actually gaining weight, rather than losing it. Her arse is now about five *Guardians* wide, and whenever Felix or I see her these days – which isn't often – she's always opening a fresh Crunchie, or ploughing through another rock bun. Sometimes she does it with a fag in her left hand, and a chocolate bar in her right.

You have to admire her, though. Breaking with convention, and all that, in her drive to be the fattest bride in Winnie's Knuckle. Resisting social pressure.

'It must be unconscious anxiety about the prospect of a lifetime's fornication with a man who has the handwriting of Satan,' Felix hisses, as she comes barrelling towards us.

If anything, though, Alison's weight gain seems to have increased the Head's passion for her, because all they ever do is roll around in the back of his Volvo, with the labrador's head intermittently popping up in the back window, with a stunned look on its face.

'Thanks for the wedding invite, sweetie,' Felix says, kissing Alison on the cheek, narrowly avoiding a Bounty coming in the other way, from the opposite side of her face. I am then forced to kiss her on the cheek too. Bastard. It's like the hugging thing with Noel all over again.

Alison smells of coconut, chocolate and – frankly – sex. Her eyes also seem to have changed colour, and turned violet – but I see why, when I get up close. She's wearing weird-coloured contact lenses. It must be for the wedding. She'll look like Pavarotti when she finally staggers down the aisle, but at least she'll have nice purple eyes.

'Tess can't come to the wedding,' she makes a face at me.

'Oh.'

Tess. Forgotten, but suddenly, not forgotten. Sad, really, how the mention of one particular name can elevate your heart rate.

Of course, I should have realised. Alison will invite everyone in the world to this wedding, from just about everywhere.

'Can't Tess just fly over?' Felix persists. 'Won't Mr Moneybags pay for her?'

'Oh, it's not that,' Alison makes a sad face, which suddenly makes her look like a bloodhound. 'It's just the time away from her school in New York. And I don't think she's with Mr Moneybags any more. Robin. So there's no question of him paying anyway.'

There isn't? She's not? This could be the best news I've had all week.

Alison finishes her Bounty, and moves on to a Twix, which is poking out of her top pocket.

'Here, Tess sent you an email,' she tells me. 'I printed it out for you. But have no fear, I didn't read it.' Felix gives me a look.

I take it, and manage to give Alison what I hope is a grateful smile. Of course she's read it. And why couldn't she just forward it to me? I mean, I've got email. Come to that, I've even got a posh new mobile phone – the old one died – which converts everything to text.

'And before I go,' Alison says, twirling on the lino, in the corridor.

'Mmm?' Felix hums his reply.

'Don't go spending too much money, you know. Tony only opened the registry at Harrods because I've got an account there. We get little free treats from them, you see, if everyone buys their presents there. But I don't expect you two to bother –'

'Oh no,' Felix insists, 'we're off to Harrods. We're going already. Aren't we Mr Buckle? We just can't get enough of Harrods.'

'Speak for yourself, mate,' I interrupt him, 'I'm just getting them new car seat covers from Asda.'

'For the Volvo, sweetie,' Felix explains to Alison, who as usual, doesn't get the joke.

'They're getting rather a lot of heavy wear and tear, your seat covers. Aren't they?'

With immaculate timing, the Head then appears at the end of the corridor, gives a discreet wave to Alison, and starts stalking towards us.

'Better go,' Felix says, gripping his wedding invitation, and quickly walking the other way.

But me, I've got an email from Tess Blake in my hand, and if there's anything I don't want to do, it's read it with Saddleton breathing over my shoulder.

'I might go for a walk,' I say to him, thinking about the sports field, and privacy, and maybe the chance of a surreptitious cigarette, away from Felix's scrutiny, behind a bush.

'You do that,' Felix says, raising his eyebrows.

It's a sunny day, so there are plenty of kids out – closet smokers, like me, from the big boys' school across the way – and some smaller kids, who run the other way when they see me coming. God knows what they're up to.

Eventually, I find a tree stump to sit on, at the farthest end of the sports ground, and allow myself the luxury of opening the email.

I'm prepared for it to be fairly dull, this friendly email from New York, so it's unnerving to see the first sentence is all about Robin.

Dear Mark,

I'm sorry I haven't been in touch until now. I know you gave me your email on a piece of paper, but Robin and I have moved so many times since we got here, it got lost. And now Robin's gone again, because he's moved to Manhattan, so some of the things that were missing have turned up. Your address was one of them.

I wonder, for a moment, if Robin Moneybags has actually been hiding my email address, all this time, but then – for what reason? I hardly think he's ever seen me as a serious threat. I keep on reading, and light my cigarette.

Robin and I have stayed friends, but if he or I were ever hoping for something more, I don't think it ever stood a chance. In the meantime, he's gone to share a place on the Upper East Side with some guys from the bank, and I'm staying here in the Bronx. I love the school, although we have had two attempted suicides since I've been here.

Children attempting suicide?

I am determined to see it out, though, and I love New York. I miss the school, though, and you too – obviously – and I'm amazed at how much things have changed since I've been gone. I would love to go to Alison's wedding, but unfortunately they won't give me time off. But I wish you well with your quest to give up smoking, and I know Felix will do a great job with the football. By the way, I have a new band – and you'll be pleased to hear it's not called Faith Lift.

And what do I read into that? Especially that last bit, about missing me – in fact, obviously missing me – and the part about me being pleased to hear she's not in a band called Faith Lift any more. Is this code, letting me know that she's dumped her Crosslink and church stuff? Or does she just mean that she knows I'm a cynical bastard, and I've always thought the name of her band was crap?

Immediately, I think of all the emails I could send back. All the things I could say, all the questions I could ask.

Clearly, Alison's been keeping her up to speed while she's been away. So, I wonder what she's been telling her about me? Wrong information no doubt, and nothing that puts me in a good light, so that will have to be sorted out.

Yeah. I've really got to write to Tess Blake. I must get around to doing something about that. Maybe after I give up smoking, as she suggests. So, Tess, yeah, I should be a new man by the time I've managed to do all that and written back to you. Some time soon.

nineteen

Veronica Roden rings me up on my hi-tech new mobile, just as I'm getting out of the bath on Sunday night. That combination of telephones and baths is still enough to make me jump, but I take the call anyway.

'I've been speaking to Noel Oliver,' she tells me, as I stand there in a towel.

'Well, you can't have been. Because then you'd know his name isn't Noel Oliver any more.'

'Oh, I know all about that,' Veronica dismisses me. 'What's he called? Mercury? Jupiter?'

'Something like that.'

'Married to a healer.'

'Yep.'

'And he's now a mini-cab driver, he told me. And an astrologer. And a few other things – he wants to feng shui my flat.'

'So are you going to let him?'

'You must be kidding. If he's so good at feng shui, how come he's still driving a cab?'

We chat for a while, about school, and about her work – and carefully avoid talking about her relationship, because her boyfriend must be in the next room – and then, suddenly, she tells me she's coming over. I nearly drop my bath towel.

This is typical of Veronica. She announces things to you, rather than broaching the subject. Basically, where I'm concerned, everything is always a done deal. Except she's the one organising the deal.

'You haven't had dinner, yet, so why don't I bring something round? I've made more than enough of this stew, I can put it in a container.'

'I'm already living out of containers. I don't think it's very healthy. And how do you know I haven't had dinner?'

'Then we can have a good talk,' Veronica says, with an air of finality.

'About what?'

'Oh for God's sake,' Veronica harumphs, and sounds like she's about to put the phone down. 'I'll see you in half an hour. All right?'

Of course, it has to be all right, because she's given me no right of reply, as usual. But I dry myself off and get dressed, anyway, resenting my own obedience, but also telling myself that the sooner she gets things off her chest, the faster I'll be off the hook.

As I scout round the house for dirty coffee mugs, old ashtrays, tabloid newspapers (she hates them) and other signs that my life is going to seed, I also find myself removing Catherine's things, too, and clearing them away into the cupboard. It's instinct, maybe. Just a sense that if we can keep her sister out of things, Veronica might be less wound up, and the evening might go a lot faster.

In the end, though, when Veronica finally arrives, it's at least an hour after she thought she'd be there, so it looks as if the whole evening will stretch into forever. I've hidden all the old Cure albums, too, and the Best of Depeche Mode. Just in case they remind her of anything.

When she walks through the front door, and immediately asks where they are, so she can put some music on, I have to lie through my teeth, and say I've given them to Oxfam, because

I've grown out of them – like my old *Whizzer and Chips* annuals. Naturally, a one-hour interrogation follows.

'But you don't just grow out of The Cure,' Veronica says, sounding horrified.

'I would have said they were one of the first things you grow out of,' I reply.

We are eating her stew now – I hate the stuff – and sitting, like adults, at the dining table, where Catherine and I hardly ever ate, but never mind that.

'I see you've gone to some trouble, then,' Veronica says, noting the empty vase I've plonked in the middle of the table. 'You just need some flowers in it, don't you, basically.'

'Shut up.'

She opens the bottle of wine she's just bought from the corner shop. I know every single kind of wine they have at our corner shop, based on varying levels of nastiness, and she's managed to choose both the most expensive bottle, and the most poisonous one.

'Tell me more about giving your Cure albums away,' she says. 'I can't believe you've done it. And the Mode!'

One of the things I had forgotten about Veronica is that she always calls Depeche Mode, *The* Mode. It's like she used to call The Voodoo Blitz, her own band, *The* Blitz. In the Veronica lexicon of modern music, Siouxsie and The Banshees are also *The* Banshees. I wonder what she calls that other, fine, late 80s outfit, The The?

'What do you call The The, Veronica?'

'Eh?'

'Doesn't matter. Do you mind if I don't eat all this stew?'

I drop a fork, then, and have to crawl under the table to pick it up, where I immediately come nose to shin with Veronica's legs, in black tights. On a purely physical level, I can't fault myself for lusting after Veronica for a reasonable percentage of my male, adult, shagging life.

She has fantastic legs. She's got the kind of skirt collection that always made me want to stick my hand up, somewhere, at inappropriate moments. And because she's so bad-tempered, she exudes a kind of heat that can often be mistaken for sexual charisma.

But would I sleep with her now? Would I even bite her left ear lobe? You must be bloody joking. I crawl back out again with the fork, and find my chair.

'Noel said you told him your life wasn't very good,' Veronica says, filling my glass.

'Well, that's no secret.'

'Don't dwell on it,' she says, as if this is some supremely original and wise piece of advice. 'Don't get stuck in feeling sorry for yourself, it's time you were seeing someone else.'

'What?'

'Even just as a friend. You know. Catherine wouldn't want you to be moping around.'

'How do you know what she would and wouldn't want me to do?'

And I half expect her to tell me that she's been receiving inside information from Catherine in her dreams, as Donna Roberts did, the other week. But instead, Veronica purses her lips, rubbing them together so the lipstick smudges, and gets on with her stew.

Then I have a horrible thought.

'You don't mean, you think you should be my new female friend,' I say.

'Oh, God no,' she says, so rapidly that I almost have a second to feel insulted.

I think about what she's said for a minute, and the way she's just analysed and picked away at my existence.

'I'm not ready,' I say at last.

'It could be a whole new life for you,' she says, peering short-sightedly at me. Like Catherine before her, Veronica needs to wear glasses, but is too vain to do it.

'Why would I want a new life? Why can't I just have the old life and graft something else onto it?'

'Because once you subtract Catherine from it, I don't think there's much of a life at all.'

'Oh yeah?'

I think about Veronica's own life for a minute. And then I realise I've got nowhere to come back from, because I don't know enough about its fullness, or its emptiness, to make any accusations.

'So what about you?' I challenge her. 'What about your life?'

And for some reason, this sets the great, frozen land mass that is Veronica Roden, into a kind of temperate zone, and she melts, and she even smiles, as she is lost in the complete happiness of telling me about herself.

'I'm not who I was a few months ago, that's absolutely certain,' she tells me.

I nod.

'I get up, I do some yoga.'

Bloody yoga again.

'I've been setting the alarm early, for about six, so I get more time to do it, you see.'

'And what's your boyfriend doing all this time, that you're contorting yourself?'

Somehow, though, in this brave new life of hers, I don't think we're supposed to mention him.

'We're quite independent, you know,' she says, smugly. 'It's a commitment that also lets us be ourselves.'

'Veronica, you now sound like you're in *Hello!* magazine, and you're Posh Spice, or someone and I'm the journalist.

She ignores me, and goes on, pulling down her skirt, which has now ridden up around her thighs.

'I cook more these days, and if there's a lot to go round, I drop it off with friends. That way I see more of my friends, you know? And they appreciate it. London can be a very disconnected place.'

Oh, my God, I think, she is doing therapy. Catherine always thought she would.

'And I'm seeing a therapist,' Veronica goes on, 'and I do a bit of Pilates as well as the yoga, and I've learned not to worry about money so much, I suppose.'

She stares at me for a minute.

'What? What? Why are you giving me that look?'

'Well, why the bloody hell are you telling me all this?'

'You seem to have had a heart-to-heart with Noel. That was fine, wasn't it?'

'Yeah, but why do we have to? And I don't call this a heart-to-heart. Like I said, it's you doing a monologue, in *Hello!* magazine.'

A long silence.

'My therapist told me I should talk to you about things,' she says.

'Oh, *things.*'

'Do you know, Mark, that if you add everything up, you and I have had a longer relationship than anything you and Catherine ever had?'

'Yeah, maybe, Veronica, but what kind of relationship? I mean, do you count lying on the floor in Canterbury and listening to old goth records? Come off it, we had sex just the once. And we were drunk. And you said it was rubbish, anyway.'

'No I didn't. I didn't use that word.'

I look at her for a second. She's way too thin again, as usual. So maybe the off-loading of food to friends has something to do with that, as well.

'I saw the therapist because of Catherine.'

'I can understand that.'

'Because of that time in the kitchen, when I saw her, after she'd just died, and she spoke to me.'

I clear away the plates, tipping my share of the stew in the bin.

'The celery in that stew's good for your colon,' Veronica says, watching me get rid of it.

'Oh well.'

'And I was wondering,' Veronica begins, more cautiously than usual.

'What?'

'Have you ever seen Catherine?'

'You've been talking to Noel D. Jupiter, haven't you?'

'Well, have you seen her?'

'No,' I lie, pouring out the rest of the wine, and knocking it back quickly, so she'll hopefully do the same, and start to feel a bit woozy and tired – and have to go home.

'Nothing?'

'Bugger all,' I say, looking her straight in the eye, which is when the stereo jumps into life, and suddenly plays *Never Tear Us Apart.*

'I thought you were getting rid of all your old CDs,' Veronica pouts. I suppose she thinks I've just turned it on by remote. Not that there's any control mechanism in my hand.

'Um. The radio just turned itself on. If you must know.'

And now, the microwave, predictably, is showing off too, flashing HELLO.

Veronica bites her lip, and gets up to unplug it.

'Don't do that. Why are you doing that?'

'Something's going on,' she says. 'I just know, something's going on.'

But she's off now, unplugging every electronic device she can find, from the blender – which I've never used since the day Catherine died – to the juicer, and the television, and the self-operating stereo, and even the lamps in the corner.

'This is weird,' she says.

'No, it's not. We're just having a power surge.'

She gives me a look.

'This has happened to you before, hasn't it?'

'No,' I lie again, shaking my head, noticing bits of stew stuck on my shirt.

'Nothing? Not ever?'

'Really. I don't know what you're all worked up about,' I tell her. And then I go around the kitchen, plugging everything back in.

twenty

Felix has now managed to give up smoking. To replace the habit, he chews bubblegum, which means his usual Russell-does-Brideshead conversations are now broken up with the sound of smacking gum.

'And it gets everywhere, as well,' he moans, as we sit in our new spot in the staffroom – a handy arrangement of chairs just in front of the heater.

'We should position ourselves here by the warmth, and claim the territory early on,' Felix observes, 'that way we will insure our physical survival by Christmas, when Blount is preparing to do his worst buggering up the central heating. Besides which, if I surround myself with moderate temperatures this winter, I may even feel brave enough to take the plunge and wear my green velvet suit to work. It's very Oscar.'

'Any more sign of Blount playing *The Archers* to pigeons?'

Felix shudders.

'You tell me, sweetie.'

I take a piece of his bubblegum, which is hard, and square,

and small – and a foul shade of pink – and start pounding it with my back teeth. I endure it for about ninety seconds, then give up.

'I don't know how you do it,' I tell him.

We walk back to his next class, which is music, and my next class, which is maths. As we approach his classroom, though, we see something almost unheard of at Rivett Street – Scott O'Grady sitting on his own, on a bench in the playground, and being quiet.

'I know,' Felix tuts, 'he's been like that for weeks now.'

Felix then does something even more unheard of. He goes up to Scott, and stands within at least half a metre downwind of him, without flinching.

Scott seems to say something, Felix says something back, and then, when it looks as if the teacher-pupil relationship can go no further, Scott wanders off.

'I'm really worried about him,' Felix says, coming back.

'Why?'

'The other kids wouldn't let him join the football team.'

'Yeah. Well.'

'No, he was quite upset.'

'He asks for it,' I say, feeling less like a teacher, and more like another one of the kids that Scott regularly tries to beat up, or steal from, or publicly humiliate.

Felix beckons me down the corridor, just ahead of the class-rooms, and we let the children file past.

'He said the other day, he can't see the point of being alive.'

I give this some thought.

'How old is he again?'

'Eleven.'

'Right.'

'I told the Head, but he's all up to here' – Felix indicates, flapping his hands, 'with the wedding.'

'What about Mrs Everly?'

She is our school social worker, and occasionally joins us in the staffroom, where she steals all the newspapers and the Cadbury's chocolate fingers.

'Mrs Everly knows about his problems. She knows about Scott,' Felix sighs.

'So she's on the case?'

'Well, yes – technically. But I've been in a school like this before. You know? In a part of Sydney, where –' and here Felix shudders. 'Anyway, I won't go into morbid details, but suffice to say, with children like Scott, at times like this, I think it's all hands on deck to help. Otherwise, we find them hanging from the ropes in the gymnasium.'

We move further round the corner, to avoid the screaming hordes of 4B who are now streaming past us, still pretending to kick imaginary footballs down the corridor.

'Tess has two kids who are suicidal in her school in New York.'

'Oh, God. Don't say that.'

'Maybe I should email her.'

'And I'll get Scott back on the football team,' Felix says, rolling his eyes to heaven.

'Although he's atrocious at keepie-uppie, and I've seen him deliberately kick at least one other child in the kneecap.'

'Oh, well. You can reinforce their shin pads.'

'What shin pads?' Saddleton dismisses me, as we finally give in and make our way to class. 'This is Rivett Street, sweetie, not Man United. They've got copies of *Reader's Digest* down their socks.'

And with that, he flounces off with all the indignation of Sir Alex Ferguson, hearing that his team budget's been cut back to only 10 million pounds.

Scott O'Grady is a good excuse to email Tess, so I do – finally. I've never been much good at the email thing. It makes me nervous. Not so much the technicalities of logging on, and logging off, and dealing with cookies and gifs, and all the rest of it. It's more the way that the first stupid thing that comes into your head ends up, permanently recorded in cyberspace, and on someone else's computer screen.

As I type in Tess's address, I tell myself off for using Scott as a reason to advance my own interests – namely, my own love life. Not that I seriously think anything will ever happen with Tess, though. Not now. Not next year, either. Maybe, if I'm very lucky, in about three years. That's probably when it will happen – the big virginal kiss. That's probably what all these other-worldly omens and predictions have been pointing to.

I suppose really good teachers would have noticed Scott's misery months ago, and demanded that the Head do something definite about it. Proper teachers would have demanded that Mrs Everly do a bit less stealing of the chocolate biscuits, and a bit more chasing of the O'Grady family, who are notorious at Rivett Street for ignoring every phone call and every letter.

I start the letter to Tess. I then re-start it. Then I get all the way through, look at it again, and hit delete. Then I find a dictionary, I am embarrassed to say, have a look at that, decide she'll blow my cover if I'm using long words, and start all over again. By the time I've finally finished the thing, and hit send, it's about an hour on from when I started.

Dear Tess,
How are you? I hope life in New York is treating you well. Every-thing's the same here, with the exception of Felix's entry into the world of non-smokers. He's replaced one bad habit with another though, and he's now a hard-core bubblegum addict. I'm still trying to give up, but I'm not having much luck. I'm writing because we've got a problem with Scott O'Grady. Not that it will be any surprise to you. But he's told Felix that he doesn't see the point of being alive. And he's sitting by himself a lot. And the other kids won't let him join the football team. I know Rivett Street is probably small-fry compared to where you are, but have you got any ideas?
Best wishes, Mark.

Then I cross out best wishes, and put love. Then I cross that out, and put salutations, which is ridiculous. Then I cross that out and put cheers. Which sort of works. Though it's hardly going to drive her wild with passion. Drag. Click. Send.

A few hours later, at home, the phone rings. And it's her. Long distance and everything. Way too late – she hasn't got the time difference right – but who cares? It's Tess. It's genuinely her voice on the other end of the phone, and it's amazing how good it feels to hear her again.

'I got your number from the Head,' she says. 'I rang Alison first, and he was with her, so he passed it on.'

'Fantastic. God, I didn't expect you to call.'

Then I remember I probably shouldn't be bandying around the word God, and clam up.

'They have really expensive rates in this place, so I won't talk long,' she says. And I listen out for any hint of an American accent, for a sign that she's changed, but she still sounds like the same old Tess to me.

'Scott O'Grady's father is abusive,' she says, all in a rush.

'What kind of abusive?'

'All kinds. I don't know. Scott was never one of my kids, so I never took it that far. But I held his hand in the loo once, when he was sick, and when I gave him my jumper to put on, because I had to wash the shirt, he had bruises on his chest.'

'Holy shit.'

Then I realise what I've just said – again – and vow to shut up.

'I talked to Mrs Everly, and she said the authorities knew all about him, and she was very good and all that.'

'Right.'

'But it's all hands on deck, you know? He's all our responsibility.'

'That's exactly what Felix said.'

'Well, he's right. And it's bad if Scott's been kicked out of the football team by the other kids.'

'Yup.'

'Is there any way you can get him back in? That would be a start.'

'And what about his father?'

'I think you'll find his mother's kicked his father out of home. It was the last thing he told me, before I left the school that day. We had a sort of talk about it, in the playground. And I meant to do something about Scott, and I didn't. I just told the Head, and I left.'

'The Head is busy organising his wedding to Alison.'

'Yes. I gathered that.'

'So he may not be entirely up to speed with the Scott O'Grady thing.'

'Yes.'

There's a long pause from the other end of the phone, then, and I suddenly realise what Tess is doing. She's passing the buck. Not because she wants to, but because she has to, because she's in New York and I'm here. And there's something else as well. I feel like she wants me to be – I dunno – good.

'He's not in my class, obviously,' I begin.

'No.'

'And I don't really have anything to do with the football team. That's Felix's gig.'

'No.'

She sounds kind enough about both these facts I'm pointing out, but still, I can feel Tess waiting, and waiting, for me to come up with something – for me to even single-handedly rescue Scott, right now, during this phone call, and prove something.

But – I don't know what to do now. I just don't. At the moment I live in a world where my primary concern is myself, so why would someone like me know what to do about a boy like Scott O'Grady? And then it comes to me. Just like that. Noel D. Jupiter.

'I've got a friend.'

Tess leaps on this.

'Go on.'

'He drives a cab. So he could pick Scott up from the football practice, or the game, and then take him home afterwards. I mean, if his dad's not going to do it – which I think we can assume he isn't. And we all know what his mother's like, so she won't care what her son does.'

'Yes. No, that's a good idea.'

'And he's a good bloke, Noel. I mean, he's a bit of a hippy, but he's okay.'

'Fantastic.'

'It's a start. I don't know what else I can do, Tess. I really don't.'

And I think, I can't be a hero for you here. I really can't. I'd love to be able to take this call now, and say I'm rugby-tackling the Head to the ground, until he deals with the issue, and I'm going to take on Mr O'Grady himself, and personally threaten him with a long jail sentence, and I'm going to adopt Scott, and make him happy, and cure his appalling flatulence problem, and all the rest of it. But in the end, Noel D. Jupiter is pretty much all I can offer. So I do. And it's enough that Tess sounds pleased, and relieved, and on my side.

There have been very few women on my side lately, after all. And I miss it.

Back at school the following day, Alison catches me up in the car park, as I wonder if I can allow myself a cigarette.

'I just wanted to tell you about the wedding!' she runs up to me. 'Yup?'

'We're having an indoor swimming pool as part of the reception, you know, so people can throw each other in.'

Oh, fantastic. Lucky I did all that hard training at Oak Street Baths, then. Lucky I'd prepared myself with my gruelling ten laps of practice.

'So you will bring dry clothes, won't you? Just in case it happens to you?'

'I'll bring dry clothes.'

The trouble is, I know it will happen to me. And why do I know this? Because Saddleton will push me in. Or he'll push both of us in together, no doubt to fuel a few salacious rumours.

'Is the Head very busy at the moment?' I ask her. I still can't bring myself to call him Tony.

'Oh, God yes. I mean, it's not just the wedding, it's his ex-wife, and his mother, and he's selling his flat, the whole thing.'

'Because Scott O'Grady needs seeing to.'

'You can say that again.'

'He's worrying us, Alison.'

'Yes, but when he does that, he also takes up all the valuable time you could be giving to the other children,' Alison observes. 'There are two hundred children alone, in our year, and none of us have time to even get the tadpoles out of their jam jars, never mind siphon off the time between Scott and the rest of them.'

'Right.'

'See Mrs Everly about him,' Alison advises me as she strides off to tell more staff members about the indoor swimming pool.

And that's it, really. So it's up to me. Frighteningly, it's up to me.

The following day, I call up Noel, who is thrilled to hear from me, and has forgiven me for not turning up to his party, and I proposition him.

'I know it's a long way,' I say, 'South London. Actually, the edge of Brixton. The O'Gradys are in a housing estate there.'

'I go there all the time.'

'He farts a lot. He'll probably do it in the cab.'

'No problem.'

Bizarrely, Noel actually sounds like a man who might be relishing the prospect of ferrying Scott around.

'I'll have to clear it with the Head,' I go on, 'and he might give you the third degree on the phone.'

'Fine.'

'And, of course, you'll have to get the okay from his mother, although really, that's a waste of time because she never replies to anything, anyway. To be honest, I'm not just asking you to give him a lift, I'm really asking you to get him there in the first place. I dunno. To encourage him.'

'Terrific.'

'There's one more thing, too,' I tell Noel, wondering if I should, but going ahead anyway. 'No, hang on, there's two more things.'

'Okay.'

'He told one of the teachers he doesn't see why he has to be alive any more, and my friend, Tess, says she saw bruises on his chest once. I think his father's been hitting him.'

'This is the father who's been chucked out by the mother, yeah?'

A long silence, as Noel takes this all in.

'Poor little bugger,' he says eventually. 'Poor Scott.'

'Yeah.'

'What can I say? You fix it, I'll do it. But, you know, get him back in the team first,' Noel says.

'Well, that's easy.'

'And thanks, Mark. Thanks for asking me.'

Noel puts the phone down.

Thanks for asking him? What irrational world does Noel D. Jupiter live in, that my exclusive invitation to him, to drive halfway across London, for no money, twice a week, in the freezing cold, to pick up a seriously disturbed, anti-social, kicking, biting, farting boy draws such gratitude?

In the face of that, though, I really do have to get off my

arse. So, in one fell swoop, I write the letter to Mrs O'Grady that she will never bother with, nor answer, and I ring up the Head – who's so distracted by the wedding, that he could care less what happens to Scott – and I leave a note for Mrs Everly in her pigeonhole, telling her about Noel – and then I ring up Saddleton and tell him to force the kids to vote Scott back on the team.

And all the time, I want to tell Tess what I'm doing – but some wiser part of me, maybe even some finer, nobler part of me – thinks that this is premature. That any vote of approval I ever end up getting has to wait, as a reward, much later on, when the O'Grady plan might even have ended up working.

twenty-one

On Wednesday night, I get a call from Pam and Tina, the two Christians from the Elvis Presley party. They are having a dinner party, at their flat, the following week, and they would love to see me.

I say I'll think about it, and then I hang up and put on another of the Saddleton football videos. Dinner with Pam, Tina and a whole lot of other God-botherers in Crystal Palace? No, I'm sorry. There is absolutely no way I'm going to that dinner party. And I don't give a shit if they'd love to see me.

The next day, I get another email from Tess. There are only two more messages in my in-box, one promising me exciting online gaming at some casino, and the other trying to flog me software, so really, there's just no contest – hers gets opened first.

Dear Mark,
I haven't heard from you, so I hope you didn't send an email and
it bounced. I just wanted to see how you got on with your friend,

the one who drives the mini-cab, who was going to help Scott. And I also wanted to let you know that Pam and Tina are planning a dinner party, at their place in Crystal Palace, next Friday. I passed on your number to them. I hope that's okay. Quite a few people from their Crosslink group will be there, so I hope that's okay as well. But I think you should have fun. Tina's got a great CD collection! Love, Tess xxx

Yeah, and I can just imagine the CDs. No, sorry Tess, no dice. You can sign off with as many kisses as you like, I'm not going to give in. Frankly, I'd rather have my a red hot poker shoved up my – no, I'd rather meet the same fate as Lucky the guinea pig – than front up to Pam and Tina's flat in Crystal Palace next Friday night.

Then, as I'm closing Tess's first email, a second one suddenly arrives.

Hi. It's me again. I just wanted to add a PS – even if you don't want to go, and I know you probably won't, my old boyfriend Troy will be there, with his wife and kid, so maybe you could do me a favour and let me know how they're all getting on.
Love, Tess xxx

I'm now not sure if this makes things better, or worse. Better, because if I meet this bloke Troy, I might be able to find out more about Tess. And that's not a bad thing. However, by the same token, if I meet Troy – not to mention his wife, and his kid, and if this all happens to a Cliff Richard soundtrack, and if there's no booze – well. It might just end up being the worst evening of my life.

A few days later, when I find myself half an hour into Pam and Tina's dinner party at Crystal Palace, I make a decision. It is the worst evening of my life. Troy is wearing so much white he is blinding me. White jeans. White spray jacket (where are we, in the middle of the bloody Atlantic Ocean?) and dazzling white trainers.

Pam has shoved candles all over the table, so that Troy is virtually glowing in the dark with all his white clothes, and his wife, whose name I can't remember – doesn't speak at all, but keeps showing me both rows of her teeth instead, in a hideous smile. The smile, of course, is also dazzling white.

Their child, whose gender is uncertain, has the kind of haircut which looks as if Mrs Troy shoved a Tupperware bowl on its head and went round it with a pair of scissors. And the child doesn't speak either. It all seems to be down to Troy, really, which means for about ten minutes, we are all treated to a monologue on how he and his wife met.

'She just wasn't interested at all when she first met me,' Troy says, 'were you?' And his wife smiles politely – but the amount of laughter this produces around the table, from Pam, Tina, various Crosslink people and even the silent, bowl-headed child, is phenomenal. Pam rocks from side to side, Tina can't breathe, glasses of non-alcoholic fruit punch get slammed down hard on the table, and even Tina's budgie, swinging violently in its cage, seems to be bent double with laughter.

Finally, silence descends again. And I feel as if my face is going to break, I'm forcing this smile so hard. Nevertheless, Troy continues his anecdote.

'You see,' (he looks politely at me, I look politely the other way), 'She was married to her golf! Every weekend she'd be out on the course, putting those shots away. So she didn't want to know about me at all. And then, she had her work as a lawyer, as well, and all these rich guys after her. I mean' – he looks at us imploringly, his captive audience, his congregation, 'what hope did I have?'

Troy takes a deep breath. 'And, as some of you know, the other thing getting in our way, for a while, was God. And it took an awfully long time to convince Mandy of that, too.'

Mandy – for that is his wife's name – now manages to smile and look sheepish, all at the same time. It's like watching one of those bad daytime Christian cable shows in the US.

Taking a sip of his mineral water – he's brought his own – Troy continues. 'I came to Christ in 1989, as you all know. And for ten long years, I prayed. I prayed that Mandy and I would be together,' he rubs his hands together, as if anticipating the arrival of pudding, 'and that God would take care of her, too. And' – he pauses dramatically for effect, bringing on another gale of laughter, 'ten years later, that's exactly what happened.

And guess what? The end of this story is, she's a better Christian than I'll ever be!' At this, Pam lets out something which sounds strangely like Billy Bunter yelling 'Yaroop!' in an old Greyfriars story, and Tina starts to clap, then gets embarrassed, thinks better of it, and stops.

And the story goes on, and on, from there. About how Mandy has now converted at least six mothers in her pre-school group, and how if God hadn't made her see the light at last, poor old Troy might even have been in danger of giving up on his maker (knowing, sympathetic nods from all around at this bit).

So – I go the loo. It's the only safe place to be. There are about eight of us there altogether, at that table, and I've got to be the only heathen. It's only a matter of time before they rise to their feet, start clapping and cheering, and drag me off to the bathroom for a quick baptism in Pam's power shower.

Or is that some other version of the Christian religion, I'm thinking of? That's the bloody trouble with it, you never know which team is which, or what the rules are. I mean, are their lot for women priests, or against women priests? Pro-Pope or anti-Pope? Is it yes to contraception or no?

I flip the toilet seat down, lock the door, and sit in privacy for a few minutes. We have only just been served the first course. Even if we have an early night, and I fully expect we all will – these are not people who go to bed after 10 p.m. – I still have two hours of torture to go.

I consider faking an illness, but realise that if I do this, Pam or Tina – or both – will want to put me in one of their beds, and flap around me for the rest of the night before, embarrassingly, calling a doctor. This lot are very big on nursing each other through illness, as I've discovered from listening to the dinner party talk tonight.

Mandy's got Troy through meningitis, Troy got Mandy's mother through cancer, someone else spent all year in hospital supervising her best friend's malaria, and the child – of course – has had a Crosslink-led prayer squad for practically everything it's ever survived, from athlete's foot to a heavy cold.

If I fake illness here, I will be thrown into one of these bedrooms, in this horrible poky flat, and not allowed to leave –

possibly for years. Moreover, I will be trapped in a room with a flowery bedspread, a lot of pot pourri, and a horrible picture of two rabbits kissing each other on a hilltop. I know this, because I have just seen the bedroom in question, through an open door.

I give in and give up, and wander back to the table. Troy is in full flight now, telling everyone about the first time he ever spoke in tongues. And as he rambles on, with me nodding politely, and Pam occasionally interrupting with a 'Wow!' or an 'Amazing!' (but never a 'Holy shit!', of course) I find myself thinking about Tess.

If someone like her, could have been in a relationship with someone like Troy, then what am I thinking, having even a modicum of desire for her? It's like Donna Roberts all over again. I'm just wearing sex goggles.

Tess is gorgeous. She's blonde, she's got the most amazing eyes I've seen all year, and for all I know, she's triggered some unhealthy, unconscious desire, deep within my soul, to sleep with a virgin. She was nice to me when Catherine died, and she sang a song for me on stage, and she's a bloody good singer. She's got the sexiest phone voice I've ever heard, and she's, undoubtedly, a better person than I'll ever be. I may even have the thought in my head that, post-Catherine, she can help save me. Help me get over it, or something. One day.

Nevertheless. She was nearly, perhaps, once Mrs Troy. And for all I know, Tess has spoken in tongues as well. This lot all think the world of her. They've been telling me that all night. So if that's the case, does she think the world of them? Because if so, I'm lusting after someone who's so far out of my range of understanding, that there's no point in even starting anything.

I stare at the wall, where there is a picture of a stallion galloping across a beach, and some sort of poem. I mean, does Tess think this kind of thing might be a great addition to an empty wall? If, in the year 2020, we ever moved in together, would I wake up one morning to find giant posters of love-struck bunnies on the bedroom wall? Or a nice brown leather-bound copy of the Bible next to my bed?

'Mark, I'm sorry, we're all ignoring you,' Tina pipes up, while Pam rushes off to get the next course. She fills up my glass with more punch, which tastes of canned pineapple juice and nothing else, and smiles at me slightly longer than is necessary.

'No, sorry, I'm just a bit tired, that's all,' I tell her.

I look down at my feet, and immediately notice someone has dropped their fork on the ground. But what happens if I pick it up? Will this also be considered hilarious, like Troy's story about Mrs Troy not wanting to marry him? Will I bend down, put the fork back up on the table, cause a commotion and have to put up with everyone wheezing and thumping the table for the next fifteen minutes?

While I am worrying about this, Tina brings up Felix Saddleton.

'Your friend was very funny at the party, Mark.'

'Oh yes. Felix.'

'He didn't quite have the best costume, but he was the best dancer.'

Yes, I think to myself, and he went home and shagged at least one of the male guests – did anyone spot that?

'You should have invited him tonight too,' Tina persists.

'Oh no. He's very busy.'

'So, what does your friend do, apart from wearing Elvis Presley outfits?' Troy asks, showing me his white teeth to match his white spray jacket.

'He's a teacher like me. And he coaches the football.'

A pause. Six heads, including the pudding-basin head of Troy's child, crane forward. And then it hits me like a brick. They want to know. They've been wondering, and worrying for weeks on end, about Felix Saddleton's alien presence at their Elvis party, and maybe Tess has said something to them about him being gay, but in any case – they want to know.

So, I tell them.

'Felix is gay. He has sex with men,' I say, chattily, knocking back the fruit punch.

Troy's wife says something to her silent offspring, and then they hold hands and leave the room.

'He's a member of the Hair Bears, in Pimlico,' I go on. 'It's a small group of gay men who happen to have an excess amount of hair on their bodies. They have spa baths together. And then they go off and shag. It's casual sex, of course. But I suppose that's okay, isn't it? I mean, God created our genitals for pleasure, let's face it. Didn't he?'

'Mark, are you feeling okay?' Tina asks, looking as worried as it's possible for a perpetually smiling woman to look.

I nod, and continue. I'm feeling almost as omnipotent as Troy now.

Then Pam comes back in with the main course – some chicken thing which smells, and looks like something Blount might cook on the camping stove in his shed.

'Fantastic!' Troy beams, and they all get up to help her – Troy, and Tina, and another Crosslink person, who looks at me as if he's going to be sick – and I sit there, wondering if I should pick the fork up off the carpet, while they leap around with napkins and serving spoons.

'Anyway,' I say, as they start piling up the plates, 'I might go to the off-licence now, and get some booze. Anyone interested?'

But no, it seems, nobody is interested.

'I mean, I think we should have something to drink with this chicken, don't you?'

Mrs Troy and the child come back into the room.

Troy puts his arm around his wife, and draws her back to the table, and the child, still holding its mother's hand, follows. They are still silent.

'Back in a minute, then,' I say, and head for the door, waiting for Troy in his spray jacket and white trainers to come bounding after me, throwing a heavy hand on my shoulder – but no, nothing. Not even a squeak of protest from Pam or Tina.

And I run down the stairs, checking that I haven't left anything – though even if I have, I'm not going back for it – and slam the door to the flats, and walk miles down to the bus stop, as fast and far as I can. And when there are no buses, I just keep walking anyway, until I'm totally lost, in a part of London I've never seen before, and have no intention of seeing again.

Later, much later – two buses and a taxi later – I get back home, to find my answering machine blinking red.

It's probably Felix, I think, wanting his football videos back, or my parents, wondering if I've finished with any of their spaghetti bolognaise containers.

Instead, though, it is Tess – and she says Pam's just rung her up, all the way from Crystal Palace to New York, because I've vanished from their dinner party, and I was acting strange, and they're all very worried about me.

I switch on the computer and send an email.

Dear Tess,
I got your message. I'm sorry if Pam thinks I was acting strange, but actually, I was acting perfectly normally, under the circumstances.
Love, Mark
PS: Troy is a prat.

Catherine used to say you should never send an email until you've read it through a few times, because there's always the luxury of the delete button. My normal reservations about using it have vanished, though. Maybe this is my own version of speaking in tongues or something, but I seem to be on a roll here, after my little talk to the Crosslink people about Felix. And I don't want to stop now. So I check Tess's address, move the mouse and press send.

After this, I check the BBC website to see if anything's happened (it hasn't – just something else about Liz Hurley, and the latest on Northern Ireland) and prepare to log off, and go to bed. It has, after all, been a bloody long night.

Before I can hit the light switch, though, my sleeping computer makes a rooster noise that indicates – against all likelihood – that someone has just emailed me. I open up my mailbox again. Tess? Yes. Tess.

If it's any consolation, I think he's a prat too. Love, Tess xxx

I could think of about ten different emails I could send, replying to this now. They would range from jokey to outraged. They might take two lines, or two hundred. In the end, though, I'm just a man who's been force-fed fruit punch and bad jokes all night, and I think it's probably better for everyone if I just go to bed.

twenty-two

A few days later, Felix tells me that the Rivett Street Junior Football Team has done enough keepie-uppie to satisfy him, and will shortly be engaged in its first practice match against its old rival, Blues Road South – often nicknamed Bruise Road South by the school.

'And the boys have agreed to let Scott sit on the bench,' he informs me, as we sit in our chairs by the heater in the staffroom, reserving our spot for the long, hard winter months ahead.

'So he's not really in the team, he's just got a plate full of cut-up oranges.'

'But he's very happy,' Felix says, waving me away. 'In fact, he's a picture of contentment, and all talk of having no reason to live seems to have vanished. The flatulence, of course, is still terrifying, but we all have to make sacrifices. And who knows, if we ever put him in goal, it could be a secret weapon for Rivett Street, used to powerful advantage.'

I nod. 'Yes, very bloody powerful.'

'And I love your friend Noel D. Jupiter as well,' Felix goes on, munching through a chocolate finger.

'So that's okay? He's being a good chauffeur for Scott?'

'He's been religious about it,' Felix comments, 'Which reminds me, have you heard from the lovely Tess?'

I pick up *The Guardian* and look at the jobs page.

'Nah, not really.'

'She sent me an email to say that you were a very erratic emailer. I think she was implying that your ability to return emails verged on the casual, actually.'

'Well, that's Christian of her.'

'And I'll tell you something else that happened,' Felix leans forward, 'I've been put on the Crosslink mailing list. How about that, for a special treat for *moi*!'

'Yeah, well, better start getting your fruit punch ingredients ready then,' I warn him, as we make our way over to the school playing fields.

I try not to feel rejected by the fact that Crosslink have gone to all the trouble of tracing Felix, and not even bothered to go looking for me. Clearly, I'm just beyond salvation.

When we finally arrive at the playing fields, there are half a dozen boys running around all over the place, shouting at each other and lobbing footballs.

Felix's team isn't exactly fit, but at least they're not sitting down in the middle of the pitch and gossiping, which is what used to happen when I was the coach.

We watch them for a minute, this weird collection of fat, thin, tall and short boys, all trying to pass themselves off as a well-oiled machine as they try five-a-side practice. And we try not to laugh out loud as someone takes control of the ball, only to fall over himself in the mud, losing both *Reader's Digest* shin pads in a puddle.

Amazingly, Scott O'Grady is sitting obediently on the sidelines, not throwing missiles, not whining, and – reading. I've never seen him read. Not in public, anyway. Admittedly, he's picking his nose, but his head is definitely encased in a book.

'He's always reading that old annual,' Felix informs me. 'I think he's got a crush on Kevin Keegan.'

'I'm sure he hasn't. Is this the book you stole from the school library?'

'Yes, so it's technically speaking, illegal goods. But then the O'Grady family feel more comfortable if they're surrounded by ill-gotten gains. I mean, Scott was telling me, two out of three generations of O'Gradys have been banged up in Brixton Prison.'

I wave at Scott across the field, and he eventually notices, and then waves back, still engrossed in his football annual.

'Take him for a run, Darren!' Felix notices one of the boys cutting in on a tackle.

I look at him.

'Where did you learn to say things like that, Saddleton?'

'Go hell for leather now, go hell for leather!' Felix yells, cupping both his hands over his mouth.

Then he turns to me and makes the familiar, excitable, flapping motion with his hands, just to reassure me.

'Your life has changed,' I say, after a minute.

'I should be so lucky, sweetie, I'm still waiting for Mr Right, you know. Or Mr Right Now, anyway.'

'You don't smoke. You're obsessed with football. You even think we stand a chance of winning the season.'

'No, I don't think, Mark. I know. I know Rivett Street will win the cup.'

'Felix, you sound like one of those cartoon strips in Scott's soccer annual. I mean' – I put on a voice, imitating him, 'I just know Rivett Street will win the cup! Hip hip hooray!'

'Oh, piss off,' Felix says, cutting me short.

'Well, come on, we don't stand a chance.'

Ignoring me, Felix steps onto the pitch and makes a weird movement with his arms, as if he was whipping an imaginary racehorse.

'Come on! Take him for a run! TAKE HIM FOR A RUN!'

I'm not about to let this drop, though. I coached this football team for over a year. I know the history of Rivett Street Junior – it never wins anything. And by the looks of things on this pitch now – with boys panting and going red in the face, even in a five-a-side match, and other players just giving up before they even manage a pass – nothing is going to change.

'Felix, just prepare yourself, okay? The standards in some of the other schools round here are pretty good. Some of them even have a proper fighting fund, you know, so the kids have real shin pads.'

'Shut up about the *Reader's Digests*.'

'I don't want you to be too disappointed,' I go on, hearing myself sounding like a prick, but charging on anyway, 'when they lose their first game.'

Felix stares at me.

'I'm afraid to say this, Mark, but I think your attempt to give up smoking might be bringing out a hitherto unseen side of your nature.'

'Like what?'

Felix shrugs irritably.

'You're behaving like a really boring and miserable bastard. Okay?'

'Oh, thanks.'

'We could get into a proper little bitch-fight about this team now,' Felix tosses his head back, 'but I'm not going to indulge, and neither are you, and besides I can tell that Scott O'Grady has stopped reading his football annual now, and is trying to hear every word.'

'I'm just a realist, that's all,' I say.

But something weird has happened here. Not so much the proper little bitch-fight that Felix speaks of, but something genuinely sour.

'You think you're a realist, some would say you're a cynic,' Felix says, watching the ball go into play.

'I never pretended otherwise.'

'You miss things by being so cynical, that's all,' Felix pouts, applauding as a boy who looks strangely like Noddy takes possession of the ball.

'Like what?'

'Oh, I don't know. Most of life. I mean, I'm not the only one who's noticed.'

'Oh, really?'

'Alison thinks you're not coming to the wedding, it's been so long since you've bothered talking to her. And you haven't sent her an RSVP to the invite.'

'Oh, for God's sake.'

'Tess sends you emails, you don't reply to them.'

'Oh. So there's been a three-way bitch session lately. Great.'

'No, not bitching,' Felix makes a face as a boy loses a tackle.

'What is it then? I mean, don't any of you fuckers – including the Christian fuckers – realise what I'm going through?'

Felix stops shouting at his team, and turns to face me.

'God forbid I should ever be so ghastly and predictable, as to tell you that Catherine is dead and buried, and that it's time to pull yourself together, but –'

'Yeah, great. Thanks for the sermon.'

'Although, Mark, if we all remember correctly, you were like this before Catherine died as well.'

Ignoring me now, Felix walks off to talk to Scott O'Grady, leaving me to watch four boys mess up a goal, and wonder if it isn't time for another piece of nicotine chewing gum.

Perhaps he's right. Maybe I am life-destroyingly cynical, or it's the absence of cigarettes, or I was born miserable – or something. But I've had Veronica, and then Troy in his white spray jacket, and now Felix, giving me little moral lectures about life, and I'm sick of it.

There's no way this team is going to win the season, either. Even with all the faith in the world. Sorry, Felix, but based on previous performances, they're not even going to make it past the whistle on the first practice match. And it's better if you're prepared for these things, before they happen.

twenty-three

The next day, I catch Alison in the car park, heading to class, and I decide to sort a few things out.

'Alison, have you got a moment?'

She is, predictably, stuffing the last of a Mars Bar into her face before returning to lessons.

'Mark! Of course.'

She is still wearing the purple contact lenses, so in direct sunlight, it's a bit like talking to an alien.

'I just wanted to apologise for not replying to your invitation. I mean, thanks for asking. I do want to go. And I've talked to Felix. We both want to get you something from the registry thing at Harrods.'

'Oh, that's lovely!'

Alison puts her hand on my arm, and at exactly the same moment, we both see that she has Mars Bar marks on her fingers.

'I've been a bit useless lately. I'm sorry,' I tell her.

'Don't be sorry,' she waves me away. 'Oh, by the way, has Tess told you her good news?'

'No. What's that?'

'She's back with Robin. So everything's back to normal.'

And with that, she flounces off across the car park, still cramming chocolate into her face, ready for another uplifting afternoon teaching kids how to twang rubber bands on shoe boxes.

Of course Alison thinks that Robin and Tess together is good news. She's in full-scale coupledom frenzy at the moment. She probably thinks I should be matched up with someone as well. And Felix. And Blount, in his hut.

It annoys me that I'm so annoyed though, both by her, and the news about Tess. I mean, why should I care? I haven't seen Tess for months, we were only ever friends – and that was only late in the piece, after Catherine was dead.

Tess has never promised me anything and I'm fairly sure I've never meant anything to her, and besides – she's on the other side of the world. Nevertheless, I decide, as I go in to tackle a music lesson, it's my turn to pick up the phone next. It might make up for those emails I haven't been replying to.

When I call, later that evening, though, she's out. Instead there is a message on her answering machine telling me that Robin and Tess aren't in right now, and could I please leave my number?

I slam the phone down. Hopefully they don't have one of those call trace things. That would be more embarrassment than I can stand, right now. And that's quite a lot.

The conversation with Tess has been rehearsed in my head, too, so it's a drag to have it turn into a non-event like this. And there's nothing on television to distract me, now. Just a programme about a hippo, or a police series, or a quiz show. John Peel isn't on the radio for hours, and I've read every single book in the house – at least twice.

So what now? Another of my record-breaking baths, maybe? Or should I just call Saddleton and force him to go to the pub with me? This last option seems best. If I get pissed enough, I may even be able to apologise to him, or he can apologise to me, for the other day.

And anyway, I want to defend myself, and point out my logic to him – that expecting the worst for Rivett Street only helps to stave off the inevitable bout of depression when they crawl out of the Bruise Street South game with a 5-0 result.

I rehearse the conversation with Felix to make sure I get this point absolutely right, too. And my argument runs along the lines of him being new to football, and not from this country – neither of which are his fault, but still – and thus unused to the peculiarly British phenomenon of healthy pessimism. If you're going to take any interest at all in football in this country, even at school level, you simply have to get real and expect the worst.

There's just no argument for behaving any other way. And I shall tell him so, as soon as we're in the pub, and I've had a few.

Then the phone rings. Tess?

Yes, definitely Tess. And once again, I hear her voice and instantly feel better.

'Your number came up on the display,' she says, 'sorry, I've literally just come home.'

'So you're living in the same place?'

'Yeah. For the moment. Thought you might have heard. Robin and I have decided to rent an apartment together. A compromise between the ritzy part of Manhattan and the grotty part of the Bronx where I live. Like, the ultimate New York compromise.'

'Congratulations.'

A pause.

'Do you mean that?'

'Um – No. Look, don't interrogate me, okay? All I've had this month is Veronica, Felix, your mates at Crosslink, the whole thing – all on my case about one thing or another.' And as I say this, I realise I'm whining, just as I used to do with Catherine, in the hopes that she would feel sorry for me.

'Veronica is Catherine's sister, right?' Tess asks.

'Yup. And she's gone into therapy since Catherine died. So I had this thing the other night where she wanted me to sort my life out. Just like her.'

'Hmmm. But were the Crosslink people really on your back too?'

'Well – No. I was exaggerating. I mean, they're sending Felix little notes, and he even got a book in the post, but no, they've laid off.'

'Well, that's good.'

'Oh yeah, it's the best thing that's happened to me all year – not being converted by a church group.'

There are certain phone conversations where you wish you were pissed, so you'd have the balls to ask the hard questions, and this is one of them.

'Tess, can I ask you something?'

'Ask away.'

'What's going on with you and Robin? I mean, tell me to shut up and mind my own business, but weren't you a virgin the last time I spoke to you, and wasn't he giving up Christianity, and . . . I dunno. I get confused.'

'Okay,' Tess takes a deep breath. 'I am no longer a virgin.'

Even though we are on the phone, I still feel myself doing something that hasn't happened for ages – I go bright red.

'I shouldn't even be having this conversation with you,' I manage to mumble.

'No, it's okay,' Tess says lightly, 'we're friends. You know?'

'Well, if it's any consolation, I can tell you, in all confidence, that since Catherine died I've become a born-again virgin. I mean, no sex, none whatsoever, for months. And I don't expect to have any in the near future, either – like, the next five years.'

And then Tess laughs at this – laughs and laughs, all the way down the line from America – so I don't feel quite so bad, and I can stop blushing.

'Robin persuaded me to see sense,' she says again. 'It took a long time, and a few long nights of debate, but – I don't know. For lots and lots of reasons, I just decided it was time.'

'So now what?'

'I don't know. I guess I'm just not as radical as I once was, you know? I mean, I believe in God. I still pray. But I'm not in church three times a week, and I'm not buying into the "one flesh" theory any more.'

'I don't know what that means and I'm not sure I want to.'

'Well, I won't bore you with the details,' Tess laughs.

Then she says something I hadn't expected.

'Actually, you had a lot to do with everything,' she says.

'Me?'

'You probably didn't realise it, but just having you around made me realise there was more to life.'

'More to life than Faith Lift?'

'A lot of things. I mean, Pam and Tina told me about the Felix speech you made. And you know what? I meant what I said in the email. Troy is a prat. And I think they're all prats for being curious about Felix's sexuality – as if it's any kind of issue.'

There is a slight American twang in her voice, now, for the first time.

'So you're a non-believer now. Eh? Is that what's happened?'

'I still wear a cross around my neck,' Tess says simply. 'Despite everything you might think or assume, because I gave up Crosslink. I mean – it's complicated. Jesus always is.'

I decide to change the subject, quickly.

'So this is it, then, with Robin. He's the one?'

'Oh, piss off, Mark,' Tess laughs, and it's the first time I've heard her ever say anything remotely four-letter-wordish, in all the time I've known her.

'Well, Robin's bloody lucky,' I say at last. And it immediately sounds wrong, and inappropriate, and I get embarrassed about it.

'Why, thankyou,' Tess says, putting on a silly, *Gone With The Wind*, Miss Scarlett voice to turn it all into a joke.

When I put the phone down, though, I can still hear her voice saying certain things – that I had a lot to do with everything, that having me around made her realise there was more to her life.

And now, Robin's going to be the beneficiary of all that, the rich bastard. So once again, God, I really have to hand it to you. I could have ended up with the last thirtysomething virgin in South London, a perfectly nice woman who also seems to be the only person in England who actually cares what happens to me, and I didn't. Instead, I'm now here in this house, alone, with photos of my dead girlfriend, a lot of Tupperware containers in the freezer, an invitation to the Head's wedding, and nothing on the television except a hippo. In short, another spectacular performance from God, and one that might even classify as a world-beater.

twenty-four

Why give up now? If you're on a roll, feeling sorry for yourself, you may as well go all the way. There seems to be a female culture of eating designer chocolate ice-cream at times like this, and watching something like four episodes of *Ally McBeal*, straight, in a row (though why that would make you feel any better, I don't know.) For men, there's really only one time-honoured solution, and that's to hold up a bar somewhere and get drunk, but frankly, I can't take the hangovers.

I suppose part of the problem, at least now, is delayed grieving. Or delayed mourning. Or whatever you want to call it. I'm not sure if this year I'm having so far fits any category, really.

Is it as bad as the very bad year, when I was eighteen and like Scott O'Grady, I couldn't see the point of going on? Not really. I do, after all, manage to get out of bed in the mornings. I can still read a book, like Bill Bryson or something, and laugh at it. I can still see a reason to teach, and a reason to go on living in this house, in London.

One thing I do know, and this was partly learned during my crap eighteenth year – very few people are interested in rescue missions. Drawing attention to yourself, by sulking, or staying in bed all day, or generally being a miserable bastard, actually achieves nothing except a bigger, emptier vacuum. People ring up less, not more, when you're suffering in an obvious way. The thing is, to do it silently. Secretly even. That just about keeps things in check.

Tess is unusual, in that Tess is the only person I can think of who did anything out of the ordinary after Catherine died. She signed an en masse card from the staff, along with Blount and various other Rivett Street fixtures. But, when the cremation was over, and the sympathy cards had started tailing off, there was a kind of lull. A lull where nobody knew what to say, or what to do – and especially what to do with me. The night she dedicated a song to me, sung in such an incredible way, has to rank as the only really important gesture anyone made.

The rest of it is expected, after all. The wreaths, and the hands on the shoulder (I think I was in danger of shoulder erosion at the funeral). The attempts at finding words, when there aren't any, because if you say something ordinary about someone dead, it sounds ridiculous, and if you try to reach for the skies by reciting lines of poetry, everyone thinks you're faking it.

So – what Tess did, maybe on the spur of the moment, maybe not – actually meant something. It's only now that she's gone, both to Robin and to another country, that I really understand what was going on at school, as well.

It would humiliate me to know this for certain, but I'm fairly sure Tess saw Alison and Felix one day, and had a quiet word. Because – don't ask me how she found out that my life without Catherine was basically no life at all – but she did. And I think she quietly decided to do something about it.

Consequently, this was the year that something almost unheard of happened. I made two new friends. Friends I moan about, and in Alison's case, friends I don't entirely understand or see eye-to-eye with – but still. I'm going to Alison's wedding and I'd say I'm even fairly proud of my friendship with Felix.

Whatever anyone else says, when they're slagging me off

these days, they can't fault me on my New Man-ness. Felix Saddleton has precisely one heterosexual male friend in all of England, and it's me.

All the more reason, then, to turn him down when he rings up later and asks me if I want to go to the Hair Bear Club.

'Felix, it may have escaped your attention but I have no hair. Especially on my head. So why are you asking me to join a club full of hairy men? And anyway, you know. I'm straight.'

'Oh, go on with you!' he tuts, affecting a camp Irish accent. 'What else are you doing right now, that I can't persuade you out?'

'For a start I've been lying here on the couch with a good book,' I lie, although I have actually been lying face down on the couch feeling sorry for myself and generally mooching about. It's not the kind of day outside where you want to be doing things, anyway. For some reason unknown to the BBC weather man, the temperature's plunged and I'm back to wearing two pairs of socks indoors.

'It's only a bar night,' Felix goes on, 'you don't have to get in a spa or anything. We're just taking over a club in the West End.'

'Oh. Okay. Well that sounds slightly better.'

'Drinks are on me, as well.'

'Wow. Well. Thanks. On your salary as well.'

Felix is doing something that I can't remember too many people in my life ever doing. He's making it up to me. We've had a fairly bad stand-off at his football practice, I was half to blame, and he's now trying to make it up to me. What a novelty. I mean, normally in these situations, the awkward politeness goes on for days. Months. With me, it's even been known to go on for years. So, how can I say no to him, now?

'Will there be any people like me there?' I ask.

'No, just wall-to-wall poofs, some of them in leather shorts with unfeasibly high voices. Is that a problem?'

'Not at all. Do I have to wear anything special?'

'Only a butt-plug harness and a lot of coconut oil on your thighs,' Felix snorts, then amuses himself by singing some horrible Village People song very loudly, in my ear.

Then something occurs to me. Something seriously worrying.

'Felix.'

'Yes?'

'I hope this isn't off the mark. But you do know – how can I put this? I have no interest.'

'Interest in what?'

'Oh, God. Accepting a transfer from West Ham so I can go and play for another team. Halfway through the season. With no prior experience or enthusiasm for said team.'

'Oh!' Felix guffaws, genuinely surprised.

'It's just that I seem to be giving out these signals lately, which invite people to convert me – to something. So I just wanted to be sure.'

'No conversion at all,' Felix assures me.

He eventually calms down and stops sniggering, and I take the number of the place – it's up some dark alleyway in Soho – and I think about taking the tube, then I give in and call a local mini-cab firm instead. My driver both looks like George Formby and seems to have his taste in music.

We drive, to Soho, while something which sounds like an army of banjos twiddling through the speakers, rings through the car, to the point where I'm gritting my teeth.

'Do you like the banjo?' the driver says finally, at the end, when he's dropping me just off Wardour Street.

'Yeah, I love it,' I smile politely, not giving him a tip. He should know. I'm English. All his customers are English. We're not able to ask him to turn the music down. It's not in our nature.

The rain is now coming down in sheets, to the point where McDonald's containers are sailing, like ships, down the gutter.

I have chosen to wear, for this – my first indoctrination into the world of rampant and unabashed sauciness, as Felix puts it – a pair of my baggiest jeans, a jumper, which I wore to my first job interview at Rivett Street, a pair of boots, which Catherine once described as my tough-guy boots, and, not that it matters, the oldest and holiest of my Marks and Spencer underpants, bought decades ago by my mother.

Should I be strip-searched tonight, they will find nary a Calvin Klein jockstrap nor a trace of men's cologne upon me. In fact, I've even taken my watch off. Just in case it's giving out the wrong signals.

As I walk down Wardour Street and turn off to the left, I see that Felix's Hair Bear bar is actually a normal bar – in fact I think I may have even staggered in there once, in my wasted youth.

After the obligatory check at the door, and the stumble through a pitch-black tunnel of stairs, the first thing that greets me is a stuffed gorilla. Wearing a giant, studded codpiece and a biker's cap, which wouldn't have looked out of place on Freddie Mercury.

Suddenly, a man runs in front of me, bollock-naked, with a fringed lampshade on his head, yelling 'Come back, you naughty, naughty man!' as another man, equally hairy, but fortunately less naked, runs the other way.

'Caper, caper, caper,' Felix complains, sneaking up to me on the other side. Thank God he's arrived before me.

'What?' I suppose I'm still recovering from seeing the second hairy man front-on.

'All they do is caper. They frolic and they caper, and they never even buy you a drink.'

'Oh well.'

I put my hand in my pocket, suddenly embarrassed that Felix has offered to pay for me all night, and that might be on his mind – but he immediately produces a fifty-pound note with a flourish, and waves me away.

'I'm going to get them. My shout. It's the least I can do after everything you've just seen.'

I nod.

'I'll go to the bar, you follow me. You can stand in an alcove, if you like. They're very comforting places.'

As I wander in behind Felix, I'm reminded of other social occasions where I haven't known anyone, or even fully understood what is going on. A rave I went to with one of Catherine's mad friends from the travel agency. A fancy-dress party when I was eleven, and I didn't realise you had to dress up. And a rollerskating rink disco, when I was fifteen, and I didn't know any of the songs, and my rollerskates didn't fit, and I was skating in the wrong direction.

I follow Felix's suggestion, and stand in the alcove, as far as I can get from the group of men huddled in there, all hunched around one candle on a table. One of them is smoking a pipe.

Another is wearing a monocle. Another, I realise is actually a woman, dressed as a man. Or is it the other way round?

My George Formby mini-cab driver would be right at home here, because there's plenty of banjo music playing through the speakers. Me? I feel about as comfortable as I did at the rave, when the bpm's got too much for me, and I had to go and lie down.

I know the vast majority of gay men lead a life that is nothing like this. I'm aware that preferring men to women doesn't necessarily involve farting around in spa baths and doing your best impersonation of Anthony Blanche in *Brideshead Revisited*, or celebrating the fact that you were born with a hairy back. Nevertheless, the particular part of Gay World that I've wandered into, thanks to Felix, is somewhere between Dante's *Inferno* and Fellini's *Satyricon*. And maybe *Planet of the Apes*, as well. And it feels weird.

A man in a chimpanzee mask, wearing a tweed three-piece suit, approaches the alcove. When I move out of the way so he can sit down at the table, though, he actually moves closer to me.

'I just wanted to say how extremely nice and original your costume is,' he barks, through the mask, and over the sound of the banjos.

'Very funny.'

'I haven't seen you before, have I?' the chimp yells.

I shake my head, preparing to shout back, but then the banjo music is suddenly turned down.

'I'm here with Felix Saddleton,' I point a hand at the bar, 'so I'm here on false pretences.'

'No, you're not very hairy, are you?' says the chimp man.

'And I'm not really keen on spa baths either,' I explain.

'Oh, we lost the spa baths,' the chimp man waves a disappointed hand. 'The management of the Pimlico establishment took a very dim view of the Hair Bears after a plumber had to be called in.'

'I can imagine.'

'This is the temporary HQ,' the chimp man explains. 'At least until the Bears ultimately get banned again. By the way, I don't suppose you can put this cigarette in my mouth, can you?' He points to his giant, grinning, pink plastic lips.

'Not without setting you on fire,' I apologise. 'And anyway, I'm trying to give up. If I do that I'll probably want one too.'

The chimp man shrugs, and goes to ask one of the men at the candlelit table. In the meantime, I scan the bar for Felix, wondering if and when I'm going to get my drink. It occurs to me that the alcove isn't quite the private haven Felix thought it was. If anything, I seem to be drawing them in, not escaping their attention.

After another long wait, Felix returns with a tray.

'I got you three double Scotches, and me four Brandy Alexanders, so I won't have to go back to the bar,' he pants.

It's hard to see what he's wearing in the candlelight, but it seems to be a cricketing jumper, which wouldn't have looked out of place on Haircut 100, a pair of women's sandals, and a kilt.

'I think you should wear that to Alison's wedding,' I tell him.

But Felix's attention has already wandered, in the direction of someone – fulfilling all his fantasies – who really does seem to be drinking from the Cup of Adonis. He has sprayed himself with gold paint, and he's wearing a toga, which I imagine might be Felix's idea of the ultimate outfit.

'Back in a sec,' he mutters, looking distracted, and putting the tray on the floor.

Meanwhile, Chimp Man has disappeared too, leaving me with a lethal amount of alcohol and nobody to talk to.

Edging back even further into the alcove, I watch the party unfold before me. It's quite interesting – because, when you're not actually in one, you get a chance to see what a load of bollocks a party actually is.

People are being so obvious, for a start. All the normal body language, or lack of it, that you see during the day goes out of the window. Allowing an extra fifty per cent hand flapping, on account of the personalities of those present, there is still way too much gesturing and oohing and aahing, and far too many people trying extremely hard to have a good time. Or, as Felix pointed out the other day, am I in danger of being a miserable bastard again?

People are sending text messages to each other, and I automatically check my own, picking up a glass of Scotch from the tray on the floor at the same time. But I don't know what I was expecting, because there's nothing there. So I check the football scores anyway, and I adjust the volume, and I muck around with the ring tone, and then I change the way the date looks.

My God. The date.

I realise, with a jolt, that it is Catherine's birthday. September 10th. If she was still alive, we would be going out for dinner tonight. Or maybe spending a quiet night at home. Or we might have booked a ticket on Eurostar.

I finish the Scotch and pick up another one. Is this what it's come to really, that I can crawl my way through the whole year, and then forget her birthday?

Around me, the man with the fringed lampshade on his head makes a reappearance, shrieking as yet more strange men chase him around the room. The guys at the table – including the one who could be a woman – look up, then go back to their conversation. The banjo music has been turned up. And there's still no sign of Felix, who has disappeared with his Adonis.

'That's it,' I say to nobody in particular, finishing my second drink. 'I'm going.' It's only when I get to the top of the stairs, though, that I notice the Chimp Man has been watching me, and following me all the way. Incongruously, he is carrying my drinks tray, which I have left behind on the floor.

'It seems a shame to waste these,' he offers, holding out the drinks.

'You have them.'

A pause.

'Oh, all right then,' he gives in.

And the chimp takes off his mask, revealing a bloke who doesn't look all that different to me. Not that this is unusual in London, of course, where every other man of a certain age wears a black coat and has a number-one haircut, but still.

'I'm Gary,' he says.

'Hi, I'm Mark, I'm just going.'

'I gathered.'

He lights up a cigarette in the corridor, and offers me one, which amazingly, I manage to refuse. Then I give in and accept.

'My girlfriend's birthday would have been today,' I tell him. A complete stranger. The Scotch must be sinking in.

'She left you? Mine left me.'

I realise, with a start, that he must be straight. The only other straight man in the place, probably.

'She didn't leave me, she died.'

Gary – Chimp Man – shakes his head, making a face, as he puts out the match.

'How did she die?'

'She had a car accident.'

'God.'

He pauses, and takes my third Scotch from the tray.

'My brother died six months ago,' he goes on. 'He had AIDS.'

'He did?'

'These are all his friends here. The Hair Bears. They did everything for him. Cooked, cleaned. Drove him to the clinic.'

'I'm sorry.'

'Yeah, you should be, it was a shit way to go. But anyway' – Gary the chimp nods his head in the direction of the banjo music, 'these are all decent chaps. He didn't die without friends. You know? And they throw great parties.'

I nod.

'Anyway,' Gary shakes my hand, 'pleasure to meet you, I hope I'll see you at a Hair Bear function again.'

'Maybe,' I tell the truth for a change.

And with that, he finishes the last Scotch on the tray, stubs out his cigarette, puts his chimp mask back on, and leaves me to it.

And how does he leave me, on Catherine's birthday? Standing in the corridor of a strange club in Soho, surrounded by naked men and one stuffed gorilla in a biker's cap, wondering how the hell I'm going to get a mini-cab back home.

twenty-five

Everyone has their own version of September 11. This is mine.

I take the day off school, because it's the day after Catherine's birthday, and I haven't slept all night, and I just can't face it.

I watch most of the housewife TV available in the morning, then I eat the last of my parent's pre-packaged spaghetti bolognaise at about twelve, then go to bed with earplugs in, because the people over the other side of the street are doing their house up, with jackhammers.

I sleep soundly until about five, when I wander down to make myself a cup of tea, switch on the news, and see that the world has gone mad.

And then, about ten minutes later, I get a call from Tess. She is in tears, and I can hardly understand her.

'Oh God, Mark, thank God you're home –'

'Are you all right? I've been watching all this and worrying about you.'

'No. No. Sorry –'

And then she hangs up.

I hit speed dial in a panic, and kneel on the floor by the phone books. The lines are busy. I keep watching the TV, showing me the same picture of the second plane, crashing into the second tower, again and again, once normally, and once in slow motion, and I hit speed dial for the second time.

Still engaged.

'Fuck.'

I call the operator, after going to all the wrong pages at the front of the phone book, and then get the same message that everyone else seems to be getting.

'Due to the present situation in New York, there is heavy line congestion on all international calls. Please try again later.'

I hit speed dial again. I go back to the TV set, look at Tony Blair, look at George Bush, then come back to the phone. Speed dial, speed dial. Nothing.

Then the phone rings and I leap on it. It's Alison.

'Mark, it's so awful.'

'I know.'

'You must get in touch with Tess, she's been trying to call you.'

'She did. And now I fucking can't get through to her.'

'Robin was in the building.'

'In one of the towers?'

'His company had a whole floor.'

'Which floor?'

'Not sure. High up.'

'Oh, my God.'

'Mark, I'm shaking.'

'Me too.'

'We must do something. I don't know what to do!'

And then I hear the Head, saying something I can't make out in the background, and she asks me to hold on.

'Alison?'

'Yup, sorry, I think we're going out. Going to a friend's place. Someone who knows someone who worked in there. Can I call you back later?'

And she hangs up, so I hit speed dial again, hoping against hope to find Tess, but like a lot of things today, there is no hope.

I look through the curtains, to see if anyone else is on the street, anyone I can talk to. Normally at this time of night, only half the lights are on, but almost everyone is at home now, televisions flickering through the windows.

I click through the television stations. Comment after comment. Will the US become more insular, now this has happened? How many people do they think were in the World Trade Centre at the time of the attack? (Surely not 20,000 – oh please, not that.) Was Nostradamus right? Is the London Underground safe?

It has that same Princess Diana feeling, that same unreal feeling, that I remember from when Catherine and I sat here, in this room, day after day, going through every single factoid, every single picture or commentary about a commentary, as if our lives depended on it.

I wasn't lying to Alison. I do feel shaky. To be honest, I'm not sure I can take so much death all in one hit. All in one year.

I call my parents, and my father answers the phone.

'We've left three messages with you,' he says.

'I'm sorry. I've been at home all day. I've had the earplugs in.'

'It's unbelievable, isn't it?'

'Yeah. Tess. My friend Tess – her boyfriend was in there.'

This is probably the first time I've ever referred to Robin as Tess's boyfriend. And I realise my heart is aching for her. Literally, physically, aching for her.

'Tess from the school?'

My father is shocked.

'He worked for one of the big banks in New York. My other friend, Alison, spoke to her, and she said he was in there.'

'Does she have any information? Has he survived?'

'I don't know, Dad. I can't get through. Tess rang me, and then she had to hang up, and I called back, and now I can't get through. All I've got to go on is what Alison knows.'

A pause.

'Do you want to come over here? Better than being on your own.'

'Actually, no, thanks Dad. I want to be here just in case she rings again. You know?'

'Well, if you change your mind later, we'll be up all night.

Chops is very upset about it.'

'Okay.'

I put the phone down, and mute the TV. The pictures of New York on the screen now make it look impossibly bright and sunny – almost cheerful. Maybe Tess will turn up on TV in a minute. Who knows? They're interviewing people who've lost people. Perhaps that's where she's gone now, after my call, down to the hospitals, where they're all waiting and hoping.

The phone rings. It's her.

'Please, Tess, please just stay on the line, I've been trying to get through to you.'

'I've called Mum and Dad,' she sobs, 'and you know, now I'm calling you again. Out of everyone I know, I'm calling you!'

'It's okay, it's okay,' I try to comfort her. She sounds half exasperated, half angry with herself – and with me. And she also sounds, not surprisingly, in total, wall-eyed shock. I let her cry for a while.

'The reason you're calling me, and I'm glad you're doing it, is because I've just had this happen too,' I explain in a rush. 'Not that I'm saying Robin is dead, because he may not be, and not that this is even close to anything I went through with Catherine. But still. I know this. I know a bit what it's like. And you know that too. So that's why you're calling me, and I'm glad you have.'

'You heard about Robin,' she says, uncomprehendingly.

'Alison told me. God, Tess, I'm so sorry.'

A pause, while she gets herself together.

It's no good. I can't deal with Tess telling me this, and the pictures on the TV screen, at the same time. It's like having massive tragedy in stereo. I turn the TV off, and rearrange myself on the floor. Not that I've noticed, but I've been kneeling the whole time I've been on the phone, to Alison, Dad and Tess, and have pins and needles in both legs.

'It's okay,' I tell Tess. 'It's okay, it's okay.'

Why am I no good at times like this? Not that I've ever had a time like this before. Tess takes another huge gulp.

'I tried to get into the church. When it was happening.'

'Yes.'

'The doors were locked. I ran downtown, to another church

I know. It was closed. I had nowhere to even pray.'

She cries herself back to calmness again.

A stupid thought pops into my head. This call must be costing her money. Isn't that what you normally say, when someone is on the phone to you from New York?

I can hear Tess blowing her nose, then she comes back to the phone.

'Have you got people looking after you there?' I ask.

'Yes.'

'Can I do anything for you?'

'No. No, I don't think so. Thanks.'

'Did you find an open church, in the end?'

And this, above all other things I say in this conversation, makes her so upset that all I hear for the next few minutes is the sound of her howling, long distance.

I remember that when Catherine used to cry like this, which wasn't very often, there was a kind of weird pattern to it. Same with Donna. There's a rush at the start, like a dam being unplugged, and then a kind of stormy bit, when you don't know what's going to happen next, and then a kind of tiredness, or calm, when they just go through the motions with you. This is the bit that Tess gets to next.

'My friend spoke off the record to one of the cops down at the site. On the record, they are saying there's a decent chance of survival. Off the record, none, zilch.'

'I'm so sorry.'

'I'm not going to give up hope because I can't give up hope. I know this has happened for a reason.'

And part of me feels like screaming then, no Tess, nothing happens for a reason. Not Catherine, not Robin, not anything, don't believe that, because if you do, it will screw you up worse than anything else . . .

I suddenly think of something. 'Don't watch the television, Tess.'

'I have to. In case anything else happens. You know, where do we run to next?'

'You'll hear it from someone else if there's a problem. Leave the radio on. Look, you're going to be fine. It's just a scary day, okay? New York is going to be fine.'

She pauses, as I realise how little I know about anything, in all my dumb ignorance and arrogance. New York's going to be fine? It would serve me right if the terrorists blew up Clapham Common next.

'Just don't watch TV,' I say. 'Okay?'

She lets this sink in for a minute.

'Okay.'

'And can you talk about Robin?'

'Yes.'

'Have you been in touch with the police, with all the hospitals, with the emergency centre?'

'Yes. Of course, Mark. Since this morning. I have no news. And the bank people are being great. You know? If there's any news, the bank will get it first, then call me. That's the drill.'

One of the things which is only just starting to sink in, with me too, is the fact that Tess is also now directly at risk. Whatever crap I'm saying to her now, that New York is fine, is probably more to reassure myself than her.

Because, as someone just said on the TV before I switched it off, there could be any number of lunatics ready to drop a bomb, or hijack another plane, or ram four trucks into another skyscraper. And Tess is there. In Manhattan. In that place I remember fuzzily from a packed weekend trip at the age of 21.

To be honest, I don't even remember seeing the Twin Towers on that trip. I probably did, because a mate and I went up the Empire State Building, but my memories of New York, like most people's, are all Times Square and cheap Levis.

'Tess, whereabouts are you exactly?'

'I'm staying with friends, on the Lower East Side.'

'So that's pretty close to the action, right?'

And I immediately regret using this phrase, because it all sounds wrong, but I let it go.

'I'm staying over the 14th street divide,' Tess explains. 'You know, that's where they've put down the police line. So I'm just there. There are hospitals taking people all over New York, but a lot of the people from the towers are ending up in downtown hospitals, because they're so close. So, I'm staying put. I want to be here, if he comes in. If he comes in, any time soon.'

'Yup.'

If he comes in. Jesus. The towers went down like dominoes. And I know they are digging, through the night, but when and if they find Robin, what kind of man will he be?

'Who is with you, Tess?'

'Robin's old flatmate, Benny, he works for the bank too, from the midtown office, so he knows what's going on. People from school, I've got my friend Sue with me, too. She wants to give me brandy!'

And Tess manages a half laugh.

'Tell Sue she's on the money.'

'I miss you, Mark.'

'I miss you too.'

'I wish you were here. Do you remember when I ran into you, after Catherine had died, and you were going for a walk, and you were trying to get some peace and quiet?'

'Yes.'

It's not a question, though, just some kind of confirmation for her – but of what, I don't know.

As we finally hang up the call, however, I do know one thing. When I said I missed her, I was giving myself permission to feel something – and that's going to take me all the way to somewhere that means a) no sleep b) no sleep and c) I just don't bloody know any more.

I think of Tess, hearing the news, maybe even hearing the plane go into the first tower, with a huge bang, and the panic on the streets, and knowing Robin was trapped in there.

And I think of her running to her church, and finding the doors locked, because it's 9 a.m. or something on a Tuesday morning, and the people who run the place think prayer should be kept on a timetable.

A few minutes later, Felix rings.

'I have an insatiable desire to suddenly talk about, and watch, football,' he says.

'Nothing but football. Isn't it odd?'

'It hits us all in different ways.'

'I know about two people in there. Do you know anyone?'

'Only Robin. Although I guess I didn't really know him.'

Then it occurs to me that Felix hasn't heard, Felix doesn't know.

231

'Tess's Robin?'

'Yes.'

'Because he worked for a bank,' Felix says, letting it sink in. 'Oh God, I was worried about her the whole time I've been watching this, and I never even thought about him. But of course – half the people in there were with banks. Oh God.'

'She's called. She's okay. She has people looking after her. She's staying in a flat near all the hospitals, near the police barricade.'

'I can't believe it.'

'Neither can I. But we have to.'

Felix starts to sob, funny little snuffles that make his voice wobble, and then he calms down again.

'Sorry. It's the shock. Christ, poor Tess.'

'Yes.'

'Do you think he's dead?'

'I don't know, Felix. I honestly don't know. He hasn't been found. It's chaos down there apparently, people just ran for their lives. She said they've checked all the hospitals and police stations, no luck so far. But, it's only the end of their day there. I mean, there's still a few hours to go before they give up for the night.'

'Yup,' Felix sniffs again, repeating that he can't believe it.

'So who knows,' I go on, 'Maybe Robin will be one of the lucky ones. Maybe he just ran out of there, or he fell and lost his memory, forgot his name, he could be in hospital with a bandage on his head.'

'Yeah.'

But we both know I'm imagining things. And don't ask me how you know when someone has gone, you just know. It's like, the millisecond before the police managed their next sentence with me, after knocking on the door about Catherine – well, I knew she was dead.

'Which floor was Robin on?'

'She didn't say. High up, I think.'

'Tess will need a miracle.'

'Well, yeah. She deserves one.'

And as Felix and I make our excuses and get off the phone, so we can crawl back to the TV again – him to distract himself with football, me to pore over all the shots of Manhattan – I think about miracles.

From a scientific perspective, they are just blips on the graph. Abormalities that, according to your perspective, are lucky – or not lucky. The mechanism in nature which may have seen Robin placed neatly in Tower Two at the time of the attack, is really not that different from the mechanism which might also have saved him.

He may have decided not to go to work this morning. They might have stayed at home for a shag – best not to think about that – making Robin late for work. Enough time, in fact, to see the first plane hit the first tower, and turn and run. Instead, everything went the other way. And now he's probably dead.

I know, somewhere in his house in Forest Gate, Noel D. Jupiter will be praying, or lighting a candle. And I can see, from the television, that candles are already appearing in Manhattan – in broad daylight, in churches, even outside fire stations.

I have no candles in the house, except for the emergency ones from the supermarket I use for power cuts – and I think Catherine and I raided them a long time ago, in a pathetic attempt to have a romantic evening at home. That's me all over, really, suggesting to Catherine that cheap paraffin candles would do for dinner.

Do you need candles to pray, though? I shouldn't think so. And so I make a sad attempt to clasp my hands together, and think of Tess – just concentrate on her, really, willing Robin to crawl out alive.

And this is how I sit on the couch for the next three hours, hands clasped, watching the news stream into my room from all over the world – the Afghanistan border, where the aid workers are already thinking about getting out, the Lower East Side of Manhattan, and London again – where they're interviewing five American men – all in tears, all of whom have heard bad news.

When I was at college, we were taught about the butterfly effect. Edward Lorenz spotted it when the first electronic computers modelled air flow, in an attempt to forecast the weather. Predictably, the weather was unpredictable. And everyone thought, the fault might be in the computer. It wasn't, though. It was in life itself, a chaotic system where the tiniest disturbance, like the flap of a butterfly's wing, can affect the course of a hurricane.

The butterfly effect of this horrendous thing, today, will no doubt be equivalent to a million hurricanes by the time the year is over. Or even next year. And it doesn't really matter what you believe, or even who you believe in, it's already begun.

twenty-six

Six weeks later, Tess comes home. September and October have been chronic months for both of us. Her, for obvious reasons. Me, for less obvious ones.

By email and by phone, I have now been sharing the last few weeks with Tess, from the little peace protest she joined at Union Square, to the day that her friend Sue spent in Kinko's at Astor Place, photocopying posters of Robin, in the hope that someone, anyone, might have seen him alive – somewhere. They spent all day on 6th Avenue sticky-taping them to shop windows.

Over the past few weeks, too, I've shared the night that Tess got really pissed, for the first time since she was a teenager, and picked up a rock from the gutter, and threw it at the church that had closed its doors on the morning of September 11. And I shared the day she was in a delicatessen in Greenwich Village, and thought she saw someone who looked like Robin, with his back to her, in the queue at the cash register. Then there was the BBC camera crew who wanted to interview her, because she was English, who she let into the apartment, then had to send away again, because she couldn't even face the first question.

I have been trying to teach my classes, to help Felix out with his football team, to get on with life again, and to be normal, since September 11. But then nobody in London has been normal. Half the teachers at Rivett Street no longer want to catch the tube, because they're terrified of attacks on the Underground, so bicycles have started appearing in the car park for the first time in years.

And now, the latest news. Both Tess and Robin's family have accepted that Robin has gone, as the authorities now recommend, and a memorial service has been arranged for him in his parents' village, in Gloucestershire. And Tess has decided to come back to London as well – permanently. The Head says she can even come back to Rivett Street if she wants to.

My last conversation with her was a few days ago, at Newark Airport.

'The queue is going round the block,' she told me, 'it's going to take me two hours to check in for this flight, and even then we're only going to Detroit. They're taking nail clippers out of people's suitcases and everything.'

'And then home to London, after Detroit?'

'Yeah.' A big sigh. 'It's one of those cheap flights that takes you halfway round the world. I'll call you when I get in, okay?'

It's been two days now, though – and I've been counting the hours admittedly – and I've heard nothing. And I don't want to call, because I'm not that kind of bloke.

'Oh, for the love of Ada, call,' Felix says, when he drops into the staffroom late on Wednesday afternoon.

'No. She's with his parents. Probably. I know what that stuff's like. Relatives, memorial services, priests. She'll call me when she's ready.'

'Oh well,' Felix sighs, 'there's no telling you. Anyway – I'm off to have a look at our goalie. He's looking rather podgy since his mother started putting P-P-P-Penguins into his school lunchbox, and I'm concerned about his mobility. Or lack of, anyway.'

'Right you are then.'

'And I'm pleased to tell you I haven't had a fag now for *weeks*,' Felix smirks.

'Oh, just go away and coach some football, will you?' I wave him away.

The next day, when I've still heard nothing from Tess, I finally give in and find a public phone box, just near the school gates, and make the call. My posh new mobile has died, just like the first one. And I suppose, if I had more time to analyse the failure of all this communications equipment around me, I might ponder if my amazing psychic energy field – at least according to John Smith – might have anything to do with it. Nevertheless, life has to go on. And this call, of all calls, is one that can't wait.

'Come and visit,' Tess says, when I ring.

'I can't.'

'Please. Just come and stay. There's a pub in the village, where they're having the service, they have rooms you can rent for the night. I'm finding it – oh, I dunno. I'm not coping with it all, Mark. It would be good to see a familiar face.'

'Where's the village again?'

And she runs through all the finer points of the motorway, and the map with me, but it's all essentially pointless. I'm asking out of politeness, not because I have any intention of being around for Robin's memorial service.

'There are some people from Crosslink here,' Tess sighs.

'But isn't that a good thing?'

'I've changed. Life has changed. Everything has changed. I'll have to explain it later.'

'Right.'

'And you know what it's like, going through a funeral.'

Well, yes, I do – except this isn't a funeral, and there's no coffin.

'Can you tell me something? Tess? This has just occurred to me.'

'What?'

'Is there anyone, among Robin's family and friends, who thinks he may still be alive?'

'Yes. Got it in one. How did you know?'

And Tess sobs down the phone, as I put more money in the

237

slot, because I don't know what else to do.

'Shit. That can't be easy.'

'His aunt, she won't give up, and she keeps on hassling me, asking me questions.'

'Right.'

'It's not her fault, she's old and doddery, but Robin was her favourite nephew. You know? And somehow, it's all coming back on me. You know, she asked me why I didn't just run up there, as soon as the first plane hit? Why I just didn't run sixty blocks and go right into the building to save him?'

'I'm sorry, Tess.'

'Please, Mark, I feel I've got to know you over the past weeks, a lot better, I don't know. Through the emails and stuff. This may make no sense to you, and you may even hate the idea, but I really would love to have you here.'

'Okay.' I mean, how can I say no? Okay. Okay.

Tess gives me the map directions again, and I tell her I'll be there as quickly as I can on Friday night, and she agrees to book me a room at the local pub, and suddenly, it seems, I'm really going. To a memorial service for Robin, who I hardly knew, who'd probably hate me if he was still alive. As Felix frequently says, you wouldn't read about it.

And there is, of course, the life-after-death element of Robin I have to consider as well. Especially after all I've been through. But I try not to think about it. Some things are just too hard.

I hire a car straight after school on Friday, and drive up. Gloucestershire isn't exactly on my list of best-known bits of England, but at least I manage to get through the worst of rush-hour traffic on the way, even enjoying the long-forgotten sensation of driving along with the radio blaring. There's a Kinks special on the radio, with songs I haven't heard for years, and I even find myself singing along to *Autumn Almanac* as I join the traffic jam past Heathrow.

The less I think about what I'm going to find at the other end, the better. My mental picture of Tess alternates between her sobbing, with her hair all over the place, and her looking like the perfect, untouchable creature she was when she left Rivett Street. Neither of those pictures makes me feel any better.

And as for Robin's family, and how they'll feel about me interrupting proceedings – well. Maybe they'll just assume I'm one of his old friends from the days when he used to be a Christian. Unless Pam and Tina are there, of course. Or even Troy and his wife and pudding-headed child. In which case, nah, probably not.

That's another mental picture it's best to ignore. Me and the outraged members of the South London Crosslink network, in church, having a stand-off and chucking Bibles and knee-pads at each other across the altar.

I find some barley sugar in the glovebox – barley sugar I have bought at the petrol station shop, especially for this exciting driving adventure – and eat two at once. I also think about Robin for a minute. If he was still alive, would he ever have invited me to a party? Frankly, no. Not after the Elvis party. I mean, we barely spoke. Why, then, with all I know about life after death, am I going to his memorial service to hold Tess's hand? I'll be lucky to get in the front door first, with the poltergeist activity that's likely to unfold.

Piss-weak private jokes aside, I decide, then and there, that there's no way I can actually be there for the service. I know Tess will be upset, and I know I'll feel like a real bastard, and be at a loose end, wandering around the village by myself for the whole day, but there are some things that even I can't bring myself to do, even for her. I'll be there before and after, but not during.

By the time I finally reach Dunstan, as the village is called, I have eaten the whole packet of barley sugars and feel fairly car sick. It's one of those hire cars where exhaust fumes leak into the front seat, which hasn't helped. And after The Kinks special they moved onto random programming of endless funk music, which just made the nausea worse.

I pull into the pub car park, and immediately see Tess, framed in the window. She's by herself, from the looks of things, and I can also see that she's cut her hair. So I feel surprised, and pleased, and taken aback all at the same time. I wasn't expecting her.

I unpack the boot, and take in my bag. The registration business – it's probably just fifty quid to the barmaid and a key – can wait. This, after all, is something that's been waiting for months. Even though I didn't actually think it would happen like this.

The pub is half empty, except for a dog lying in front of the fire, and two men playing darts, and some noisy women in the corner.

'Tess.'

She turns around, and smiles, and waves me to come over. When we kiss, though, it's nothing like some of the kisses I'd imagined. She pecks me on the cheek, and rubs my arm in a half-hearted sort of way, and then just flops down in her chair again.

'It's good to see you,' she says at last, taking a sip of her drink – orange juice, I note.

'Have you been waiting long? I mean, I didn't expect you to wait for me. You know.'

She nods. 'I thought you'd get in somewhere between nine and ten, so I decided to plant myself here and surprise you. I can't be there, at home with them, anyway. It's just too much. You know?'

I nod back.

She gets up. 'I'll get you a beer. Okay? And I'll get one for me as well.'

I watch her go. Her hair has been cut into a funny, neat kind of bob, and some of the wild frizz has gone. She looks thinner too, especially in the face. And older.

In the background, the noisy women cackle at some joke that nobody can hear. I wonder if they're part of village life – it's a small place, judging by the look of the high street – and if so, whether they've been invited to Robin's service as well. I suppose everyone who can go, will go. He died, after all, in a very famous way.

Tess comes back with the beer.

'Can I tell you something, Mark?'

I nod, and take a sip. She's got me something horrible, some hand-pulled pale ale from the barmaid, but then I guess she's new to drinking, just like she's new to sex, and everything else, so she can be forgiven.

240

'I don't miss him as much as I think I'm supposed to miss him.'

And she sighs with relief, as if she'd been holding this in for a month – which she may well have been.

'Okay. No, that's normal,' I shrug. I mean, what would I know?

'With Catherine, I know you were together for years, and you were happy, and with Robin and me it was only months, and we fought a lot – but . . .'

I tell her what she wants to know.

'I would say with Catherine it's gone from missing her, to not missing her, to worrying about it, to craving her, to actually managing to forget that it was her birthday –'

'You forgot that?'

'Yeah, and I had the worst guilty night of my life when I remembered.'

Tess looks down for a minute.

'I think I'll be able to remember Robin's birthday. It's just other things. I feel like I'm supposed to be more upset than I am, in front of the family. And his friends.'

'Ah, yes, well I felt that.'

'But grief is all the stages mixed together isn't it? I mean, nobody does a straight line of anger, denial, acceptance, all those things.'

'No, they don't.'

Especially when you have fairly solid evidence they're still around, I think – but at the moment, this is the last thing I need to talk about with her.

'It's fantastic you're here,' Tess reaches across the table and taps her fingers, not on my arm, but just in front of it. 'It's great to just be able to let go and talk to you.'

'Well, that's good.'

'And I know it was a long drive, and I know you have to stay in this pub tonight, so –'

'Don't worry about it. You'd do the same for me.'

And that's just it. She would. Any day of the week. That's something I do know about Tess Blake.

The noisy women have another cackle at something, and Tess tries to drink too much beer at once, and chokes on it.

'God woman, you're pathetic.'

She smiles, once she's tidied herself up and wiped her mouth.

'It's such a relief to be able to talk to you,' she says.

'Why, specifically?'

'Because I don't have to pretend.'

'About Robin?'

'Exactly. You know, the thing is, somebody dies, and they're in a particularly horrible, tragic thing like this – and suddenly you get the whole religious thing shoved down your throat, and people who hardly knew him being more upset than you, and then, your own guilt at not missing him more. You know what the worst thing is? I'm actually angry with him.'

'Well, that's normal.'

I'm still absorbing the information about her feeling like religion's being shoved down her throat. Who would have thought?

Tess takes another, smaller, sip of beer.

'I'm angry at him for having such a boring morning, if you must know. The morning he went off to work. We probably said four words to each other, he had some toast, he asked me to pick up his dry-cleaning –'

She chews on her bottom lip for a bit.

'– And that was that.'

I let her sit and stare out of the window for a while.

'We used to have these very intellectual arguments about my virginity,' she says, eventually. 'They went all night, in the apartment. That was the first apartment we were sharing. And I could see his point. It was hard for him to be kissing me in the kitchen one minute, then saying goodnight the next. You know, we had separate rooms and all that.'

I nod again.

'I'd always thought that sex had to wait until the commitment was there, the marriage was there, because otherwise there was always this risk that we would break up, and that both of us would get hurt. Badly hurt, I thought, because I always thought sex was something sacred. Not, you know, shagging and bonking, and what everyone else calls it –'

'Okay.'

'At Crosslink, we were taught that if you have sex, you become one flesh, and then when you get torn apart, it leaves really bad scars. And more than that, too – if you get pregnant, for example, you might end up with an abortion, or you have a kid, and the kid ends up getting hurt if you separate.'

Suddenly, for no real reason, I think of Noel's stepdaughter, that gangling, moody teenager in the kitchen.

'I mean,' Tess continues, 'as I used to say to Robin, does the world really need another potential Scott O'Grady? Because that's what so many of these casual relationships amount to.'

I think about this for a minute, drink some more beer, and then decide to tell her about Donna.

'I got a woman pregnant and I didn't know. She had to have an abortion. She didn't tell me for years.'

'That's awful.'

'But Tess, there are plenty of couples who waited to have sex until they got married, and divorced anyway. Or, they stayed together – fine in the eyes of the church, just fine – but underneath, there was all kinds of shit going on. Child abuse. The lot. I mean, you read the papers, don't you? Tess, leaving sex until the honeymoon really isn't the key to the kingdom, you know?'

And then something else occurs to me.

'And what about all those perfectly virginal Catholic men? All those teachers in the Catholic schools, dragged up on paedophilia charges? I mean – virginity's not the magic word, you know. At least, I don't think so. The technical act of not doing it for fifty years doesn't exactly solve all the world's problems.'

'That's almost what Robin said,' she tells me.

Tess looks at me with a strange expression on her face for a moment, and then looks down.

'Mark, the other thing nobody talks about is your own libido. When someone dies.'

'Well, there's no little poem about it on the Hallmark sympathy cards.'

'In New York, when I left' – Tess looks around her. 'People were going nuts. This big city, where everyone is so hands-off all the time, it just became one big love-fest. Since September 11, four of my friends started new relationships. One of them, this guy in the bank who never did anything with anyone, has just gone mad.'

'Like the Second World War,' I tell her.

'Yes, I've heard that too.'

'Not that many people talk about it, but when the killing started happening en masse, so did the shagging. It's simple biology, when you think about it. Survival of the species, and all that.'

Then I stop myself, because I sound like a teacher again.

Tess takes a deep breath.

'I've had death en masse, for the past two months, along with death singular, so maybe I can be forgiven then.'

'Forgiven for what?'

For a horrible moment, I think she's about to tell me that she's steadily worked her way through the male population of lower Manhattan, or even the village of Dunstan in the past two days, but instead she just smiles, and looks coyly away.

And what am I supposed to do, now how am I supposed to react? This is a gorgeous woman, who also happens to have become a friend, who seems to be dropping large hints, in a pub, in the country, and there's nobody else around except us to witness anything.

'I don't know whether it's finally having sex, after years of never doing it, or just reacting to September 11 along with everyone else in Manhattan, or maybe it's something they put in the bagels, but anyway . . .'

She looks at me, and I look at her, as if a line has been crossed.

'For what it's worth, your name has been coming up a lot lately.'

'Who with?' Tess leans in slightly, to hear me over the top of the cackling women, and the pub jukebox.

'There's a bloke called Noel, who I knew when I was a kid, who's become an astrologer, or something. Actually, he's a jack of all trades. He drives a mini-cab in Forest Gate as well. Anyway, he said something about you to me. And he doesn't know you, he's never heard of you.'

'Wow. What did he say?'

I shake my head.

'That's the trouble with these people, they're all hints and no hard facts. I dunno. Just that you were, somehow, important in the scheme of things.'

'Well,' Tess pouts, suddenly looking and sounding like a girl, 'I hope I am.'

'And there was another bloke, a medium. After I had all those weird experiences with Catherine, I rang him up. My doctor told me to, actually. And he said someone with the initial T would be important.'

'Well,' Tess bites her lip again. 'What can I say?'

For as long as I can remember, I have always responded to girl signals. Also woman signals, because otherwise Veronica would never have got me past the first stair to the bedroom – but even the slightest indication that a female is willing to play the old Hollywood Marilyn Monroe-Dean Martin game of eyelash-batting and shyness is enough to reel me in.

Catherine always said I liked flirting, and I do. And even if we shouldn't be doing this now, because Robin is dead, and Catherine is dead too, I can't see anyone else in this pub who cares, except the nattering women, and the dog in front of the fire. There's nobody out there in the village tonight either, to peer through the curtains at us, and point a finger.

'You think your libido has gone mad?' I tell Tess, 'Let me write you a few essays about mine, some time. I was even forced to go swimming, to try to deal with it.' Tess smiles.

'But I thought it might just be me. You know. Because I didn't have sex for so long, then I finally started, and it was so much fun.'

'So much *fun*?'

Tess laughs. 'Sorry, I know I must sound like Pollyanna or something, Mark, but you know what I'm like. And then, suddenly my world collapsed, and Robin had gone – but my body had woken up. Really woken up, with a vengeance. And in New York, everyone around me was suddenly in this frenzy, so I thought – well. I thought the libido thing was just my problem.'

'Tess, it's not a problem. Please, never call your desire for me, or anyone else, a problem.'

There, I've said it. Thrown down the bait, or placed the trap.

But, as if this information is a given, all she does is blink a little, and smile, and keep staring out of the window.

'Yes, it is a problem, Mark. We are burying Robin tomorrow. And you still miss Catherine.'

'Okay, yes I do, but bugger it, Tess, why should we suffer more? What are we, less than human, less than deserving somehow, just because we're officially the bereaved? I mean, what do you think half the guests for the service tomorrow are doing tonight?'

'Wow. I'm not sure I want to think about that,' she says.

'Your ex, Troy, do you really think he'll be sitting at home with his wife and kid, watching a wildlife documentary and twiddling his thumbs?'

'Well, you don't know Troy. That's not a good example.'

'Well, Tess – people from Robin's work, anyway. All those people who've booked into luxury hotels in the next town, do you think they'll be feeling guilty if they decided to actually use the big king-size bed the night before his memorial service?'

'Don't use that phrase, king-size bed,' Tess whispers, with her lips almost touching the top of the beer glass.

'I think we should Stand Up For Your Love Rights,' I tell her, quoting an old song that The Bottom Line used to cover. 'We are bereaved, you and me, but we can be bereaved any way we want to. I mean, what the fuck would any of them out there know about it?'

'This is just your way of getting me into bed,' Tess giggles, doing her Marilyn thing again.

'But that's the whole point,' I say, looking at her lipstick, which she never used to wear, and which has ended up smudged around her lower lip.

Our eyes lock in, and make that silent click that has always, happily for me, meant the point of no return.

'Tess, the whole point of life, and living, especially when all this is going on around our heads, the war against terrorism, or whatever they want to call it, is this. You and me, in a pub, getting a bit tipsy – well, you getting a bit tipsy, anyway – and us deciding to go to bed.'

There. I've said it.

'But it won't be king-size up there,' she points at the ceiling, and laughs.

'No, it will be some horrible single bed with a cast-iron mattress that's probably riddled with bedbugs, but that's never stopped any human being before.'

She nods, taking this all in.

'The only problem is, I know the barmaid will gossip. This is a really small village, Mark. And I don't know, I'm beginning to feel guilty.'

'Well, don't do it then.'

'No, no.' She finishes her beer. 'I want to.'

'Well, then. I'll get the key.'

Her reservations are right, of course. Even me, who has never been in Dunstan in his life, can tell that this is the kind of town where everyone will know about this in the morning. Tess can creep into Robin's parents' house as quietly as she likes, but they'll still know she was out suspiciously late. The barmaid has already clocked us, or rather Tess, giggling and as near as damnit flirting with me at the table. And even the dog probably talks.

Nevertheless, it's time. Even if this is a disaster, it's time.

As I sort out the money and the key, Tess waits for me at the bottom of the pub stairs, below a clock which is supposed to look like a ship's wheel, and is showing the wrong time.

'I can be up there and back to Robin's parents' place in half an hour,' she stage-whispers.

I'm just realising the effect a pint of beer can have on a woman, who's hardly ever drunk.

'Half an hour?' I react, in mock outrage. 'Clearly you've got a lot to learn, Tess.'

When we are out of sight of the bar, and the noisy women, she takes my hand, and we creep up the stairs together, on carpet which seems to be all threads and no actual carpet.

The room, as I suspected, has one single bed, one lamp, one sink, and a wardrobe with two bent coathangers in it, and a lot of grey fluff in the corner.

'It's so typical of my life,' I say to her, 'that my first time with you should be in a place that looks like Brixton Prison.'

'Don't,' she laughs, and it is she who grabs me, not the other way around, as we lean against the wardrobe.

She has the most phenomenal skin I have ever touched. It's bloody freezing in here, because there's no central heating, and neither of us has actually managed to turn on the bar heater yet. Even her goose pimples are soft, though, on her arms. And she tastes of beer, which is strangely wonderful.

Tess squeezes my arm, suddenly and pulls herself away.

'Cold?'

She is making me feel like I'm in my own private Hollywood movie, circa 1955. I want to invite her to waltz around the room, I want to tell her she looks pretty.

'Um, not cold. Can we just sit down for a bit?'

I lead her to the bed. Of course she can sit down. Maybe all night, if that is what it takes, because I know, in a moment, that all this is too much for her now. Why on earth did I ever think that she was serious?

'Catherine,' I begin talking to her, then stop myself short.

'You called me Catherine,' Tess says. 'Ouch.'

And suddenly, there's nothing either of us can think of to say. No magic breaker for the ice, no normal way to make things as good as they felt five minutes ago.

'I'm sorry. I'm tired. Not quite with it. I'm really sorry, Tess. Catherine was actually the last thing on my mind. It just slipped out.'

'No, it's okay.'

She looks at me for a minute, and takes my hand, as we sit side by side on the hard wooden bed.

'Tess. I'm sorry. Just because my head was thinking about you, and my mouth was saying Catherine, doesn't mean a thing.'

'Really?'

'Trust me.'

She yawns, then, and slowly lets herself fall sideways, until she is lying in my lap. And we lie there for a while, her cutting off my circulation, which I'm extremely happy about, and me stroking her hair. It's as soft as her skin.

'We can just fall asleep,' she says.

But I've heard this one before, this we-can-fall-asleep thing. It seldom works. Either one of you wakes up at 3 a.m. and desperately wants a shag, or all the good intentions – to have a little nap, then set the alarm, and get up, and go home – disappear.

'You have to make an appearance back there tonight,' I tell her. 'You really have to be seen to go home.'

'I know. Hey, Mark, I feel really happy at the moment.'

'So do I.'

'I feel right. You see, I always suspected that. When I looked at you properly for the first time, that day you were walking across the playing fields, there was just an instinct that you were right for me, on some level. My kind of person. Not because I had any other motives, of course, because I didn't. I felt sorry for you, because you looked so alone, and I knew Catherine had only just died. I truly, honestly didn't fancy you.'

'And no wonder,' I cut in. 'With this lack of haircut?'

'But still,' Tess ignores me, 'I knew you were one of those people who would just fit in. Who I would fit in with.'

'Well, you had a better idea than I did.'

'Instinct is always right,' Tess sighs, stretching back in my lap, and reaching up to rub my neck.

'Can I tell you what I instinctively feel now?'

'I know. I should be leaving you in peace.'

'You should be leaving, certainly, but you should also be coming back. To London. I think you should stay in my house.'

Tess sits up, and stares hard at me.

'Wow.'

Then she looks down for a minute, at her hands in her lap, and thinks about it.

'No, it's a brilliant idea,' she wins the argument with herself. 'Mark, thankyou. Thankyou.'

'No, thankyou. I mean Tess, you have no idea . . .'

We stay there on the bed for ages, and I go through things in my mind.

Robin is being buried tomorrow, or remembered, anyway. Veronica and the entire Roden family will hate it, if they see Tess come to stay, and they see her clothes one day, hanging in Catherine's side of the wardrobe. The Head's not going to like it, either, this state of cohabitation. And Alison and Felix will act pleased for us, I know, but be secretly shocked. All those things. And yet, and yet –

'This is good,' Tess stands up and looks at me seriously. 'This is a good thing, Mark. You know, I've had kids trying to kill themselves in my school this year, in New York. I've lived through that, and I've lived through the Towers. I know bad things, like those, and I know good things, like this. Or, at least I think I do. This is good.'

'It's going to hurt people's feelings if you come to live with me.'

There. I've said it now. Not stay with me, live with me.

Tess nods and is still for a minute.

'You can't deny people will be hurt,' I go on. 'Robin's parents, for one.'

'Do unto others,' Tess replies, 'that's what I believe. That's what I always have believed. Honestly, if this was Robin, and it was me in those towers or what's left of those towers, I would say, under the circumstances, just go. Try it. Be with that person, if you want to be with them, and they want to be with you.'

She bites her lip.

'Okay, I will admit, I'm fighting with myself over this too. But then, it's only Robin and Catherine who count, you know? So – what about her as well? Do you think, if you had died in the crash, and not her, she would let you be this happy, this soon? Even if it is complicated?'

I hold Tess tight, and gaze at the bare, yellow walls.

'Yes, and I've known it all year,' I tell her. But that's all I want to tell her, at the moment.

twenty-seven

Soon after Tess moves in, with her two big suitcases, and her four heavy boxes of books – the rest of her stuff is still in storage – we have our first argument. Not surprisingly, it's about religion. This is later followed by an argument about Catherine, then an argument about Robin. And also an argument about politics. All these arguments frequently end up in bed, which is great, and no – just in case anyone is wondering – late starters don't always lag behind. Well, not in Tess's case anyway.

The religion argument is easy. We're at a local restaurant when it happens, an Indian place up on the high street.

'If you're not comfortable with the idea of God,' Tess challenges me, over the curry, 'then what are you comfortable with?'

'It's just so typically arrogant of white, middle-class, Western society,' I argue back. 'Of course your God is the only God. What about Native Americans, and their belief in a Great Spirit? Or Australian Aborigines and what they believe? Is that worth any less? What about Hindus and all their beliefs, seeing as we're in an Indian restaurant? What makes your lot so much better, or your version of the truth so much more accurate?'

'Hang on a minute,' Tess stops me in mid flight, as two waiters move to offer us more pappadums, then nervously move away again.

'What you're assuming,' she says, 'is that I have a particular version of God. Something that you seem to be relating to the churches. And I don't. Whatever I thought a year ago, I don't think any more.'

'And why is that?'

'Loads of reasons. I don't know. Maybe I just grew up and got over my dad dying,' she sighs.

I look at her for a minute. We haven't really talked about her dad up until now, although it was one of the first things she ever told me about herself – that sometimes, when she prays, she thinks she hears him.

'If you must know,' Tess goes on, 'I liked the idea of a Heavenly Father because I really didn't have a real one. This idea that God was organising and controlling things was a comfort. It made sense.'

'The same God who seems to have organised and controlled the Americans now bombing the shit out of Kandahar, yeah? That is, if we believe certain speeches now taking place on the US Bible Belt. And the same God who was behind the Holocaust, not to mention, I dunno – England never winning anything since 1966? The same God who brought us the African famine, maybe, or that boon to all humankind, the stinging nettle?'

'Don't,' Tess gives me a warning look. 'Just don't even start.'

'Well, what are you saying then?'

'I'm saying, there is a creative intelligence in our world, and it sometimes unfolds over a long period of time, which is why we can't always comprehend how it's working. And if you call yourself any kind of science teacher at all, then you have to accept it, Mark. Maybe God was the wrong label, that's all. You can't blame human beings for misinterpreting a few things, and we've had a few thousand years to get it wrong. I mean,' she goes on, 'God hasn't got a beard. I don't think that, and I'm insulted you'd assume it. And clearly, He's not a he. And I don't think we should just throw ourselves down on the floor of the church and submit our will the whole time, to whichever priest or politician appears to be interpreting the message at the time. I mean, I was in a church in New York, and they were citing God as a reason to bomb Afghanistan!'

'But of course. They always do. But anyway, Tess. Back to the science bit for a minute.'

'Yes.'

'Why do I have to believe in a creative intelligence, in order to believe in science?'

'An order in nature. Even if humans only understand a very small part of that order, in order to do science, and definitely to teach it, you still have to accept that there's some kind of natural law or order out there. Something intelligent.'

'What if I just think it's all random chaos and anarchy, though? What if I secretly think The Sex Pistols are in charge of God's garden?'

'Shut up,' Tess says, pressing her lips together like a little old lady.

'No, come on, I'm enjoying this. I never used to do this with –'

And I break off, but she has already heard the word, like a thought balloon above my head. Catherine. Which is how the second argument begins.

The next morning, while Tess is obligingly making me something to take to school for lunch, and I am enjoying the bizarre sensation of having some kind of Doris Day figure cooing over my ham sandwiches, it starts all over again.

'I'm over Robin,' she says sharply, cutting the ham on the chopping board.

'Well – yes. If you think so. I mean, what's brought this on?'

'No, I know I'm over Robin. Or as over him as I'll ever be. But you're not over Catherine.'

'Tess. Hang on a minute.'

I go over to her, and she stops chopping the ham.

'Where has this come from,' I ask her, 'and anyway, what do you mean by "over"?'

Tess makes a face at the knife, and looks teary-eyed for a minute.

'Her name keeps coming up, you know?'

'Look. I'm sorry. You're thinking about last night, at the Indian restaurant. I didn't even think about it before I said anything to you.'

'Stop making comparisons with me and Catherine. Who cares if it's different with me, or if it was different with her. It's so childish.'

'But I'm not, Tess, honest, I'm not.'

In the end, I go to school with ham sandwiches, which are made inside out, with bits of bread sticking to the side of the brown paper bag.

Tess then rings me in the staffroom, later in the day, to apologise – and we have another argument, on the staff telephone, with everyone listening.

'I've just been watching the lunchtime news,' Tess says, on the end of the phone.

'What's happening?'

'I just want to know why you think the war is such a good idea, that's all,' she sniffs.

'Oh, for God's sake Tess, not now.'

'No, come on, let's have it out. I've been sitting here watching these bloody women from the BBC all afternoon, being all nice and polite about all this killing – not that we ever mention the k word of course – and I'm sick of it. I want to know. I have a right to know, because I'm sleeping with you. Why do you think this war is such a good idea?'

'I'm in the staffroom,' I say, in a ridiculously chatty, casual voice. 'It's lunchtime.'

'I don't care where you are, why are innocent people being killed? And why do you think Blair and Bush have got it right?'

'I can't talk to you about this now.'

'Well, come home and talk to me about it then.'

'I can't. Tess. It's not possible. You know it's not.'

At the mention of Tess's name, a few ears swing my way, like air-traffic control radar, then swing back again. The fact that she has moved in with me is still hot news in this place, even now, which shows you exactly how much goes on at Rivett Street.

'I'll come home later and we'll talk about it then,' I tell her. But she has already hung up.

One of the things I have been discovering about Tess, and it's a good discovery, is her passion. Noel D. Jupiter says it's because she's got Pluto on her Venus, whatever that means, but whatever the reason, it's a bigger part of her personality and her life than I'd ever guessed.

Because she's not working at the moment, for example, she's developed a passionate interest in cooking. It's weird for her, because she's never cared about food before, but her entry into this house has sparked a kind of one-woman mission in the kitchen that would put Nigella Lawson to shame. She has a way of licking her fingers, too, like Nigella, that immediately makes me want to turn the stove off, and take her upstairs instead.

The passion explains the Crosslink thing to me, as well. And more besides. Since she gave in to Robin in New York, and gave up on her virginity, she has developed passionate arguments for her personal brand of faith, because she's still a believer, at heart, just as much as she's found passionate arguments against the conventional churches.

'I told you Jesus was complicated,' she says to me, one night, after we've had the kind of three-course dinner that men like me can only dream about.

'So tell me. What do you believe?'

'Simple. I believe in life after death. I believe that Jesus Christ was real. I believe he healed people, and I believe he really did multiply loaves and fishes, and I also believe he was sent to save us. Society at that time –'

'Oh, please, Tess. I mean, I'm listening, but I can't have the big run-down on the corruption in Roman society, you know?'

'Okay.' She gives me a fierce look, beneath her curtain of hair – it's growing back now, the blonde frizz, after having been banished for so long in New York.

'Three, I believe in the life force. I believe that you can't stop it, no matter how much you try to kill, and maim, and fuck people up, and all the rest of it.'

One of the other things that has happened since Tess moved in with me, apart from the cooking, is also this – she is beginning to swear like me.

'It's like that Dylan Thomas poem we do at school,' she says. ' "The force that through the green fuse." You know. I believe in the force.'

255

'Tess, you sound like Luke Skywalker.'

'I don't mind. I believe in Jedi knights as well. Do you know, millions of people put that down as their religion, on the last census? Sounds like the kind of thing you'd write down.'

I chuck a cushion at her, which is a nice thing to do. I miss throwing cushions at grown women. I've missed it all year.

'So what don't you believe now?' I pester her. 'I mean, what have we decided to dispense with?'

'You can't stop the life force, and I include Felix in that. His Hair Bear Club that you were telling me about. Just because gay men's life force doesn't end up in human reproduction doesn't mean it's wrong.'

'Yes, but Tess, I've seen the Hair Bears' life force, and you haven't. They put a stuffed gorilla in a butt-plug harness. It's not a pretty sight.'

'And I think it's wrong to keep the churches all-male,' Tess continues, 'what a load of crap that is, and I think anyone who kills anyone else and says God is on their side doesn't have the faintest idea of what God is.'

'You don't need to convince me, Tess,' I tell her, as she crawls along the sofa to fold herself in my arms. 'I mean, I was the anti-religion bloke first, remember?'

'You said something to me once, at school, about my dad being dead, and me still thinking he was around.'

'I didn't actually. You told me. I was just asking a question.'

'And we still haven't really talked seriously about Catherine. Have we? About what happened after she died?'

'I thought Catherine was black-banned.'

'Piss off. You know what I mean. So what do you really believe, Mark? Come on, I'm curious.'

'I dunno.'

And I'm not being difficult, or deliberately obtuse, or any of those things that Tess normally accuses me of. I really just don't know. If you ask me what I believe, in the light of what Tess has just told me, it really comes down to one thing. I have evidence, my own evidence – which no scientist would touch with a barge pole – that people who die can send tele-pathic messages, fit themselves over my face in the mirror, say my name on a mobile phone, communicate at length during meditation or dreams, and make microwave ovens say HELLO.

The stereo then kicks into life. *Never Tear Us Apart.* Inevitably, *Never Tear Us Apart.*

'It always does that,' Tess says, 'just turns itself on and turns itself off. Oh. It's the song.'

'Yes, it's the song.'

She gives me a look.

'Sort of our song, if you think about it. Something's going on, Mark. Have you just pushed a button?'

'No.'

'Well what's going on then?'

'It's on the radio. I don't know. I thought I'd turned it off.'

'Weird.'

She snuggles into me and closes her eyes, while I stare at the wall, and smell Catherine's perfume, Joy, wafting into the room. I check Tess's face, but I don't think it's registered. So this is a private thing, then, from Catherine, just for me. One of those occasional visits John Smith was talking about.

'I thought I was happy with Robin, or – a bit happy,' she mutters, half her face in my jumper. 'It wasn't anything like this sort of happiness, though. Maybe that's why I've stopped beating myself up over it – over me moving in. And Mark – is it the same for you?'

And I don't reply, even if she was expecting one. If I was going to be truthful, though, I'd probably tell her it was a different kind of happiness. A new angle, perhaps, on old feeling, that was taken away from me a long time before Catherine died, and then vanished for good. Or so I thought, anyway. My God, maybe there is a God.

twenty-eight

Soon after this, Tess invites me to dinner with some of her friends. She refuses to tell me if anyone from Crosslink will be there, although she reassures me that Pam and Tina, and for that matter, Troy and his family, will be absent.

'Mainly because they're so shocked at the fact that I'm here with you,' she says.

'Ah well,' I reply, 'if they're not going to be there, it just means more lovely fruit punch for me. Doesn't it?'

Tess rolls her eyes – nicely, but she rolls her eyes.

'I mean, I assume we're going to dinner with a bunch of believers,' I tell her.

'I'm not even going to tell you anything about them,' she says, crossing her arms in mock outrage. 'And anyway there's only two of them. Polly and Ted, two of my oldest friends.'

'Polly and Ted – sounds like they crawled out of the *Play School* toy box.'

'Just shut up, will you? I love Polly and Ted, and it's time you met them.'

'So will I have to perform under Stalin-like scrutiny then, at this dinner they're having for us?'

'Just have your bath,' Tess sighs, 'and get ready.'

Polly and Ted live in one of those houses that Catherine and I often fantasised about buying, but could never save up enough cash for. Even by the time my dad had helped me out, her life savings had been cashed in, and we'd borrowed far too much from the bank, we still couldn't quite manage one of the old Victorian mansions that Polly and Ted now live in, just around the corner from Tufnell Park tube.

The hallway is full of those original Victorian tiles that most people got rid of in the 60s, and they even have a real fireplace. With a real, blazing fire. One of my fantasies, in fact.

Polly is a ceramicist, so there are plenty of weird-shaped sculptures and ashtrays around the place – not that I'm smoking much any more, and I've been banned from smoking tonight, by Tess, so there's no point.

I don't know what Ted does, and I don't ask, until it's been twenty minutes since I stopped telling him all about myself, and I suddenly realise it might be polite to make an enquiry back.

We're sitting at the biggest dining table I've ever seen, with the kind of huge, expensive lamp overhead that would kill anyone immediately, if it decided to detach itself from the plaster ceiling and crash onto our heads.

'So what line of work are you in, Ted?'

I can't help noticing his beard. It's long, and it's straggly, and it's practically in his soup. Maybe that should give me a clue, I think, but it doesn't. Certainly not a barber, anyway. And definitely not a male model.

'I've just come back from Afghanistan,' Ted explains. 'I work for a couple of aid organisations.'

Polly nudges him, looking embarrassed.

'Hence the beard,' Ted goes on, 'which I realise makes me look like Papa Smurf. Sorry, I haven't had time to shave it off yet.'

While Polly and Tess talk nineteen, or possibly nineteen-million to the dozen, Ted explains that the Taliban don't let

259

anyone into their refugee camps, unless they're suitably hairy. Plus, it's freezing in Afghanistan at the moment, so the aid workers need all the facial hair they can get.

In turn, because I think he'd appreciate the joke, I tell him about Felix and the Hair Bear Club. Ted thinks this is funny enough to almost choke on his soup, which is gratifying, so I spin out the story and tell him about Felix coaching the football team, until he is begging for mercy.

'Brilliant!' Ted says, then Polly goes and gets the next course, which means he's still on soup while we're onto roast chicken.

It's amazing that I should be sitting next to someone who's actually part of the action – as in the action you see on *World In Action*, or on those Channel 4 documentaries about war zones – and he's even laughing at my pathetic Felix stories.

I can't ask Ted all the questions I'd like to ask, though, about the Taliban and the Northern Alliance, and all the rest of it, because he's still cramming soup into his mouth, trying to catch the rest of us up for the next course.

'Speed eating,' Polly observes, making a face. 'You've heard of speed dating, this is speed eating. He's very good.'

Making a mock-annoyed face at her, and trailing his beard in the soup, Ted goes on, cramming spoonful after spoonful into his mouth, trying to catch up.

'Actually I know someone who used to do speed dating,' I tell Polly, and Tess suddenly looks interested as well, and before I know it, I have a captive audience for my Alison story. Very smoothly, I feel, I don't give her name. But I tell them about someone who was looking for labradors and cocaine in no particular order, at a speed-dating dinner in Chelsea, and then Tess immediately guesses anyway.

'Did Alison really do that?'

I give her a look, as Ted continues to speed-eat next to me.

'Thanks, Tess, I did think I was managing to be discreet about this, but yeah, it was Alison.'

Tess explains to Polly that Alison is marrying the Head, and that there's going to be a heated swimming pool at the hotel where the reception is being held, so we're all expected to spontaneously fall into it, fully-clothed.

Polly laughs at this, a kind of a 'hur hur' laugh which you

don't normally hear women doing, and then Ted joins in too, not laughing at the heated swimming pool story, but laughing at Polly, making the hur hur noise.

I'm not really one for being introduced to people. Catherine used to do it sometimes, and we'd always end up with total strangers from various British airline or hotel industries, trying too hard with each other, and putting up with crap food in a restaurant, usually worrying about splitting the bill at the end, and not really having a very good time.

So, this is a first for me. Tess has introduced me to Polly and Ted, and I like them. I genuinely like them. They're not Christians, Ted is actually one of the few interesting people I've met this month, or even this decade, and best of all, they think I'm funny as well. Or at least, we all think the same things are funny. And they've got stuff on the stereo that I like, and I can see from the bookshelves that we've even been reading the same things lately, so I almost feel – I dunno. At home.

Tess has problems opening the wine after this, in the kitchen, and calls me in to do the manly thing with the corkscrew.

'Aren't they great?' she asks, while I wrestle with the cork.

I nod.

'And they're both believers, you know,' she says casually, as the cork comes out.

I shrug. She's not getting me that way.

'Why should that bother me?' I ask.

But suddenly it does. It puts a whole different spin on Ted, and the conversations I'm about to have with him, and Polly, and how I feel about her.

Tess watches me carefully, and then points a finger in triumph.

'You see? You're going to get all thingy about them now, aren't you?' she whispers. 'I can see it in your eyes. You think they're weirdos now, don't you?'

'It's just that I'm now worried about every four-letter word that's come out of my mouth in the past hour, not to mention the approximately two million times I've said Jesus to illustrate a point.'

'They don't care,' Tess says smugly.

'Well, whatever, I don't feel comfortable now, thanks a lot.'

As the wine flows, though, and the food just gets better – home-made chocolate pudding, with fantastic coffee and even cheese afterwards – I find myself relaxing.

Ted is telling me stories about the time he stuck a camera down his underpants in a place near the Iranian border, so he could smuggle out photographs of one of the refugees, and how he discovered you could get camera rash, the same way you could get prickly heat.

Polly is getting out the photos now, too, finding embarrassing old shots of Tess for my benefit, shots that show her with very bad 80s hair and even a ra-ra skirt.

'You were the spitting image of Kylie Minogue at that New Year's Eve party,' is Polly's verdict. 'You don't know what you were missing, Mark.'

And then, all too soon, after the photos have been put away, it's time to go. I don't think we've talked about God once, or any of the other Christian stuff, come to that. I've got away with constantly using the worst expletives available to humanity all night, and they've laughed at more of my Felix stories – the one about Blount and the pigeon soup made Polly fall off her chair – and I just don't want to go back to my own bed, if you must know.

For the first time in my life, I find myself inviting people round. Not in a vague way. Not in a way that merely backs up what my female partner is saying. And not even in that way that lets both of you know, instantaneously, that it's never going to happen, not in a million years.

'Why don't you come to dinner, next Friday or Saturday, if you're free?'

And Ted and Polly act like this is the best invitation they've had all week, and say they'd love to, and Ted says he'll have his beard shaved off by then, and Polly says he'd better, because it's like getting in the sack with Osama Bin Laden, as well as Papa Smurf.

Tess and I say our goodbyes, and then walk back to the tube, feeling warm and well-fed, already preparing ourselves for the massive shock of the Northern Line and the trip back to our place.

'So what do they actually believe?' I say at last, as we do a complex manouevre that involves her putting one hand in my left pocket, with my hand, and keeping her right hand firmly wedged down the front of her jeans, under her coat.

'I could tell you were dying to ask,' she says, beneath her scarf.

'Well, tell me. Put me out of my misery.'

Tess takes a deep breath. 'Ted used to go to school with me, and he's always been a Christian. One of the aid organisations he works with is linked to Christian Aid.'

'Right, so they go in and feed refugees, on condition that they'll learn how to do the missionary position straight afterwards. It's the Pacific Islands all over again.'

'Shut up Mark, you don't know what you're talking about. Anyway, Ted is a Christian and Polly is a Buddhist.'

'Oh, now, that's a good one.'

'Why is it a good one?' Tess gives me a baleful stare, from underneath her curtain of hair. 'You're making it sound like a joke or something. "Heard the one about the Christian and the Buddhist?"'

'They're just playing for opposite teams, that's all,' I say. 'I'm just pointing out that they're strange bedfellows. I mean, literally with Polly and Ted. They're strange bedfellows.'

'But the main thing is, at least those two believe in *something*,' Tess says, breathing out little puffs of air into the night. 'Otherwise, how do you think Polly could stand turning up to the airport, and saying goodbye to Ted? How do you think Ted could even think about going into Afghanistan, when the Americans are missing their targets and killing aid workers, and the Taliban are executing people like him?'

I shake my head. 'I have no idea how he does it. I am full of admiration, Tess, but I have no idea. And Polly too. I mean, he told me he was going back there, before the winter sets in. How the hell is she going to deal with that? Although,' I go on, having a conversation with myself, 'I suppose it makes their time together more precious.'

Tess walks faster, pulling me along with her.

'Some people say that Jesus Christ and Buddha were the same person, it's just the historians who got it wrong,' she says.

'Impossible.'

'Okay then, try this. In separate parts of the world, at separate times, two very similar people turned up. They had the same way of seeing the world, and were even peforming the same miracles. Sort of, Uri Geller to the one thousandth degree.'

'He's a fake,' I cut in.

'Whatever. Let's just say that these two men were part of the same thing, a kind of arrival of new ideas, new ways to be human. And they had special powers to prove it.'

'Right.'

'And then a whole bunch of rich and powerful blokes, and occasionally a few downright nasty blokes, started interfering, and distorting the message, and then over a thousand years or so, it got so twisted and warped that we've ended up with two different belief systems.'

'More than two if you count all the other fruit in the big supermarket trolley of life. I mean, there's Moslems, and Jews, and – oh I don't know – people like Noel's friends, who are Rastafarians.'

'Well, maybe everyone distorted the original information,' Tess concludes, 'to suit themselves. Because it was such power-ful stuff. That's what I think anyway.'

'Not that I notice you started this conversation with Ted and Polly,' I say, as we approach the tube station.

'Oh no, we've already been through it. A million times,' Tess says. 'Especially since I got to New York. There've been a lot of long emails going backwards and forwards between us, let me tell you.'

'My friends send me email about football and what was on TV last night. You and your friends talk about the meaning of life. Tess, I'm sorry,' I make a mock face of disappointment, 'I just can't compete.'

'You don't have to, you idiot,' she says, pretending to whack me around the head, and we walk into the glaring fluorescent strip-lit paradise that is Tuffnel Park tube, and head home.

twenty-nine

A few days later, we are driving down the motorway – again in a hired car, with the novelty of barley sugar and the radio blaring – towards Winnie's Knuckle, for the wedding of the century. Tess is in the back seat with the map, and Felix is in the front seat with a collection of old Bronski Beat tapes that I am refusing to let him play.

'I can hit all the high notes in *Smalltown Boy*, and still, he refuses to let me entertain you,' Felix turns around in his seat and grumbles to Tess.

'What I want to know is,' Tess yells back, over the sound of the engine, 'how come you're in the front seat, Felix?'

We have laid our money down at the Harrods' wedding registry, we have hired our suits, and in Tess's case, just paid two weeks' salary for a new frock, and we are on our way. Felix has hired a suit which is pale blue velvet, thus making him look like Peter Rabbit, according to Tess.

'Every time I look at you, I wonder where the carrot is,' she tells him.

'Every time most people look at me, sweetie, they're looking for the carrot. And it's never where they expect either. Because it's a very *special* carrot.'

'You're getting a bit Hair Bear, Felix,' I warn him. 'We're practising you being straight for this wedding, okay? There are army people there. Alison's father. And all his mates, and besides,' I go on, 'If you get in some straight man practice, Felix, it will help you at the football next week.'

Miraculously, or perhaps through sheer bloody-minded determination, Felix has got Rivett Street through the practice games, and into the quarter finals of the first practice cup. Something like that, anyway, they keep changing the rules of schoolboy football every other season.

Because Felix has not allowed me to forget that Rivett Street saw off Bruise Road South the other week – in a respectable 1-0 result, too – we now have a gentlemen's bet in place. It revolves around a 3-1 result against Hackford, who are the next opposition team that we face, and also a fanciful notion that Scott O'Grady might actually be pulled off the benches, and put into the squad.

'Are we there yet?' Tess says hopefully. She's already waded her way through most of the papers, and I can tell she's not enjoying being crammed into the back seat, either.

It takes a bit of time, after this, and a lot more of Felix singing Bronski Beat songs than either Tess or I would like, but we do eventually find Winnie's Knuckle. Better still, we find our bed-and-breakfast, just by following all the other cars.

I don't know why we didn't think of that in the first place. Spot a landdrover, or something with a horse box, or a Tory car sticker and just trail it every inch of the way as if you were the metropolitan police trailing the Great Train Robbers.

'Do you think the Queen will come tomorrow?' Felix asks us, and we ignore him.

'Alison said this is a very nice B&B, Tess reassures us, as we catch sight of our accommodation for the next twenty-four hours – a cottage with two big white-painted cartwheels next to the front door, and a lawn that looks like it's been shaved, rather than mown.

It's okay though, once you get inside, and not as expensive

as I'd feared, and they've put Felix in a room by himself downstairs, so at least we won't have to put up with him squealing if he manages to pick up any potential new Hair Bears at the reception.

Alison, according to Felix, has been 'looking out for him' and more than one desperately bent former public school boy will be in attendance. Consequently, he's full of hope. Especially because he thinks his Peter Rabbit suit is what he calls 'a dead cert' and 'one hundred per cent guaranteed result wear.' Neither Tess nor I want to disillusion him.

The Head has decided against a stag night, which everyone is very relieved about.

'I have to go out with Alison, though,' Tess tells me. 'Her friends have organised something. I think we have to wear hen beaks, or devil horns, or something. And we have to drive her blindfolded to some pub.'

'Male stripper alert!' Felix says, and we can both tell that he's wondering how to pass himself off as one of Alison's female relatives, and smuggle himself in for the night.

'You can use my hankie as a headscarf if you want, Felix,' Tess tells him. 'And you can even borrow my good tweed skirt. But even if you do get away with it, remember you're risking being proposed to later, by one of the local farmers.'

'A peaceful married life in the country,' Felix ponders, 'with a man in a flat tweed cap and wellies. A simple Sydney boy like me could do a lot worse.'

In the end, though, Felix and I settle down in the B&B living room, surrounded by bowls of pot pourri, over-loud television speakers, old Morecambe and Wise videos, and the fussy female owner, and Tess goes off with Alison by herself.

'Wish me luck,' she calls, as she walks down the gravel driveway to join a carload of screaming posh women.

'Oh, my God, one of them has her bare arse out of the window and it's only quarter past eight,' Felix observes.

It is, however, a false plastic bottom, which one of Alison's mad relatives is wearing on her head, so we retire to watch Morecambe and Wise, greatly relieved.

The wedding the next day is pretty much what we all expected. Because weddings are planned over so many months, and always in the same way, I suppose that even the cock-ups and the mistakes end up being predictable after a while.

In other words, the same generalised butterfly effect applies to all of them. You can just about bet that the bride will have a hangover, or be nervous, and consequently she's going to forget to say the groom's full name properly – which Alison does.

And in turn, this flap of the butterfly's wing will mean that some relative thinks that this bridal omission is the funniest thing she or he has ever heard, which results in them going on about it, endlessly, at the reception – resulting in another butterfly flap, which is the person next to them getting drunk so they won't have to listen – and on it goes.

Flap, flap, flap. A predictable wedding day for Alison and the Head, full of speeches we don't understand, food that somehow falls short, either in quality or quantity, and a kind of raw nervousness in the air that affects everyone. There are tiny chain reactions happening all over the place.

Part of the predictability of the event is also that the Head will see Tess and me together, and give a hearty fake wave – which happens, moments after we find our seat at the reception and sit down in front of our name cards.

And the other thing we're expecting, as predicted by Felix this time, is endless questions about our own nuptials. To the point where Felix, who is fairly cut on champagne, swings around and tells one of Alison's relatives that neither of us can get married yet, because we've only just buried our partners and we're both infidels in the eyes of the church, and worse than Camilla and Charles any day.

Alison and the Head are seated, just a little bit like Camilla and Charles, perhaps, at their own special table, with disposable cameras littered in front of them, and two bottles of booze, just in case Alison gets through the first one too quickly and needs another supply.

The Head's labrador has a white ribbon around its neck, which looks ridiculous, although it also seems pleased to finally be out of the Volvo.

'I notice Blount didn't turn up,' I tell Tess.

'Alison told me. It's just that he said he had other things to do.'

'Other things?'

'Pigeon noodle soup things,' Felix says, looking tired.

I can tell he's going to have to go back to the B&B and collapse soon, even if there is a heated swimming pool waiting a few steps away. Despite Alison's promise of former public schoolboys who are ready, willing and able, he's scoured the place and found nothing resembling a potential Hair Bear at all.

'You two go cavorting and carousing,' Felix waves a tired hand at us. 'What with the speeches, and the poisonous prawns, and this cheap champagne the Head's paid for, I don't think I can go on. Plus,' he adds, 'I have nervous exhaustion from worrying about what the future holds for Alison's sex life.'

With that, he staggers off, looking like Peter Rabbit after Mr McGregor's attacked him with a rake, and he makes his goodbyes, stealing disposable cameras as he goes.

'The Head is looking at us in a strange way,' Tess says, a little later.

'He thinks we just told Felix to nick those cameras.'

'No, it's not that. It's just – I don't know. The Head's not happy.'

'He's marrying Alison. Any clues there?'

'No, it's us,' Tess says, ignoring me, 'He's not happy with us.'

'But why? You don't work at Rivett Street any more. It's got nothing to do with him if we're living together.'

We've crossed that line now, too – she's no longer staying with me, she's living there.

'The Head wants me to come back to work as a teacher's aide again, and he thinks that if we're together, it can't be done,' she explains. 'Alison sent me this email about it. According to her, he doesn't mind the fact that we're the infidels of South London –'

I nod.

'It's just that some of the parents will inevitably find out and complain one day. The Head couldn't care less what we've decided to do with our lives. It's more popular opinion on the accepted time it should take before you leave behind one person in your life, and go onto the next.'

'Bloody hypocrite. He's only just got the divorce through from his wife, and he's shacking up with Alison. And she's a full-time teacher, and he's her boss! I think that's worse.'

Tess swills her champagne round in the glass.

'Felix is right,' she says. 'This is cheap. I thought Alison's parents were loaded.'

'They paid for the food, the Head did the booze. Mind you, the food's rubbish as well.'

'Oh, well,' she says heavily, 'there's always the heated swimming pool to look forward to.'

At the end of the day, though – and it's a long day – we find ourselves watching, at a safe distance – while Alison goes into the pool (she's changed into jeans and a jumper especially for this mad act of spontaneity) and then the Head goes in in his suit (it's a crap suit anyway, so it probably doesn't matter), and then various kids, animals and military types jump, or are pushed, in the deep end.

'What larks,' I say to Tess.

'Oh no, Blount has turned up,' Tess gasps, as we see a familiar figure staggering towards the pool, with an alsatian in his arms. 'I hope he's not going to jump in the pool with that dog. The Head will have a fit.'

But he does, and minutes later, the labrador with the white ribbon follows.

thirty

Rivett Street Junior School FC are trailing Hackford 0-1 and Felix Saddleton is about to lose his bet. Scott O'Grady is still stuck on the subs' bench as well, upping my chances of winning ten quid.

It's a cold – but thankfully not too cold – Saturday morning, and most of the school, including the Head and Alison, have turned up for the game.

'I suppose we have to call them Mr Head and Mrs Alison now,' I tell Tess, who gives a weak smile at this weak joke.

We are nearly at the second half, and despite Felix's generous donation of new *Reader's Digest*s the Rivett Street boys are running as if their legs are made of jelly.

Felix himself looks exhausted, bounding up and down the touchlines like a man possessed, yelling the occasional 'Go for a run!' and 'Go hell for leather!' as the parents look on, mystified that one man could get so worked up about their sons' sporting destiny.

'I can't stand the tension,' I tell Tess, as Rivett Street fumble another pass. 'I know I said we wouldn't win, and I meant it, but – you know.'

'You really want them to win though,' Tess nods. 'Well, so you should. Who cares about the ten quid?'

'Where can I get a fag, though?' I interrupt her, suddenly gripped by a serious craving. I've been off cigarettes for five days' straight, but the stress of the game is beginning to get to me.

'Ask Alison,' Tess says, making a face as another Rivett Street boy makes an obvious foul.

When I go up to her, though, she says she's all out of Silk Cut, and even her Benson & Hedges have gone, because the Head's had the lot.

'Shit.'

'That bad?' Alison tuts.

'I'll have to ask one of the parents,' I say, hoping the Head won't hear, but he does.

'Don't ask the parents,' he warns me, staring at the opposition as they kick a Rivett Street player hard in the shins.

Alison gives me a look, and I give up and try Felix instead.

'Felix, are you sure, when you gave up, that you didn't just keep one up your sleeve for emergencies?'

'No. Come on. Be strong. Resist. OH, GOOD PASS!' Saddleton suddenly yells, as we take control of the game again.

The cravings are impossible now. But if I can't ask one of the parents in front of the Head, who can I ask? Alison, me and Felix are the sole three smokers at Rivett Street, and that's it.

There's only one thing for it. Scott O'Grady. And if I'm subtle about it, I might just get away with it. He's sitting on the grass, reading his Kevin Keegan annual, just far enough away from the Head and Alison to make it safe.

'Scott?'

'Yes,' he says thoughtfully, eating an orange.

'Don't tell anyone I'm asking you this. Got any fags?'

Without even blinking, Scott reaches in his pocket for a packet of tobacco, some cigarette papers, and a little plastic machine which lets you roll them.

'Shit. Put it away!'

'It saves time,' Scott says, calmly. 'Do you want me to roll you one?'

'No. Put it away!'

'I've got a light too,' Scott says.

'Great,' I say. 'Look, let me work out how to do this. It's well out of order.'

'You're desperate,' Scott smiles, with wisdom beyond his eleven years.

'Yes, I am desperate.'

'The Head's coming over,' Scott says, immediately flicking his attention back to the football annual.

'Shit.'

I concentrate on the game, while the Head trudges into my peripheral vision.

'Mr Buckle, can I have a word?'

He leads, I follow. All the way back to the Volvo, which I quickly realise has some kind of special significance for the Head. Part sanctuary, part living quarters, part official HQ, it seems to be the place where most of the important things in life happen. Like serious professional conversations, for example. We hover around it, as the Head leans up against the bonnet, giving him a chance to scrutinise me and the game at the same time.

In vain, I look for Tess. She is now in a huddle with the team, and Felix, and she appears to be massaging Scott O'Grady's shoulders.

'Scott is a very special boy,' the Head begins.

'Yes.'

'He's not the only child at this school, but he is one of the most important. Scott is a kind of Everychild for us. Do you understand?'

'Yes.'

Clear as mud.

'You and I are Everyman, Scott is Everychild. If he fails, many more will fail. And then we've all failed. And I think I know what you were up to then.'

'Up to what?'

'When you've been in the teaching business as long as I have, Mark, you develop a kind of sense for these things.'

'I was talking to him about the game.'

'And another thing,' the Head warns, before I can escape,

273

'It's the other influences on Scott as well,' he continues. He stops, and gives me a look. 'A friend of yours has been teaching Scott witchcraft. Did you know this?'

'What?'

'Your friend, who so kindly offered to collect Scott after his football practice, has been showing him all sorts of tricks. How to cast his mother's horoscope. How to use a crystal to make money. How to use feng shui' – the Head struggles with the pronunciation of this a few times, then gives up – 'how to use the black arts to get himself on the football team.'

And I look up and see Scott O'Grady, getting the thumbs-up from Felix, and running onto the field, at exactly the same time that the Head does.

'Anyway,' the Head continues. 'Your friend has also got him reading Harry Potter, which you know I'm dubious about. And even worse, Scott seems to have a near obsession with Kevin Keegan.'

'What's wrong with Harry Potter? What's wrong with Kevin Keegan?'

I can feel myself getting bolshie now.

'Noel's harmless. He's a great bloke. I grew up with him. I'd trust Noel with my own child. With my own Everychild, even!'

The labrador is now going mad in the Volvo, so the Head unlocks the door, letting it bound into the front seat, where it pokes its head through the gap between the car door and the ground, with its tongue hanging out, trying to escape.

'There's also a rule about dogs on the playing field,' I say, feeling the bolshie-ness rise up. 'I mean, are you going to let that thing out there, just because it's your dog?'

In return, I get another look.

'I can't have Tess back at the school if you continue to live together,' he says at last.

'And is this really what this talk is all about? I mean, is it really the key issue?'

'The second half is starting,' the Head says, watching Rivett Street run onto the field as fast as their shin pads will carry them. 'I don't want to miss it, and I don't want you to either.'

Phew, then.

'But,' the Head says lightly, as he closes the door in the

labrador's face, 'you can consider this a warning. I'm not happy with your role in school life at the moment, Mark. Not happy at all.'

Then he wanders off to stand next to Alison, while I try to find Tess.

'So what happened?' she says, as I stand rigidly beside her like a soldier, not daring to touch her unless another lecture follows – or the sack.

'It's a drag,' I tell her. 'I'll tell you later. Bloody hell, look at O'Grady!'

Felix, screaming up and down the sidelines, is shouting at Scott as if his life depended on it, yelling at him to take on the entire Hackford defence at once, and he is – in fact, he appears to be winning.

'He's put him on as a striker,' I say, 'I don't believe it.'

Tess shakes her head.

'I know. Scott was down in defence, first of all, but then Felix suddenly had this vision, and he went all misty-eyed and strange, and then, pow, he swapped the boys around, and sent Scott straight on.'

'And look,' I say, not quite believing what I'm seeing, 'he's about to score, too. Look at Hackford! They're useless!'

It's such a perfect goal, the Scott O'Grady goal, that neither Tess nor I, nor the yelling, hysterical parents, can quite believe it. But Scott knocks it in, with no help at all from the rest of his team, until they hit that magic moment when they actually realise the whole thing is real, and just like on TV, start throwing themselves on the ground, and kicking their legs in the air, and hugging each other, and jumping on Scott's back, four at a time.

Instinctively, I look at Felix, who has his arms folded, hugging himself. One of the mothers has rushed up to him, to pat him on the back, and he looks as if he's going to cry.

The scene on the field is indescribable. We've equalised. There's plenty of time to go, for Scott to keep on going – and he's clearly on a roll – and we've equalised. This almost never happens. Well, it certainly never happened when I was coach.

Suddenly, I get tapped on the shoulder. It is Noel D. Jupiter, wearing a Rivett Street Junior school tie around his head like a bandanna.

'I just got here. I just saw him. He's a genius,' Noel says, jerking his thumb at Scott, as he stands straight and tall, taking his position back on the field.

'Well, maybe not a genius exactly,' Tess interrupts, smiling and introducing herself to Noel. They've spoken on the phone, but they've never met.

'What did you do to him Noel?' I ask, 'and more importantly, before you tell me your state secrets, have you got a cigarette?'

Noel makes my day by producing not one, but two brands to choose from. 'I don't smoke, of course,' he tells Tess, 'people just leave them in the cab and I pick them up.'

While we're busily choosing from a selection of Marlboro or Silk Cut, though, and finding matches in Tess's coat pocket, we nearly miss the second miracle. The second goal. And it's one that comes so close to hitting the post that nearly every Rivett Street player has a cardiac arrest on the spot, but nevertheless, it is – a goal. Pronounced goaaaal!, just like in the Kevin Keegan annual.

'Scott set that up for them,' Noel says proudly, sizing up the players.

'He did too,' I agree, 'and look at Felix! He's going apeshit!'

Saddleton, in true Hair Bear fashion, is indeed doing some kind of primate imitation, in front of all the parents, jumping up and down like a monkey who's been shown a good tea party, and making strange, guttural baboon-like yells of excitement, which we can hear from the other side of the ground.

'I hypnotised Scott,' Noel says, after a while, 'I must confess. I did it mainly to get rid of his farting, actually.'

Tess catches my eye, and laughs.

'It was Ruth, though,' Noel goes on, explaining to Tess. 'My wife is the real healer in the family, and she did the laying on of hands about a week ago, just to help with Scott's stomach really. But it seems to have done all sorts of things. I mean, did you see that goal?'

'Incredible,' Tess agrees. 'Your wife must be a miracle worker.'

We are now officially winning, the sun has come out from behind the clouds, and although I am probably about to be sacked anytime soon, this is already turning out to be one long, great day, in a run of long, great days lately.

The fear of immediate unemployment is there too, of course, gnawing away at me that the whole time the Head is standing there. I don't think anybody quite gets over the fear of losing a job. Especially anyone who lived through the 80s. But then I think – fear of *what,* exactly?

There are other teaching jobs. And above all things, I am a teacher. I am what I teach, in fact – I pass on bits of myself to the kids, and not just page 49 to 59 of the National Curriculum.

Frankly, if I I can't pass on Noel to Scott, and if I can't fuck up occasionally in front of the kids by having an illicit fag, and if I can't have Tess in my life, at the same time that I'm trying to teach the kids about the life cycle of rabbits, then what's the point?

Tess squeezes my hand.

'I think we're going to win,' she whispers.

'I know. It's unbelievable,' I whisper back. 'What was it you said happened, Felix went all misty-eyed and had a vision about Scott?'

'I'm not sure,' Tess makes a face. 'Let him tell you. I don't know. *Something* happened. Have you got any clues, Noel?'

But Noel D. Jupiter just stands and stares, almost as if he's just seen the invisible man, at an empty spot on midfield which seems to fascinate him all of a sudden.

'Maybe,' he says. And at that moment, Scott O'Grady scores his final, triumphant goal.

thirty-one

There is a depressing little pub near our school, which hardly anyone goes to, mainly because it looks like a place where you go to die, rather than a place where you go to get a drink. Nevertheless, one of the parents decides that this will, in fact, be the Rivett Street celebratory pub of choice, so that's where we all head, in our dozens, in a fleet of cars, all honking at once.

The kids are parked outside in the beer garden with their parents making extravagant orders for double orange juices, and salt and vinegar crisps, and one of them even tries it on by asking the Head for a Red Bull – 'It's non-alcoholic, Sir' – but doesn't get away with it.

Noel, Tess and I grab a table by the window, and plonk ourselves down, while the Head and Alison hover uncomfortably in the corner. Moments later, Felix joins us, with his hair standing up like a porcupine's quills, from much head-ruffling by the team. He looks exhausted, but happy, like a man rescued from a death sentence at the last minute, and then given strawberries and cream.

'Did you see it?' he asks me.

'I saw everything,' I tell him. 'Here's your ten quid.' I push the money over the table. 'A triumph, Felix, is the only thing I can say about it.'

'Thanks,' Felix whispers, emotionally, as one of the football parents shoves a large Scotch under his nose. 'Thanks, Mark. I feel –'

We all look at him, for his Match of the Day-style verdict.

'I feel grotesquely victorious!' he shakes his head. 'I mean, is this what it's like for everyone? This repulsive feeling of omnipotence?'

'And this ain't even the final,' Noel nods his head, grinning.

Felix holds out his hand for Noel to shake.

'We meet again. You're the knight in shining armour, in the mini-cab.'

Noel grins.

'We've never really met properly, have we?'

'No,' Felix shakes his head, 'only in the context of O'Grady, and that can be a very distracting context.'

Tess looks up, as she hears cheering coming from the beer garden.

'That sounds like Scott now,' she says. 'I can hear him singing. I'd know that voice anywhere.'

'So would I,' Felix says, 'And I'm the poor bastard who's been doing Crazy Shoe Music with him all year.'

Scott is singing *You'll Never Walk Alone*, why I'm not sure, but the other boys sound like they're joining in, and the parents too.

I light up another of Noel's wide range of cigarettes, anyway. I'll give up another day.

'So what's the story?' I ask Felix at last. 'You put him on as a striker, and bingo. He's been sitting on a bench all year getting intimate with oranges. What happened?'

Felix shakes his head. 'I can't say.'

'No,' I persist, 'come on. What's the secret?'

Noel laughs then, a great big belly laugh that seems to come up from nowhere – considering he's even skinnier than me.

'Felix is getting help,' Noel says, and to my amazement, Saddleton actually blushes.

'Noel's a bit spooky,' Tess explains to Felix. 'I think he knows a few things.'

'Damn right I know a few things,' Noel smiles. 'But the question is, does anyone else want to know about them?'

Felix looks at Noel nervously. It's unusual seeing Saddleton this anxious about anything, but Noel D. Jupiter seems to be having a strange effect on him.

'My wife Ruth is a healer,' Noel tells Felix. 'She works with her spirit guides to sort people out. That's how I got cured. That's how a whole lot of people got cured. She set to work on Scott the other week. And after about ten minutes, she called me into the room and said, "Look at this" – and you'll never believe it.'

'I already think I do,' Felix sighs, staring hard at his double Scotch.

'There's only' – and Noel names a very famous, very dead footballer – 'working on him!'

I look at Tess, to see how she's taking the news, but she is fascinated now, leaning forward so she can hear every word.

Felix wriggles uncomfortably.

'Okay, game's up,' he admits.

'You've been in touch with him, with this footballer, the whole time, haven't you?' I challenge him.

Felix nods. 'How do you think I ever understood about offside?'

'He comes to you in your dreams, doesn't he?' I go on, and Felix nods again, finally looking me in the eye.

'Wow,' Tess says. 'Spooky. Weird. Amazing. Shall I go and get us some more drinks?'

Felix barely seems to hear the offer, though, as he starts staring at a fixed point somewhere above Noel's head.

'He's coming in on my vibration,' Noel offers, as if he's telling us about the weather. 'Your man is coming into my aura.'

I turn my head, and see a patch of white mist. But nobody else in the bar seems to have noticed anything.

'Oh, my God, I can see him!' Felix bursts out.

'And I saw him too, on the field,' Noel says, 'running around, having a great time. Ask Scott about it. Ask the kids. Children are more sensitive, I bet you someone picked it up.'

Noel shakes himself, and goes back to his drink.

'Sorry, can't keep it up,' he apologises, somewhere over his left shoulder, and Felix and I gather that his vibration – wherever and whatever that was – has fizzled out.

'He's gone,' Felix looks disappointed.

'You've never seen him materialise before?' Noel asks.

Felix shakes his head. 'I just dream about him,' he says sadly. 'I feel like a hideous fraud,' he goes on. 'Because I dream about him, you see, and he just tells me what to do. And it's like this sort of super-brainwashing, because I wake up and I just *know* everything.'

I shake my head.

'It's so hard to believe,' I say. 'But there can't be any other explanation.'

'Well, you would say that,' Noel laughs.

'This guy' – and I say the name of the very famous, very dead footballer again, hardly comprehending – 'why on earth would he take an interest in Scott O'Grady? Not to mention Rivett Street Junior FC? I mean, assuming this is all real, and not some gigantic piss-take from both of you.'

Noel laughs again.

'Well, hasn't this bloke got better things to do?' I persist.

As Tess comes back with the drinks, Noel shakes his head.

'Why shouldn't he take an interest?' he asks. 'I mean, he can be anywhere, any time, any place, this chap. He can be with his old team one minute' – and he names the team, which I remember has just miraculously moved up a division, to the amazement of all the sports pundits – 'and then he can be with Scott. It's whatever's required. And whoever is open to it at the time. Felix, as it happens, is open to it.'

Saddleton nods. 'I am, I confess,' he says. 'When you're desperate, you'll accept anything, even the advice of the deceased, wearing shorts.'

'And you shouldn't feel like a fraud, or a fake, or whatever you said,' Noel encourages him. 'You've done the work, man. You deserve the credit. You're just being helped.'

'Thanks,' Saddleton mutters.

'It's true,' I say, hearing myself assume my teacher voice. 'Even if we can accept the hypothesis – some would say, the cracked hypothesis – that some very famous, very dead centre-forward from the glory days of English football is giving you help, and even dropping large hints in Scott O'Grady's ear, the fact remains – it's you who's been getting out there in the wind and the rain, making them do the keepie-uppie.'

Noel jabs me in the ribs.

'Yow.'

'You know more than you're letting on, Mr Buckle, so don't give me that crap,' Noel grins, and hands over the remaining cigarette packets.

And, while they talk amongst themselves – Tess, Noel and Felix – about how miracles occasionally do happen, and how I've always been wrong about them being blips on the graph, I remember something else.

It's a vague memory at first, but then it slowly becomes clearer. So clear, in fact, that I immediately want to tell someone – but I also know I can't, that it's impossible.

The day in the Tuscan garden, when I was talking to Catherine and I saw my grandmother, looking so young in her flowery dress, there was a footballer there too. Looking thoroughly out of place. And I half-recognised him, but then dismissed it. And he was a long way in the distance, this footballer, so I could only just make out the long shorts and old-fashioned jersey, but if I put two and two together and make forty-six . . .

'So what was the Head's lecture about?' Felix interrupts me.

'Oh – he's just pissed off that I tried to cadge a cigarette from O'Grady.'

'My wife is working on Scott,' Noel says, 'he's got to give up the cancer sticks, you know, he's only a kid.'

'Your talk with the Head looked serious from where I was standing,' Felix goes on, 'in fact, my devotion to the game was even interrupted, while I saw him chastising you.'

'He wants me to go back to Rivett Street,' Tess interrupts. 'And he's not keen on me and Mark sharing a house together, or living together, or whatever you want to call it. That's the main problem.'

'Plus, he doesn't think Scott should be reading Harry Potter, or fan-worshipping the young Kevin Keegan,' I add. And I think about mentioning the Head's fear of feng shui as well, but

I let it go. It's not the kind of thing that Noel needs to know about.

'Can you bring him back?' Felix says suddenly, ignoring what we've just said and making a pleading face at Noel.

'Your magic man is your own business,' Noel says, and I guess he means the myserious footballer. 'He'll be back, though. Don't worry. You get things in your dreams, Felix. So stay tuned at night time. But one day, who knows, you might even see him on the pitch too.'

'C'est incredible!' Felix says, shaking his head slowly from side to side.

'I think your wife should do some healing on Mark,' Tess tells Noel, as Felix gets up to buy the next round of drinks. 'And get rid of his terrible smoking addiction.'

Noel laughs. 'And anything else?'

'Oh,' Tess jokes, 'don't tempt me, Noel. His appalling cynicism. His refusal to believe in anything except quantum physics, and Galileo Galilei.'

And then, inevitably, we are treated to a round of *Bohemian Rhapsody* by Felix, who never can resist lapsing into bad imitations of Freddie Mercury, at the slightest provocation.

thirty-two

Tess and I stay up most of the night talking, and then we doze off just after 4 a.m., then wake up at 8 a.m. and keep on talking more. We already know I'm going to be late for school, at a time when I should probably be on my best behaviour – but given what we've just decided, it's probably irrelevant.

Tess can return to Rivett Street, which is what the Head wants, and I'll do something I should probably have done ages ago – go back to college, and get on the proper road to science.

'There's no money in it,' I tell Tess.

'Robin left me some money,' she says suddenly.

This takes some time to sink in.

'You didn't tell me because you thought I'd be upset,' I say, as we sit up in bed, nursing cups of coffee, and listening to people start their cars, ready to go to work.

'Not that.'

'Why then?' And I manage a weak joke, 'And more to the point, how much?' Tess smiles.

'Robin was a smart investor. It's quite a lot. Enough to pay off this mortgage, anyway.'

'Right.'

'I sometimes wonder if Robin's around actually. Given that we're in this mood, where we're talking about dead footballers, and ghosts and stuff. Funny things happened in New York, with the money people, and the bank. Put it this way – doors opened, very quickly. What I thought would be complicated, wasn't. So he's seen me right, financially. And Mark, I want to do my bit. Pay off the house.'

I nod.

We sit there in silence for a bit. 'So you'll tell the Head, then?' she finally asks, 'today?'

'I'll do it today. He'll be in a good mood after the win yesterday. And anyway. He wants you back.'

Tess makes a face.

'You're an inspired teacher, Mark.'

'Yeah, but being inspired involves thinking for yourself, and being a human being, and all those other things. I don't think the Head's much keen on that.'

'So we're going to do this thing, then?' she puts on a silly voice, and finishes her tea.

'Yes. Just let me have a little kip, and –'

When I wake up again, it's because Tess is shaking me.

'Go to school! Go to school!'

It's like being seven years old again. The very worst kind of flashback.

Standing in the Head's office, an hour later, also gives me flashbacks. It's that age-old fear that any moment now, he's going to tell you to stand in the corner with a book on your head.

'I'm feeling manipulated,' he says, after I've given him the spiel that Tess and I spent all night working on.

'Don't be like that.'

'You're presenting me with a fait accompli, and I'm not sure that's appropriate.'

'Whatever. Tess is a really good teacher's aide, and you need her.'

'I know that.'

'Think of it like a football side. Move me out, put her back in. She's fit. And you'll get another teacher to replace me.'

'Mark, I'm really not that keen on football.'

'Sorry.'

The Head shuffles around in his drawer, looking for something.

'Well,' he says at last, 'technically there's no reason it can't be done. As long as the children's timetables aren't affected.'

'Good.'

'You're an unusual man, Mark.'

'Thankyou.'

'I used to teach at a Catholic school, in the early 80s. We had a nun there. You remind me of her.'

'Thankyou once more.'

'You affect this cynicism, but I get the feeling you're a conversion waiting to happen.'

'You do?'

'There's more to you than meets the eye,' the Head finishes, putting his papers back in the drawer.

And it would be great for me to say that it finishes right there, with me belting down the corridor, yelling 'I'm free!' and throwing my books up in the air, and sprinting through the school gates. It's not over yet, though. Not by a long shot. And I've got to take the kids through the cross-section of a light bulb this afternoon. Oh, the giddy joy, as Saddleton would say.

As soon as I get the chance, I call Tess from the staffroom.

'Done it,' I tell her. 'He said yes.'

'How fantastic.'

'So, a lifetime career in science awaits me. My God, what am I thinking?'

She pauses.

'Have some time off first,' she says. 'You need it.'

'Yeah.'

'Help Noel out with his mini-cab or something. It might be good to flex some different muscles for a while.'

'Well, it would mean endless supplies of free cigarettes from the back seat.'

'No,' Tess says firmly, 'that's the other thing we talked about last night. Remember? You're giving up. Nicotine chewing gum, and lots of Smarties. That's the plan.'

'And what a plan,' I moan. 'I already feel like a fag, and that's just from talking about it.'

'Well, what else do you suggest, then?'

'I'll think of something,' I tell her. 'Don't you worry.'

So, when school finishes for the day, I go and see Noel D. Jupiter. Or, more specifically, Mrs Noel D. Jupiter.

'You've just missed Noel,' she says, ushering me in past all the bikes and trikes in the corridor.

'Sorry, it was just on a whim really. I should have called.'

'Not at all,' Ruth smiles, 'we were sort of expecting you.'

Well, of course. Why would I have predicted anything less from the dynamic mind-reading psychic duo? Noel's step-daughter appears then, at the foot of the stairs, waving an armful of dirty laundry at her mother, then thinks better of it when she sees me, and rushes back up again.

'Shy,' Ruth says.

The other children are sitting in front of the TV watching cartoon videos, so Ruth leads me into the kitchen, where there is more funny curry-smelling stuff on the stove, and a big pile of dough on a wooden board, waiting to be rolled into something.

'How are things?' Ruth asks.

'Good. I just resigned from school.'

She nods, and looks at me thoughtfully.

'You're in transition,' she says, making it sound like one of my school experiments with tadpoles.

'I've been in transition all year, if I'm being honest with myself.'

'You're a Gemini.'

'Did Noel tell you?'

'No, I can tell from the way you can't sit still. You're very jumpy. Do you still smoke?'

'Can't give it up.'

'Yes, you can,' Ruth says firmly. 'Close your eyes.'

My first thought is, she's got flour all over her hands, my second thought is, will I open my eyes in a minute to see a large, famous, dead footballer, in a baggy pair of shorts, waving at me.

Ruth doesn't even touch me, though. Instead, she seems to be standing behind me, or to the side of me, and whatever it is she's doing, she's sending up a fantastic wave of heat, right across the centre of my head, then around my neck.

'I didn't even realise I had that headache,' I tell her, 'but it's almost melting.'

'You don't have to talk,' Ruth says. 'You Geminis, you always talk!'

I shut up then, damned by my own star sign. I never liked it anyway.

'I'm going to remove any need you have for a cigarette,' Ruth murmurs. In the background, I can hear the kids' cartoons, but then the noise drifts away, and all I can register is the incredible warm heat, now rising up somewhere under my ribcage.

'Can you feel that?' she asks, and I nod. It's like drowning in honey. A fantastic way to go, if you're going to submit to the notion that a Forest Gate housewife might have healing hands.

'There,' she says, after a minute. 'You can open your eyes now. Have a little shake, get yourself back to normal.'

Obligingly, I do what the children are always doing after they've been lying on the mat, and shake my fingers, and my toes, and then suddenly feel ridiculous.

'You waste a lot of time,' Ruth says kindly, 'worrying about what you think of yourself. Most people worry what others think, you drive yourself mad with your own doubts.'

'Yes. Okay. You're absolutely right.'

I clear my throat, which feels like it's about to dislodge something big, like a giant furball.

'That's your impulse to smoke,' Ruth says. 'It's going.'

I half-cough, and then it turns into a full cough, and then I'm hit by a wave of nausea, so horrible that I think I'm going to throw up on her kitchen floor, there and then.

'Every time you feel like a cigarette now, you'll be sick,' Ruth shrugs.

Then there's the sound of a man falling over two tricyles in the hallway, and Noel comes in, hugging himself from the cold.

'Mark!'

The great thing about Noel is, every time you see him, you

feel as if you've made his day. Though I have no idea how he could think that about me, of course.

'I just dropped in,' I said.

'Well, we knew that,' Noel smiles at his wife.

'You lot know too much if you ask me,' I say, and Noel puts the kettle on, while his wife goes in to talk to their kids.

'So what's up?' he asks.

'I quit my job.'

'Good, good. And you've been talking to Ruth?'

'She's been – healing me, I suppose. Getting rid of the cigarette cravings.'

It occurs to me that I have just told Noel I've resigned from my job, and he doesn't appear to think it's any more important than the fact that Ruth's been working on my throat.

'I had to leave the school,' I tell him, 'the Head was just too much.'

'Funny school,' Noel shrugs. 'Scott had a hard time there, he says.'

'Yeah.'

'He's bringing his mother to meet me next week,' Noel tells me. 'They're coming round here for dinner.'

'Is she pleased? About Scott being on the team?'

'I think she's just pleased he's still alive,' Noel says, 'you know?'

I know if I hang around for much longer, they'll ask me to stay for dinner too, which is the kind of people they are – but really, even though I am impressed by the way Ruth can generate huge quantities of heat just by standing next to me, I don't much fancy her vegetarian curry.

'I have to go,' I say.

'So soon? Hey, stay in touch.'

'I will. I might need to take over one of your mini-cabs shortly. While I work out what I'm going to do with the rest of my life.'

'Feel free. Be my guest.'

We say our goodbyes, and Noel even manages to refrain from bear-hugging me, and although the children don't come out to say goodbye to me this time, they press up against the window instead, squashing their noses against the glass, while

Noel and Ruth wave frantically behind them.

And as I go home, on the tube, even though I'm standing up along with the other million human sardines on the Victoria Line, I start to feel good. So good, in fact, that I wonder if Ruth has been working on my brain, as well as my body.

Life hasn't often felt this right for me. Maybe when I first found the house with Catherine, or even when I first got the job at Rivett Street – but it's an unusual sensation, this feeling of rightness, and I suppose I'm starting to panic about losing it.

thirty-three

I still love Catherine Roden at the core of me, and nothing is going to change that. I realise it when Tess gives me a funny look on Saturday morning, straight after I've woken up, after dreaming about Catherine and me, swimming together, on our camping trip.

'You were talking in your sleep,' Tess says, sitting up in bed with a book on her lap – but not reading it.

'Probably rubbish,' I yawn. I'm still half asleep.

'What were you dreaming about?' she asks, but she already seems to know.

There's no point hiding it.

'I had a dream about Catherine. About the time we went camping.'

'Is that what that photo's all about then?' Tess asks. She means the photo of Catherine and me, holding up our tin mugs of tea, outside the tent, which is still on my bedside table.

'Tess. Don't be like that.'

'No, I'm fine. I was just curious.'

She goes back to her book.

Polly arrives a few hours after this, when I'm in the bath.

'We're just going to Brighton,' Tess yells through the door. Unlike Catherine, she doesn't hang around in the bathroom talking to me.

'What for?' I yell back. Probably because they've read how exciting it is in *Time Out* and they want to catch a glimpse of Fatboy Slim, just like everybody else.

'Polly wants to go to the markets!' Tess yells again, so I shout my goodbyes back, and then lower myself back into the bath water, as I hear the front door shut downstairs.

Tess and I hadn't made any particular plans today. I assumed we'd just be hanging around the house, which is normally what we do on a Saturday. And of course I have no objection to Polly taking Tess to Brighton, or in fact, taking her anywhere. There's a slight chill in the air, though. No doubt about that. Whatever it was I was saying in my sleep – and I'm worrying about it now – I don't think Tess is particularly happy about it.

The dream is still with me. Not like a Catherine-in-Heaven dream, where you know it's real, but more like the kind of thing where you want to stay with the sensation as long as possible, just to hang onto the feeling while it's still there.

I can't deny it, although I may have been doing a fairly good job so far. I love Catherine Roden. I love Tess too, of course, and I've even managed to tell her this. But this feeling now is – I dunno. Are you supposed to lose your love for the first real woman in your life, just because the second one has turned up?

This will be with me for years. I haven't thought about it much, because the last few months have been a blur, but now, it seems, I'm ready to accept it.

On paper, sure, I can write down a hundred things that weren't right for Catherine and me. Maybe two hundred. If anyone ever wants to interrogate me about the health of this relationship now, with Tess, and the good things it's producing in my life – as opposed to the stuff with Catherine, and Donna, and the rest of it – well. There is no contest. Logically, the Tess days win over the Catherine days, every single time.

Nevertheless. I miss Catherine. And I know I'll always love her.

So, in the afternoon, I go to the church where we had her service. The ashes have been put in a family plot reserved by the Rodens, just to the left. I know where it is, because a long time ago, Veronica told me exactly where to look. Not that I've ever bothered until now, of course.

It's more than not bothering, though. It's a kind of disgust. When she died, and when they cremated her in front of me, I felt a sort of anger at the whole proceeding. Anger at her being boxed up like that, and stuck in the ground next to a church which meant nothing to her. A faint sense of repulsion at the process. Or maybe just the way she was *processed*. Like everything else in this world, from cans of baked beans, to traffic laws, you die on other people's terms.

Catherine was never in a small (too small) hole in the ground for me. And even less so, after she first appeared, all those months ago, sitting on the bedroom chair. So it's wrong to say I haven't been back to see her grave, because I haven't bothered. The truth is, a mixture of fear, anger and something worse than both those things has kept me away.

I wander round the churchyard, noticing the way so many graves lean forward, and so many names have been erased. They must have run out of space years ago, and it looks as if the modern section is filling up fast, too. I wonder, despite myself, how much the Rodens paid for their bit of land. I suppose everyone wonders that.

The set-up around the side of the church is ridiculous, because unless you want to literally step on other people's small, square headstones, you have to tiptoe up against the stone walls of the church, squashing yourself flat and shuffling forward.

I eventually find Catherine's name though. It's very simple. Just the usual – in loving memory. And that's accurate, even if it isn't original. I feel a stab of anger, again, as I realise that nobody asked me about the wording. Nobody rang me to find out. It's like I admitted to Donna, at the very beginning. I was kept well out of it, by the Roden family.

'I'm not in there,' Catherine said, when her coffin was being carried into the crematorium.

And she's not in here, either. She's nowhere near this church.

I can feel Catherine, when she's around. I know her perfume, I know her personality. This is an alien place for her to be in. Maybe Donna was right. I should have dug a hole in the back garden and just put her there. It would have made more sense.

I take the bus back home. Polly and Tess will be away all day, and probably half the night, if they decide to stay and have fish and chips on the Pier. I think about calling Ted, to see if he wants to have a grand day out as well – I need something to distract me.

But the impulse fades as the bus crawls towards our street, and I realise that Ted won't do it for me, today. Neither will Noel, nor will Felix. Even sitting in front of the TV with a beer won't get me to where I want to be, and all the CDs and books in the world, or at least in this house, aren't going to help either.

I miss Catherine. In fact, I miss Catherine like you wouldn't believe.

I look at the stereo, willing it to kick into life. I think about John Smith, and if he could stand another call from me, and then I decide against it. I put a cup of tea in the microwave, half-hoping it will say hello, but all it does is boil the tea in a minute flat, leaving me with the worst cup of tea I've had for months.

I decide to give up and go back to bed. Maybe I should be nicer to myself. Isn't that what Noel's wife said? I'm my worst critic. Something like that, anyway. So if I feel like I'm falling apart now, and I shouldn't – well. Perhaps I should just ignore myself, my Gemini twin self, for a change. The twin that wants to obsess about Catherine so much, should be given a free rein by the twin who just wishes it would all go away.

Despite my better instincts, I reach over to the bedside table, for the photograph of Catherine and me, standing outside our tent.

It's not there.

Tess must have put it away, I think, slightly shocked at this fact, and annoyed at her, all at the same time. I search through my side of the drawers, then hers. Endless amounts of paperbacks, splayed out in the middle, and a few condoms, and the odd bar of half-eaten chocolate, but nothing apart from that – except the other photo of Catherine, lying topless on an

Australian beach. If Tess was going to get rid of stuff, I think, why didn't she take that as well?

I think about trawling through the wardrobe, but I haven't got the energy. If Tess wanted to hide the photo she would have thought of a more sensible place.

And then I see it. At about the same time I hear the birds, going crazy outside the window, and I see the cat, running backwards and forwards in front of the bed, I see the photograph. It is in Catherine's hand, and she is holding it up, to show me. She is wearing the pink dressing gown. And the light is shining not through her, but around her.

'I've come to say goodbye,' she says, and I feel the tears start in my eyes.

'Was that you in the dream?' I manage, at last.

'No. It was just a dream. Some dreams are just dreams, you know?'

'I love you,' I tell her.

'I love you too.'

'Will I see you again?'

'Not for a long time,' Catherine says. 'But yes, you will. Be happy with Tess.'

'You want me to be with her?'

'Everyone does.'

'Everyone?'

'It's the right thing. You're going to be a scientist,' Catherine says.

'Do you know?'

'A lot of people are going through this. You have a lot of questions about what's out there, so do they. You'll become a scientist.'

'You're right,' I say at last. 'I have endless questions. *Endless*, Catherine. Why is this all happening to me? You, and the footballer the other day, and the stereo, and the microwave?'

But Catherine has gone, and all I am left with is the clock, flashing 12.00, and the cat, which jumps on the bed and starts nagging me for food. I suppose Tess left it up to me to feed it, this morning.

The birds have gone anyway. And the picture is back – the photograph of Catherine and I, camping with our tin mugs of tea – and it's even where I left it, on my side of the bed. Still, some things are meant to be put away, aren't they? To tell you the truth, I hadn't even realised it was there. And if Tess had a photograph of Robin next to her bed, *well* . . .

I take the photograph of Catherine and me, and wrap it in one of my old T-shirts, and put it in the bottom drawer. It will make me happier, anyway, if I keep it for special occasions. Something to treasure, and remember. Which is probably what Catherine would prefer, anyway.

I wonder, for a moment, if she and Tess would ever have been friends. It's an impossible question, of course. I would always have got in the way. But without me, would there have been any chance?

I suppose the answer to that question is, Felix Saddleton. Catherine thought he was great, Tess thinks the same – so, Saddleton would have been the middle ground. I don't think Catherine would have had time for Tess's theory of life, the universe, Jesus and everything – she was too pragmatic for that. But then, look at her now, appearing in a haze of white light and everything. Maybe Catherine, post-death, is exactly the person Tess *would* get on with.

It's a strange thought. I feed the cat, twice as much food as usual, to shut it up, and then I sit on the sofa for the rest of the afternoon, wondering what it would be like to actually be a scientist.

The mini-cab driving bit seems easier for the moment. And maybe that's not a bad way to start. The Communists always said the intellectuals should get their hands dirty from time to time. Not that I see myself as an intellectual, though. But Catherine was right. I do have questions. Eight million questions. I start jotting them down on a piece of paper.

1. Was Wittgenstein right? If the limits of our language set the boundaries to our world, maybe we just need a fuller language – eg, ghost, spirit, spectre etc. not sufficient.

Then I cross that bit out and write again

1. Never mind limits of language, is Catherine's world like quantum world – eg, things disappearing and appearing,

electrons behaving like bouncing snooker balls, reaching pockets and then reversing?

2. Are natural laws – momentum, cause and effect, action and reaction etc. etc. part of Catherine's world? And Noel's world, eg, karma?

I hate that word karma. It still reminds me of Catherine's yoga friends and their crappy sympathy notes, after the funeral. But anyway – I keep writing.

3. Does God play dice with the universe? eg, Einstein? Assuming there is a God?

And then Polly and Tess pull up in Polly's car, laughing and carrying on like the very worst of the girls in 4B, so I put my piece of paper to one side, and try to sit up straight, and look normal. Then I realise that nobody sits up that straight on the sofa and looks normal, so why am I bothering?

The key turns in the lock, and I can hear Tess offering Polly tea, but she wants to get back to see Ted, and there are a lot of girlie goodbyes – why do they always take about ten minutes to actually make any kind of departure? – and then the door closes.

'Hello,' Tess says, and I can tell in a second that her morning mood has lifted.

I kiss her. She tastes of candy floss. And vinegar.

'We ate everything on Brighton Pier we possibly could,' she explains, kissing me back.

'Good day?' I ask.

'Amazing day,' she smiles. 'We went to see a fortune teller, a tarot card reader, down on the beach.'

'Oh, God. And? Did we get the lottery numbers?'

'He had a lot to say about you,' Tess smirks.

'Like what?'

'You're going to be a famous scientist.'

'Oh, *famous* even.'

'We're going to move to America, you and me, and you're going to be a famous scientist. In the year 2015.'

'Oh, not too long to wait then. Anything else?'

'We're going to have twins.'

'Not if my sperm has anything to do with it, Tess. I can't afford it. Even when I'm a famous scientist – they don't earn much, you know.'

She pushes me on the couch, and we lose ourselves in each other for a while.

'I'm sorry about this morning,' I say at last.

'Don't worry.'

'I put the photo away, by the way.'

'You didn't have to.'

'If it was a photo of you and Robin next to the bed, I wouldn't like it.'

'I don't even have a photo of me and Robin together,' Tess says, looking sad for a moment. 'That's the problem.'

Then she changes the subject for herself, and looks at my list.

'I see your quest to be a famous scientist has already begun then,' she says, reading the Einstein quote.

'Tess. I need to tell you something.'

'Yup?'

'It's about the stereo playing *Never Tear Us Apart* all the time. And it's about me. And it's also about Catherine. I don't want you to get upset.'

'No, go ahead.'

'She didn't die, Tess.'

She nods.

'I mean, I tried, in a roundabout way, to tell you this before. That day we were in the staffroom. But Tess – she was talking to me a few days after she was killed. I heard her. I've seen her. I mean, I've even been to the place where she is. The other world. And she didn't die. In fact, nobody dies.'

Tess looks at me, hard.

'You smell her perfume, don't you?' she says.

'I thought it was just me.'

'No, I've often caught it round here. You know? It's always when you're quiet. And happy. I think I know the smell.'

'It's called Joy.'

'And what else, Mark?'

I shake my head. If I start now, I'll either never stop, or I'll start getting teary-eyed again, and Tess has just had a great day out with Polly, and neither of those things are a good idea.

'It's Sunday, tomorrow,' I tell her. 'Can we do it then?'

And she nods, and starts rubbing my shoulders, in a way that only she can do, and I fall into her, on the couch.

'I never want you to stop loving her,' she says at last, when I've relaxed enough to almost fall asleep.

'Thanks.'

'And I love you.'

'Thanks again.'

She switches on the news, and we watch film of a charity – maybe even Ted's charity – flying sacks of wheat into Afghanistan.

thirty-four

I wake up early the next morning, and slide out of bed as quietly as I can, so I won't wake Tess up. Then I start adding to my list of questions, picking up where I left off.

By the time Tess comes down in her dressing gown, yawning, with the David Bowie cat over her shoulder, I have managed to write down four hundred and nine questions.

'It makes no sense to me,' she shakes her head, as she holds my piece of paper up and stares at my notes.

'I'm not surprised. I've been up since the crack of dawn doing this, and I hardly understand it myself.'

'4. Anthropic principle 5. Chaos 6. Newton 7. Auras 8. Quarks,' Tess reads out loud. 'What on earth are you up to?'

She pads into the kitchen in her bare feet, followed by the cat, and makes some toast.

'You'd better tell me from the beginning,' she calls, over the sound of the kettle whistling. 'If I'm going to have twins with a world-famous scientist in America, like it said in the tarot cards, then I'd better have all the facts!'

'Very funny,' I reply.

Tess comes back in with the tea and toast – her Nigella Lawson fetish must be fading, because she'd normally turn her nose up at mere toast, and come in with home-made bacon muffins.

'So anyway,' she says, sitting next to me on the sofa. 'How about it? Just very slowly, because I'm not at my best on Sunday mornings.'

'I know.'

And so I tell her the whole story, as she requests, from the beginning. Including the birds going mad in the park, the night of the Elvis Presley party, and the way every DJ in the country seems to want to play *Never Tear Us Apart*, any time I'm walking past a radio. I tell her about what John Smith said to me, and what Noel said to me. I explain about our velvet armchairs, in this living room, being transported to Catherine's sunny meadow. And I tell Tess about Veronica seeing Catherine in her kitchen, though not what Catherine said to her about us.

'Phew,' Tess says at last. Our toast has gone cold on the plate.

'I'm sorry,' I say. 'I didn't mean to have this big, complicated secret.'

'No, I understand why.'

'You always say you understand, Tess, and it's nice of you, but really. I don't feel too good about this.'

She looks at me for a second.

'At what stage did you cross the line?' she says.

'What from?'

'Not believing and believing.'

I think about it.

'When I saw you in the pub.'

'With Faith Lift?'

'Yes. To be honest. When I saw the auras around you, and the blokes on the stage.' She shakes her head wonderingly.

'And every time I sang to you, my throat went blue.'

'Yup.'

'How fantastic. I love that bit,' she says, like a child wanting to hear the same story, over and over again.

'Of course, I've felt like two people the whole time,' I explain.

She nods.

'The believer, and the non-believer, sort of having a fight. And then another one of me, trapped in the middle, just totally confused.'

'Well, yeah. I mean, you weren't trained for any of this, were you?'

Tess is quiet for a moment.

'I'm a bit jealous, to tell you the truth,' she says at last. 'Or, envious, even. What you've been telling me is what we used to spend hours hoping for, praying for, at Crosslink.'

'Really?'

'Oh, God yeah,' she says, and then laughs at what she's just said.

She eats the cold toast.

'It's going to be fascinating watching you work out what you really believe,' she says.

'But I do.'

'No, beyond the fact that you believe in life after death. Or that consciousness survives, or whatever you want to say, in that scientific way of yours. I mean, next, as Ted and Polly always say, you have to go looking for the moral framework.'

'Tess, I don't have to do anything.'

She shakes her head at this.

'No, Mark. I know you. You might pretend to be this man in a white coat, this detatched teacher type in the laboratory, but sooner or later you're going to have to be a human being about this. What is it for, all this microwave oven stuff, and this dead footballer man from half a century ago, and the armchairs in the meadow, and the auras around people's throats? I mean, come on, Mark. What's the point of it? What's the moral point? Unless you start with what Noel and that other chap have been saying –'

'John Smith.'

'Yes, the spook with the name like a beer. Him.'

'I'll make up my own mind,' I say, at last. 'Who knows, Tess, maybe it's all just random, after all.'

'Shut up.'

'I'm just teasing.'

I lean forward, over the cat, and kiss her.

'You do have some idea, though, don't you?' Tess persists.

'Nope. None at all. That's why I've just been up since the crack of dawn writing down about four hundred questions.'

'How can I have twins with a man who has no idea?' she sighs.

'Shut up about that charlatan in Brighton, for God's sake.'

We settle down into silence, finishing the toast, and I think about America, and what it would even be like, in the year 2020, or whatever it was her fortune teller told her. And she thinks about – well, I can tell what she's thinking about now. Robin. You don't have to be psychic to pick that up, when the look on her face shifts ever so slightly, and her eyes lose their focus on the room.

'Everyone wants us to be together,' I tell her.

'That's nice.'

'No, not everyone, as in here in this place. Over there. Catherine told me. I think it's one of the last things she ever wanted to tell me.'

'Yesterday?'

I nod.

'And who did she mean, everyone?'

'Well, that's the next question on my list, isn't it?'

'Big questions,' Tess muses.

But I can tell I might have given her a little of what she's looking for. Because, after all, she's a believer – in everything, pretty much – and I'm just a rank beginner. I've got the facts, I suppose, but I don't see the point.

One of the reasons I love her is that she's never even needed the facts to see the point.

'Mark?' she says, after a while.

'What?'

'I know you said the fortune teller was bollocks, because that's the kind of thing you would say.'

'Where is this leading?'

'But part of me wants it not to be bollocks. You know?'

'Well, maybe I do believe, then,' I tell her. 'If it makes you feel any better.'

'What I mean is,' she struggles, 'I don't want the fact that you think someone on the pier at Brighton is a charlatan, to get in the way of all my little dreams.'

'He's not.'

This seems to satisfy her, and she goes off to make more toast, coming back a few minutes later with a proper Nigella-style feast.

'You haven't asked me what the tarot cards said about *me*,' she mock-complains.

'Go on then.'

'I'm going to be in a new band,' she says.

'What, another one? And with the twins to look after?'

'No, before all that.'

'And will it have a name as crap as Faith Lift?'

'That's the question isn't it,' she says, smirking as she drinks another cup of tea.

So I put that down on the list as well. Question 410. Will Tess's next band have a name as crap as Faith Lift? I might as well. Before I spill my tea on the list, anyway, and it all becomes a blur.

author's note

I should like to thank Michael Witheford for all his football expertise, although any mistakes are mine. Margaret Dent, author of *Love Never Dies*, for her expert advice on the spirit world, and Terri Bradley for connecting us. Maggie Alderson, Imogen Edwards-Jones and Nick Earls for doing such a fantastic job on *Big Night Out* at the same time that I was finishing this book. Emma Marlin and Andy Cowles for being so amazing during the fortnight that I spent on Greenwich Street, after September 11. Stephanie Cabot at William Morris, and Fiona Inglis at Curtis Brown, for first-class agenting. And finally, to all those in spirit who have been hard at work behind the scenes of this book – there have been times when the temperature in my shed has been at freezing point, but I wouldn't have it any other way!

Jessica Adams, Bellingen, 2002.